Waterspell Book 2:

The *Wysard*

Deborah J. Lightfoot

Seven Rivers
Publishing

Seven Rivers Publishing
P.O. Box 682
Crowley, Texas 76036
www.waterspell.net

First Paperback Edition: October 2011
First Electronic Edition: December 2011

The characters and events portrayed in this book are fictitious. Any similarity to real persons, living or dead, is coincidental and not intended by the author.

Waterspell Book 2 — The Wysard: A Fantasy by Deborah J. Lightfoot

Summary: After blundering into the last stronghold of magic, Carin discovers that she is right to fear the wizard Verek. He is using her to seal the ruptures in the void, and she may be nothing more to him than an expendable weapon. What will he do with her — or to her — when his world is again secure? Or has he erred in believing that the last bridge has been broken? The quest may not, in fact, be over … and Lord Verek may find himself not quite as willing to dispose of his fiery water-sylph, Carin, as he once believed himself to be.

ISBN 978-0-9728768-5-8 (E-book)
ISBN 978-0-9728768-6-5 (Paperback)

*For Gene, who gave me the gift of time …
and never grumbled when I asked him to read the
whole thing "just once more."*

CONTENTS

To have a new vision of the future,
it has always first been necessary to
have a new vision of the past.

— Theodore Zeldin

Prologue

The Path Between

The heartbeat couldn't be hers. She was dead.

Maddeningly, however, the sound persisted—a strong, steady *whump, whump* in Carin's left ear.

Through the blackness within her mind, half-formed impressions drifted like moonmist. They teased her with sensations to which she struggled to attach meaning. Her body lay sprawled across a surface that was hard enough to bruise her corpse. But her head and one shoulder rested on matter more yielding. Had her drowned remains come to rest on a rocky ledge in a supernatural ocean? Was this a pillow of seaweed cushioning her skull?

No, a thought whispered from a corner of her torpid brain. *Seaweed and rock have no heart beating in them.*

The rhythmic pounding in Carin's ear hammered at her until a crack opened to admit a sliver of comprehension:

She lived.

If the heart-sounds were hers, then she wasn't dead. If the heart beat in another's chest and she heard it, then she was not only alive, but also pressing very near some other undead being.

Her eyes jerked open. They beheld what might have been a rumpled snowdrift bathed in the light of a blood-red sunset.

She stared.

Whump, whump in her ear deepened the crack, penetrated to the core of her cold-shocked mind—

Lucidity flashed through the breach, and abruptly Carin knew: the rumpled whiteness that pressed against her face was Lord Verek's linen shirt. The reddish tinge on it was no natural light from a setting sun, but the glow from the walls of Verek's

1

vault of sorcery. The wizard lay on the cavern's floor of polished stone. Carin lay atop him, her head pillowed on his chest, her ear to his heart, and her slowly focusing eyes inventing wind-drifted snow from the wrinkles of his shirt.

She gave a violent start, put both hands to the floor, and heaved herself off Verek's unconscious body — so forcefully that she nearly toppled back into the ensorcelled pool behind her. She teetered on the pool's rim, waging a brief, desperate struggle for life. To fall again into those glacial depths would kill her. The intense cold had cast her faculties into an abyss that must have no rival but death itself. Without the sorcerer to drag her up from that oblivion, Carin stood no chance of surviving a second dunking.

And her rescuer was in no condition now to extract her from the unnatural waters of his wizards' well. Verek lay like a corpse. Carin's sudden movement hadn't roused him to consciousness. He appeared as lost in the abyss as she had been.

She kept her balance. Carin stumbled to safety, treading between Verek's body and the enchanted pool that imperiled all living flesh, whether mortal or magian. She reached the nearest of the four stone benches that ringed the wizards' well. Upon that seat carved with the symbol of a fish she collapsed, but she took care to avoid the shape that was cut into the stone.

The symbol, precisely centered and deeply carved, might be nothing but decoration. Like its fellows on the other benches in the cave — the image of a key chiseled into the seat across the pool from this one, a radiant sun on the bench to Carin's left, a crescent moon to her right — the fish might be only a token of magical art. Maybe the four symbols were a wizard's badge of office, as a king's crown and scepter were emblems of his royal authority.

Or, Carin thought, *maybe there's magic in every line and curve.* The events of her three weeks' imprisonment in Lord Verek's

2

house had led her to suspect sorcery in all elements of his domain. She distrusted the blighted woodland outside his manor walls and the shape-shifting books in his library. But here in the cave below the library rose the undoubted wellspring of magic. Power flowed in the waters of the enchanted pool and in the lifeblood of the sorcerer who had submitted himself to it.

From her uneasy perch, Carin studied the blacked-out wizard at her feet. Verek's shirt, though white enough that her addled wits had mistaken it for snow, was sweat-stained down the front and under the armpits. His blue wool vest lay crumpled on the floor where he'd thrown it.

Half rising from her seat, Carin bent to pick up the vest. The garment, previously soaked through with Verek's perspiration, wasn't even damp now. She and the wizard, one as near-dead as the other, had lain together on the floor long enough for the sweat to dry on Verek's clothes and hair.

The wizard's black hair, falling around his ashen face, set off features that Carin had never seen so still and so unguarded. The jaw with its close-cropped beard was slack. The parted lips, so pale, were framed by a thin mustache that met the beard below the corners of the mouth. Closed lids hid the fierce, dark-flaring eyes that had excited terror in Carin's soul since her first meeting with the wizard. Only the slow rise and fall of his chest showed that his body held life.

The glossy blackness of Verek's hair, graying nowhere but at the temples, suggested a man of fewer years than forty-four. *How bizarre,* Carin mused as she looked at him, *that I know more about this warlock's life than I know of my own.* Between his housekeeper's yarns and Carin's own discoveries in the wizard's library, she'd pieced together Verek's life story enough to know that her captor was almost thirty years her senior—in mortal terms. But wizards live long. When his age was

3

calculated by the standards of his kind, the gap between them narrowed considerably.

And what are the odds, Carin wondered, *that in just three weeks I would discover more of Verek's secrets than he's revealed to most people in a lifetime?* In the brief period since her blundering across a boundary that should have repelled her, Carin had learned more than even Verek's fellow wizard, the venerable Jerold, could know. Certainly that old elf was unaware of tonight's events, which had dropped Carin into the lethally enchanted pool and sent Verek diving after her.

Why had he done it?

Done which? interjected another thought, spilling in on the first.

It was a measure of her bewilderment that Carin was almost as unsure of her question as of its answer. Which of Verek's actions was, in fact, the most inexplicable? That he would send her on a magical errand to steal a trinket from another world, and nearly kill her doing it? Or that he'd risk his own life to save a serving-girl who dreamed of destroying him?

The wizard's right hand twitched.

The sudden movement brought Carin out of her reverie as if an arrow had whizzed past. She sprang to her feet and stared at the warlock, searching for signs of returning consciousness. There were none.

But though it wasn't repeated, the spasm in the hand that Verek commonly used to raise his enchantments was a warning Carin could hardly miss. Fate had given her an opportunity that wouldn't likely come again.

Do I want the warlock dead? she demanded of her tattered courage. *Did I mean it today when I offered to knife him through his heart? Now's my chance.* If she acted quickly, before the wizard came to, she could rid herself of this enemy who was otherwise invincible.

Carin dropped the crumpled vest and darted behind the fourth bench, that of the crescent moon. She raced for the stairs that spiraled steeply to the library.

But at the foot of the steps lay an object that brought her up short. It was the crystal trinket on a golden chain that Verek had sent her to fetch — first casting her on the surface of his wizards' well as though she were a wraith who could walk on water, then dropping her through into frozen nothingness.

What was the crystal doing here, lodged against the bottom step, its chain loose beside it? Before lobbing the trinket to Verek's waiting hands, Carin had snugged the chain around the pendant, making a tidy package that had reached him intact. The moment he'd got his hands on it, he'd let her fall into oblivion.

From the depths of that void, Carin had had no glimpse of what he did next. But the evidence at her feet — the pendant and its now untidy heap of chain — suggested that the wizard had flung his treasure away, with force. Crystal and chain had piled up against the bottommost step like a runaway comet with its tail crashing into it.

Carin was bending to pick up the trinket when a whisper of apprehension stopped her. Just before Verek had let her fall, he'd shouted: "I cannot withstand its pull on you!" And in fact, she had seen in his grimacing, sweat-streaked face the strain of *something*, some invisible force that opposed him as he drew her back from her raid on an unknown world.

Had the crystal been pulling Carin away while the wizard fought to return her to his domain? If the trinket at her feet was imbued with such supernatural power, then she would be a fool to touch the thing again.

She snatched her hand back and glanced over her shoulder for reassurance that Verek still slept. Then Carin stepped over

5

the crystal and hurried up the stairs, trying not to think about her plans for the wizard.

Her pausing, though, to mull over the evidence of the crystal, had given doubt a chance to undermine resolve. It would seem simplicity itself to kill Verek where he lay. But would the presence which haunted that cavern of sorcery — be it ghost, water-spirit, or other sort of disembodied intelligence — allow Carin to harm the wizard, its servant? The power that had once summoned her into its company might turn on her in Verek's defense, were she to enter the cave armed with a knife.

The dragon, Carin reminded herself. *I have the puzzle-book dragon.*

If she spoke the incantation that conjured the Jabberwock, those fangs and claws might rise from wizards' waters. But the presence that seemed part and parcel of those waters might rise, too.

Maybe she was deluding herself, to think that she — an inept mortal, and no sorceress — could successfully wield her own magical being against wizardry as powerful as Verek's. In spellcraft, he was the master, and she not so much as an apprentice.

Carin reached the top of the winding stone stairs and let herself into the library where she had labored to bring order to the wizard's disarrayed books. Through hours of stolen study, she'd also gained a knowledge of everything from archery and alchemy to Ladrehdinian geography.

And haven't I also learned, she reminded herself, to draw her thoughts back from the direction they appeared to be heading, *that the House of Verek has been badly served by its current master? Didn't Verek's own grandfather describe him as "the tainted seed"? And didn't Lord Legary hide his words on a high, dark shelf as though he never wanted his grandson to find them?*

Carin almost regretted her discovery of the *Book of Archamon*. On the day she tugged the ancient book into the light, she thwarted the wishes of the long-dead Legary and abetted Verek's own designs. By delivering the volume into her captor's hands, Carin had — she suspected — accomplished Verek's true purpose in setting her to work in his library. He must have hoped she would find the words that were lost to him for twenty years.

The library, as Carin entered it now, was a black pit in the night. The lamps of evening had been put out hours ago, and the hearth-fire had dwindled to a few glowing coals.

She felt the darkness, felt her fear of it, in the prickling along her spine. But she ignored the sensation, long enough to grope her way to the nearest of the two high-backed benches that faced one another before the fireplace. This was the seat that Verek always took when he interviewed — or interrogated or upbraided — her in this room.

Carin rounded the end nearest the hearth and felt for the low table between the benches. Her searching fingers closed on a candle. She put the wick to an ember on the hearth, and with that new-kindled flame she touched off two oil lamps.

Feeling safer in the light, with her breath coming easier, she settled on the bench across from Verek's and returned to pondering his fate. Could she kill him? If she didn't do it now while he lay bereft of his senses in the cave below, she might never get another chance. But would she be permitted to harm him?

Perhaps the real question was: Would Carin's sense of justice allow it? Verek, after all, had extracted her from his wizards' well — evidently damaging himself while saving her life. He should have recovered his wits by now, unless the shock had injured him worse than it had hurt her. Certainly he'd gone in knowing how painful it would be to submerge his

7

living flesh in that glacial liquid. His distress had been obvious on that other occasion, weeks ago, when Carin had seen him swept into the pool and hadn't been sure he would survive.

As her eyes adjusted to the oddly cheerless light of lamp and candle flame, Carin detected a dark blanket opposite. It lay draped over the cushions of Verek's bench, a vestige of a late-afternoon nap.

I was right about one thing, anyway. Her face warmed at the realization. *That warlock was dozing in here, all cozy and snug, while he had me scared out of my mind.*

Carin's gaze roved from the blanket back to the table between the benches and found the kitchen knife she'd tried to use on Verek before tonight's adventures began. The sight of it irritated her—to know that the wizard, after easily disarming her, had brought the knife in here and tossed it on the table. Then he'd stretched out on his bench, blanketed and peaceful for an hour's nap. Carin had spent that same hour in an agony of fear, expecting it to be the last of her life.

But as she studied the weapon, no new impulse urged her to pick it up. The hot anger that had once fueled her had cooled. In fury's wake, reason and—could she admit it?—principle now prevailed over emotion. Try as she might ... and try, she did ... Carin couldn't picture herself stabbing the narrow blade into Verek's heart, stilling the beat that had roused her from the blackness.

"Good work," she muttered aloud so she would hear and fully appreciate the contempt in her voice. "You've talked yourself out of it."

She wouldn't try to kill the warlock, and everything about her decision smacked of cowardice. She was afraid of angering the specter in Verek's cave of magic by going there armed, and in any case she didn't have the guts to drive the blade home.

Couldn't she come up with a reason that suggested wisdom, not just weakness?

Yes, she could. There was the captive woodsprite to consider. Verek had promised to release the creature when Carin had done his bidding to return the *Looking-Glass* book to … wherever she'd been tonight … and bring him the crystal trinket. The trade had been accomplished—at less cost to herself, it would seem, than to the wizard who had threatened to destroy the sprite if she failed.

Now that Verek had what he wanted, he must keep his promise to free the woodsprite. If Carin were to kill the wizard, the spells imprisoning the sprite might become unbreakable, assuring the creature's death.

"For the sprite's sake then," she told herself with a little less shame. "It's as good an excuse as any, if I need a reason not to murder a warlock tonight."

Carin stood, but then hesitated anew as another dilemma presented itself. Should she go to bed, as she very much wanted to, and leave Verek as he had fallen? Or should she try to help him?

With her head tilted to one side, as if to force her contradictory sentiments to settle one way or the other, Carin walked to the small cabinet in the bookshelves where the wizard kept his liquor. The tart *dhera* that tasted of currants would warm a body, as she knew firsthand, from tongue to toes. From the cabinet she took a flagon of the glowing red liquid, but no goblet. If the warlock wanted the liquor, he could drink from the bottle.

Carin gathered the blanket from Verek's bench and threw it over her shoulder. With the bottle in one hand and a candle in the other, she retraced her steps through the library and down the stairs. She descended quickly, unwilling to linger with her thoughts.

9

At the foot of the stairs she stepped over the crystal trinket, then approached the wizard's inert form. Verek's right hand now lay over his heart, where Carin's head had rested. Otherwise, he was as she'd left him.

Carin set the flagon of *dhera* on the bench of the fish, where the wizard must see it when he woke. She spread the blanket over him and tucked it close around his body. Verek's wool vest, retrieved from the floor and folded, made a serviceable pillow. Carin lifted his head to slip the vest under it, and her fingers buried up in his hair. It was satin smooth and, oh, so cold. To the touch he was a cadaver.

But she'd barely lowered Verek's head to the pillow when he began to shiver lightly, with a motion as slight as the trembling of an aspen's leaves on a still day. Her ministrations were bringing him around—

—And she had no wish to be there when the sorcerer regained his senses. The morning would be soon enough to speak to him of promises to be kept and an odd woodsprite to be freed.

Carin grabbed her candle. She didn't need its light in the cave's ruddy glow, but the way to her bedroom would not be so preternaturally lit. She took a step toward the library stairs. Then she paused and studied the wall opposite, behind the bench of the carved key.

Nothing in the wall indicated a doorway. But four times Carin had passed through a concealed portal in that expanse of stone—thrice with Verek's permission, and once in a dangerous turn of spying. The secret doorway led far more directly to her bedroom. If she could go that way, it would save another stiff climb to the library and get her to her bed that much sooner.

Carin glanced back at the wizard. His shivering had grown more pronounced; he would rouse soon. She looked toward the library stairs, and almost elected to make her way up that

10

familiar ascent rather than risk detection by the awakening Verek.

But then, like a rift forming silently in a canyon wall, a portion of the stone face swung inward, opening to a lightless stairwell. Carin stared, and didn't try to suppress the shudder of mingled fear and awe that traveled her length. Whatever it was that haunted this cave had evidently chosen to grant her unspoken wish, perhaps reading her thoughts in her quick glances around the room. If that were so, then the presence must be watching her right now.

"It" — Carin did not dare say its name, even to herself — must follow her every move in the cave. It would have seen her throw a blanket over its servant Verek. Could it know that she had contemplated murdering the wizard, but she'd lost her nerve for fear of what that unfathomable force might do to her?

Unwilling to disturb the silence, Carin only nodded her obeisance to the invisible presence. Keeping her eyes lowered, she walked to the portal. The moment she passed through into the stairwell, the door swung shut behind her. The gap sealed itself as completely as if it had never been.

Exhaustion weighed on Carin by the time she climbed the last of three flights and gained the upper corridor that would take her to her bedroom door. She slipped along the chilly, unlit hallway, holding her candle barely an inch from the wall. Her free hand trailed over the stonework, feeling for any break that might reveal the entrance to Verek's private rooms. But his wizardry of last evening held firm: the bespelled doorway remained as hidden to Carin's touch as to her sight. She wouldn't be fetching the sprite from its prison-tree in Verek's sitting room as long as the sorcerer's concealing magic prevailed against her.

Staggering the last of the way, Carin reached her own door and pushed through into shadows. She stripped and crawled into bed, and cradled her knife-hand close to her body. Despite the severe wrenching Verek had given it when he disarmed her, Carin was vaguely aware, as she drifted off, that her wrist barely hurt now.

The knocking came from the underside of a black lagoon. It sounded both muffled and remote, like a diver with a mossy hammer tapping the hull of a ship below the waterline. The tapping, repeated again and again, brought Carin swimming up from deep sleep.

And when she roused enough to know the sound for knuckles rapping at her door, she also knew whose hand made the fist. On those rare occasions when the housekeeper bothered to knock, the good-natured Myra never waited for an answer, but simply let herself in. Only the master of this house condescended to give Carin some privacy.

"Just a minute," she called, thick-tongued. She fumbled back the bedcovers and reached for her clothes, leggings first. The light outside her window was the colorless paling of the sky before cockcrow. She'd not been permitted much sleep.

The fist rapped at her door.

"Wait! I'm coming," she snapped, louder, and hurried to pull her oldest, shabbiest shirt over her head. She drew her long auburn hair from under the neckline as she walked barefooted to the mortised timbers that closed off her bedroom from the corridor. Her hand on the latch, Carin sucked in a breath and held it as she opened the door to the warlock she knew was standing there.

The apparition who faced her across the threshold was hardly recognizable, however, as the wizard Verek. His hair hung around his face like lank seaweed beached by a storm. His skin was pallid. Bouts of shivering shook his lean frame as though a fitful wind assailed him. He clasped around his

12

shoulders the blanket Carin had spread over him in the cave. A faint scent of *dhera* intimated that he'd also accepted her gift of his liquor.

Verek's eyes, which could burn like white-hot iron when he worked wizardry or lost his temper, were subdued. His gaze expressed only a weary surprise as he studied her from the doorway.

Carin let out her breath but said nothing. Just because she hadn't killed him didn't mean she was happy to see him.

Verek eyed her for a moment more, as silent as she was. Then, braced against the doorpost to keep on his feet, he addressed her in a voice that had more life in it than the rest of him appeared to possess.

"So—it goes easier with you than I had foreseen, and worse with me than I might have imagined. It seems you do not suffer so deeply the wasting cold of *wysards'* waters.

"Tell me, then," he growled. "As you have endured the trials of this night with body whole and mind sound, why didn't you take the opportunity that was laid before you to do me violence? Shall I dare to hope you have at last divined that I am not the enemy?"

Chapter 1

Ghostly Reflections

Carin knifed the wizard in the neck.

She riddled the stableboy with arrows and gloated as Lanse's corpse tumbled off his horse into a pile of wind-drifted leaves. His blood tinged them more brightly than autumn had colored the forest when this miserable journey began.

What are you going to do to me now? she silently demanded of her captors. *What could be worse than this mad errand you've dragged me on?*

As if in answer to Carin's unspoken query, the wizard Verek turned in his saddle and glared at her. "I tell you for the last time: ride up and join our company." His voice was as brittle as the leaves under her mare's hooves. "To lag behind with your sullen face hiding your black thoughts is a fool's pastime. These woods harbor cutthroats."

Like me, you mean? If only, she thought, and suppressed a mirthless smile.

"Leave off with daydreaming," Verek ordered, "and put your eyes and ears to use. These woods have ears and the scheming eyes of scoundrels who may watch us even now."

To have died so many times in Carin's imagination, Lord Verek and his groom remained irksomely healthy and in charge of her. Carin heaved a sigh through clenched teeth. She tapped her heels, urging Emrys to a brisker walk that brought them quickly up to the leader of this small expedition.

But before the mare was well settled behind Verek's mount, an arrow — this one real — thudded into a birch tree so close to Lanse that the boy could have touched the shaft with his fingertips.

Verek jerked his bow up and sailed an arrow toward the unseen attacker. Lanse's shot followed hard on his master's. The wizard's cry of "Cover!" was wasted breath. The three riders were off their horses, diving for the underbrush, even as the forest returned the echo. Carin ducked behind a tree near enough to her captors that she could watch where they watched and, straining her eyes, probe past them into the gloom at their backs.

All was peaceful. The sudden disturbance had interrupted the quiet of the forest as might the brief, bounding flight of a deer. Now the hush of early winter descended again. A chill breeze brought to Carin's ears no hint of booted feet trampling dead leaves. Nothing flitted past bare branches to betray a concealed archer or to suggest any renewed attack upon the party led by Lord Verek of Ruain.

While their riders waited motionless, the horses of Verek's company nosed aside fallen leaves, searching for tufts of grass that the lateness of the season hadn't rendered unpalatable. The almost-silent skirmish and the quick dismounts had not alarmed the beasts. Verek's dark-gray hunter, called Brogar; Carin's trim little mare, Emrys; Lanse's nameless gelding, and the packhorse that carried the bulk of their supplies browsed placidly, as though glad for this chance to rest.

Silent minutes later, Verek nodded to his groom. Both stepped from behind their trees. Lanse caught the horses' trailing reins and tied them beside the forest track they traveled. Then he stood with his bow bent, an arrow on the string to answer any thief who might have designs on the animals.

Verek worked his way, soundless as a thought, in the direction of his bowshot. Carin glided after him like a slim shadow, preferring the wizard's company to the society of his servant or the hidden dangers of this remote but inhabited forest.

16

And anyway, she reflected, *it isn't as though I have any say in who I stick with.* The ensorcelled band of iron that Verek had fastened around her right ankle ensured she wouldn't stray far from him.

Before they'd left his lands in Ruain, Carin had put his wizardry to the test and discovered why Verek had full confidence in the iron's ability to keep her from escaping. The farther she traveled from her captor, the tighter the band drew about her ankle. It snugged up appreciably when she ranged out of his sight to change her clothes or relieve herself. Beyond those limits, she began to know the extremity of pain that such an instrument could inflict. Should Carin stray too far, the iron would tighten its grip until it severed her foot from her leg.

The wizard couldn't make much protest, therefore, against her following him now. Indeed, Verek seemed too intent on his quarry to even notice her.

Watching the black-garbed warlock slip like a night-bat from tree to tree, Carin was glad not to be the one he hunted. Verek had ferreted her from hiding, espied her through walls—even read her mind, she suspected—often enough to prove that he perceived things mortals couldn't. His magian senses were acute, and not easily eluded. If the bowman who had shot at Lanse lacked the good sense to take himself far from this place, then Verek would find him.

The wizard dropped to a crouch.

Carin froze.

In a moment, Verek straightened and strode boldly between two leafless alders, making no further effort at concealment.

As she hurried to join him, Carin nearly tripped over the reason for his lack of caution. A body already on its way to becoming a skeleton lay in the leaves. Verek's arrow protruded from the thin chest. The wretch's clothes were threadbare, his feet wrapped in rags. So emaciated was the corpse, Carin marveled that the man had had strength enough to draw the bow that sent an arrow Lanse's way. It was clearly an act of desperation. A half-frozen derelict on foot attacking a mounted party of three—two of them well armed—could hardly have hoped to succeed.

Carin looked away as Verek put his foot on the bony chest and yanked out his bloodied arrow. She returned her gaze to find the wizard bent over the body, taking the bow from the dead man's hand.

"Fool!" Verek spat the word with such vehemence that Carin slid him a look to be sure he indicted the slain bowman and not herself. Very often, the wizard called her a "young fool." But he generally did it with a sort of half-tolerance, and not in the tone he was using on the corpse at his feet.

"Better for all, had this half-wit laid aside his weapon and made petition as a beggar," Verek grumbled, partly to Carin and partly to the forest around them. "His folly has cost us time, and himself his life. Had he stood at the wayside to beg a meal, pity would have moved me to give it to him. Prudence now demands that I take the wretch's only treasure, this well-made bow, to keep it from the hands of those who might use it more tellingly than he did." Verek glanced at Carin, then away. "Drisha take this fool's soul and leave the body to the wolves. We've no time to dig a grave."

He shouldered the dead man's bow. "Come," he ordered. "Thanks to this vagabond's error, we'll have a harder ride than we once faced to reach Deroucey by nightfall."

Returning to the horses and their guardian, the wizard slipped the confiscated weapon into the case on the packhorse's back that held Carin's own indigo-blue bow. That beauty was "hers" only in the sense that she'd loved the weapon from the moment she found it leaning against the door of the bedroom where she'd slept during her month under Verek's roof.

She'd been allowed to use the bow for only one afternoon, while the wizard tutored her in shooting. That afternoon's archery lesson remained among the more astonishing of all the events Carin had lived through in Verek's labyrinthian manor house. Why the wizard had indulged her, if only briefly, in her desire to master the bow had never been made clear.

Why he would bring "her" weapon along on this crackbrained expedition was even less apparent. Both he and Lanse used their own bows with surpassing skill—the boy's ability proof that his master had trained him well. Besides their bows kept at the ready, both wore dirks at their sides. And Verek carried a longsword in a saddle scabbard.

Even if he were willing to let Carin go armed—which he was not—the wizard didn't need her inexpert bowmanship to bring another measure of protection to their company. Quite apart from the weaponry he carried was the formidable arsenal of magic that Verek commanded.

Fear whispered to Carin—a vestige of recent terrors—as scenes flitted across her memory: the wizard conjuring fire … summoning a knife to his hand with a snap of his fingers … draping spells over the woodlands of Ruain to make an impassable curtain of enchantment … or—most dreadful of all—trafficking with bodiless spirits.

And if cold iron or wizard's cantrips should fail to protect this expedition, they might fall back on Verek's uncanny mastery of the healing arts. By such craft alone he could keep his companions safe from the ordinary hurts to which mortal flesh was subject. Carin's gashes and bruises had healed within hours when the wizard applied his herbal remedies. If the vagabond's arrow had found its mark in Lanse's back, the wizard's skill as a healer would have mended the boy within a day, she didn't doubt.

Weaving with Carin's thoughts were the words of Verek's housekeeper, the talkative Myra: "So long as the wound doesn't reach the vitals, dearie, the master's healing dusts will stitch it up in no time. My good master can stir up a potion to cure 'most any ailment."

Myra's "good master" — the woman's estimation of him, not Carin's — mounted his horse and led their party off down the forest track at a brisker pace than before. As they chased the winter sun that dropped low in the sky, the breeze out of the north freshened. Carin reached with a gloved hand to pull up her hood and tuck it around her face. Then she retreated again into her ruminations, much as she withdrew into the folds of the cloak that Myra had sewn for her from napped woolen in a green "to match your eyes," as the woman had said.

If I've got to go adventuring when the winds and snows of winter lie ahead, Carin mused, *at least I'm not going afoot and threadbare.*

In the days before this journey began, Verek's small household had been frantic with the preparations for it. The wizard's own wardrobe and trappings had needed few additions to have him ready for travel. But Carin, and to a lesser extent the stableboy Lanse, had required much new clothing and gear. Besides the cloak Myra had made for her, Carin had received three pairs of felt-lined wool breeches, knitted stockings and linen smallclothes enough to don fresh every day for a week, three linen shirts, overgarments of soft, warm wool, a quilted underjacket, and a coat with twenty pewter buttons down the front. Her mid-calf boots, crafted of soft-tanned horsehide, were made-to-measure to cover her small feet as comfortably as their own skin.

No doubt, I'll be the best-dressed manservant to accompany a noble traveler into Deroucey tonight, Carin congratulated herself wryly. Her roving thoughts replayed the fit that Myra had pitched when Lord Verek ordered the woman to transform his maidservant into a footboy.

"Cut the girl's hair!" Myra had exclaimed. "Nay, my lord, I cannot! I pray you, do not ask it of me. Bob her lovely hair? That great ruddy mane? To comb and dress it gives me much joy. Would you cause me sorrow in equal measure, with this hateful act you bid me do?"

The wizard had been surprisingly tolerant of his housekeeper's opposition. Carin—eavesdropping from the unlit passageway between the minor wing of Verek's house and Myra's kitchen—had been ready to step up and get it over with, if the woman seemed in danger of provoking her master's temper. But Verek had replied patiently:

"Answer me this, Myra. Would you have the girl ride from here to the western mountains with that great ruddy mane drawing the eye of every man she meets? Will you trust in the gentlemanly ways of each rogue whose path crosses hers?

"I tell you distinctly, mistress: I look for rougher manners in our fellow wayfarers. Indeed, I can scarcely vouch for the honorable conduct of both riders in whose company she'll travel. The resentments that bear potent sway with Lanse have stripped him—as you well know, Myra—of any regard for the civilities owed a lass of his own station.

"Tell me, then," Verek had continued. "Would you send the girl on this journey with that remarkable mane inviting unwelcome glances? Or will you do as I ask, and shear it to a length befitting a gillie who is newly come to his lord's service? So scrawny is the girl from neck to heel, she'll pass handily for a boy—once shorn of that hair. Though it's a fair-faced lad she'll make, I grant you. But do you not think, Myra, that I may more readily defend her against those lechers who might fancy a pretty 'footboy,' than against all the rakes who would desire such a gloriously tressed servant girl?"

Lurking unseen in the passageway, Carin had felt the blood rush to her face. From Myra's silence, she gathered that the gray-haired matron was also disconcerted. The housekeeper, however, soon found her tongue.

"Well, now, m'lord," Myra had begun, in a tone that said many minutes would pass before silence again filled her kitchen. "As you've asked me what I think, I'll tell you. Surely it is I who must say it. I think it exceedingly unwise, sir, for a man to leave his snug, warm home long after the last straggling geese have fled this northern country—with a cold wind behind to help the feathered twits on their way. 'Tis too late in the season by far, my lord, to be riding forth on any foolish errand to the western mountains. If you don't die in a blizzard or break your bones falling from some icy precipice, then it'll be Providence alone, and not your own good sense, that saves you.

"And 'tis the greater folly still, good sir—if you'll suffer me to say it," Myra went on, emboldened by her indignation, "to drag along a girl who's had more than she needs of such adventures—the very waif who came to our doorstep not a month past, in rags and tatters, bravely fending for herself in the middle of nowhere but half starved. After all the time and trouble I've been put to, to get meat on that spare frame of hers, she's so thin even now that a stiff wind could blow her away. 'Tis a wonder that coddled mare of hers hasn't mistook the stripling for a handful of wheat-straw and gobbled her up, so spindly is she.

"'Twas in my mind, master," Myra had continued in disappointed tones, "to have a great feast at Mydrismas, such as hasn't been seen in this house since your noble grandsire feasted his cohorts and their households for leagues around. 'Twas in my mind to sit the girl down to the Mydrismas table and not let her rise ere she had put some curves on that stick-thin figure.

"And if I may speak my mind" —

At this, Verek had snorted, as if expressing his doubt that the woman could address him more frankly.

— "I'll say this, too: For all your talk of that great mane of hers drawing men's eyes, I think *you* see none but a child when you look with your own eyes at that girl's frame. What else could you see in her, my lord? She's hardly more than skin and bones … she might be elves' kin — all wide eyes and lanky limbs.

"But I wonder, master," Myra had rambled on, as was her wont, almost losing Carin as she jumped from thought to thought. "Do you see how much like yourself is that lonely, clever girl? Do you see how she buries herself in your grand library, filling her head with all the learning to be found in those musty old books?

"Do you see what a pair you are, my lord, you and that well-spoken child, who earns her place in this household as the only soul to speak keenly to you of books and puzzles and mysteries? You've no sense in your heads, the one or the other of you, when it comes to those dusty old books.

"And of a certainty, my lord," Myra had concluded, finally making her point, "*you've* no sense inside that skull of yours, sir — though whipped I may be for saying it — to be thinking of taking that girl on a journey halfway across Ladrehdin in the dead of winter. For I'll tell you a thing that maybe you've given no thought to, in all your scheming for this enterprise. Though I call her a child and you may think her one, the girl is no infant. She's a young woman, with a woman's body and womanhood's ways.

"Will you be stopping in some fleapit inn or filthy hole every month of your journey while the girl is in the dark of her moon? Or will you make the lass ride on, sick and bleeding and hurting, through the cold and the snow? 'Tis not to be thought of, my lord!

"Abandon this reckless venture, I beg you. Let winter find you safe at home, with Lanse tending his horses and the girl her books. But if you must go on this foolish journey, then leave the girl behind in my care. 'Tis neither wise nor proper that she be on the road for months with two men—neither of them a husband nor a blood relation to her."

Though hidden in the passageway, Carin had wanted to disappear through a crack. She could only guess at Verek's reaction. In the silence that followed the housekeeper's speech, Carin had imagined the wizard sipping his ale, his unquiet eyes glimmering while he considered his reply. Then he had sighed, but in a manner that expressed no change of heart.

"It is with a thought for the wisdom—and the proprieties—of traveling in the company of a young, unwed woman that I command you as I do," Verek had said, a flash of anger evident in his clipped tones. "Obey me, then. Cut her hair. Dress her in boy's garments. Speak to me no more of the trials of womanhood. Do you think me blind, or so long bereft of my own lady's companionship that I cannot distinguish between an unfledged youngster and a lass of marriageable age and condition?"

When Myra—a woman who was seldom speechless—made no reply, the wizard seemed to repent of his brusqueness. Addressing one matter that she had raised, he added in a voice less edgy:

"There are herbs, good woman, to stem the flow of the female humors in the dark of her moon. It will do the maid no harm, only ease her journeying, to drink each day a draught that I'll prepare. Spare me, therefore, further argument, and see to your duties. There are provisions to be secured and clothing to be sewn. You've work enough, mistress, that you needn't add to your burden by harrying yourself into such a state as you've fallen today."

The sudden scraping of a seat pushed back and the ring of hard-soled boots across the kitchen floor had signaled the end of that singular exchange between Verek and his housekeeper. Carin had fled down the passageway and upstairs to her bedroom, herself and her spying barely avoiding detection.

Alone in her room, she'd dropped onto the bed to consider her limited options. Should she try again to get away from Verek, to spare herself any part of a journey that promised as much danger as misery? For weeks already, she'd sought a way out of his manor and found none. Her one, earlier attempt at escape had ended disastrously, landing her in a "root cellar" that was worse than any dungeon ...

Recalling that episode now, as Carin followed her jailer through the somber forest, she tightened her cloak around her. Yet she couldn't suppress a shudder at the memory of that pit of black horror, utterly lightless and cold enough to chatter the teeth in a moldering skull.

And so I chose to go along on this madman's errand, she chided herself, *thinking I could easily escape when I'd gotten clear of Verek's lands.*

Her plan had seemed simple. Stay with the wizard and his groom until they reached a western country that was as unfamiliar to her captors as to herself. Then steal Emrys and flee, using the forest and the dark, narrow lanes of its scattered settlements to evade Verek's pursuit.

But then the wizard had snapped his cursed band of iron around Carin's ankle, binding her to him. In her mind's eye she had begun to see the magic as an infinitely strong thread, thin as a hair, tying her to the wizard. She could neither slip the knot nor break the thread, but must stay always tethered to her captor.

Carin stared at Verek's back. *Clop, clomp* came the hoofbeats of the mare she rode, striking the ground as steadily as a timepiece, marking the passing of these minutes among all the dismal hours she'd endured on this journey. And yet she had left Verek's lands in Ruain barely two weeks ago. The village he had named as their goal for tonight, Deroucey, was only a minor objective on a quest that threatened to last through the winter and—if she lived to see it—into the spring.

Peeling her gaze off Verek, Carin pushed her hood back and glanced around. The late-afternoon light was dimming into the gray of evening. High overhead, thin clouds hid the first few stars. Twilight spread gloom through the trees.

The wind ran cold fingers through Carin's cropped hair. As befitted her station as Lord Verek's lowly "footboy," she now had the shortest mane of the party. Myra—the woman's face dark with disapproval—had done her master's bidding and bobbed Carin's auburn hair. Once halfway down her back, now it lay in a face-framing pumpkin-shell cut that barely brushed her earlobes. In contrast, Lanse's long brown curls tumbled over his coat collar. The wizard's straight, black hair fell to his shoulders, swept back from his forehead and held off his face by a silver fillet.

But did the narrow band on Verek's brow serve more than a utilitarian purpose? Carin had never seen him wear it to keep his hair out of his eyes when he rode to inspect his land holdings, or when he engaged Lanse in swordplay. Might the coronet announce to strangers his rank? Or was it the ensorcelled mate to the iron band that encircled Carin's ankle? Except for the metals of which the two were made, her shackle resembled Verek's headband.

Or was it, Carin wondered, a bespelled shield that kept the wizard from working magic when ordinary methods would serve him better? The possibility had come to her about a week's travel past the borders of Ruain, when she realized that Verek had worked no wizardry — nothing overt, anyway — since leaving his own lands. Was he deliberately hiding his abilities? Or was he forgoing the use of them now so he'd have the fullest measure of his powers later on?

The prospect gave Carin pause. If Verek expected to have his mastery tested, that said much about the dangers they might face before this quest ended.

Her roving thoughts lit upon a flash that illuminated the forest track ahead. She tensed, prepared to spring from the saddle and into cover at Verek's first warning. But the wizard didn't slow.

Carin, following close behind, stood in her stirrups to peer past her captor. Ahead she made out a flaring torch that jutted from a timber-built stockade. As they rounded a slight bend in the path, a second torch came into view. The fitful light of the pair played over a gateway sealed by iron-strapped doors.

Deroucey, she realized, and heard Verek mutter the name like an echo of her thought. "At last," the wizard added, and Carin detected a note of relief in his voice.

He rode up to the gate. "The Lord of Ruain wishes to hire rooms for the night," he announced, loudly, to the unseen guard. "Will you open to an honest traveler who pays in coin?"

"Gladly, my lord," came the muffled reply. One door screeched inward, opening just enough to admit Verek and his servants and horses. The silver that Verek dropped into the gatekeeper's palm elicited a heartfelt "Drisha bless you, sire!"

Inside the walled town, the streets were nearly deserted. Evidently the people of Deroucey sought the comforts of their evening hearths as soon as night fell. Guided by one of the few natives who were still abroad, Verek led his party to the finest accommodation in town — an inn called "The Grand." It was more meek than magnificent, but entirely satisfactory to Carin.

After two weeks of sleeping blanket-wrapped on the ground and washing sparingly, she was eager for a bed and an all-over bath.

They dismounted at the inn. Verek stepped inside to arrange their lodging, leaving Carin alone with Lanse.

Watching him from the corner of her eye as she struggled, with gloved fingers, to untie her satchel from the packhorse, she saw Lanse jerk his saddle-roll off his gelding. He swung it, hard, into the packhorse's face. The gray, shying from the blow, plowed into Carin and knocked her to the ground.

Wordlessly—she didn't even mutter an oath—Carin got up and dusted off. She stroked the startled beast, quieting it until it would let her claim her baggage. She didn't so much as look Lanse's way again, but mentally she tallied another mark against him.

This new offense joined the dead branch with thorns as long as Carin's middle finger that had found its way into her bed-blankets and her flesh. It aggravated the hurt from the pewter mug with its handle turned so long to the fire that she'd burned her fingers. It deepened the rancor between them, as had the scorpion that fell out of her boot two mornings ago. Carin had, prudently, shaken her boots out before pulling them on, thus avoiding the sting of that particular trap.

How many rocks must Lanse have turned over to find the vermin stirring this late in the year? That he would go to such lengths to harass her didn't bode well for the remainder of their journey together, especially considering that Lanse had punched her once—only once, but hard enough to break Carin's cheekbone.

Remedying that injury had required a benign bit of spell-weaving from Verek—spellcraft the wizard hadn't been certain would work on the "peculiar foundling" from elsewhere who had washed up on the shores of Ladrehdin. It was only Verek's threat of dire punishments, should Lanse lift a hand to her again, that had saved her, Carin knew, from suffering worse from him than pranks.

Tonight, apparently satisfied with his mischief, Lanse didn't trouble her further. By the time Verek rejoined them, the boy had the bags off his gelding and the wizard's hunter. Carin stripped her personal gear from the mare and unburdened the now-calm packhorse. The gray showed by the droop of its head the fatigue that all four horses must feel after the day's forced march.

"The stable is there." Verek laid his hand on Lanse's shoulder and pointed to an unlit structure down the lane. "The innkeeper instructs you to give a shout at the gate, and you'll raise two sturdy lads to help you tend these beasts.

"Here," Verek added, and reached into his leather belt-purse for two pieces of silver. "Give the lads these. Coin buys the best care. When you've seen to the horses, claim your supper from the innkeep and be shown to our lodgings. Our host offers nothing but cold meat and day-old bread, but perhaps you'll find it to your liking after a fortnight of your own cooking."

In the dim light from the open door of "The Grand," Carin eyed the wizard. Was it possible? Had her dour, unsmiling captor made a joke at his groom's expense? Drisha knew—as did Verek and herself—how poor a cook the boy was. Carin never complained, however, for fear of getting the job. Her one hotheaded attempt to stab Verek with a kitchen knife had apparently disqualified her for cook's duty, and she didn't want to be reconsidered for the post. Let Lanse wield the pots, pans, and butcher knives.

If Verek's words were meant in jest, they provoked nothing from his groom but a short nod. The boy led the horses off down the lane, leaving Carin and the wizard to haul their baggage up steep stairs to their rooms.

The innkeeper was there before them, spreading their evening meal on a trestle table in the front chamber. He had already kindled a fire on the hearth; the leaping blaze would soon have the chill off the room. The round, bald hosteler faced them wide-eyed and wrung his hands nervously.

"'Tis an honor to have you with us, m'lord," the man rumbled in deep, hearty tones. That he spoke bravely to cover his uneasiness was obvious. Carin had used the tactic too many times in her own dealings with the wizard not to recognize it in another.

"I fear, good sir," the innkeeper went on, "that you'll be thinking this a house unfit for gentry, seeing as how you've caught us with nary a lad on hand to carry up your packs, nor a lass to wait on you at table. May I hope, m'lord, that you'll forgive such poor service to a noble guest, seeing as it's Mydrismas Eve that you've come to us? Not a lad or lass will work tonight, if they've any living soul in Deroucey to call kin. But on the morrow, sir, all me lads and lasses shall be at your service, ready to fetch and carry as you may command them."

Mydrismas Eve? Carin gave no outward sign of surprise. She stood quietly beside the hall door, her eyes lowered as was proper for a gillie in his master's presence. But her thoughts raced back over the past two weeks, searching for the moment when she'd so thoroughly lost track of time as to forget the major festival of the season.

No wonder the streets were deserted tonight, she realized. All who honored Drisha had been early to temple with their prayers and tithes, and then had got home before sundown to feast with their families. Mydrismas Eve was a night, as the innkeeper said, for young and old to gather with kin to celebrate and retell "the stories," the traditional legends and fables of Ladrehdin. None but the friendless, the destitute, and the desperate were abroad on Mydrismas Eve.

What must this fat man think, Carin wondered, glancing sidelong at their host, *to be serving cold meat and common ale to the Lord of Ruain on Mydrismas Eve?* If Verek hadn't wanted to draw attention to himself, he couldn't have done worse than to enter the town on this night, of all nights. His unorthodox behavior would be the talk of Deroucey tomorrow.

As Verek thanked the innkeeper, however, Carin detected nothing in his manner to suggest the wizard regretted the timing of his party's arrival.

"Do not trouble yourself a moment longer, good man," he told their host—with more warmth than Carin generally heard in her captor's clipped voice. "I'll ask nothing more of you this evening. Such hospitality as you are able to extend on Drisha's night is both welcomed and admired, and a credit to your house. I had hoped to reach your fair town some days ago ... a lame horse is to blame for the delay that's imposed myself and my servants on your kindness and torn you from the comforts of hearth and family on this night of nights. Now—I pray you—return to those things that are the proper business of the devout in this season of joy."

The effect of Verek's lie was, Carin suspected, exactly what the wizard had anticipated. Their host puffed up, a proud bullfrog, visibly pleased with himself for treating his troublesome guests so indulgently, and delighted with Verek's intimation that fault lay entirely with the traveling nobleman and his party.

There goes a man unlikely to spread tales tomorrow, Carin thought. She watched the bullfrog happily bow his way out of the room, pausing to accept a coin from Verek just before he shut the door. Should any man of Deroucey speak ill of the nobleman for breaking with tradition on Drisha's night, their host might be counted on to give out Verek's fiction about a

31

lame horse, to silence rumor, innuendo, and unwelcome questions.

When the innkeeper had gone, Carin stepped to the table and raised her eyes to the wizard's. What she saw in them wasn't satisfaction for the way he'd handled the bullfrog. For an instant — until he realized that Carin was studying him — Verek's dark eyes were clouded.

With pain? Guilt? Regret? From what Carin knew and suspected of the wizard, any one or all three would answer. But on a night devoted to family, this man who had no one — motherless since childhood, with his grandsire, father, wife, and child all dust in the tomb — must feel pain above all else.

Verek's eyes regained their guarded look. His face settled into the unreadable expression it usually wore. But when he spoke, his words confirmed Carin's notion that he thought of the past — of Mydrismas Eves spent with a family long lost to him.

"A poor night it is to be abroad, as our host has said," he addressed her quietly. "Had Myra won the custody of you, that woman would have spread before you such a feast tonight as would founder an ox. Tell me, for I know little of the customs of the southern country: How did you keep Drisha's night in the wheelwright's household?"

Carin shook her head. "Sir, I was not privileged to celebrate the festival with the wright's family," she said, coolly formal. From a filled pitcher on the table she poured water into a basin. "I was only a servant in that house," she reminded Verek as she washed her hands. "I didn't have anywhere to go on Drisha's night — no one to be with. Why should someone like *me* … who's alone and without a family … care about the customs of Mydrismas?"

Verek's silence said her barb bit. Neither of them spoke again as Carin knifed the slabs of meat and cheese the innkeeper had set out. Vigorously, angrily, she hacked off chunks to pile on a slice of stale bread. But as she pushed the unappetizing meal across the table toward the wizard, she felt a little ashamed of herself.

I should respect the memory of the dead, Carin thought, *especially since they died so horribly.* Although Verek's wife and child had drowned years ago, his pool of magic had retained images of their bodies, like ghostly reflections. Carin's glimpse of those images had stayed with her: the woman — Verek's young wife — with the skirts of her gown and the tendrils of her hair floating in the water; and the boy, their five-year-old son, his body grotesquely bloated.

Other things that Carin had seen during her month under Verek's roof came back to her. Vividly she remembered discovering the family tomb in an overgrown section of the garden behind the house. Buried in that tomb, near his wife Alesia and his son Aidan, were Verek's father, Hugh, and his grandfather, Lord Legary.

Carin tried to shake off the memories by renewing her attack on the cold beef and greasy mutton. *If that man still had his family for Mydrismas,* she thought as she sliced portions for herself, *he wouldn't be dragging me along on this mad trip.*

The wizard who occupied Carin's thoughts ignored the food she'd served him. Instead, Verek walked to the door behind her, pushed it open, and stepped through into the second of the two rooms that he'd taken for their party. Carin cast a glance over her shoulder, through the open doorway — and gasped, her heart sinking.

The second room was not the twin of the first. The front room was small, simple, furnished plainly with a wooden table, two backless benches, and two barely adequate cots on either side of its fireplace. But the adjoining chamber made "The Grand" live up to the inn's name.

That room was twice the size of the antechamber. Tapestries dressed its stone walls, and thick carpets half covered the floor of oiled oak. Near the room's large fireplace stood a cushioned bench with a curved back. Cloths of linen and lace draped a table that was elegantly appointed with silver candlesticks and place settings. Across from the fire a tall, canopied bed had curtains of wool to draw round the sleeper, for keeping out drafts and guarding privacy. Clearly, that room was meant for gentry; its antechamber was servants' quarters.

If the second room had been no finer than the first, Carin might reasonably have hoped Verek would share the front chamber with Lanse and put her in the back room, out of his way. But given a choice between luxury and austerity, wouldn't the Lord of Ruain take the quarters to which he was entitled?— leaving Carin to spend a restless night on a cot three steps from Lanse's.

I'll sleep with a knife in each hand, she vowed.

Verek spared hardly a look for the chamber's furnishings. He walked to the room's one window and threw open its shutters. In the glow from the fireplace, nothing appeared against the night sky beyond but a cluster of bare branches. They congregated so near the back of the inn, a person could clamber onto them through the unglazed opening. To do so, however, must put the climber far above the ground. Carin's legs still felt the strain of hauling packs up the long, steep steps that led from street level to these upper-story rooms.

The wind blowing through the opening was icy. Whatever curiosity had led Verek to investigate the window seemed quickly satisfied. He closed and latched the shutters. As he returned through the bedroom, he paused to throw another log on its fire. Then he rejoined Carin in the front room.

"Take what you wish of this rough fare and eat it in there." Verek jerked his head to indicate the luxurious chamber. "Take also whatever you'll need for the night." He pointed his thumb at the bags and satchels that were piled near the front room's entrance. "Once that door closes behind you, I do not wish it to open before morning. I wouldn't have Lanse see that your accommodation for the night is finer than his. I'll say to him that you are sent to bed without your supper. That should gratify his spite and gain us all some few hours' peace."

Carin stared at Verek, too deeply wary of her captor's motives to accept such generosity at face value. The nobleman would relinquish to his "footboy" the comforts that suited a person of rank, and sleep tonight on a servant's hard cot? Why would he favor her to such a degree?

Verek sat down to his cold meal. When he looked up from the table to see Carin wavering, balancing her supper on a slab of bread and not sure where to turn, he frowned but he didn't bark at her. Briefly he studied her face, and when he spoke again it was as though he'd divined her unvoiced questions.

"I'd lose a night's rest, were I to take the better quarters and leave my two young warriors alone together in this room. Which of you would forfeit such a golden chance to harm the other?"

Carin's surprise must have registered on her face, for Verek continued: "Well do I know the enmity that's between you and the boy. And well-deserving would I be of a sleepless night, were I fool enough to throw together in one small room the pair of you, unarbitrated, like combatants off the tournament field. It's for my own sake, not yours, therefore, that I choose a straw mattress above a featherbed. So get within, as I've commanded, with your supper and your baggage. Bar the door, and be as absent from my sight as is the sun itself until tomorrow comes."

This time, Carin didn't hesitate. Spinning on the ball of her foot so quickly that she nearly scattered her supper on the floor, she rushed it to the linen-clothed table and dumped the mess on a silver trencher. Then she grabbed her packs and lugged them into the bedchamber—a room that had never sheltered a less august personage than herself, she suspected. Finally she poured a mug of the innkeeper's cheap ale, to wash down a meal that looked to be as bad as anything that Lanse had served up.

With her free hand on the bedroom door, Carin paused and looked again at the wizard. Verek sat tearing at the meat and chewing grimly, as if engaged in battle against a tough opponent. Between bites, he stared into the fire. He was so obviously lost in thought that Carin didn't dare speak to him.

She stifled a sudden, insane urge to apologize for alluding earlier to the losses that he'd suffered. If she said "Sorry," Verek would make her explain what she knew and how she had learned about the deaths in his family.

Carin's empty hand slid from the doorlatch to touch, through her layers of heavy clothing, a pocket of her trousers. Nestled within were three sheets of writing taken from Verek's library. Two pages of it, she could read. But one remained a puzzle she hadn't solved. Upon those pages was written the greater part of Lord Verek's family history—a history as dark and brooding as the eyes that stared into the fire. Carin wouldn't willingly confess to her captor how much she knew of his private torments, nor how much she had guessed.

Leaving him to his thoughts, she closed and barred the door. With her ale-mug delivered to the table and both hands committed to the unswathing, Carin shed her cloak and every garment underneath, down to her chemise. Only with privacy could she enjoy such freedom. She hadn't been alone for fourteen days.

Too hungry to care what she ate, Carin swallowed whole that part of her supper which couldn't be chewed, and sluiced it down with ale. She poured a little water to wash her face and hands. The rest of the room's ample supply, she set aside for a morning bath.

The bed under its goose-down coverlet was a cloud pinioned to earth. Carin, now stripped of every stitch, slipped between smooth sheets and sank into a mattress that was too soft to be the work of human hands, or so her tired thoughts imagined. She drifted into sleep as if carried there on wings.

* * *

Scratch … scratch … scratch …

It might have been a beetle gnawing wood. It could have been a mouse nosing through dry leaves. But the sound — incessantly repeated until it dragged her out of the clouds — announced itself at last, in Carin's waking brain, as bony fingers on the shutters, seeking admittance through the room's latched but unbarred window.

Chapter 2

A Droll-Teller's Tale

She slipped out of bed and into her cloak. From the fire irons beside the hearth she removed a poker, withdrawing it with such care that the crackle of burning wood masked the ring of metal on metal.

Carin hefted the poker and studied the shutters at which something still persistently scraped. Her gaze went to the door that separated this room from Verek's. Should she call the wizard to deal with this visitor in the night?

Certainly not, snapped the voice of reason—or was it self-respect? Her inner protest bumped up against Verek's words of perhaps an hour ago: "Be absent from my sight." Prudence would dictate that she not go running to the wizard for protection—not without first discovering what threatened from the outside.

Carin glided across the carpeted floor, holding the poker before her like a pike. She brought her face as near the bony scratching as she dared. In a hoarse whisper she demanded: "Who's there? What are you doing at my window?"

"Carin!" came the reply, in a squeak so muffled by the shutters as to be barely audible. "Words fail me. I am more pleased to hear your voice than I can say!"

The heavier end of the poker slipped from Carin's grasp and thudded on the windowsill, jolting her out of the shocked conviction that she heard speech from the grave. She grabbed the iron before it could clang to the floor and rouse the sleeping wizard …

Are you asleep, warlock? Or are you still staring into the fire? With her head cocked to catch the smallest sound, Carin listened for any stirrings from her captor's direction and thanked Drisha when all remained silent.

She put down the poker and unlatched the shutters. A breath of cold air ghosted into Carin's face. But mercifully, the stout wind of earlier had let up. She wouldn't suffer frostbite to be out in the night with a fey creature she had thought dead at Verek's hands.

"Shh!" Carin hissed as she swung one shutter past bare tree branches. She didn't give the living spark that flitted over them a chance to shrill another word. "Woodsprite!" she whispered. "I can't believe it! You're alive. And you're *here*."

She reached for a limb as thick as her arm and grasped it so tightly her knuckles whitened. "*How*, sprite?" Carin demanded. "How did you not die? And how did you get here, so far from the little tree where Verek locked you up? You can't possibly have made it in one jump, all the way from your prison to this huge old thing."

Sighting down the tree's bole, Carin understood why Verek's curiosity about the bedroom window had been promptly satisfied. To reach the ground below would be at risk of breaking bones. The tree's lowermost branches ended well above the surrounding roofs. And light spilling from several windows at ground level showed the venerable tree to tower above an enclosed courtyard. Even if Carin could clamber down among the lower limbs, and from there drop to the ground without crippling herself, she would still be trapped by stone walls.

Trapped, and shackled too, was the thought that flitted through her mind, bringing with it a vague uncertainty. Why regard this window—or any other—as a potential escape route, when the ensorcelled anklet that Verek forced her to wear must keep Carin close to him? Did the wizard's concern for this window hint of a weakness in his spellcraft?

Carin had no time to ponder the possibility. Her lost friend, the sprite of the wood—that nameless, flickering spark among the branches—was shrilling at her in its reedy voice, commanding her attention.

"My friend!" the creature piped breathlessly, its whisper like a flute trying to make music without air. "Though I've trailed you for a week through wintering woods, I've had no chance before tonight to speak up and tell you the means—or, indeed, the fact—of my escape. How closely the mage guards his last captive! I despaired of having a moment alone with you. How is it that he gives us this chance to talk together, free of his presence?"

Carin glanced over her shoulder for reassurance that they were in fact spared the wizard's company. Then she answered in a whisper that was almost as thin as the sprite's.

"It's because of Lanse. I never thought I'd be grateful to that idiot for anything. But Verek shut me in here by myself to make Lanse leave me alone." She dropped her voice even lower. "We have to be careful, sprite, to not let the wizard know you're here. Give me a minute to get dressed and I'll come outside with you."

Carin threw on almost as many layers of clothes as she'd earlier shed. Then she pushed open both shutters and sat on the windowsill. From there it was a moment's work to climb into the branches beyond. Cautiously she pushed the shutters almost closed behind her, but not so far that the latch would catch and strand her in the tree.

"Now, sprite," Carin addressed the spark that fluttered eagerly beside her. "We can talk while the whole town's indoors getting drunk." A glance at the ground below found no one in sight, but snatches of laughter and song drifted up from the night's festivities. "When they get enough wine in them, they'll be seeing things that aren't there and telling wild tales. If we're spotted up here then, no one will believe that we're not just another fairy story."

"Indeed," the sprite replied, catching her drift so quickly that Carin guessed this wasn't the first Mydrismas Eve the wight had passed at the window of an unsuspecting reveler. "But it would make a good story, don't you think?

"'Now here is the tale, children,'" the creature put forth in tolerable imitation of a wandering droll-teller, "'of Fair Carin from a Far Country, who was spied on Drisha's night high in a tree, speaking to a fay the like of which has ne'er been seen in Ladrehdin before or since. Sprite! cries she. You have won free! Clever creature, tell me all! To which the wight replies: Ah, dear girl, I confess to trickery. I did deceive your worthy friend, the plump and graying goodwife who keeps her master's house in perfect order.'"

"Myra?" Carin interrupted, quite forgetting that she was meant to be the "droll-teller's" audience. The sprite seemed not to mind, but dropped its playacting and took up the story in its own reedy voice.

"The same, my friend. The lady who showed you such kindness proved as gently disposed towards myself—though she did approach my prison-tree no nearer than she must, our first few days together, to sprinkle water on its roots. But I soon put her at ease with praise for the fine needlework that trimmed her, ahem, *roomy* garments. So pleased was the woman with my words, she began to visit me throughout the day, though the mage had charged her only with a morning watering and a throwing back of the curtains so the sunlight might reach my leaves. We got on famously. How I wish I'd heeded your advice and made the lady's acquaintance long before the wizard made me a hostage in her care."

Carin almost laughed aloud at the picture the sprite's words painted. She perched more comfortably amid the branches,

41

tucked her legs under her cloak, and patted the limb in which the flitting spark had settled.

"I knew you'd like each other," she said. "In all of the north country, there are only two that I trust, and either of you could talk the ears off a mule. Together, you must never stop. No secret could be safe with two gossips like Myra and the woodsprite. But I tell you everything, and only hope you'll hold your tongue when you need to.

"But sprite, I'm dying to know: how did you escape? The last time I saw you, you were stuck in that potted plant in Verek's sitting room. I imagined him doing horrible things to you."

"Be easy on that point," the sprite said. "Though I chafed at captivity, I could not complain of my treatment in the mage's house. Indeed, it was his command to Myra—he told her she must keep me alive through the winter—that let me slip away."

"While she was tending you?"

"Just so. From the tree that was my prison, I caused the leaves to wither and fall. 'Alas!' I said when Myra came with her watering can. 'Look how my host sickens! Soon it will die, and I'll perish with it.'

"'Oh my, uncanny creature!' the woman cried. She swept up the fallen leaves and fretted over me. 'What's to be done? My master bids me preserve the sprite. I daren't disobey him, and I shouldn't like to see such a cheerful fay pass from this life. Tell me the remedy, wee goblin, and I'll fetch it as quick as I may.'

"'The remedy,' I said, 'is a young, healthy sapling brought to me forthwith. Dig up a vigorous sprig with a great ball of roots, pot it, and hasten here with my new prison. Quickly, dear lady, I beg you. Another day will see the death of this sickly shrub, and my own demise as well.'

"I'd hardly got the words out before the woman was bustling forth to do my bidding," the sprite went on gleefully.

"And within the hour she came again to me, with a slender branch of rowan in a flowerpot.

"'Oh no, my lady!' I greeted her in consternation. 'Not the rowan tree! Never rowan! Do you not know the rhyme? *To rowan, amber, and red thread / Weirdling wights cannot be led.* I must have a sapling of hazel—a scion of the limber tree, fairest in the woods.'

"With a cry of dismay then, Myra snatched up her potted rowan and flew to the door with all the speed such a plump goose could make," the sprite continued. Carin heard amusement in its voice. "And with a great leap, like so"—the creature sparked away in the night, coming to rest in a distant limb—"I flung myself from my prison-tree and into the twig in the lady's hands."

The sprite flashed back to Carin, with a light like steel on flint, to finish its story. "For as you well know, my friend, the wood of the rowan holds no terrors for such a one as I. Safely hidden in the vessel of my escape, I was as silent as a buried root until the woman had carried me from the mage's rooms down the stairs and out to the garden. There I sparked away, happy in my freedom and lingering only a moment to reveal the trickery and beg her pardon.

"I'm not proud to have deceived Myra," the creature said. "But I couldn't stay behind while you, my friend, journeyed into danger. I cannot doubt—having tasted of the mage's treachery—that he may yet throw you into harm's way. A month ago, I believed the wizard to be your protector. Now I suspect that you've had the right of it all along, to doubt him. The mage doesn't scruple to deceive; he deserves no one's trust. Didn't he break his word to you, by keeping me captive though you did the task that was to win my freedom?"

"He certainly did," Carin replied, her voice low and strained. She felt her anger rise again, as blistering as when she had first realized that the wizard would not honor their bargain. "He went back on his word the very next morning, after he and I both had almost drowned in his pool of magic. Like I told him then, 'I did what you wanted. Now you *have* to let the woodsprite go. That was our deal.'"

"But how did the mage presume to justify his reneging?" the sprite asked, flickering hotly.

Carin sniffed. "He didn't. He just went around in circles." In her best imitation of the wizard's clipped voice, she repeated Verek's reply: "'I will fulfill my obligations when you have fully met yours.'" She shook her head. "I should have known I couldn't trust him. Sprite, I'm really sorry I let him trick me in the first place. If I hadn't brought you into his house—right into that trap he set for you—he never could have taken you captive."

The sprite flared up. "If I hadn't been *such* a coward," it cried, "I would have thrown myself into the fire that night. My self-destruction would have broken the mage's hold on you. It was hardly the act of a true friend, to value my own life above your safety."

"Dead friends aren't much use," Carin retorted. She put her palm on the branch where the sprite flickered. "I prefer you living." Before she slipped her hand back into the folds of her cloak, Carin tucked the hood closely around her face and throat. Then, trying to ignore the cold that deepened with the night, she went on with her story.

"Anyway, sprite, you'll be glad to know that the wizard ended up in worse shape than I did that night. When the painful part was over, I was standing and he wasn't. But soon enough, he got on his feet—and he came after me."

As Carin talked, she relived every moment of that night. She heard again the wizard knocking at her bedroom door. Verek's insistent rapping had brought her out of sleep the way the woodsprite's scratching had roused her tonight.

It occurred to Carin then to wonder how the creature had made the sound. The woodsprite possessed no fingers with which to scrape at window shutters.

She'd ask later. The agitated sparking in the tree limb at her side spoke of a listener who was impatient to hear her tale.

"I didn't know what to expect," Carin went on, "when the wizard came to my door. Was he going to be furious that I'd gone to bed and left him in a bad way? Would he light into me for falling into his wizards' well—like it was somehow my fault? Or could he possibly be happy that I'd managed to trade the puzzle-book for a trinket that he wanted from that other place? But everything else aside," she admitted, "I never expected him to ask why I hadn't killed him."

"Carin!"

The sprite's shriek nearly startled her off the branches. She grabbed for the nearest limb and avoided a fall, but threw her tucked cloak into disarray. Winter's frosty breath swept up her legs and down her neck.

"Sweet mother of Drisha!" Carin swore. She drew her cloak tight before cold air seeped through every stitch. "You scared me out of my skin. Keep your voice down!"

"Your pardon," the sprite said. "But your words—or rather, the mage's—have me wonderstruck. What did he mean when he spoke of *you* slaying *him*?"

Carin sighed, and half wished she'd omitted that part of her story. But the sprite—whose destiny might lie in the wizard's hands as her own fate did—deserved to know how Carin had thrown away her one chance to destroy the sorcerer.

"Verek was helpless," she muttered. "The way he'd just collapsed, after getting me out of his pool of magic, I would have thought he *was* dead—except for his beating heart."

That heartbeat: Carin might have stilled it with a single stroke. But she had chosen not to. And when Verek's wits returned, he'd come to her to know her reasons: *Why had she spared him?*

The woodsprite held its peace during Carin's preoccupied silence. But it signaled by a rapid fluttering in the branches that it wanted her answer, as Verek had.

Did the sprite need to know all of her reasons? No. The same half-truth she had told the wizard would do.

"I was afraid to finish him off," Carin said, "because I didn't know what would happen to you, sprite, if Verek died while you were still his prisoner. I thought the spells holding you captive might become permanent, like walls without doors. Then you'd never get out. When your prison-tree withered away, so would you."

"How did the magician answer," the sprite asked, "when you'd stated your grounds for showing him more mercy than he deserved?"

Carin shrugged. "He hardly ever gives me a straight answer. All he said was: 'I am heartened to find so much wit in you, that you'd give thought to consequences and choose your way with reason, not passion only.'"

She leaned against a branch. "What do you think he meant? That I was right? That I would have ended up killing you, too, if I had knifed the wizard? Or is Verek just glad that I let myself get distracted? If I hadn't worried about 'consequences,' he wouldn't be alive now. And you and I wouldn't be up this tree, hiding from him."

"Perhaps not," the sprite replied. "Who can say? You and I cannot know the wizard's mind—not without more practice than either of us has had. You've known the mage—how long? Some six weeks, if memory serves. My acquaintance with the wizard is of longer standing but lesser intimacy. You speak with him daily; I, hardly ever. Indeed, he held aloof from me until you astonished us both by entering lands so bewitched that no natural being of this world may walk there.

"But I digress," the creature interrupted itself. "I have questions yet to ask you, of what transpired in the cave of magic that first night of my imprisonment. But for now, I'm satisfied to know that no irreparable harm befell you.

"What of the second night, however? Did I only dream it, or did you come to my prison-tree long after sunset that next night, and speak a few words?"

"You weren't dreaming," Carin said. "I was there. But I didn't get much out of you—just mumbles and yawns, you were so sleepy. That's all I needed, though, to know that you were still alive.

"By that time, sprite, I was ready to scratch Verek's eyes out. There he'd made me think that I only had to run the one 'errand' for him, but I was realizing how he'd double-crossed me. That next night, he wanted me to go off again, somewhere else. He said I'd have to, or he wouldn't ever release you."

She sniffed. "I told Verek I wouldn't go on any more magical journeys to 'other worlds' until he proved to me that you were all right. I wasn't taking his word for it. He's such a liar," she grated.

"He burned with anger, and I thought he would blow up at me. All the signs were there." A shudder hunched Carin's shoulders like a spasm, not entirely from the cold. "But he gave in. He took me up to his rooms and let me see you."

She shrank deeper into her cloak. As Carin told the woodsprite of that second night's confrontation with the wizard, she was, for long moments of mental flight, out of her high, cold perch and back in Verek's library ... the scrabbling of the wind against the room's windows conspiring with the hiss of the hearth-fire to lull her into sleep ... her head sinking to the cushions of the bench where she had sat reading ... waiting ...

It wasn't a noise—no tapping or scratching—that had woken her then, but an uneasy sense of no longer being alone in the library. The hairs rose on the back of Carin's neck like waking thoughts starting up from a bad dream.

Her eyes flew open to see a glowing witchlight orb resting on the back of the bench opposite hers. Just below and to one side of the orb gleamed a head of dark, glossy hair. Verek's eyes like coals of fire looked back at her from a face half in shadow. The witchlight shining on the right side of his face was the only light in the room.

Carin's wide stare traveled, from the orb and the unsettling face it illuminated, down to Verek's right hand. In it he held a glass of *dhera* that reflected the witchlight like liquid rubies. His left hand rested on his leg, with his fingers hooked over a slim stick that was so highly polished, it seemed to glow in the magical light.

She knew the stick. It was the honey-colored wand with which Verek had baited his trap—the well-laid trap that had made the sprite a prisoner and Carin a slave to the wizard's schemes. Was the wand really a piece of the woodsprite's homeworld, as the creature so desperately wanted to believe? The lure of the wand had been the fay's undoing. It had wagered its freedom against a chance to touch the artifact, and it had lost.

Verek said nothing of his captive, but with the flat of his hand he idly rolled the wand along his leg.

"You've missed your supper, and I'm to blame," he remarked almost conversationally. "I persuaded Myra to let you sleep, which she was pleased to do. She saw you dreaming in here. Now the woman reproaches herself.

48

"'I've overworked the girl,' she said to me. 'The chores I give her are too much for the lass.' Though I knew of other reasons for your fatigue, I kept silent and let the woman blame herself alone. For if our Myra knew of the errands I send you on by night, running you ragged until the wee hours, I'd get an earful."

Verek sipped his drink and regarded Carin over the rim of his glass. She gazed back less boldly. Of the ashen-faced, shivering, disheveled man who had slumped in her doorway early that morning, no trace now remained. The wizard was himself again—neatly groomed; dressed in a fresh white shirt, dark vest and woolen trousers; and fully possessed of all his faculties, both magian and mortal, to judge by the light of sorcery at his shoulder and the mockery in his words.

Lowering his glass, Verek said, "If you're hungry, go now to the kitchen and eat. Myra will have set aside your portion. But if you've worried yourself out of an appetite, then come with me to the cavern of *wysards* and journey again as you did last night. You will not, I trust, delay again in the otherworld as you delayed at your last destination."

The wizard leaned forward, casting his face into shadow as he left the illumination of his witchlight orb. "Didn't I warn you in the strongest terms to hurry back from that other place?" he asked, an accusation in his voice. "Were my instructions not precise and firm upon that point? Yet you tarried over a book— began to read it, as though you had all of eternity to spend beneath that other sky!

"I tell you distinctly: you very nearly lost yourself in the oblivion between the worlds. And such losing would have been for all eternity. Once parted from you, I haven't the means to bring you forth from that emptiness. Do not, therefore, risk again such a fate. From the world to which you will journey tonight, return at once, delaying not for the wink of an eye to marvel at whatever oddities may present themselves."

Verek leaned back against the cushions of his bench, back into the light, and Carin forced herself to meet the gaze of those darkly brilliant eyes. Slowly, she shook her head.

The wizard frowned, then took another sip of his drink. As Carin's silence lengthened, the muscles of Verek's jaw tightened visibly. His quick anger, always just under the surface, was threatening to explode. In the face of it, Carin receded into her cushions but still said nothing.

"Tell me," Verek snapped. "To which of my instructions do you mount the resistance signified by a wordless shake of your head? Surely you don't mean to disobey me in a matter that bears so directly upon your safety? When I tell you that any delay in your return may mean the death of you, I expect your thanks for my concern—not your defiance of the warning."

Carin swallowed in a dry throat and found her voice.

"I'd return right away, sir, just like you say—*if* I was going anywhere. But I'm not. I'm staying clear of the wizards' pool and any journeys that start or end down in that cave. So I don't need to take your advice—though I'm *sure* you're offering it out of a *deep* concern for my safety."

The wizard, scowling, leaned toward Carin across the low table between their two benches. He set his half-full goblet down so hard that *dhera* sloshed over his hand. Heedless of the drops he flung Carin's way, Verek flicked the fingers of his right hand at her—exactly the gesture he'd used to subdue the spells that guarded the boundaries of his woodland. Did he think he could control her, as he controlled his conjurings?

Triumph flashed in the midst of Carin's fear. The warlock's gesture had no effect. Though it might bend the forces of wizardry to his will, it brushed past her as harmlessly as air.

Carin allowed no hint of gloating into her face, however. She couldn't let Verek see how much it pleased her to thwart him. Her immunity to much of his magic — apparently a consequence of her otherworldliness — had been a goad to him since their first meeting.

The wizard stared at her, as if seeking a sign that Carin would yield. Finding none, he settled back and sighed. He raised one booted foot and rested that ankle on the opposite knee. With his *dhera*-stained hand Verek massaged his propped ankle as though kneading sprained ligaments.

It was a pose Carin had seen him adopt before, when he sought to curb his temper or restrain his impatience.

"So," he addressed her finally, his voice sharp with displeasure. "You have chosen to let the woodsprite die. Never doubt me: I *will* kill the creature, as I've promised, if you resist me."

Carin sprang from her seat with a ferocity that caught the usually self-controlled Verek by surprise. He recoiled as if a viper had struck at him.

"Never doubt you!" she exclaimed, almost strangling on the words. "Never doubt *you?* How can I do anything *but* doubt you! You're a man without honor."

She rushed on, ignoring the look he gave her. "I have such a deep mistrust of you now, after your dishonesty of these last two days, that I wouldn't believe you if you said the sun sets in the west. We had a bargain. Last night I kept my end of it — and I thought I would die before it was over. But now, you're refusing to honor your promise to turn the woodsprite loose. You're just a two-faced liar."

Although Carin had more to say, she paused as Verek rose and stood over her, glaring. His gaze threatened to sap her courage. She hurried to finish while she could.

"I think the sprite is dead. I think you've already killed it. Why bother to keep it alive, after you blackmailed me last night into doing what you wanted?" Carin flipped her hair back defiantly. "If you've got rid of the sprite already, then you've made a big mistake. Without it, you can't force me to do anything."

Verek heard her out, his hands toying with the polished wand. The bright stick had the look of crystal in the witchlight. He pinned the wand between his opposing palms so that the whole of its length lay open to Carin's view, only its tips pressed into his palms like a crossbeam between two upright posts.

Then, with a sudden movement of his left hand skyward, the wizard tilted the wand from the horizontal to the vertical. He grasped it right-handed like a club. Carin braced for the blow.

But he only tapped the wand's tip against his lower lip. After a moment of that, Verek shook his head almost imperceptibly.

"I shouldn't dignify your first accusation with an answer," he snapped, his voice brittle. "When you agree to a task with ill-defined limits, you have no grounds for complaint when the work goes on. Did I tell you the task would span one night only? No, I didn't. If you think it's a poor bargain that you've struck, blame yourself. I will not alter the terms simply because you've decided they displease you."

Verek punctuated his next words by loudly popping the wand into his left palm. "As for your second charge, that I've killed the sprite: it's easily disproved. Come upstairs and discover for yourself that I have not played you false. The creature lives. But hear me when I speak this warning, for I will not repeat it: When you have seen the woodsprite, you will descend with me to the cavern of *wysards*, there to travel tonight as I decree, or your friend won't know another daybreak" —

"May the villain *roast* on a bonfire of oak, alder, blackthorn, and russet aspen!" the sprite cried.

A curse so black coming from the normally mild woodsprite brought Carin up short, halting her tale. She put a cold hand to her face, a little dazed by her abrupt return to the present. She'd almost forgotten the fay's presence and might have been sitting in a tree talking to herself, remembering that second night with Verek, back in Ruain.

"I tremble with anger to know how the brute has used our friendship as a weapon against you, dear girl," the sprite went on. Indeed, the tree seemed to shake as the creature spoke—but it could have been just her own shivering that Carin felt. She tugged her hood over her half-frozen face.

"Abject apologies," the creature added, "for my thickheadedness when you came to speak with me that night. As one accustomed to sleep in the wild woods and open air, I found that the closeness of a curtained room made me deeply languid after sunset.

"But tell me now, my friend: what happened next? The mage—dark villain!—spoke of your journeying that night from the cave of magic to a world beyond. Did you go? What did you see? Did your travels take you to the land of the bright wood? I burn with eagerness to hear of your adventures."

Carin shifted on the branch under her. The discomfort of her perch and the frostiness of the night were getting hard to ignore. As she debated the wisdom of returning to bed and leaving the rest of her long and tangled story for another night, a voice cut through the air. She couldn't make out the words, but she knew the inflection: Verek's. It didn't come from indoors. His voice shafted up from the lane between the inn and the stables.

"Shh!" Carin cautioned the sprite. "I hear the warlock. We can't let him catch us out here. I've got to go in now, and tell you the rest of it later."

"A moment," the sprite begged. "I would know the business that has drawn the magician to the streets at this hour."

From the treetop, the creature sparked to a shrub that grew in the corner of the innkeeper's courtyard. Its next leap took the fay out of sight, but not for long. Before Carin had done more than unwind her cloak and begin to inch toward the window, the sprite was back, bearing news.

"The mage seeks the stables. There is, I think, some trouble with a horse. He casts no glance this way. I take it your absence has not been noted.

"But perhaps we would be wise to end this meeting while our secret is safe. I confess a need to sleep, and I suspect that you would prefer your bed to these branches. Such a chance as we've had tonight, to speak together through the midnight watch, may not soon come again. But I'll be at your back day and night, my friend, and follow wherever your journey takes you."

Carin hugged the tree and promised to finish her story at the next opportunity. As she reached for the shutters, a loose fold of her cloak tumbled down and fell against the planks. The shutters swung inward ever so slightly, but too far. With a soft *click*, the latch dropped into place. The window was sealed, and Carin was out in the cold with a disturbed wizard prowling the night.

Chapter 3

Possibilities

Her first thought was to coax one of the Mydrismas revelers below into coming upstairs to let her in. She considered sending the sprite to find out whether Lanse had joined his master in the stables, leaving the way clear for a rescuer to pass unchallenged through Verek's rented rooms. Should the incident be mentioned in the morning, Carin could deny it all: "High in a tree, m'lord? Climbed through the window and locked myself out? What nonsense! Our host has been in his cups."

But then she realized the futility of her scheme. Her bedroom door was barred from the inside. The wizard might have a means of lifting the bar from his side of the door, but no drunken mortal would manage it.

The sprite, however, had a plan of its own. "Higher in this tree is a dead branch, its wood dry and hard as stone," the creature said. "A sliver of it should serve you to slip between the shutters and lift the latch. Were the wood alive, I wouldn't dream of violating it. But I think this old giant will not begrudge you a splinter of its dead flesh."

Sparking upward a short way, the sprite set to work. There was a ripping sound, similar to sailcloth tearing, then three sharp snaps like twigs breaking. When the creature called her to claim the tool, Carin only had to stand on a branch and work her hand up through a cluster of small limbs. The sprite's eager sparking guided her until her fingers closed on a strip of wood the length of her hand and paper thin.

Only an ironsmith could have forged a stiffer blade. Amazed, Carin tried to bend it but couldn't.

The sprite's been keeping secrets, she thought. *It can do more than talk and jump through trees.*

Maybe this example of its talents shouldn't come as a surprise, though. Weeks ago, the fay had broken off tree limbs and sent them crashing down on the wasteland dogs that had threatened to tear her apart. And then the creature had wanted to drop a branch on Lanse's head. Carin had stopped the sprite when it first proposed cracking Lanse's skull open. But as she slid this newest example of the creature's handiwork between her fingers, she reconsidered. With the sprite on the loose again, maybe it could serve her as a weapon.

The slim crack between the shutters admitted the strip easily. Carin flicked the latch up, took her leave of the sprite, and climbed through into the welcome warmth of her quarters. She disrobed, crawled back into bed, and was asleep in seconds.

* * *

She woke to a sunlit room and a fire that had dwindled to embers. The light that streamed in through four diamond panes high up the wall was the clear light of day full broke. But the morning had brought no pounding at Carin's door, no shouts ordering her to rise and make ready to ride. Why hadn't Verek roused his party at dawn to continue their journey?

Carin slid out of bed and padded to the door that separated her from her captors. She pressed her ear to it and caught no sound from the adjoining room. She seemed to be alone.

How lucky can I get? she wondered. First a comfortable bedroom all to herself, then a long reunion with the woodsprite, and now the prospect of time for bathing and for washing out a fortnight's worth of dirty clothes.

She built up the fire and found a cake of soap. Water by the pitcherful made for a better bath than Carin had had since leaving Verek's manor. It was a delight to wash her hair—for the first time since its bobbing—and to slip her last set of clean clothes over scrubbed skin.

Carin reused her bathwater for her laundry. Linen shirts and smallclothes soon hung from the mantel and the furniture, making her quarters look like a scrubwoman's shop.

The warmth of the fire and her exertions drove her to the window for a breath of air. She pushed open the shutters, admitting brittle cold but bright sunshine. It would have been a good day for traveling. Why was Verek's party still in Deroucey?

Curious as well as hungry, Carin returned to the door, this time not just to listen at it but to crack it open. The antechamber beyond was empty, but obviously not yet vacated. On the unmade beds were saddlebags and satchels that belonged to Verek and Lanse. The ashes on the hearth had not been raked up, nor a new fire laid, but the remains of breakfast on the table suggested that the innkeeper hadn't wholly neglected his guests.

Carin closed the door on the sight of her dripping laundry and sat down to breakfast. The mutton was cold, the cheese and bread were beginning to dry out, but the food was much better than their host had served last night. She ate appreciatively and cleared the table of nearly every scrap that Verek and Lanse hadn't consumed.

Clean, warm, and well fed, Carin sat relaxed and sipped at a mug of milk … and wondered again what had stopped a journey that had been dawn-to-dusk hard riding for two weeks.

Some trouble with a horse, I think.

The woodsprite's words from last night popped into Carin's head and dispelled the sense of ease—almost of well-being—that had crept over her.

"Not Emrys!" she whispered. Carin's stomach twisted around her breakfast. "Merciful Drisha, don't let it be the mare that's gone down!"

She plunked her mug on the table so hard that the milk splattered out. Carin sprinted for the door to the stairs. She yanked it open, took a step toward the landing—

—And fell, grabbing for her ankle.

The ensorcelled band of iron had tightened like the garrote in an assassin's hand. It sliced deep. Blood welled up, wetting Carin's clean stocking. The sensation, in the first few seconds, was more a stinging than real pain. But quickly the wound began to throb. It sent pangs to her toes and all along her leg. By the time she pulled herself up the doorjamb, got her good leg under her, and hobbled back to a bench at the table, the pain in her ankle was agony.

Carin peeled off her bloodied stocking and clawed at the iron. It was embedded in her flesh, girdling her ankle. She couldn't get it out.

She fumbled for a basin and knocked over the mug of milk, but she managed to get a bowl off the table and under her foot. With what little water remained in the only pitcher within reach, she bathed the wound. Carin gritted her teeth and tried to marshal her thoughts. She had to extract the iron, but how?

Footsteps sounded on the stairs. They climbed toward the landing where Verek's instrument of torture had crippled her.

"Help me!" Carin shrieked through the open door. "I'm cut to the bone!"

The firm tread on the stairs reached the top. It was not the innkeeper or a servant who appeared in the doorway, but Verek, scowling.

As the wizard's gaze slid from Carin's face to her ankle, however, a look of shock replaced his frown. "Death of my life!" he swore.

He closed and locked the door, then rushed to the saddlebags on his bed, to take from them a linen bundle and a leather wallet. These he set on the bench beside Carin. Then he knelt at her feet and encircled her ankle with his right hand.

"When I release the *chalse*," he said, looking up at her, "the pain will worsen. There's no help for it—the ring must be loosened. I will remove the device from the wound, and you are to stanch the bleeding as best you can." He jerked his chin at the bundle of linen.

Carin's hands shook as she pulled out a length of cloth and held it ready. She gulped a shuddering breath and tried to prepare for what was to come. If the pain worsened much, she'd faint.

With his left hand, Verek gripped the calf of Carin's leg. His other hand tightened around her ankle, then began slowly to open. She felt the iron mimic his slackening grip. It crept out of her flesh.

The pain was savage. "Agh!" Carin cried. Black spots danced before her eyes.

The wizard slid the loosened band up her shank. He kept it hidden under his right hand. Then he slipped it under his left, still out of Carin's sight. For a moment his hands stayed still, both holding her leg well above the ankle, both concealing the cursed band. Did its form change so much, when the warlock subdued the magic in order to move the thing, that he didn't want Carin to see it? What *was* the ensorcelled iron, in this other guise?

Carin twisted linen around her ankle and squeezed, trying to stop the bleeding. The pain was so bad, she could barely breathe. Deep in her throat, she whimpered.

Verek leaned aside, giving her room to work. While Carin soaked up an alarming amount of her life's blood, the wizard slid the basin out from under her foot. The water in it was red with gore, but he rinsed his hands in it, then dried them on the corner of a bedsheet. When he reached around Carin for the wallet that he'd laid beside her, his face brushed hers as she bent double.

"How did this happen?" Verek murmured, looking straight into Carin's eyes.

What an extraordinary question from the one who had inflicted this torture! Still bowed at the waist, Carin glared at him, clenched her teeth, and said nothing.

Verek seemed to take her meaning. He shifted his gaze to the wallet in his hands, undid the thongs that closed it, and rephrased his question.

"What I wish to know is, where were you when the *chalse* tightened?"

"Leaving!" Carin grated out.

Her reply made Verek frown again.

"Had you no warning? Didn't the band contract by degrees as you neared the door?"

"No, it did not," Carin snapped. "The damned thing was fairly loose until I stepped over the threshold. Then it clamped down like a bear trap, so hard I thought it'd break my ankle."

The wizard shook his head but said nothing. From the wallet he removed two packets and opened them. One held bronze powder; the other, green.

Carin bit her lip. From previous experience with the bronze *cyhnaith*, she knew it would burn like damnation's eternal fires when Verek dusted it into the wound. But it would also stop the bleeding and heal the cut. A deep gash on her knee—an injury Carin had suffered within an hour of first meeting Verek in Ruain—had closed overnight after a single treatment with his medicinal powders.

She didn't resist, therefore, when the wizard unwrapped the blood-soaked linen and liberally dusted her ankle with the

60

bronze powder. A shriek erupted from her as the compound seared her flesh. Verek did not look up. He poured more powder into his hand and cupped it around the back of her ankle so the medicine would reach the whole, encircling wound. Then he repeated the application with the green dust.

Carin cried out again—in sheer relief—as the green powder's painkilling qualities took hold. *Cyhnaith's* fire died. Her ankle went numb. Deadened nerves no longer screamed at the assault on her flesh.

She raised a shaky hand to her face and found her cheeks wet. At what point she'd surrendered to tears, Carin didn't know.

Verek wiped at the blood that was congealing around the wound and on Carin's bare foot. He dipped a clean end of an otherwise gory piece of linen into a little clear water, and with it removed the worst of the stickiness. With fresh linen, he bound her ankle.

When the dressing was done, Verek closed his right hand around the ensorcelled iron. The band had hung just below Carin's knee throughout the tending of the injury it had made. Now Verek slid it back down to her ankle. He held his hand around the iron until it had shrunk nearly to its original size and rested on the bandage over the wound.

"For the love of Drisha," Carin swore, but softly, almost under her breath.

Her tone seemed to get Verek's attention more readily than angry, loud cursing would have. He jerked his gaze up to hers.

"Take that evil thing off me," she whispered to him. "The next time, it could cut clear through. I'll lose my foot."

The wizard shook his head. "The next time you provoke the *chalse* to tighten, you will have warning. I was too hasty, it seems, in setting spells upon the threshold when I left this morning. I was distracted by last night's business in the stables

61

and didn't linger to be sure the spellcraft was properly done. I will make certain that the protections which must accompany this wizardry are well in place, if I must again leave you confined."

Apparently unwilling to accept all of the blame, Verek added: "The ring would not have roused, however, if you hadn't attempted to run away."

"I wasn't running!" Carin protested, her voice rising. "When my foot crossed that threshold I was on my way to the stables, to be sure Emrys—"

She stopped herself just in time. *To be sure Emrys wasn't hurt*, she'd nearly said. But why should Carin have concerns about the mare being injured? How could she know anything of last night's "trouble with a horse" unless someone had told her about it? It would have been exceedingly stupid of her, to let a slip of her tongue tip off Verek to her secret informant.

Carin quickly amended: "—to be sure Emrys was doing all right this morning. She was worn out when we got here last night, and I wanted to check on her." Carin lifted her shoulders, stretching as she shrugged. "I hope she got to sleep late, like I did."

"Late it is," Verek muttered. "And getting later."

He stood, gathered his supplies of curative powders and clean linen, and returned them to his saddlebags. Then he took off his coat and moved a bag aside so he could sit on his bed, with his back to the wall.

Carin twisted around on her bench to face him, working clear of the shambles on the table: the gory rag, basin of bloody water, and film of dried milk amongst the remains of an hours-old breakfast. She'd just wedged her elbow into a relatively clean spot when she looked up to see Verek studying her.

His eyes were hard, like two black crystals. And though his gaze was intimidating, it held none of the luster that had often made Carin doubt the wizard's sanity. That gleam in his eyes, which had flickered like a candle's flame from the depths of a cave, had been absent since Verek paused outside the borders of Ruain to settle a silver fillet on his brow. In the same way his party had kept the campfire turfed each night of this journey, to subdue the glow, the silver band seemed to bank the wizard's magian fire.

"This delay that you have enjoyed," Verek said, continuing with his train of thought and apparently oblivious, for once, to what Carin was thinking, "will hold us here only one night more. A careless fool of a stableboy—drunk last night, with all the town—let the packhorse into the oat bin. The foundered beast is at the knacker's now, and Lanse bargains for a nag to take its place."

"Is Emrys all right?" Carin asked, safe now in letting her worry show. "And Brogar?" The wizard's hunter was every inch its master's steed, but the horse had let Carin on its back when she was too sick or injured to walk, and would stand patiently when Verek ordered her up. Though it was not a friend like her Emrys, in whose ears Carin could whisper secrets, Brogar was nevertheless a stalwart companion she wouldn't want to lose.

"The three from my own stables are unharmed," Verek answered, as if to remind Carin that the mare was his, not hers. "The loss of one from among their number would be grievous. I regret less the ruin of the pack animal than the time wasted in securing its replacement.

"Still," Verek added, "man and beast can do with a rest. I don't doubt that the survivors among the horses will be as pleased to remain another night in the stables of Deroucey as you will be to sleep again in your stately quarters."

Carin ducked her head to hide her smile. *He doesn't know the half of it*, she gloated. For not only would she enjoy another night of comfort, in her privacy she could also have another talk with the woodsprite.

Her smile faded as her gaze found the anklet that ringed her bandage. Her pain was gone, but Carin's dried blood coated the iron. She brought her foot up, rested it on the bench, and began chipping at the blood, flaking it off with her thumbnail.

"Please." Carin looked up at Verek. "Take this ankle iron off me. I give you my word that I won't try to get away."

Verek laced his fingers together, the full count of his right hand covering for the missing little finger of his left. He slipped his hands behind his head and leaned back. For a moment he studied her in silence. Then he replied coolly, "What good is your word to me?"

Carin stiffened, and returned her benched foot to the floor. She tried to look equal parts insulted and bewildered.

"When have I given you a reason to doubt it?" she demanded. "Haven't I answered your questions and kept my promises?"

Darting into Carin's thoughts were all the times she'd given Verek the truth—about the wisewoman who had sent her northward from the plains, about the blank in her mind that her childhood memories should fill, about the "puzzle-book" in the alien tongue that she could read. Had the wizard forgotten how Carin had confessed to spying on him and seeing him almost drown in his own magic? Did it also mean nothing to him that she had shared a confidence? She'd told Verek, probably unwisely, that she and the woodsprite were of two minds about returning to the worlds from which they had come.

When Verek replied, however, he made it clear that he was remembering other episodes from their six weeks' acquaintance.

"You hadn't been two days under my roof when you gave me cause to mistrust you," he snapped, eyeing Carin with an unsettling directness. "Didn't you thank me prettily when I set you the task of sorting out my library? Didn't you say you would do the work, and do it gladly? And had the sun gone down on another dusk before you were fled, leading me on a cold, hard chase through the night?

"What of your pledge to travel where I sent you, across the waters of the *wysards*?" Verek continued, jumping to the exact matter that Carin hadn't yet discussed with the woodsprite. "Didn't you stand on the brink of those waters and refuse the second journey that was yours to make?"

Carin hesitated to answer. If she admitted now that she had deceived Verek that second night, he'd never trust her enough to unshackle her.

She countered with an accusation of her own. "You weren't honest with me," she said, "about the sorcery that brought me to Ladrehdin. Kidnapping someone from another world—that's just *way* beyond your abilities, right? Only a 'master wizard' could conjure up that kind of magic. And the name of this master magician has to stay secret. I can never know it."

Carin scoffed, and returned the wizard's gaze as levelly as she could. "But it's easy enough to guess, isn't it? *You* sent me back to the bedroom that used to be mine in some other life— out there." She pointed off into space. "So I know you've been lying. You've shown me that you have the power of passage between the worlds. You can do it—you *have* done it."

Verek stared at her. Slowly he took his hands from behind his head and sat up from his slouch on the bed. The face that seldom betrayed his thoughts showed surprise and sudden comprehension, as though Carin had just cleared up some mystery for him.

"I am flattered that you think me capable of such magic," he growled. "But you are mistaken."

He shook his head. "Let us drop the pretense. We're now far enough from the waters of the *wysards* that honesty cannot alter our course. Enlighten me, won't you, and spare me further conjecture about your failure to summon from those waters an image of the woodsprite's world. Was it truly your 'failure'? Or your *refusal*, as I have suspected since that night?"

Carin sighed. Hiding a subterfuge from Verek was never easy. She counted it a feat to have kept him guessing this long. But did she dare admit that his suspicions were correct? That she'd stood on the rim of his wizards' well and tricked him? Would such an admission rouse that punishing temper of his?

"Come," Verek said, as though he'd clearly heard every question that darted through Carin's mind. "If I did not—in my grave dissatisfaction—thrash you that night, am I more likely to beat you now for telling me what I need to know?"

Carin returned her foot to the bench and resumed scraping the blood from her anklet. It gave her hands something to do while her thoughts ordered themselves. Finally she looked up at the dark eyes watching her, and told Verek the truth.

"I couldn't do it. When you took me down to the cave of magic that second night, I couldn't do what you wanted. That stick you handed me … the woodsprite is—was—convinced that it's a piece of the creature's world. But when you told me to use the wizards' well to find out if that's where the stick really came from … no, I didn't even *try* to do it."

Verek tilted his head. "Why? Why did you not try?"

Carin shrugged. "If I'd gotten it right—if I'd conjured up a picture of the woodsprite's world, made it rise from the pool of magic—what would you have done?" She held Verek's gaze. "You would have made me go there, wouldn't you? You would have sent me across to that world, just like you'd sent me into the child's bedroom the night before."

She shook her head. "I couldn't go through that again. I couldn't risk falling into the wizards' well. Sweet mercy!" Carin swore with quiet urgency. "It's horrible. The water in that pool doesn't feel anything like water. It's black as death down in that well — and so *cold* — a cold that bites to the bone." The memory made her flinch. "No, sir. I wasn't going to risk drowning. What if you weren't able to get me out in time?"

Carin narrowed her eyes at the wizard. "That's assuming, of course, that you would have been willing to dive in, like you did the first night. Maybe you wouldn't come after me a second time. You might just leave me to suffocate in that ocean of nothingness."

Verek lifted his chin. "Your fear of *wysards'* waters? That was your sole reason for refusing to summon an image of the woodsprite's world?"

"No," Carin said, still eyeing the wizard critically. "I was afraid you'd abandon me in that other place. If I had actually managed to call up the sprite's world, you might have left me there. If you weren't planning to send me on more journeys across the pool of magic, why bother bringing me back to Ladrehdin?

"Besides, I owed the woodsprite," Carin added. "You might have made me ditch the wand out there, like you had me leave the puzzle-book in the child's bedroom. I think the wand is — was — the sprite's way home. But if I'd conjured up the creature's world and then dumped the wand there — while you had the sprite locked in your rooms — I would have doomed it to the fate that it feared more than anything. The sprite never would have seen its natural home again."

I'm talking too much, whispered the voice in the back of Carin's head. But having revealed some of her thinking, she might as well confess a bit more, while she had the wizard's full attention. Verek was studying her with such interest, he was making her self-conscious.

"So now you know," Carin muttered. She dropped her gaze and pinned it on the blood-encrusted anklet that she scraped with her thumbnail. "When you ordered me to 'see' whatever glimpse of the sprite's world the wand could show me, I pictured instead … nothing. I made my mind a blank. I wasn't sure I'd get away with it—you might figure out what I was doing. But when the pool of magic stayed still, when nothing rippled its surface and no images appeared, I thought I'd pulled it off.

"Later, though," Carin added, and tentatively met the wizard's eyes again, "I thought of another possibility. Didn't the sprite say it couldn't feel anything in the wand? The sprite desperately wanted to find traces of its old home in that stick, but it got no results either." Carin shrugged. "Maybe I didn't actually blank out any images. Maybe the wand is just a stick, with nothing to show and no bridges to build to other worlds. That's possible, isn't it?"

"You little artificer!" Verek snapped. Carin still had his complete attention, only now he was looking at her angrily. "Of course it's possible. That is *precisely* the question I sought to answer when I bade you summon an image from the wand: did the fault lie with the relic or with the sprite? Would a mind more open than the sprite's perceive more in the wand? I left the cavern of *wysards* that night thinking the wand must retain no trace of the world whence it came. But there was, in your long looks and silences, something that made me wonder: had you played me for a fool?"

The wizard glowered at Carin a moment longer. Then, with an air of resignation, he settled against the wall at his back.

"Your deception has robbed us both of knowledge that might have proved a boon before this journey's done. For the questions remain unanswered: Is there any part of the sprite's natural home in the wand? Does there yet linger in the stick some bond with that other world? Heed me, you witless sprat, when I say to you that the time may come when you will go in search of those answers—and you'll be wishing then that I still stood, a safe anchor, at your back!"

Carin only stared at Verek. She had no idea how to reply to such an assertion.

The wizard seemed to expect no answer. He got off his bed and crossed the room to stand looking out the window. The sunlight through it gleamed off Verek's black hair almost as brightly as from the silver band that circled his brow. The light made the streaks of gray at his temples as silver as the metal.

Turning away from the window and back to Carin, Verek resumed their conversation—the longest between them since his party of three had left Ruain.

"You accuse me of a lie," he said, "when I claim for myself no such extraordinary powers as you have witnessed in the waters of the *wysards*—no such supreme mastery of magic as that which whirls living flesh through the void between the worlds. But I swear by the oath of my House that I do not deceive you in this. It lies within my power to convey only lifeless objects through the void—like the looking-glass book that I sent back with you to the child's bedchamber, and the crystal amulet I bade you bring me from that place. You yourself, I could not—and did not—send through the void.

"Do you not remember," Verek asked quietly, "the words I spoke to you that night? Didn't I tell you that only an intangible part of yourself would walk on that other world? That your essence—your life's breath, I think I called it—would remain with me in the cavern of the *wysards*? I cannot explain the matter more clearly. It is not a thing that lends itself to words.

"But you may believe me when I tell you: I *cannot* send living flesh through the void. The power that brought to Ladrehdin the living spark we call a woodsprite—and that plucked a young girl from a comfortable home to deliver her, stripped of childhood memories, into a mud-banked millpond—is a power beyond my craft and almost beyond my ken."

The wizard rested his hands on the windowsill behind him and half sat on the ledge, his lean legs stretched out before him. He did not take his eyes from Carin's.

"I am not so dull, however," Verek continued briskly, "that I cannot imagine the possibilities which would open to a master *wysard* who wields such ability. Tell me: have you given much thought to the significance of the second whirlpool that you witnessed in the cavern of enchantment? The vortex that carried vermin and another bit of debris from a storm of magic—debris that seemed more exotic than a book or a driftwood wand?"

Carin shook her head. "No, I haven't thought about it at all. I'm more interested in my own two trips across the void. All I know about the first passage is what the wizards' well showed me—that first magical whirlpool slinging me to the millpond when I was a child. I still can't remember a thing about that journey."

She rubbed her bandaged ankle. It was starting to itch—a sign of healing.

"But I've given a lot of thought," Carin added, "to the 'errand' that you sent me on not a month ago, to return the puzzle-book and steal a trinket. I keep wondering: What's so special about a little crystal dolphin that you'd nearly kill us both to get your hands on it?"

Verek lifted one hand from the windowsill, stroked his close-trimmed beard, and eyed her sharply.

"Do your thoughts still follow their narrow tracks and miss the broader path ahead? Tell me this, then: Last night in the room behind that door"—the wizard lifted a finger from his chin to point at the closed door to Carin's private quarters—"did you open the window to the winter night? Or did you keep it shuttered against the inrush of such elements as might do you harm?"

Chapter 4

The Fiends of Night

He knows! Carin fought to keep her panic from showing. *He knows the woodsprite came to my window last night, and he thinks he'll make me betray the creature a second time.*

Their eyes locked. For a skin-prickling instant, Carin felt her mind laid open to the wizard's scrutiny as nakedly as her ankle had been.

From the stairs came a sudden commotion. A small army was advancing on them, to judge by the din of voices and footsteps.

Verek's gaze shifted from Carin's with such dizzying abruptness that she had a sense of falling backward as his eyes released her.

"Cover your ankle," the wizard snapped. He swooped from his window perch to scoop Carin's bloodied stocking off the floor and thrust it at her. "Remember who you are meant to be. If you have managed, in the space of one short night, to give your bedchamber the look of a lady's bower, then remedy that error now—and be quick about it, or find yourself the object of much petty gossip before we are gone from this place."

Carin whirled to go, but a firm hand on her arm arrested her.

"Refrain," the wizard breathed into her face, "on peril of your life, from revealing to these people anything of your true identity—or mine. Don't think to seek sanctuary in this village. These simple souls cannot help you."

With a rough shove then, Verek rushed her in the direction of the bedroom where her washing hung. Carin yanked her still-damp clothes off the room's furniture and stuffed them into her satchel. She pulled her bloodstained stocking over her bare foot and over the instrument of torture that Verek had refused to remove.

She had barely buckled on her boots when a call of "Enter!" rang out from the other room, an edge of long-accustomed authority in the wizard's voice. An army of servants erupted through the door from the stairs as though Verek's summons were a battle cry.

Carin began to clear the hearth, to make that the "footboy's" reason for being in "his master's" bedroom. She was shoveling up ashes when the door between the two rooms opened to admit a chambermaid.

"Don't you be troublin' yourself with that, young sir," the girl said cheerfully. "I'll make up th' fire soon's I change th' bed-linens and tidy up a bit."

As Carin stood awkwardly at hearthside, the scoop in her hand, not knowing what to say or whether she should speak at all, the smile on the maid's face turned to a look of dismay.

"Arrah!" she exclaimed. "You poor lad! That awful master of yours has been beatin' you, 'asn't he? The tracks are plain on your face where th' tears have trickled down, and if that's not a smear of blood there"—the girl touched her own cheek to indicate the spot on Carin's face—"then I'm blinder than a *blencathar*. Is that your blood, young sir, on th' table and th' floor in t'other room?"

Carin nodded.

"Poor lad!" the maid exclaimed again. "I wonder you're not flat on your face after such a flayin'. The skin must be plumb off your back." She stepped a little closer and lowered her voice. "Get away from that villain, soon's you can, and come back to Deroucey. My mother'll put you up and find you work."

Carin gave the girl a weak smile. If only it were that simple. She turned to look out the window, leaving the maid to get on with straightening up.

The "poor lad" tried to sort out a pack of conflicting emotions. Should she, despite the wizard's warning, reveal everything to this girl—Verek's secret as well as Carin's own—and hope that such a revelation would rouse the townsfolk against the sorcerer in their midst? But how dearly might such an uprising cost the people of Deroucey? For all of Verek's denials that he was a great master of magic, Carin had seen the desolation the wizard could wreak upon a landscape.

And although he had restrained himself lately—he hadn't threatened to kill her for a good three weeks now—Verek was capable of violent rages. His earlier fits of temper had instilled in Carin a dread that went deeper than the bruises he'd given her. In her weaker moments, Verek only had to turn his penetrating gaze upon her, and terror would grab at her heart. He'd made Carin fear his anger. Would she risk his full fury now, to betray him to these townspeople whose ability to protect her was highly questionable?

No, she wouldn't. Quite apart from the calamities Carin might call down upon herself and the villagers, there was the matter of the woodsprite and its desperate desire to return "home."

Though it's good having the sprite back, the creature does complicate things, Carin realized. *I've got to look out for it now, and not just myself.*

Looking out for the sprite meant helping it to go home. As long as she had a hope that Verek might give her both the means and the opportunity to fulfill the creature's wish, Carin must seem to go along with the wizard's plans ... and watch for an opening to free herself when she had what she wanted from him.

More of the trooping servants came through from the front room, bearing armloads of firewood and fresh water by the pitcherful. Carin hobbled aside, on an ankle that was beginning to ache now from overuse, to let a sour-faced woman toss her morning's bathwater out the window. It splashed the trunk of the old tree that grew outside the building. *That's a cold wake-up for the sprite,* Carin thought, *if the creature is trying to sleep out there.*

Having put the room to rights, the servants withdrew. The chambermaid paused to tap Carin's shoulder as the mistreated "footboy" went back to gazing out the window.

"Leave that devil quick as you can," the maid whispered into Carin's ear, "and circle back to Deroucey. Don't be long about it, or you'll be slogging through snow up to your arse. Winter comes fast to these parts after Mydrismas."

The girl was gone. Carin stood another moment at the window, then shuttered it against a breeze that felt decidedly wintry already. The fire that the servants had built on the hearth brightened the room but didn't cheer Carin. With the departure of the innkeeper's troops, she had little to do but hang up her clothes to finish drying, and then return to the front room, where Verek waited.

The antechamber was as tidy now as Carin's quarters—the beds made, a fire dancing up the chimney, the scrubbed table bearing dried fruit, fresh bread, cheese, and a bottle of the best that the inn's wine cellar could offer. Carin walked in to find Verek frowning over a bundle of clean, pressed clothes. One of the servants who had descended upon their lodgings was evidently the washerwoman to whom he'd sent his own laundry and Lanse's.

Verek drew the top shirt off the pile and tossed it at Carin.

"It's ripped," he growled. "Can you do anything with it?"

She stuck her fingers through a parted shoulder seam, and nodded. "I can't sew like Myra, but this I can fix." Carin got the mending kit Myra had packed for her. Then she settled at the table with her foot propped up. The green powder's painkilling worked best with her weight off the wound. Carin threaded a needle and waited in silence for Verek to return to the subject that he'd raised before the housekeeping horde interrupted them.

He was not long in doing so. Verek took the bench opposite Carin's at the other end of the table. The wizard poured himself a glass of the innkeeper's wine and swallowed a small, dubious sip. Carin felt his gaze on her but she didn't look up as he asked the question that had been left hanging:

"So—how do you plead in the matter of your bedroom window? Did you shutter it last night, or throw it open to wraiths and night-horrors?"

Hmm, Carin thought. *That's no way to talk about the sprite.* But she gave Verek the answer she had prepared while servants worked around her in the next room.

"To convince you—if I can, sir—that you can trust me, I'll tell you exactly what I did. I opened the shutters long enough to see what was out there. Then I did what any sane person would do: I closed them against a dark, cold night."

Verek nodded. "A sensible course of action."

The wizard seemed primed to say more, but he held back at the sound of boots on the landing and a hand on the latch. Through the door from the stairs entered Lanse, wrapped in coat and cloak.

Carin glanced up at him briefly, then returned to the shirt in her hands. She'd never speak to Lanse if she didn't have to.

"What news, boy?" Verek asked him. "Do you horse-trade with the best in Deroucey?"

"I do, my lord," Lanse answered, cocky. From inside his coat he drew out a leather pouch and set it on the table. "Before nightfall, there will be delivered to the stables a strong sorrel gelding, a healthy four-year-old that shan't balk at any load strapped on it. And from this purse, sir"—Lanse tapped the pouch on the table—"you are missing but a single piece of gold. It needed only that, with the price I bartered from the knacker's for the foundered brute, to buy a beast two hands the dead gray's better."

"Well done!" Verek exclaimed. "You've a good right to be proud of so keen a bargain as that."

Lanse shed his hood and his coat—basking in his master's praise, he hardly needed them—and joined Verek at the table. While he ate, the boy related in tedious detail the particulars of his horse-trading.

Carin ignored him. She bent to her needlework with resolution. Taking small, even stitches, she managed to make the job last until the wizard and his boy had finished their meal. Then they rose for a walk to the stables to see that the sorrel gelding's owner honored his end of the bargain.

At the exit, Verek paused and sharply cautioned his captive: "Stay clear of the door. I won't take time now to correct the imperfect spellwork that guards it."

She gave him a curt nod.

The moment the door closed behind the pair, Carin knotted the thread and tied off the mended seam. She folded Verek's shirt and laid it on his bed. Then she stepped into her room and barred its door. To remove the tracks of her tears and the streak of blood that had earned her the maid's pity, she dampened a kerchief and wiped her face.

At the window, Carin pushed open one shutter. No one stirred in the courtyard below. Now that their duties were done, the innkeeper's servants were probably sleeping off their

Mydrismas hangovers. She and the woodsprite could talk privately again.

"Sprite!" Carin hissed, too softly to rouse a human sleeper. "Are you there? Woodsprite?"

Nothing answered at first but the wind in the branches. Then a spark raced across the yard, arrowing to the bole of the tree. It flickered its way up the trunk like a will-o'-the-wisp and came to rest in a branch that Carin could touch from her window.

"I'm here, my friend!" the sprite piped, sounding out of breath. "But do we dare to meet so boldly, with the afternoon sun shining on our secrets?"

"Sometimes it's safest to hide in plain view," Carin replied. "Don't worry, I'm alone. The wizard isn't here."

Quickly, she shared her suspicion that Verek might know about the woodsprite's escape and its appearance at her window last night. "If you have to go anywhere near that warlock, move as fast as elf-fire," Carin cautioned the sprite. "Don't give him a chance to recapture you."

"Be easy about me. I'll stay as distant from that villain as he is from goodness.

"But now," the sprite added in the same breath, "keep your promise from last night, and tell me of your journeys from the cave of magic to worlds beyond. Where did you go? What did you see?"

"I saw another life."

Though her words couldn't do justice to the weirdness of her travels, Carin described her journey to the child's bedroom on an unknown world: her crossing of the wizards' pool ... how she'd traded the *Looking-Glass* book for the crystal pendant that Verek wanted ... how a book half-hidden under a pillow had caught her eye, and how she'd lingered to read from it. Carin told about the ocean that she'd discovered lapping at her feet, when she'd put down the *"Wonderland"* volume and looked round for the sorcerer who held her life in his hands. She tried to explain how the space between them had seemed enormous then, as though the wizards' well had become a universe.

"I thought I was lost," Carin murmured, "when Verek let me fall. Drisha's teeth! Sprite, try to imagine a winter rain that freezes as it hits and coats the tree limbs in black ice. Imagine yourself frozen in that ice, so achingly cold that you don't have a spark of life in you. Verek's pool of magic is even colder than that. I couldn't stand it. I blacked out." Carin swallowed. "When I came to, it took me a minute to realize I wasn't dead."

"How miserably I've failed you, Carin!" the sprite cried, its distress thinning its voice. "It was for care of me that you suffered wizardry's cold agonies. I may not be forgiven for causing you such pain."

"Of course you may," Carin retorted. "You didn't drop me into the pool. The warlock did."

She paused to listen for sounds of Verek in the next room, but he remained absent.

"Then that second night," Carin resumed her story, "when you were still his prisoner and Verek ordered me off on another magical errand, I was determined to get out of it. But I had to find a way to disobey him without making him so angry that he'd kill you, sprite."

Carin repeated to the creature what she'd confessed to Verek: how she'd emptied her mind when he'd ordered her to conjure with the wand an image of the world that had produced the artifact.

"If you had been with me in the cave that night, my friend, I might have gone on the trip," Carin added. "If I had been able to see your world across the pool, then maybe you could have made the crossing and found your way home. But for me to go alone while you were locked in your prison-tree—that was too big a risk. I could have lost the wand out there." She signified "out there" with a vague wave of her hand.

"Sprite, from talking to Verek I get the feeling that the wand must be a kind of bridge. If I'm right to think that it ties this world to yours, then you should be glad that I didn't let Verek get rid of it—the way he used me to get rid of the puzzle-book."

"Carin!" The sprite's voice was low and horrified. "Do you hear what you're saying? Have you caught the drift of your own words? If the wand is the 'bridge' that I must take to return to my home, then surely your path lay by the book. But the book is gone. Aren't you stranded here now, upon this world called Ladrehdin?"

Carin stared at the branch that had spoken. The creature had put its finger, so to speak, on an obvious parallel between her book and its wand—assuming that either object had, in fact, once belonged to "footboy" or woodsprite. She hadn't missed the drift so much as ignored it. Carin, after all, wasn't the one who nursed thoughts of "home" so tenderly. But the sprite's consternation at her loss of the puzzle-book stirred her misgivings.

Had Verek ditched the book to keep Carin from ever going back to "her" world?

What had he said to her, the night he bade her conjure that forgotten place from the pool's mists? When she'd told him that she had no desire to regain that world—not like the sprite, who could speak of little else—Verek's response had been: "Good. That will render the task ahead of you less distressing." The task being, as he had emphasized, to *return* the book and *retrieve* the crystal.

How had she missed what the wizard's choice of words clearly implied? That the puzzle-book, in its alien language, belonged to that other world—but the crystal's destined place must be here, on Ladrehdin.

Carin nodded—not at the sprite, but to herself—as a bit of the puzzle seemed to slip into place. *The book and the crystal … they're both bridges. But they no longer link two worlds.* In trading one for the other, she may have destroyed the unearthly pathways between the two places—and cut herself off for all time from the land of her birth.

The sprite was making inarticulate sounds of woe.

"Easy there," Carin said, trying to soothe the creature before the innkeeper had half his staff looking for the moaner. "Don't be sad for me. I can't grieve for a life that I don't remember. But I promise I'll help you look for your 'homeworld.' And I'll escape from Verek, too—I'm determined to be free of him. For now, though, we're both in his power. He's got the wand that may be your only way home, and he's got the key to the shackle that keeps me a prisoner."

For a long moment more, the sprite gave vent to its emotions. But finally the creature quieted and took its leave of Carin. Though still sounding a bit teary, the sprite renewed its promise that it would follow wherever Verek was leading her on this journey—and however early in the morning the travelers might depart, now that last night's "trouble with a horse" had been remedied.

After the sprite's departure, Carin latched the shutter and stood in her bedroom, chafing her arms. She threw another log on her fire, then went into the front room for a glass of the innkeeper's passably good wine and a nibble at the cheese and fruit that Verek and the boy had left untouched.

What now? Walk the floors? Sit and stare into the fire? The hour was only a little past mid-afternoon. The wizard and Lanse might be out past dusk. Was there no good way to use this rare gift of private time?

Have a go at that mystery you've been carrying around in your pocket – and your head – for a month.

The thought was barely framed before Carin was retreating back to her bedroom and barring the door behind her. She cleared a space at the room's white-linen table, then drew from her trousers pocket the three compactly folded sheets that nestled there.

One sheet, she returned to her pocket unread. She knew it almost by heart. The other two, she spread flat on the table.

Carin wasn't quite able to focus on the sheet that bore the longer inscription. A wilder jumble of meaningless marks and characters couldn't be imagined. The writing was not foreign. She had penetrated its secrets far enough to know that its author—Verek's grandfather Legary—had penned it in the common Ladrehdinian script. Upon the page, however, the old wizard had placed a spell of concealment so powerful that it had survived when Carin—praying that no lethal enchantments protected the book from such desecration—had torn the page from the sorcerous text that held it.

Smoothing it now, she relived the astonishing spectacle of the stolen page rebuilding itself in the *Book of Archamon* like a lizard regrowing its tail. Within seconds, she had been viewing two identical but unreadable manuscripts—one on the torn sheet in her hand, the other on the left-hand page of the two leaves to which the book lay open.

The work on the right-hand page hadn't been bespelled. Carin had easily read and written down the words Lord Legary had placed there. Her fair copy of his narrative was on the sheet that had gone back into her pocket. Deciphering that twenty-year-old account wasn't the task that faced her now. If she wanted to know the genesis of the tragedies that had struck Verek's family, Carin had to make sense of his grandsire Legary's older work. The ensorcelled writing dated to the year when Verek's mother had disappeared and left the boy-wizard orphaned, at ten.

81

Carin slipped the case off a pillow and used the linen to cover the bespelled writing. Would the trick that she had devised in Verek's library—of concealing the characters, then quickly revealing them—work on this purloined page far from the magic that permeated Verek's strange old manor house?

Yes. As she snatched the pillowcase away, the word *corruption* rose from the chaos, briefly legible.

Carin jotted it down on the third paper that made up the secret archive she had smuggled from Verek's library. That paper held only a smattering of deciphered words and phrases—the fruits of many hours of tedious labor. For all her determined probing with her cover-and-reveal trick, she'd lifted from Legary's bespelled writing only a handful of terms. Among them were *sacrificed, sorceress, evil, a worthy heir, the adept, ungifted, Morann, craggy heights, grieving widow*, and *wife of Hugh*.

That the "grieving widow" and the "wife of Hugh" were one and the same, seemed evident. Myra had told Carin that Legary's son Hugh had married at eighteen, fathered a child—the present Lord Verek—at nineteen, and gone to his grave that same year. Master Hugh's untimely death had left a young widow—surely the grieving widow of the narrative—to raise their son … but not alone, for the boy's grandfather had taken an active part in young Verek's education.

What had happened to that widow? What had taken her from Legary's household when her son was only ten?

The few words Carin had picked out of Legary's cloaked narrative hinted that the lady might have met a sad end. Had she fallen to some "evil sorceress"? Was she the one "sacrificed"? Or had the old wizard been describing other players in this drama?—the unknown beings he called "worthy," "adept," "ungifted."

And who was "Morann"? Legary had named that entity in this account and again in the later narrative that he would pen on his deathbed.

In that second, unconcealed work, which he had written when his grandson and heir Theil Verek was no longer a boy but a nobleman of twenty-four, Legary had warned the mysterious Morann away from Verek in the strongest terms. *By the oath of my House, I command thee: Touch him not!* the dying sorcerer had written.

The phrase "craggy heights" hadn't seemed significant when Carin first extracted it from the depths of Legary's spellcraft. But now she wondered. Verek had made it no secret that he was leading his party into the western mountains. Could the "heights" in his grandfather's decades-old narrative be their ultimate destination?

The rattle of the outer door's latch announced her captor's return. Hurriedly, Carin refolded the bespelled page of writing and her sheet of notes. She stuffed them in her trousers pocket, then re-covered her bed pillow and curled up with it.

Footsteps tramped into the front room. She heard the clatter of cutlery and serving dishes. Low voices exchanged remarks Carin couldn't make out. After a time, silence reigned again in the antechamber. A safe guess was that the innkeeper's servants had been and gone, bringing supper.

No one disturbed her. No knuckles rapped at her door. She was not summoned to the front room.

Lying on the bed staring into the fire, Carin felt the strain of the day fall away. The pain in her ankle was no more now than a bad memory. Verek's healing dusts had worked their magic. Her reunion with the woodsprite had left her much encouraged. She wouldn't continue this journey friendless. Together, they might manage to get what each wanted: Carin, a way clear of the wizard; the sprite, its passage home.

She woke with a start. How long had she slept? The world was dark outside the diamond-paned eaves-light over the bed. The flame that had blazed high on the hearth when she'd drifted off was sinking low among the embers. Carin bounded up and tossed a fistful of oak chips on the fire, then another log.

Hunger pangs were reminders that the two in the front room had not asked her to share their evening meal. Should she invite herself?

Carin inched her door open. The modest blaze that licked at the firedogs on the antechamber's hearth showed a motionless form on the far bed. Just enough wavy hair fell over his blanket to identify the sleeper as Lanse.

But when she widened the crack enough to get her head through, Carin discovered Verek still awake. He sat cross-legged on his bed, in his shirtsleeves and stocking feet. Before her intrusion, the wizard might have been staring into the fire, as Carin had often caught him doing on this trip. Now, however, his gaze was full upon her — and an unnerving gaze it was.

She started to retreat. But Verek gestured toward the laden table, which he and Lanse had not nearly cleared of meat and bread.

With a short nod, Carin accepted his invitation. Quickly but quietly, she loaded a platter for her cold, late supper.

Verek reached for his saddlebags at the foot of his bed and in the same motion got to his feet. He preceded Carin into the bedroom that she had come to regard jealously, in the space of a day, as her own private retreat.

Get out! she wanted to shout at him. But she said nothing, only trailed Verek into the room.

The wizard shut the door behind them, but he didn't bar it. He set his bags down, drew out the wallet of medicinal powders and the rolled linen bandages, and put them on the table.

"I would see how your wound fares," he said, his voice low. "Be pleased to bare it to my examination."

Carin hesitated, but then sat down and bent to remove her boot and stocking. She started to shift the ensorcelled anklet so she could unwind the bandage underneath it. But Verek was a falcon stooping to the attack, so swiftly did he crouch to take over the unwrapping, leaving his patient staring uneasily — and skeptically — at the top of his head.

Was this change of dressings really necessary? Was the injury so severe that it needed another dose of Verek's curatives?

Carin glanced up at the shuttered window. The wizard was here, she suspected, not for her health, but to check her quarters for the escaped woodsprite.

Verek wadded the cast-off bandage in his hand, moistened the linen with cool water, and bathed Carin's ankle more thoroughly than she could have stood that morning, when the wound was fresh. Now the gash had almost closed. The wizard dusted it anyway with pinches of the bronze and green powders. The *cyhnaith* stung, but its effect on a quickly healing wound was nothing like the inferno it touched off in a raw, bleeding cut.

He rewrapped her ankle with clean linen. Then he stood, and dodging Carin's hanging laundry, spread the damp, stained bandage on the hearth in front of the fire.

"In the morning, when the cloth is dry, burn it," Verek instructed.

He looked at her with something peculiar in his gaze, which suggested that Carin's ankle wasn't the only thing occupying his thoughts.

Verek turned to the shuttered window. He pushed the leaves open and stood gazing into the brittle night.

Carin reached for her plate of cold supper and smiled at the warlock's back. If he expected to catch her talking to the woodsprite tonight, he'd be disappointed. Her exchange of news with the sprite had been so satisfactorily completed that afternoon, she and it wouldn't need to risk another meeting for days. The creature only had to follow at a safe distance as Verek led his little band westward, until Carin and it got the chance to talk privately again.

She did away with her smile as the wizard pulled the shutters closed and turned at the window to face her.

"It's late," he said. "You and I must speak of many things, before this journey's done, but tonight you should rest—for we'll be off on the morrow before the sun is over the world's edge." He canted his head. "Pray favor me, however, with a bit of thought in that nimble brain of yours, and consider the words I spoke to you today. As the sleeper shuts the window against the fiends of night, and the gateman hoists the drawbridge in the enemy's face, you may be called to like service. Perhaps your thoughts have not yet ordered themselves as mine have, but you possess knowledge enough to reckon as I do. Think on what I say."

The wizard retrieved his bags, strode to the door and was gone, leaving Carin to finish her supper in solitude. She gnawed her way through it, then barred the door and stripped to her skin for another night of luxury between smooth sheets.

Sleep did not come easily, however, on top of a cold, greasy meal and Verek's odd speech. His words echoed in Carin's mind. Was it a coincidence that the wizard had mentioned a "drawbridge" hard on the heels of her own remarks to the woodsprite, that the wand might be the creature's "bridge" home? And why did the warlock speak so pointedly of evil things crawling through the night, as though he wished to fill her dreams with frights?

The last misty notion in Carin's head, before sleep nudged it away, was a vague impression of a wobbly rope bridge—its near end anchored to the side of a mountain, its far reaches seeming to float on a mirror-smooth ocean—with an army of demons and firedrakes, corpse-candles and creeping horrors, massed on that far shore and making ready to cross.

Chapter 5

A Worthy Heir

Ten days out of Deroucey, thoughts of bridges, night-crawlers, and other matters of conjecture competed for Carin's attention with the monotonous concerns of the traveler. When would they stop to rest the horses and eat a little? Where would they camp tonight? Would the weather hold, or give them reason to regret their late start on this journey?

The days since Deroucey had been cold; the nights, freezing. So far, however, the woolly clouds overhead had not dumped sleet or snow on them. No blizzard had come howling off the distant mountains to turn an uncomfortable ride into a deadly one.

Since Deroucey, Verek's party hadn't seen a village, only a pine forest that sheltered a few deer. Once, Lanse's quick shot had downed a buck. Fresh venison that night was a welcome change from their trail diet of jerked meat and ash-baked oatcakes.

Lanse had almost stopped harassing Carin, these days. He ignored her when he could. When he had to talk to her, he spoke curtly and contemptuously. But he had quit playing tricks on her. The boy seemed to feel himself so securely back in his master's good graces that he had less spleen to vent on Carin.

Verek had shown great faith in his nineteen-year-old groom, to give him a purse of gold and leave the horse-dealing entirely to Lanse. The boy's choice of the sorrel gelding had proved sound. The packhorse didn't balk at the pace the wizard set. Lanse's success in that trade must have pleased him almost as much as hearing Verek praise him for it.

Too, the boy had jumped at the chance to be in his master's company without Carin at hand. Lanse never complained about Carin having a room to herself in Deroucey. He'd happily occupied the servants' quarters with Verek, glad to shunt his "rival" aside.

His *rival?* Carin, as she rode through the pines behind the wizard and his stableboy, had to shake her head at that idea. She would not willingly deprive Lanse of *any* of Verek's company. Quite the contrary. She kept out of the warlock's way as much as possible. Lanse had little reason to see her as his competitor.

But Myra had thought otherwise. "What the boy begrudges you are the hours you spend with our master," the housekeeper had told Carin in confidence. "He fears to lose, to you, his place at the master's side. Lanse fancies himself angry with you for drawing to yourself the notice that he craves."

The woman's fondness for talk had led her into other revelations as well. "Once," Myra had whispered when she and Carin were alone, "Lanse did aspire to learn the arts of alchemy and magic. But that was not to be. The boy hasn't the gift."

The gift. It was revealing of Myra's long service to the House of Verek that the woman would speak of sorcery as a gift, not an evil. How many among the ancestors of the current Lord Verek had been as "gifted" as he was? Verek's grandsire, Legary, was reputedly an adept of fantastic power—"a wizard beyond compare," Myra had called him, reminiscing about her early years with the family.

The hairs prickled on the nape of Carin's neck as she thought of the old wizard, dead these twenty years. In the narrative that the dying Legary had written—his words unconcealed in that treasury of wizards' lore called the *Book of Archamon*—one stanza hinted that he had put himself in the grave with his own magic:

I have paid the dearest price
To invoke the forces primal;
They draw me now into the tomb,
Where lie the first son and the third.

The "first son," if Carin's speculations went anywhere near the mark, was Legary's child Hugh. Teenaged Hugh had died when the present Lord Verek was only an infant. Counting Verek, then, as the second generation, the "third son" had to be Verek's little boy, who had drowned with the child's mother, under mysterious circumstances, in a lake within walking distance of the wizard's manor house.

When Verek found their bodies tangled in the water lilies, his grief had turned violent. "'Twas a terrible thing," Myra had said, moved to tears by her memories of that day, also twenty years past. "He raged, and cursed the lake, and drove the life from it. He sorrowed night and day for the loss of his wife and child."

The wizard, Myra confided, had appeared to go quite mad. And in his madness he laid such a malignant curse on the woodland bordering his home that it became an empty, silent ghost forest. Nothing lived in those woods now but the trees themselves. *As barren as a tomb*, Carin thought with a little shiver, recalling her unintended trespass into those woods — the mistake that had thrown her into Verek's power.

How much of Ruain would Verek's curse have blighted, if Legary hadn't stepped in to halt the devastation? What unimaginable powers of wizardry had the old lord summoned to his service, to keep his grandson's derangement from destroying the estate that had been the blood-right of that lineage for generations? With his own hand, Legary had written of "invoking the forces primal" — and paying for it with his life.

An eyewitness to those events had also testified that nothing less than the "magic of life" protected the lush garden at Verek's house from the desolation of the adjoining woodland. Old Jerold—master gardener, minor magician, and onetime sorcerer's apprentice to the powerful Legary—had chosen his words tellingly.

Jerold ... scowling at Carin over his pink rosebushes ... a wrinkled, grumpy elf ... perpetually sad, with an air of resignation about him that was worlds away from Verek's aura of angry melancholy ...

A new idea careened into Carin's musings, so unexpectedly that it brought her hands up in a gesture of surprise. She jerked the reins that hadn't so much as twitched on Emrys' neck for the last several miles.

Startled, the mare threw up her head and almost stumbled.

"Easy, girl!" Carin exclaimed, and stroked the trim black neck. "Please excuse your rider. My mind is wandering. It's just come across an interesting thought. Would you like to hear it?"

A glance, however, toward the black-cloaked wizard a few steps up the trail showed further conversation with the mare to be unwise. Verek was glaring at her over his shoulder, his meaning clear: *"Stop your noise."* Carin satisfied herself and Emrys, therefore, with a few reassuring pats, and returned to her silent meditations as soon as Verek quit scowling at her.

Think, ordered reason. *What do Jerold and Lanse have in common?*

Both could be considered failed magicians. Myra had described Jerold's gift as "slight"—not a dead loss like Lanse, but nearly as inept.

So Legary had been disappointed in artless Jerold; and Verek even more disappointed in his would-be apprentice, Lanse. This family of adepts seemed fated to attract only ungifted disciples.

Ungifted …

As the word lingered on Carin's mind, her hand stole to her breeches' pocket where three sheets of paper nested. The term "ungifted" was among the few she had wrested from Legary's ensorcelled narrative. Up from that murk had also come "the adept" and "a worthy heir." Would an ungifted child not satisfy the House of Verek as a "worthy" heir? Must the line of succession in a house of wizardry pass only through an adept?

Was that why "the first son and the third" of Legary's noble house had died before either boy reached his majority?

Carin shuddered. The day was growing increasingly overcast. And with the clouds came a harsher cold than the riders had endured, at least during sunlit hours, since leaving Deroucey. But it wasn't the sharp breeze alone that made Carin hunch deeper into her cloak. In her mind's eye she saw, as clearly as if the page were in front of her, the narrative Legary had penned on his deathbed. Four lines from the end he had written: *"The lad is slain, the infant drowned; / The tainted seed is future's hope."*

The tainted seed. Elsewhere on the page, Legary had left Carin in no doubt about the identity of *that* one. One stanza of his poem could hardly be viewed as anything but a description of Legary's grandson, Theil Verek:

The second — the troubled, the tainted seed —
Vented wild rage upon the living wood.
Dead and barren, as his heart within,
Left he the woodland with fury spent.

Carin narrowed her eyes at the wizard riding ahead. Then she dropped her gaze, for fear that Verek's magian senses would detect her staring a hole in his back as her thoughts unfolded …

The tainted seed is Legary's only surviving heir. The future of an ancient house lies with that blackheart Verek. He's an adept, no question. But what about his son, the child who drowned? Did the boy bear the mark of his ancestry, or was he "ungifted"? What about Verek's father, Hugh, who was laid in the tomb before Verek's first birthday? Did he have the gift, or didn't he?

"The lad is slain," Legary wrote, hinting that his son was murdered. But by whom? And for what reason? Did Hugh die because he was judged an unworthy heir?

Did Legary kill him?

Carin's sharp intake of breath was loud enough to provoke a twitch of the mare's ears. Had her first impression of the old wizard's narrative been wrong? As Carin had read the unsteady handwriting that slanted across a page of the *Book of Archamon*, she had seemed to feel Legary's sorrow—his heartsickness at the tragedies besetting his family. But was she really sensing his guilt? His remorse for the murder of his own son?

"My crimes are great, my penance vast," the dying sorcerer had confessed. Was he thinking—not of the sorts of regrets any man might have, as he looked back on his eighty years of life—but of crimes more explicit, and foul? Had Legary gone to his grave burdened with guilt for what he had done, unable to confess it except through a vague line in a poem?

Maybe …

Carin tried to stifle her thought before it was fully formed. But there was no stopping this next conjecture that flowed naturally out of the first. Maybe the tragic history of Legary and his son had repeated itself in the lives of Verek and *his* boy. Was it possible that the warlock had caused his own son's death by drowning?

She chewed her lip as she mentally recited the opening stanzas of Legary's narrative. In them, Carin searched for clues that might support or refute this new and disagreeable interpretation. When Legary wrote of an *"evil that slew the first*

93

and tainted the second" that *"hath no power over the third,"* he seemed to suggest that a force outside the family had wreaked destruction upon it.

But was Carin misreading the clues? Had she missed the real meaning of two passages in Legary's narrative? They were several lines apart, but apparently related: *Dead was the first by guileful craft; / Dead was the third by blackest art* … and its echo near the work's end: *The lad is slain, the infant drowned.*

She had been imagining a nameless evil that was bent on the destruction of House Verek. She'd pictured an external force—the Fates or the Furies—taking two of the old wizard's heirs. But maybe Legary and his grandson had killed their respective offspring because neither Legary's son nor Verek's infant were "gifted."

Carin threw back her shoulders in a joint-twisting stretch. She was stiff from riding. For hours she'd sat astride Emrys, barely moving, woodenly staring into the middle distance.

And her head ached from filling it with questions she couldn't answer. She rubbed her forehead.

Stop this! Carin pleaded with herself. *Leave off before your head explodes. If you must think, then think of a way to get off this horse's back.* Was that blackheart up ahead never going to call a halt?

As Carin's thoughts swung round on this new heading, she became intensely aware of her cramped muscles and sore backside crying for rest. Could she make him hear? Could she make the wizard read her mind when *she* wanted him to, not the other way round? She locked her gaze onto the back of Verek's head, and consigned to the space between his ears the wailing of every nerve in her body.

If Verek heard the distant, unhappy chorus, he ignored it. But still Carin kept her eyes and thoughts fastened on him. The attempt to reach his mind kept her own from wandering back to the endless questions that gave her no rest.

A mile or so after the exercise began, Carin gave it up as a failure; Verek never shot her a glance. But when she tore her gaze from the wizard, she discovered a landscape that was markedly different from the thick forest that had surrounded them twenty minutes ago. They were about to leave the pines. Ahead lay an expanse of tall, coarse grass.

"My lord!" Carin called sharply to the rider up ahead. "Please give me a minute before we lose the cover of the trees. I need some privacy."

Verek rode on, advancing several steps. Gradually then, he eased his horse to a halt. For a moment, he sat still. Slowly, as if he wasn't paying attention to what he was doing, he reined Brogar around to face Carin. But his eyes seemed to have trouble finding her. They stared vacantly over her shoulder before finally moving to Carin's face and seeming to see her. Then, with a curt nod, Verek acknowledged her.

"Very well." He dismounted with easy grace, showing none of the ache that afflicted Carin's muscles. "You may have your moment alone. Be quick about it. We must press on, or fall short tonight of a creek where we may camp and water these beasts."

Carin climbed down stiffly, and hobbled off to a cluster of pine saplings that promised better cover than the scattered mature trees. In the heart of the grove, where Verek and Lanse couldn't see her, she pulled off her gloves and called softly to the woodsprite. The spark that had been flitting through the trees behind her like a tenacious firefly would have found a way to follow her here, even through the spread-out trees at this forest fringe.

The sprite did not disappoint. There was a tiny flash, then:

"My friend!" an anxious voice piped from a sapling at Carin's elbow. "How pleased I am to see this caravan halted before you'd left me behind. Into the field that stretches away beyond these trees, I may not venture. It would be the death of me."

"I know it, sprite." Carin flung her cloak back and worked her bare, rapidly chilling hands through the layers of her clothes to get at the drawstring of her trousers. "I'm glad I woke up in time—I was daydreaming." She gasped as she bared her nether regions to the cold. But she forced her bladder to avail itself of the last chance it might have for a thorough emptying, for who knew how long.

"Sprite, how will you go from here?" she whispered. "Can you stay in the edge of the trees and work your way around, and catch up to us on the other side?"

"No." The sprite was only a mouth muttering from a sapling's trunk, with nothing like eyes peering out to violate Carin's privacy. "I dare not let myself be far separated from you. If the trees do not circle, if they end here while the grass stretches on for leagues, I would be stranded in this forest—never, perhaps, to see you again. No, I could not bear that."

"Me either," Carin said. "So what do we do?"

"What I propose," the creature piped, "is this: Pull up by the roots—carefully!—one of these tiny pines. Bundle the roots snugly against this cold, dry air to keep the life in them—and thus in me. I'll leap within the bantling, and in the safety of it I'll ride with you, hidden in your cloak."

"In s-safety!" Carin hissed as she yanked up her trousers. "Sprite, you're daft! What happens if the grass *does* go on and on, and it takes us days to cross? By the time we find more trees up ahead—maybe in the mountains, where Verek's headed—it could be too late for you. If your little pine dries up, and if I can't find a shrub for you out there"—Carin pointed at the prairieland ahead—"then you'll die. Will you risk it, just to stay with me?"

"Indeed I will. I don't doubt that the mage has his reasons for making this journey. And if he thinks it's necessary to have one of his otherworldly 'guests' with him, then I count it no great mental leap to believe that the other—myself—may also have cause to attend him. I pray you, let's waste no more time arguing. What do you have that would make a fitting wrapper for a ball of roots, to hold the moisture in them?"

That was a good question. If Carin gave up a stocking, her foot would freeze to her boot. Her gloves were equally indispensable. The only item on her body that might be superfluous in this cold was the chemise that she wore next to her skin.

"Watch those two." Carin jerked her head to indicate the men who were waiting for her. "I'll be as quick as I can."

She threw off her cloak, coat, quilted doublet, and linen shirt, then pulled her chemise over her head. Already shivering violently, she restored all the layers of her clothing, except that her frozen fingers had trouble doing up the buttons of her coat.

"Hurry!" the sprite urged her. "The mage looks this way with a frown upon his face. In another minute, he'll be tramping over here to see what's keeping you."

Carin left her coat mostly unbuttoned. She reached for a seedling that was small enough to conceal under her clothes, and pulled it up so gently that its roots lost only a few grains of moist soil. She wrapped the roots in her shed chemise.

"Your carriage awaits, sprite." Carin held the seedling up for the creature's inspection.

"And a fine one it is!" the woodsprite declared. The seedling twitched as the sprite leaped into it. "Slip me now inside your coat," the creature said, its voice humming through the needles, "and I'll travel comfortably indeed. No more sparking through cold trees for this wight!"

Carin did as it suggested. Then she wrapped up in her cloak to hide both her unbuttoned coat and the green pine needles that were bristling out of it. Fresh misgivings flashed upon her. She was putting the woodsprite within Verek's reach once more. But there was no backing out now. She grabbed her gloves and dashed out of the grove, just in time to meet Verek arriving at its edge.

"At last!" the wizard exclaimed. He glowered at her. "What have you been doing all this time? Are you ill?"

Carin shook her head. To avoid meeting his gaze, she focused on the task of regloving her cold-whitened hands. "No, I'm all right. I'm ready to ride on, if you are."

Verek said nothing. He stood blocking Carin's way until her gloves were on and could no longer command her attention.

Reluctantly then, she looked up to find the warlock studying her. His face betrayed no hint of what he was thinking. Did he come by that enviable skill naturally? Or was it the product of careful practice?

Don't make him suspicious, Carin told herself. *Think of anything except the creature that hides next to your heart.*

In Carin's thoughts, however, the woodsprite's seedling rooted itself firmly, allowing nothing else to come to her mind. On her face the secret might already be plastered, as plainly as if she'd pulled the little pine from her coat and brushed Verek's nose with it.

Carin's shivering intensified until her teeth began to chatter.

Still Verek gave nothing away, by word or look. What did he know? What did he suspect?

At last the wizard turned and stalked away. "Come," he snapped over his shoulder. "Small use standing here until you freeze. Get on your horse and don't let me hear you call for a stop again before nightfall."

Carin found that her knees had locked, and she was gripping one hand so tightly in the other that both ached. The tension in her body thrummed almost audibly as she broke herself loose and hurried to Emrys. But when she was remounted and trailing Verek at a lengthening distance, her muscles began to uncord, and she felt safe in working the seedling up into the light, a little way out of her clothes until its topmost needles tickled her throat.

"This is delightful!" the sprite whispered, too airily to be overheard. "I haven't been so warm since I left the mage's sitting room in Myra's potted rowan."

"You feel the cold?" Carin whispered back, surprised. "I wouldn't expect it to matter to you. The trees you live in don't seem to mind whether they're hot or cold."

"They might not, but I know the difference. When I leap into the heart of a sleeping oak, I find the timber disagreeably cold. Winter's breath drives down the sap. But the wood of an evergreen is always pleasant, for those trees keep their needles all year.

"On balance, though," the sprite added, "I'd rather be chilled than roasted. A stupor comes over me when I am overly warm. And I'm sure you remember, my friend, how I yelped when the mage passed the roots of my captured hazel twig through the fire on his library's hearth. Wet enough, those roots were, to protect them from burning, but feel the heat I assuredly did.

" — Which brings me," the woodsprite interrupted itself, "to a point I would impress upon you with some urgency, if I may. Pray favor me with a moistening of this seedling's roots, as soon as you'll not be put to trouble to do it."

"Sprite!" Carin hissed at the creature in alarm. "It may be *hours* before I get a chance to water you. Are you shriveling already? Drisha! I knew we shouldn't have done this."

"Pray do not distress yourself!" the creature squeaked. "I assure you that I am in no danger, and shouldn't be for days. The sprig in which I travel is young, fresh, and full of life. My desire to keep it so is the reason I ask that it be watered—but only when you may find it convenient."

The pine needles poked Carin in the throat as she heaved a sigh of relief. She worked her hand inside her coat and grasped the seedling by its bundled roots, intending to draw it down a little, away from her face. But for a moment her hand stayed where it was, her irritated neck forgotten, as she caught sight of Lanse gesturing up ahead. The boy pointed to his left, calling Verek's attention to something southward.

Carin followed their gazes, then began tugging the seedling deep out of sight.

"We've got company," she whispered to the disappearing needles. "Three riders spurring toward us. I'll stick close to Verek and Lanse in case there's trouble—so keep quiet."

"—As a green bud," the sprite promised.

Both of the horsemen ahead of Carin had removed their gloves and unshouldered their bows. As she caught up with them, a frowning Lanse tossed her the packhorse's lead rope. Then he and Verek drew arrows from their quivers and nocked them. Neither bent his bow, only held his weapon lightly at rest.

The three riders who were kicking up dust from the south were similarly armed—bows in hand but not drawn. As the trio neared Verek's party, their scruffiness was the most striking thing about them. Though they rode good horses and carried well-made weapons, the men were dirty and unkempt. Their clothes had been unscrubbed too long to ever be clean again. Carin wrinkled her nose as an errant breeze brought her a whiff of the strangers.

"Halt!" the trio's leader cried.

He rode in so tight in front of Verek that the wizard had no choice but to comply. Lanse reined in at his right hand. Carin brought up the rear.

"In the name of my Lord Attis of Imlen," the stranger said, "you are hereby commanded to leave his land at once."

Verek looked the scruffy spokesman up and down. "I take it ill that a baseborn hireling should presume to command me to any action," he growled. "As it happens, however, my path takes me off this ill-favored plain as quickly as these tired beasts will cross it. Move aside and let us pass."

The leader of the opposing party shook his head. "Nay. You'll go no farther. Turn those nags around and ride back the way you came."

"And if we do not?" the wizard asked. He leaned forward in his saddle.

Though Carin couldn't see Verek's eyes, the stranger's reaction told her the wizard had fixed him with one of those deep, menacing stares that could unstring her own nerves instantly. The rider flinched and averted his gaze.

Quickly, however, the man collected himself. He scowled back. "If you do not," the rider barked, "then you'll end your journey here, with the vultures plucking out your damned eyes before the sun is set."

"Destruction on you!" Verek spat the curse. He straightened. "Provoke me further and it's your worthless carcass that the scavengers will feast upon. Move aside, or have but a moment to regret your error."

The rider laughed. He cut his eyes at his companions. Then he ran his stare appraisingly over Verek's two.

His gaze lingered longest on Carin. She gripped Emrys' reins and barely mastered the urge to back the mare away. The stranger's leer made her feel as violated as if his hands were on her.

The rider returned his attention to Verek. "Those are brave words for a rich fool who's backed by a cub and a pretty boy." He scoffed. "I think we'll spare the pretty one for a bit of sport.

A fair-faced boy will please like a strumpet if he's all there is to be had. But it's to *farsinchia*, sir, that we send you and the cub!"

Before the last word was out of his mouth, the rider and his men had their bows drawn and their arrows leveled.

Only Lanse was as blindingly quick with his own weapon. The wizard's bow still rested on his leg, held casually in his disfigured left hand. Verek did not appear to have twitched a muscle, except he'd raised his right hand. He held it out before him, the long fingers spread.

Carin's stomach heaved. Under all the layers of her clothes she was cold but damp with sweat. She gawked at a scene that seemed frozen in time, as if painted on a canvas of colorless sky and winter-killed grass. The three ruffians and their horses didn't move. But then Lanse drew his arrow back a little further, and Verek began to raise his own neglected weapon.

It's too late! screamed panic inside Carin's head. *They'll be killed. Get out of here!*

She dropped the packhorse's rope, yanked Emrys around, and kicked the mare to a run. She didn't look back to see whether Lanse could down one of the riders before he himself fell—alongside Verek. The wizard, so carelessly caught off guard, was sure to take an arrow before he could loose his own shot. Verek and Lanse were done for. But at least two of their killers would survive—to come after her.

The ensorcelled band on Carin's ankle clamped down, hard. "*Aaahhh!*" she shrieked, and hauled back on Emrys' reins before the iron could bite deep and cleave her foot from her leg.

As the horse skidded to a halt, foam flecking its mouth, Carin slumped over the mare's neck. The blood roared in her ears. All but witless with terror, she was powerless to choose:

Which fate? Run, and be dismembered? Or surrender to the ruffians to be raped and murdered?

Chapter 6

An Unpardonable Offense

Her ankle iron loosened.

Verek is dead, and his spell dies with him! Carin clutched at the possibility. She hazarded a glance backward to the scene of the wizard's murder—

—And discovered his doppelgänger approaching at a trot. The ghost saw Carin gaping at him. He reined Brogar to a halt and called out, in familiar clipped tones that said he was no apparition:

"Why do you weary that poor beast with a hard run in the wrong direction? You must know by now which way is east and which, west. Kindly recover your bearings and get yourself back here."

A stunned and half-strangled "Uhh ..." was the sum of Carin's response. But Emrys heeded the wizard's call. The mare's breath fogged the air as, chuffing and snorting, she took them to Verek at a slow walk.

When they were still a few steps from him, Carin bent from her saddle and vomited. The full contents of her stomach splashed to the ground, steaming in the cold. Emrys never paused, but carried her to the wizard's side.

"Steady!" Verek exclaimed. "What's all this?"

The sky seemed to press down on her as Carin dug for her water costrel. But before she could get at it, Verek had leaned across the slight space between their two horses to hand her a different bottle—one that didn't hold water.

"What you appear to require is a swallow of this," he said. "*Dhera* is a great comfort to those who are sick with fear. In these symptoms of yours, I read no other malady. You needn't be so anxious as this, however. I should not have left Ruain if I meant to be stopped by common ruffians."

Carin took a long pull of the liquor. Its warmth spread through her belly, calmed her retching, and helped her to stop shaking.

"Come," Verek ordered as Carin silently gave him his *dhera* back. "There's little now to hold us here. We must be away."

She followed him too closely to allow even a whispered word to the sprite in its seedling. They rejoined Lanse. The boy was waiting impatiently astride his gelding, holding the packhorse's rope. As Carin rode up, he shot her a black look. She ignored him. Her attention was all for the three bodies that lay on the ground, already stiffening in the cold.

The dead riders' horses stood as they had at the moment the men raised their weapons. The animals might have been statues, except for their eyes. These rolled in terror, the whites showing.

The spell of stone, Carin thought, beginning to make sense of events. With the spread fingers of his right hand, the wizard must have cast horses and riders under the enchantment at the instant the men brought their bows up. Verek and Lanse had been free then to dispatch each motionless target with an unhurried shot through the heart. The blots of blood in the center of each chest testified mutely to a single arrow entering, then being pulled from the flesh the way it went in.

Merciful Drisha. What a way to die. Carin felt certain that the slaughtered men had been fully aware of their peril, if they experienced the spell of stone the same way she had. Each of her three brushes with the magic had deadened her limbs but not her mind. She had known exactly what was happening to her.

Verek dismounted and approached the three frightened horses. He spoke softly to them and placed his bare hands on the foreheads of the first two. With his eyes closed, he held that pose a moment, then dropped his hands.

The two horses started back, snorting their uneasiness. But they did not run. Their goggle-eyed fear diminished to a nervous curiosity. They watched as the wizard touched the third animal's forehead. That horse, also released from the spell, joined its mates.

Verek spared no glance for the bodies on the ground. He pulled on his gloves, remounted, then led the way westward at no quicker a pace than he had set before the three riders challenged them. The entire episode—from the initial confrontation to the executions and the release of the horses— had cost the party from Ruain little time. Now Carin found herself as before, trailing Verek and Lanse, just behind the packhorse that the boy led by its rope. For a time, she kept close.

Hoofbeats sounded behind her. Carin twisted in her saddle to find the three newly riderless horses almost at Emrys' heels.

Gluttons for punishment, she thought.

But after an hour or so of uneventful riding, Carin dropped back and joined the trailing herd. She loosened her clothing to get at the sprite's seedling.

"My friend!" the sprite shrilled with the voice of a cracked pipe, the moment its topmost needles cleared her coat collar. "What has happened? For a long while, I could hear only the pounding of your heart. 'We've met with some grave misfortune!' I thought. When your heart finally quieted and I could make out a few sounds from the outside world, I heard the mage speak of ruffians. Were we attacked? Does danger threaten still?"

"Easy, sprite," Carin said. She patted the bundled roots under her coat. "The three men who came at us lived hardly long enough to regret their mistake." In a whisper, her voice masked by the beats of hooves all around her, she told the creature what had happened.

"It's a bad end for those fellows," the sprite said, "but perhaps no worse than they deserved. Though the mage is hardly less villainous than they were, I am glad to be under his protection when such scoundrels are abroad. But tell me now: do you see a tree anywhere? Are we to leave this plain by evening, do you think? Or must I spend the night in this sprig?"

Carin scanned the line where brown grass met gray sky, saw nothing reminiscent of a tree, and said so. The sprite took this news cheerfully, but asked then to be tucked back inside her coat to rest.

"It might be prudent of me to save my strength. We could be days crossing this land—as you warned—and I'll be a sapless wight at the end of it if I'm careless of my health. Too, it's been a bit of a strain, leaping through the trees all this way from the mage's house. I could count it a fine piece of luck that we came to this wide plain when we did. Now I have the chance for a good long rest, going horseback for a change. So if I'm quiet for a time, don't be anxious for me. I'm only sleeping deeply, the way some trees drowse through the cold months."

Carin returned the creature's "Good night." She slid the seedling down in her coat and pulled her cloak around them both. What was left of the afternoon plodded by, with not so much as an interesting new thought darting into her head to break the monotony.

Just before sunset, they reached the creek that Verek had named as their night's stopping place. *Does he know the way only from maps and travelers' journals? Or has he made this trip before?* Carin wondered. Was it, perhaps, a sort of pilgrimage for the wizards of Ruain? The "craggy heights" of Lord Legary's ensorcelled narrative suggested that possibility.

The creek was a ribbon meandering across the plain, frozen over at its edges. But seven thirsty horses soon had the ice broken — the three newcomers as eager to drink as Verek's four.

They left the beasts saddled for warmth, but Lanse slipped the bits from seven mouths so the horses could graze. The four without riders, including the sorrel packhorse, had to make do with grass. Only Brogar, Emrys, and Lanse's gelding got rations of oats in nosebags. As the horses munched their feed, Lanse moved among them, checking their hooves and feeling for swollen tendons.

"The boy will be a while with that lot," Verek commented as he dropped his saddle-roll and bags on the ground. "Be pleased to fetch me wood off that pack animal. The evening's too cold to wait for a fire."

"All right."

Carin went to the sorrel and discovered a number of tree limbs, bundled in canvas. Most were longer than her arm and thicker than her wrists. Evidently Lanse and Verek hadn't been idle at the forest fringe while she'd attended to private business in the pine grove. They had packed enough wood to see them through two suppers on this treeless plain, if they used the fuel sparingly.

She returned along the creekbank with an armload and found Verek clearing a circle at the water's edge, a precaution against any sparks from their campfire setting the grassland ablaze. Carin dropped the wood there, then walked back to the packhorse for a frozen slab of stewed venison and strong sage tea. Above the horses' watering spot she broke the ice and filled two pots.

Within the circle at the creek, when Carin got back, the wizard already had a small fire laid and lit — no great feat for one who could summon a flame with a snap of his fingers. By the time the tea was made and the first cups drunk, the meat was thawing at its edges. The two of them sat on their blankets to eat it. They did not wait for the preoccupied Lanse to join them.

"I'm curious, sir," Carin ventured, trying to sound casually conversational. "Why are the dead men's horses following us? Wouldn't most go back to their stable when they've been given their heads?"

Verek scowled. "Have you added horse-thievery to your list of charges against me?" he growled, with his maddening habit of answering a question with a question. "At last count, I believe your indictment of me alleged only lunacy, villainy, fiendishness, and murder."

Carin shook her head. "I'm not saying you did anything wrong—about those horses, I mean. I just think it's strange that they've come with us."

The wizard sighed—whether to express or to subdue his irritation, it was hard to say. But perhaps more the latter. He took a bite of half-thawed stew, then gave Carin a fuller answer than she expected.

"So that we need not kill the beasts, I placed upon them the spell of forgetfulness. For the next four days they will not remember to whose stables they belong, but will trail us. On the fifth day, their memories will reawaken. Then we'll see which yearning is strongest in their simple intellects: the desire to stay with this new herd they've joined, or a wish to return to their familiar places."

Carin thought it over as she chewed her supper. Then she asked the obvious question.

"Sir, the spell of forgetfulness ... Couldn't you have cast it on those three men to make them forget they'd ever seen us? Did you have to kill them?"

Verek sipped his tea and eyed Carin over the rim of his cup. Uneasily, she traced the rim of her own with her fingertip, hoping she hadn't made a misstep.

The wizard, though, proved to be in a patient mood this evening. He lowered his drink and answered her, again at some length.

"It's not as simple with men as with horses. When these beasts regain their memories, they may return to their owner, but they will tell him nothing of what took place. Stripped of saddles and their riders' gear, they'll offer no clue to the fate of the three. If some enterprising comrade of the dead men chooses to mount a search, he may discover their corpses on the plain. What conclusion will he draw from what he finds there? That thieves murdered the three for their horses and goods. He'll think the horses somehow escaped—perhaps while the killers drunkenly divvied up the spoils.

"Were the men themselves to return to their master, however," Verek went on, "they would return in full possession of their memories—and their tongues. Those placed under enchantments—even with the spell of forgetfulness upon them—do not forever unknow what has happened to them. Don't you recall very well the times you succumbed to spellcraft?" he asked, watching her.

Carin nodded. Her brushes with the supernatural under Verek's roof were etched into her memory. Those recollections would be with her always.

The wizard took another sip. Then he continued, with no prodding from his listener.

"The returning riders would raise a cry of 'Sorcery!' from one edge of this plain to the other. The ignorant and the superstitious would be rallied against us until every bowman and dog in the country were on our trail. I could deal with them, but at the cost of many lives. The result of such a bloodbath would inevitably be war." Verek's voice hoarsened, and he swallowed more tea to clear it. "The wounds have not yet healed from Ladrehdin's last 'Wizards War.' I have no wish to start another. But neither would I choose to burn."

"Burn?" Carin asked. "Like … at the stake?"

"Yes. If I allowed a mob of the mindless to fall on us, such would be my fate. Yours could be worse. The worthless *spriccts* might find it amusing to brutalize for a day, or a week, a lass who was found to be masquerading as a lad. But they would also, in time, consign you to the flames."

Carin reached for the steaming pot of tea. Wordlessly she refilled Verek's cup, then her own. The lull in the conversation stretched on. She didn't know how to react to the wizard's use of the coarsest swearword in the Ladrehdinian tongue. Nor could she comment on her fate at the hands of those to whom he applied the obscenity. So she returned the pot to the fire, and kept quiet.

Verek, however, seemed reluctant to let the matter go until Carin had conceded the point. He pressed her:

"In light of what I say, do you believe that Lanse and I were wrong to kill those scoundrels? Had they more right to their lives than we three to ours?"

She shook her head. "No, sir, I don't believe they did have. I understand that it was self-defense. They raised their weapons first and left you no choice."

Carin glanced around, looking for Lanse. He was still with the horses. She turned back to Verek and asked, "Both of you killed those men, right? I mean, *you* put them under the spell, of course. But then Lanse didn't just watch while you shot all three of them, did he?"

Verek was looking at her almost warily.

"Why should you wish to know that?" he asked, his head atilt. "Would it surprise—or trouble—you to learn that two of those ruffians died with Lanse's arrows in them?"

Carin studied Verek's silver headband to keep safely at the edge of his glances. "I wonder whether Lanse had ever killed anyone before," she muttered.

Slowly, the wizard shook his head. He did not take his eyes from Carin.

"To my knowledge, no, he had not. But it's a long lane that has no turning. None of us is likely to end this journey unchanged from what we were when we began it."

Surprised into meeting Verek's gaze, Carin held it for a moment. She tried to read a deeper meaning there. But the wizard's face did not betray him.

She continued then on the subject of Lanse's first kill, not quite sure why it interested her so much. "Was Lanse reluctant to do it? Did he hesitate at all? Or did he kill those men willingly?"

"Not willingly," Verek said, his voice quick, his words clipped. He inspected Carin narrowly. "One does not take another's life willingly, nor casually. Lanse did what he had to, bravely and without hesitation. We all do what we must—if we would not be guilty of shirking our duty."

The wizard fell silent while he studied Carin. Then a gleam of understanding seemed to flash in his eyes.

"I begin to plumb the well from which spring these questions about the boy. No very great while ago, you might have taken a life, but you found that you had no stomach for murder. You were weak. You hesitated, and the chance was lost. Isn't that what troubles you? Haven't you been seeking in Lanse's actions some grounds for excusing your own? But in that hope, you have been frustrated. For Lanse did not hesitate. He acted, while you dithered."

"Yes," Carin muttered. "Something like that."

The wizard shook his head. "Your reasoning is faulty. To say that you should have done as Lanse did is to compare the way of the root to that of the leaf."

Carin started, and almost put her hand on the roots of the pine seedling that nestled in her clothes. To hide the gesture, she deliberately rearranged her cloak, snugging it tight around her.

Verek seemed to see nothing in her fidgeting. He went on with his argument.

"It best serves the root to burrow downward, toward rich, well-watered soil. The leaf, however, prospers upward, reaching for the sun. It would not behoove either to behave as the other. They follow their contrary paths because it profits each to do so.

"Lanse had good and urgent cause to kill those men. He was preserving not only our lives, but also this venture in which we are joined. You, conversely, had sound reason to stay your hand, the night in the chamber of the *wysards* when you found me gone into darkness. It is not for my sake alone that I commend the good judgment you showed that night. If you had acted rashly, the consequences would have fallen on the shoulders of many besides yourself and me."

"And the woodsprite," Carin added. Again she resisted the urge to touch the bundle near her heart.

The wizard paused, as if finding her remark worth heeding. Then he nodded. "And the sprite."

M'lord Verek is in a talkative mood tonight, Carin thought. Now might be a good time to get some answers—if she could avoid asking the wrong question, the sort that got his ire up.

Verek hadn't frowned when she'd mentioned the sprite. Maybe that subject would be safer than others Carin could raise, given that Verek might think the fay was still imprisoned in

Ruain. Or if he suspected otherwise, the wizard might hope to extract the truth from her. The creature that was hidden in her coat would enjoy hearing itself talked about, if it were awake enough to attend to this exchange.

So Carin ventured on. "You call it my 'good judgment,' sir. But I think I probably made the worst mistake of my life, when I didn't knife you through the heart that night. I told you why I didn't do it—I was afraid the sprite would be trapped if you died. Was I right about that?"

Verek raised his mutilated left hand to his chin. He stroked the formerly close-cropped beard that had grown ragged since Deroucey. His three bare fingers did not linger there, but slid quickly back among the folds of his cloak.

He shook his head. "No, you were mistaken. The spells that safeguarded my apartments would have failed at my death. Many kinds of enchantments will retain their full potency long after their crafters are no more. The spells on my doors, however, were not magic of that sort. Had you killed me, you might simply have walked in and carried the sprite away.

"But I suspect," Verek added, "that this news does not trouble you overmuch. For it wasn't solely your regard for the sprite's welfare that stayed your hand, was it?"

Carin sighed. Slowly, she shook her head. Since she was the one who had sent the conversation down this path, she might as well speak openly—where both the warlock and the woodsprite, if the creature was listening, could hear her confession.

"No, I had other reasons. Mainly, I doubted that the pool of magic would *let* me hurt you. If I'd walked into the cave carrying a knife, wouldn't the power that lives in the water have stopped me before I got anywhere near you? Same with the dragon," she added. "If I had tried to call up the Jabberwock from the *Looking-Glass* book, wouldn't the pool of magic have

113

destroyed the dragon from another world to save a wizard from this one?"

Carin questioned for effect, not expecting Verek to answer. But when she paused to sip her tea, the warlock gifted her with a surprising reply.

"In truth, I cannot say." He cocked his head as he spoke, but his gaze was direct—disturbingly so. "To my knowledge, never has the chamber of the *wysards* been visited by such a one as you—nor by any otherworldly dragon. You were a witness to my astonishment when first you summoned the creature to those waters. A participant you were also—though unwilling, as I recall—in my efforts to know the beast's nature. Surely you cannot profess to wonder at my own uncertainty upon the points you have raised. Until the question is put to the test, I am no more able than you are to say whether the waters of the *wysards* will rise against your uncanny dragon to protect an adept of Ladrehdin."

'Whether the waters will rise'? Not 'would'—but 'will.' Verek made it sound like the question wasn't a conjecture from the past, but a puzzle for the present and a test for the future.

Carin barely had time to wonder about Verek's phrasing—and to note his use of the word "adept"—when the wizard redirected her attention to the subject they had strayed from.

"I fear my case stands bootless," he said, "in defense of the decision you made in the cavern of enchantment. Of the two reasons you have given me for sparing my life, I tell you that the first was mistaken and the second debatable." Verek shifted on the blanket under him. "Perhaps I may do better, if you have a third to offer."

Indeed she did. But she hesitated to reveal it. Carin looked at the ground and began to pluck at dead, dry grass. She couldn't stand the cold for long; it forced her hand back under her cloak.

She didn't look up then as she answered Verek. "My third reason will probably sound lame to you. But I felt like it would be" — she searched for the word — "*dishonorable* to murder someone who had just saved my life. I would have drowned if you hadn't come in after me. You knew you'd get hurt. That pool is an ocean of pain." Carin shuddered as she recalled it. "After what you did, getting me out of there even as hurt as you were, I felt like I owed you … especially when I saw you afterward. You looked awful.

"So instead of finishing you off that night, I just walked away." Carin shrugged. "Now you know all my reasons for not trying to kill you. Take your pick. None of them is very good."

She awaited his scorn. But Verek withheld it.

"No reason serves better than this last one as grounds for any decision," he replied, softly. "No higher justification is there than the voice of conscience. To commit a deed that is dishonorable in one's own eyes is an unpardonable offense. The criminal may more easily make amends for a lifetime of unscrupled crime, than the man who forsakes his conscience — even once — will rid himself of that shame."

Are you talking to me, warlock? Or are you talking to yourself now? Carin wondered.

She lifted her gaze and studied Verek's face. For the first time since this exchange began, he had turned away from her. He was staring into the fire.

Have you done something that shames you in your own eyes? she asked him silently. *Are you responsible for the death of your little boy? And years ago, when you were a child yourself, did the voice of conscience whisper to your grandfather Legary of his own dishonor?*

"Did your grandfather kill your father?"

In the stillness that followed, the crackling of the fire was loud. *Drisha take my tongue from my skull!* Carin cursed herself.

Her question had cut through the cold air. But she clung to the hope that she had only heard her thoughts inside her head.

The look on Verek's face dispelled that delusion, however, the way a pouncing cat scatters the pigeons. His head snapped toward her, and his right hand shot out to close on a fold of her cloak so quickly that she barely had time to flinch.

"What?" Verek barked. He jerked Carin toward him until she was off her blanket and her face was less than a span from his. "What is this that you dare to ask me? What do you know of my grandfather *or* his son? And how does such an accusation come leaping off that tongue of yours, as though it has waited there, eager for the moment when it might be given voice?"

Carin heard these questions with her eyes tightly shut. It took nerve to look the wizard in the face even when he was calm. But now he was flushed and furious, and Carin's courage failed. She swallowed, her mouth as dry as the winter grassland around them.

"I'm—I'm sorry," she stammered out. "I didn't m-mean to say that to you. I don't know what m-m-made me say it aloud."

Verek held her another moment in his ironhanded grip. Then he returned Carin to her blanket with a neck-popping shove.

"Small use running after the arrow once it's loosed," he growled. "Do not try me with your regrets for having uttered such a thought. Explain to me, rather, how such an abominable notion comes to be lodged in that brain of yours."

And how was she to do that? Carin couldn't tell him about the stolen pages from the *Book of Archamon* that held the verses from which she had drawn her clues—and her suspicions— regarding the death of Verek's father.

But those narratives weren't Carin's only sources of information. She had others. And to admit to them might provoke Verek less than confessing to her desecration of his book.

"Myra—" she began, but was immediately silenced.

"Myra!" The warlock thumped his hand on the blanketed ground as though it were his housekeeper's ear that he cuffed. "The woman has a weariless tongue, and she betrays precious little sense in wagging it. But even she cannot unbosom more than she knows. Tell me: what says the old gray goose of my father and my grandfather?"

"Please don't be angry at Myra," Carin pleaded. "She only told me that your father married young and died young. You were just a baby when he died, so your grandfather Legary helped your mother raise you. Myra said Lord Legary was a great wizard. She admired him. But I got the idea that your grandfather had a guilty conscience. Jerold seemed to think so, anyway."

"*Jerold?* He said that to *you?*" Verek almost spluttered. He stared at Carin in open disbelief. "No! Jerold speaks rarely, and never to gossip with prying chits. You won't persuade me that you've heard aught of my private affairs from that old conjurer."

Carin ran her hand through her hair, which was somewhat grown out from the ear-length bob that Myra had given her four weeks ago.

"No, Jerold didn't say anything to me—not directly," she conceded. "But one time in the garden at your house, I overheard Jerold talking to you about your grandfather. He said that Lord Legary was to blame for the harm that's been done to your family. I didn't know what he meant, but I heard Jerold say that your grandfather had done something so wicked that your family still isn't over it. Lord Legary carried his guilt to his grave, Jerold said."

Carin locked her gaze onto Verek's left shoulder and kept it there. No force existed that could have raised her eyes to his at that moment. She drew a steadying breath, and hurried to finish.

"With Jerold blaming your grandfather for some evil deed, and Myra telling me that your father died suddenly when he was only nineteen, I started to wonder. What you said just now, sir, about never forgiving yourself for doing what's dishonorable—it made me think: what's worse than killing your own flesh and blood? Is that what happened? Did your grandfather kill your father?"

And you, Theil Verek: do you have your own son's death on your conscience? she added, taking care this time to keep the thought private.

In the hush that again descended, the sounds of the horses grazing the creekbank came clearly through the evening air. The twilight showed Lanse still moving among them, adjusting a buckle here, smoothing a saddle blanket there, working the snarls from untrimmed manes. Though the boy would never presume to question his master's judgment, his concern for the horses on this long, hard trip was obvious. Even that great brute Brogar could not continue forever at the pace Verek set.

The stewed venison that the wizard and Carin had not eaten was beginning to congeal in its pan. With movements that were as small as she could make them, she stirred the fire and added another stick of wood, then put the pan in the revived flames to reheat. Hunger must drive Lanse from the horses in another few minutes.

Carin's motions roused the warlock from his brown study. He arched his back as if working out the kinks. Then he drew in a long breath through his nose and let it out as slowly.

When he did not otherwise break the silence, Carin risked a sidelong look at his face. She found it to be an impassive mask. Her glance, however, stirred Verek to speech.

"Your talent for weaving elaborate tapestries from a few torn scraps is truly remarkable," he said with a carelessness that sounded forced. "Perhaps this journey will lead you to your true vocation—that of the wandering wit and tale-giver. For it seems you can spin a yarn most bizarre from the slimmest threads of half-truths and hearsay.

"But until I release you to follow that trade, you will refrain from inventing slanders against the House of Verek." He leaned slightly toward her. "You will, rather, train that restless mind of yours upon the matters which concern you—the matters I have set before you for the most careful consideration that you are capable of giving them. I will not ask it again. Widen your gaze. Occupy your thoughts with perceiving your purpose in this venture, and you'll find me ready to aid your understanding of it. But waste your days spinning fantasies of evil sorcerers and murdered children, and I won't fail to give you other things to think about."

So quickly that Carin didn't see it coming, Verek's left hand shot out and plucked hers from the folds of her cloak. His other hand went for his knife. He crushed her palm in his three-fingered grip and bent her little finger back painfully far, pinning it with his thumb. Against the first joint of her finger, Verek laid his knife.

"The monks of Drisha have a ritual that concentrates the mind wonderfully." The warlock's voice was a low murmur, and as menacing as the roar of an avalanche. "Do you know of it? The rite is performed over twelve days—one for each of Drisha's commandments. On the first, the monk cuts off his small finger at the first joint. He mustn't let the pain intrude upon his thoughts, but must ponder the meaning of the First

Commandment until the wound clots. On the second day, he severs the finger at the middle joint and contemplates the Second Commandment. The next day, he rids himself of the stump while meditating upon the Third. And so on, day by day, until his four fingers are removed piecemeal and he has shown himself so disciplined in mind that no agonies of the flesh will disturb his reflections upon the will of Drisha."

Verek pressed the knife in place. On Carin's taut, bloodless skin, the bend of the joint showed clearly as a thin red line that might have been drawn on, so straight and distinct was it — an easy mark to follow for the first cut.

Her breath came in short bursts. The only part of her that wasn't shaking was the hand that Verek gripped in his own. His fingers were surprisingly warm ...

Carin's free hand slid out of her cloak and shivered upward to close around the fingers that held hers. She watched her hand with a feeling of detachment, as though it moved with a will of its own, determined — despite its trembling — to mount a rescue of its opposite number.

For a long moment they stayed that way, Verek's hand enfolding one of Carin's and embraced in its turn by her other; his free hand holding the knife. Then Verek lowered the weapon. He released Carin's little finger from its painful backward arch, but he did not pull free of her grasp. He only slipped his hemmed-in fingers between her two hands until they rested in her palms.

"Perhaps the fingers matter more to *wysards* than to monks," he muttered, and studied the tangle of hers and his. "For I have not known any true adept of Ladrehdin to employ the monkish method to center a distracted apprentice. I trust that it shall not be necessary in your case."

His hand twitched between hers. Carin let it go.

"Now," Verek said and rose from his blanket to stand looking down at her, "go to bed. And sleep with something on your hands, or risk losing fingers to a hazard other than this knife." He flashed the blade at her before he sheathed the weapon. "Your digits feel as frozen as this night air."

The warlock tossed the last ration of wood on their dwindling fire. Then he walked down the creekbank toward Lanse and the horses.

Carin stayed on her blanket, her hands stuck in her armpits, concentrating her thoughts—not on the mysteries that Verek had commanded her to ponder—but on restraining her racing heart and pumping lungs. When both had slowed to a saner pace, she fished a clean stocking from her saddlebags and got her water costrel.

Through the owl-light Carin walked out onto the plain, away from her captor and the horses. Beyond the circle that the campfire lit, the tightening of her anklet warned that she was as far from Verek as his sorcery allowed. She backed slightly toward the fire to loosen the anklet's grip, then drew the pine seedling from under her coat and splashed water on its linen-wrapped roots.

"Hew me!" the woodsprite swore in a thin, sleep-slurred voice. "Are we drowning?"

"I'm just soaking your roots, sprite," Carin whispered. "Now do you mind if I cover you up, pine needles and all? If I slip a stocking over you, it may help keep your 'feet' damp longer. And it will stop the rest of you from shedding. I don't think it's good that you're losing your needles in my clothes. Besides, they stick me. Would you smother, wrapped up in wool?"

"No ... not smother. Be warm ... so cozy ... so sleepy ..."

"Then go back to sleep," Carin whispered. She slipped the seedling, bundled roots first, down into the stocking. "Maybe tomorrow we'll get off this plain."

* * *

The next day — and the next — brought nothing, however, but hours of riding across an unchanging landscape. On the third day, they came to a jumble of rocks that were piled on the grassland like the falling-down ruins of a temple. There Verek and Lanse stripped the saddles from the horses of the three slain ruffians. Under the rocks they buried the saddles and the dead men's gear, so deeply that no passerby would catch a glimpse.

By the fourth day, Carin could get nothing out of the sprite except an occasional sigh. The sound was faint, and more like a breeze than a living breath.

On the morning of the fifth day, the enchantment left the horses that Verek had bespelled. Two of them suddenly wheeled, threw up their heads, and stared wide-eyed back the way they'd come. With nary a glance at those who had been their companions for the better part of a week, they trotted away with their ears pricked as though each heard its master's voice.

The third horse watched the first two go. It bobbed its head and danced sideways, but it didn't take off after its stablemates until Brogar rushed at it with his teeth bared. Evidently that showed the beast where its path lay. The horse galloped off to join the others.

In the late afternoon of that same day, Verek's party, absent its camp followers, reached the western edge of the plain. The grassland ended at a wide, partly ice-choked stream, the opposite bank of which sloped upward.

Carin's heart leaped. Dotting that slope were pines and firs.

The riders crossed the stream single file, Verek leading the way on Brogar, breaking the surface skim of ice. Carin had to lift the hem of her cloak and take her feet from the stirrups; the frigid water was deep enough to brush her mare's belly. But Emrys crossed without mishap, only splashing the fringes of the mare's thick saddle pad.

In the trees streamside, they stopped for the night. Carin heated a pot of water over their campfire and carried it downstream to have privacy for a wash-up.

As soon as she was out of sight, she pulled the seedling from under her coat. She stripped off its wool and linen wrappers. The withered little pine left most of its needles in the stocking. All but a few hairlike roots came away with the linen.

"Sprite!" Carin hissed. She pressed the seedling's remains to the trunk of a green-needled fir. "Wake up. Here's a fresh tree for you." She gave the seedling a little shake and knocked off more dry needles. "Come on, sprite! Get moving."

There was no answer. The only sigh in the forest was a cold wind through the treetops.

Chapter 7

Vermin in the Vortex

Carin flattened her hands against the seedling. She crushed it to the fir as though to force it inside the tree's living heart. Still there was no sign of the sprite—no spark, no whimper, no faint quivering.

It's dead, murmured her rational mind.

No! Her silent shout put to flight a possibility that she would not entertain. *The sprite is only asleep—dormant, like an oak tree in winter. I have to find a way to wake it up.*

Carin eyed the pot of water that she'd heated to wash with. It steamed on the ground beside the half-frozen stream.

Hot and cold—the sudden shock—

She kicked a rock onto the ice at the stream's edge. It broke open a hole; Carin plunged the sprite's seedling through.

Her hand burned in the icy water as though in the superheated air of a pottery kiln. She stood it as long as she could, then jerked the seedling out, shook it, and dunked it into the steaming pot. Again she held it there, long enough to let the heat seep in but not so long that the sprite would drown—Carin hoped.

She snatched up the dripping seedling and pressed it to the fir. "Sprite!" Carin whispered. "Come on! Wake up." Her lips touched the few green needles that still clung to the dying pine.

Her wet hands were freezing, aching almost beyond endurance. But Carin jammed the seedling tight against the fir tree, willing the spark within to make the leap to safety. She rested her forehead on it, as if to entwine her thoughts with the sprite's. But nothing came from the seedling—no reedy voice, no flicker of light.

Carin clenched her eyes shut. Tears squeezed out and beaded in her lashes.

Blinking the tears away, she sighted a stone on the ground at her feet. It was almond-shaped with a blunt end for gripping and a sharp, broken edge for cutting—a perfect hand ax.

Pain. What the dead can't feel may save the living. She would hurt the sprite enough to rouse it—or kill it with the effort.

Carin flipped the seedling over and pressed its thicker root end against the fir's trunk. Slowly but firmly, she sliced the seedling open, working from its roots toward the few remaining needles that dangled off the seedling like green icicles.

At first, the cut revealed only dead wood. But as Carin sliced toward the cluster of still-living needles, the wound oozed sap. A faint cry rose from it. A dull glow appeared in the needles. The light dripped into the fir tree as gradually as a pat of butter would melt on barely warm bread.

When the glow was entirely gone from the seedling, Carin dropped the dead husk. She put her lips to the light that splotched the fir's bark.

"Sprite!" she breathed. "Are you all right? I haven't hurt you? I didn't know how else to get you moving."

The creature glowed with a feeble and faintly yellow light. But it made no sound.

"Talk to me, sprite!" Carin pleaded. "Sweet mercy! What have I done? Did I cut you?" She turned her head and put her ear to the tree.

A snowflake falling to earth would have been only slightly less audible than the voice that reached her then. But Carin managed to pick out a few words from the sprite's whisper:

" … not cut … so weak … need rest."

Carin leaned against the tree and closed her eyes. "Thank the stars above!" she murmured. "I thought I'd killed you." She was shaking with relief, but also from the cold. Under the trees beside the stream, the air was frosty. Her hands felt numb.

"Sleep well, sprite," Carin whispered. She opened her eyes and straightened. "I'll check on you in the morning."

The woodsprite made no reply. It oozed deeper into the tree until its glow was hidden, like a firefly in tall grass. Carin patted the fir.

In the twilight she made her way back to the campfire. Verek and Lanse were already wrapped in their bed-blankets, stretched on either side of a dying blaze. Both seemed asleep. The wizard drew deep, even breaths. The boy wheezed through a stuffy nose.

A house cat might have padded its way between them to lie by the embers, but Carin could not curl up small enough to fit. She tiptoed past, got her bedroll, and carried it to the opening in the trees where the four horses were picketed. Brogar, Lanse's mount, and the pack animal only eyed her sleepily, but Emrys whickered at her approach.

"Easy." Carin stroked the mare's neck. "Shh. I'll get an arrow in my back if those two at the fire mistake me for a horse thief. They haven't left me anyplace to get warm, so I've come to you." Carin stood close, sharing the mare's body heat.

"Would to Drisha that you could tell me where we're going," she whispered into Emrys' ear, "and when we'll get there. What's going to happen to you and me? Will your dark master take you home to Ruain eventually?" Carin scratched the mare's forehead. "He promised to free me when spring comes. I just hope I'm alive then."

The mare's white blaze caught the moonlight as Emrys brought her head up to peer over Carin's shoulder. For a moment, the animal seemed to study the fireside sleepers as though pondering her rider's questions.

But then Emrys swung her head the other way, toward the thicker growth of trees up the slope from the streambank. Her nostrils flared. Large dark eyes and sensitive ears fixed on the timber, searching for … what?

Carin stood still, hardly breathing, probing the moonlit scene. Deep in the shadows under the trees—was that a shadow blacker than the rest? And had it just moved?

Emrys snorted. The other horses trained their gazes on the same stand of timber that the mare studied. They showed their uneasiness with low nickers and hesitant foot-stamping.

Carin backed away. She dropped her bedroll, whirled—

—And ran straight into the outstretched fingers of a hand. The fingers jabbed her in the face as the hand reached for the hood of her cloak, closed on it, and hurled her forward with bruising force. She fell on her knees, rolled, and came up in a crouch, her fists raised.

Lanse's voice cut through the night. "Witch! Stay away from the horses. What are you about, creeping around in the dark? Hexing the beasts so they'll come up lame tomorrow?"

By way of answer, Carin picked up a rock, and from her crouch launched herself at the boy. He sidestepped, and she lunged past him. Lanse helped her on her way with a boot to her behind. As Carin hit the ground again, the rock did not leave her grasp. Twisting, she flung it with all her might.

The rock streaked past Lanse and struck Verek a blow to the chest as the wizard came up behind his groom.

"Umph!" Verek huffed like an angry danbuck. He started back. "What in the Kingdom of Greatrakes is going on?" he bellowed. "By the powers! Can't I close my eyes for three minutes without I find the two of you at each other's throats?"

Lanse got in the first word. "The trull was out here in the dark bothering the horses, my lord. As sure as I stand here, she's been bewitching the beasts."

"You gilded ass-end of a black dog!" Carin swore at him. She scrambled to her feet.

The moonlight couldn't show her their faces clearly, but in her captors' silence she read surprise. It seemed she had astonished them both by refusing to hold her tongue at this latest abuse from Lanse, the way she'd resolutely remained silent in the past.

"Lord Verek," Carin snapped. She looked past Lanse to the wizard. "I'm not the one who's bothering the horses. Something is out there—up there." She pointed to the sloping ground above their campsite. "I'm not sure what I saw, but Emrys saw it too."

She turned toward the horses and found both the mare and Brogar still watching the black patch up the slope. Though the other two animals had lost interest, Emrys and Verek's hunter had their heads up and their eyes on the trees. Each flicked an ear toward the quarrel behind them, as though wondering when their riders would leave off squabbling and attend to business.

One glance at the pair, so obviously on alert, and Verek was striding toward them. He brushed by the boy's shoulder.

"Get your bow, Lanse. It seems we have company."

Carin stepped aside to let the wizard and his boy pass. Then she withdrew to the nearly dead fire. She kneeled beside it, listening. What was out there? Nothing now seemed to move, either on the slope or among the horses. Only a breath of a noise reached her, a muffled whisper as Verek and Lanse conferred.

The two were no more than a quarter hour returning.

"A wolf, I think," the wizard said. He crouched near Carin and the embers. "Alone, and not so desperate for meat—before storms and snows are upon the land—as to stalk humans or horses. It looks us over more from curiosity, I'll wager, than from hunger.

"Be that as it may," he added, "prudence demands that a sentry be posted. As you seem to be the liveliest among us tonight" — by the moon's rays, the look Verek gave Carin was ill-defined — "you will stand the first watch. Wake me at once if the horses grow restless. If all remains peaceful, call me when the moon is overhead or lacks but a hairsbreadth of it."

Verek did not await her answer. He reached for his blankets and stretched out beside the embers. Lanse returned sulkily to his place opposite.

Carin didn't protest. The evening's string of alarms had her wide awake. She'd be on the lookout, whether Verek wished it or not.

She walked back to the horses, retrieving her bedroll on the way. With her hands gloved and her blankets drawn round her shoulders, she sat with her back to a tree at the edge of the clearing. From there she could see the horses and the stand of timber that might yet hide a prowling wolf. Though after the commotion that Lanse had raised, the animal should be long gone.

Was this a hopeful sign, Carin wondered, to be trusted with this guard duty? *Stay awake, see your watch through, don't annoy the warlock,* she told herself, *and maybe he'll agree to take that damned iron off you.*

She felt for her anklet. The iron made a hard ring under the soft leather of her boot. The wound the thing had given her in Deroucey had healed completely, leaving only a pink scar where it had cut her. But the next time she "goaded" it, the iron might strike with such force that even the wizard, with all his skill as a healer, would not make her whole again.

Carin looked over the horses that dozed now in the moonlight. Her gaze traveled up the slope, but she saw nothing except trees and motionless shadows. Even the moon seemed stilled. It progressed little along the climb to its zenith.

129

The cold seeped through the layers of wool swathing Carin. It crept up with special vigor from the ground under her. She folded one blanket to put more layers between herself and the frozen soil. Then she resettled against the tree, her eyes watchful and her mind far from sleep.

The woodsprite's condition worried her. Would morning find the creature fit to travel? Or would the spark be too weak to follow as they resumed their journey westward through these trees? Carin wouldn't be hiding the sprite in a seedling and carrying it as she had across the plain. The creature could not stand much more of that "cozy" form of transport.

If the sprite wasn't strong enough tomorrow to keep up with them, then it must rest here until it felt able to follow. It could trail her. Of course it could. After all, the sprite had caught up with Carin in Deroucey despite the fortnight's head start that she'd had.

Were these western woods as unfamiliar to the sprite as they were to her? Carin wondered. The wandering woodsprite had been none too clear about recollecting its first weeks—or even years—on this world of Ladrehdin. Could it have arrived in this realm so far from the wizards' well under Verek's library—the pool that had coughed up the honeywood wand that was, presumably, a relic of the creature's homeworld?

Carin could believe it possible. Her own landing on the shores of this world had been at the edge of a millpond far to the south of Ruain—five months, to travel it by foot, away from Verek's estate in the highlands and from the wizards' well where "her" puzzle-book had washed up.

The sprite was lucky, Carin mused, *that it didn't have to climb half-drowned out of the same millpond that received me into this world.* The creature might have found shelter in the willows that shaded the pond's banks. But beyond them, it could not have forged a path. The grasslands of southern Ladrehdin stretched treeless around the millpond where Carin had been found.

She'd been a cold, wet, terrified child "rescued" by a wheelwright into years of servitude. Given that the sprite remembered no time when it wasn't flitting unfettered through the trees, it would seem that the creature had had the good fortune to live freely in woodlands since its first hour here.

What was the force that had brought woodsprite and wand, Carin and puzzle-book, to this world—from wherever they had once called "home"?

The question, more properly, she corrected herself, *is not "what," but "who." Who is the "master wizard" who made the magic that awes Verek?*

Every word her captor had said in Deroucey played now in Carin's thoughts. "I cannot send living flesh through the void," Verek had maintained. He'd marveled at the power that had seized the life-spark of the woodsprite, and then snatched a child from distant shores, stripping the memories from both and depositing the two otherworldly beings here on Ladrehdin.

What else had the warlock said that day?

He spoke of possibilities ... the possibilities that would open to a master wizard who wields the power of passage between the worlds. And in the next breath, he asked me about the whirlpool that I saw in his cave of magic—the vortex that carried vermin from a nightmare.

Carin gasped. She sat forward from the tree at her back. She scanned the pines on all sides—behind her toward the stream, as well as up the slope where the supposed wolf skulked.

What if Verek's "wolf" was *not* a natural beast of Ladrehdin? What if the creature that stalked the horses—and their riders?—was in fact a freak, a horror from another realm?

If it's a question of possibilities ...

Who knew where that maelstrom of sorcery might have disgorged its cargo? In Verek's cave of magic that night six weeks ago, the wizards' well had shown them a powerful image of the approaching whirlpool. But it had not shown the vortex's ultimate arrival in Ladrehdin. The alien monstrosities that rode the storm of magic could have landed anywhere—maybe on the banks of the very stream where Verek's party now camped.

The thought almost brought Carin to her feet to rouse the wizard and tell him what she suspected. A glance at the horses, however, showed no cause for alarm. All four dozed peacefully, bathed in moonlight. The silver glow revealed the plain east of the stream to be the same empty landscape that Carin had come to hate in the days it had taken to cross it. Westward, the trees formed crooked ranks on the slope, a motionless army of conifers.

The trees were silent except for the occasional hoot of an owl and the rustlings of small creatures that were out hunting a meal. Once, Carin nearly came out of her skin at a cry, like a baby's, from deep in the woods. It was only a hare dying in an owl's talons. If any beast larger or more menacing stole through the timber, it moved as noiselessly as the stars above.

Carin pulled her blankets up to her nose and checked the moon's position. Another hour, and it would reach the top of its climb through the night. Another hour, and she could turn this cold duty over to the wizard and get the sleep that she was finally beginning to want.

When she woke Verek, should she tell him her speculations about the whirlpool and the vermin it had carried?

The warlock is way ahead of me there, Carin realized with a flash of insight. Why else would Verek have urged her to remember the maelstrom?

Her thoughts returned to that night—the night the voice of the wizards' well had summoned Carin to the cave to witness the oncoming whirlpool. The vortex had carried a matched pair of monsters—creatures so huge and hideous that Carin had dubbed them *mantikhora* after the similarly misshapen vermin of an old folktale she'd once heard.

Together she and Verek had watched the whirlpool spin faster and grow larger, until the wizards' well engulfed the vision. For all its violence and thunder, what they had seen had been only an image—a distant view of the magical storm that had surged to shore elsewhere on Ladrehdin.

The flotsam the storm had left behind in Verek's cave was not, however, mere vision or image. Carin only had to close her eyes to feel again the texture of that artifact ... tough yet limber ... a weight like a pane of split horn as she picked it up from the rim of the wizards' well ... but thinner and more translucent than any sheet of polished horn ever was. And in its graceful teardrop shape, it showed a tracery of veins. If the artifact—a fragment as long as Carin was tall—resembled anything earthly, it seemed to be the wing of a dragonfly, but almost big enough to support a horse.

Emrys' soft, questioning snort blended with Carin's reverie for the briefest moment—long enough to bemuse her with the thought of the mare sporting wings. Then another snort brought Carin's eyes fully open, like a dousing with cold water wakes a sleeper.

She jumped to her feet. Her gaze swung from the horses to the shadowed stand of trees that again claimed the animals' attention.

Carin dropped her blankets and raced to Verek. Though she made no effort to be quiet, the shed pine needles under her boots were a cushion that muffled her steps.

The wizard heard her anyway—or sensed her coming, by whatever means he used. Verek was throwing off his blankets and grabbing for his bow and quiver before Carin reached him. Neither spoke as he trotted at her heels back to the clearing. He stopped beside her at the tree where Carin's blankets lay spilled in a heap.

"The wolf is back," she whispered. "But I don't think it *is* a wolf. I think it could be the *mantikhora*. You know what I mean—those scorpion-alligator vermin that came across the void right before we left Ruain."

The wizard seemed not to hear her. He held his bow ready as he ran his gaze over the trees that Brogar and Emrys studied. Those two seemed more curious than alarmed. The other horses, as before, had lost interest. Both were grazing. Whatever lurked in the trees up the slope was undetectable to Carin's human senses and almost beyond what a keen horse's hearing and eyesight could perceive.

If Verek made out more than his animals did, he kept it to himself. He lowered his weapon and let down his draw. Then he questioned Carin, in a whisper barely above her own.

"Why do you say that our prowler is no beast of this world? Have you glimpsed it tonight? Was there, perhaps, a flash of the moon off an armored claw?"

Carin's face warmed. She shook her head. "You don't need to mock me. No, I didn't see a *mantikhora* in the moonlight. I didn't see a wolf, either." She stared at the trees. "To keep myself awake, I've been wondering about the magic that brought the woodsprite to Ladrehdin. I've been thinking about the wand that supposedly arrived at the same time as the sprite … like the *Looking-Glass* book drifted to you when I surfaced down south. Mostly, though, I've been thinking about the *mantikhora* and that weird piece of a flying wing that washed up in your wizards' well.

"It's made me wonder: where are the *mantikhora* now? If they'd landed near a town, the people would be up in arms. We might have heard something of it in Deroucey. But what if those monsters came to ground up here? They might be hiding up in these trees … stalking us."

Verek didn't scoff. Somewhat to Carin's dismay, he nodded as though her every word had merit.

"Good!" he exclaimed. "Excellent. I am heartened to find your thoughts turning at last upon matters that may not be neglected much longer. You've done well tonight. But now I would counsel you to put those *mantikhora* devils from your mind and get some sleep."

Verek leaned his bow against the tree and collected Carin's blankets from the foot of it. "These covers, I claim for the rest of this short night. Mine at a cold fire will be yours. There's little enough to recommend the one above the other."

Carin eyed him. Verek did not seem concerned about venomous monsters infesting the forested slope above. But he hadn't denied that the possibility existed.

In the act of arranging her confiscated blankets over one shoulder and under the other so that his bow arm wouldn't be hampered, the wizard paused. In the moonlight, he studied Carin's face. The look she gave him wasn't meant to hide her misgivings.

As though in answer to it, Verek reached for her and rested his ungloved hand on her shoulder.

Through the layers of her clothing, Carin could barely feel his touch. But her heart quickened. It was a gesture that Verek used often when speaking to Lanse; never, until this moment, when addressing his "footboy."

"You say that I mock you," he murmured. "You're mistaken. I do not. It is quite possible that the phantom in the trees is a thing that belongs not to this world, but far beyond the void. I have a notion, though, that the monsters you and I witnessed in the vortex are—at this moment—firmly in the grasp of the one who brought them to Ladrehdin. Surely the adept who wields

135

such weapons would not suffer the beasts to roam at large, this far from the castle keep."

Verek tipped his head to indicate the hillside that hid some unknown creature of the night. The prowler seemed once again to have withdrawn. The horses were easy, dozing on their feet or nosing aside fallen pine needles in search of grazing.

"I do not say that we won't meet up with the devils before this journey's done," Verek went on. "But all that threatens tonight, I believe, is a restless wolf or maybe a mountain cat out hunting hares and finding us instead—interlopers in her territory. Curious she is, and puzzled, but not so dangerous to armed, well-mounted travelers as is more of this cold air and broken rest. So to bed with you now, or be hard put to rise in the morning."

Carin nodded. She tiptoed back to the spot beside the stream where Verek and Lanse had spread their blankets. She slipped into the warlock's and pulled them over her head. The wool smelled of him—like an herbalist's workshop musky with the odor of calendula oil and earthy vetiver. Her eyes closed. She breathed in his scent …

… And felt a hand on her shoulder, shaking her awake.

"Get up," Verek ordered. "Day breaks. We ride on."

Carin sat up amid her borrowed blankets and looked around groggily. For a moment she didn't know where she was. Then her head cleared at the sight of the frozen stream, the plain beyond it stretching to the horizon—the plain that had nearly killed the woodsprite.

And by the look of their rapidly disappearing camp, she had only a few minutes to discover whether the sprite would accompany them this morning. Lanse's blankets and gear were gone from their places opposite, across the rekindled fire. Verek was pouring the last of the hot tea into Carin's mug. He waved the empty pan over her mug and over a crust of bread beside it.

"Eat, and get on your horse," he ordered. "Or eat while you ride. However you choose, look alive. We tarry here no longer."

She sprang up from the wizard's blankets, shook them out, folded and rolled them into a tight bundle. Then she grabbed her tea and bread and rushed into the trees downstream.

"Quickly!" Verek's shout followed her.

Once out of the wizard's sight, Carin hurried to the fir that the half-dead woodsprite had crept into.

"Wake up, sprite!" she whispered. Her lips brushed the tree trunk. "How do you feel?"

Where the bark, last night, had absorbed a yellowish mass resembling butter melting, there now appeared a flicker more like the sprite's old self. The spark was duller, however, than the fay's usual sparkle, and it moved with less vitality.

"My friend!" the creature said in a barely audible trill. "Once more I am in your debt. Had you not delivered me to this wholesome tree, I wouldn't have lived to see the sunrise. How am I to repay you?"

"Just follow me, sprite," Carin mumbled around the bread she wolfed down. "Get your strength back and come on. Can you catch up with us again? You know what direction we're going—west, toward the mountains."

"Indeed, I know it. I shan't be likely to lose you now, after so many weeks of traveling with the sun. I'll find you, be assured."

"I hate to leave you, sprite." Carin put her hand on the tree. "But Verek won't wait. So long, for now."

She heard the sprite's good-bye—a faint but spirited piping—as she gulped the last of her tea. Carin ran back to the campfire and found it gone, its ashes scattered over the streambank. Verek and Lanse were on their horses and riding upstream. They pulled away so rapidly that Carin's ensorcelled anklet began to tighten, even as she mounted to chase them. She urged Emrys into a trot until the iron relaxed. Then she settled into the saddle to pass dreary hours that grew into days.

They followed the stream up into the foothills, winding through a succession of slopes ever steeper and more thickly wooded. Three days above the plain, the stream was only a slice at the bottom of a high-walled, heavily forested canyon. From the canyon floor, it was impossible to glimpse either the wide grassland they'd left behind them to the east, or the towering, snow-capped mountains that loomed ahead to the west.

Six days into the foothills, the weather lost patience and gave up waiting for Verek of Ruain to come to his senses. Before that sixth day was well begun, a fierce wind sprang up. The canyon walls funneled it straight at them. A few hours after sunrise, clouds built and began to spit ice. The wind drove the sleet into their faces.

Carin pulled her hood over her eyes, but she couldn't avoid the stinging pellets. She bent low over Emrys' neck, making herself a smaller target for wind and ice to pummel. The gale whipped away any words of encouragement that she tried to speak to the mare. From time to time she forced her head up, her eyes seeking the riders ahead but tearing so fiercely that she couldn't always make them out.

The wind howled in her ears and drowned all other sounds. Nothing of the world remained except the icy blast that beat at her. It drove pins into her skin and seemed to pack her brain in a freezing slush.

Then another sensation arose, a feeling that gradually intensified until it rivaled her other miseries. Carin's ankle iron was tightening. Second by second its grip grew more painful, until the ache cut through her cold-induced stupor like a hot wire through frost.

Ride up! cried the corner of her mind that wasn't lost in the storm. *You're falling behind – too far! Close the gap.*

But Carin's body wouldn't straighten from its slump across Emrys' neck. Her unfeeling hands refused to twitch the reins. Her knees gave no little squeeze that was all the mare required to know Carin's wishes. Was Emrys still under her? She couldn't feel the little mare struggling onward, into the teeth of the gale. There was only shrieking wind, needles of ice ... frozen ground rising to meet her.

The tempest stilled. All that remained was a deep, silent cold.

Chapter 8

A Water-Sylph

Lanse was shouting: "… unnatural creature! Kill the witch, my lord! She is dangerous. She intends harm to us. Look how she puts her power upon knives and sends the fire leaping, from this trance into which she betakes herself."

"A 'trance' you call it, boy?" Verek's voice was harsh. "We find her blue with cold, dripping blood on the ice, and you reckon it a trance? I think your wits stand shakier than hers, and with slighter cause. You speak like a superstitious rattlebrain who never saw spell cast or conjury done. I'll hear no more of this nonsense. Go search in the snow for your courage — and cool your head while you're out there, or I'll show you what it is to fall into such a 'trance' as has made off with this one's senses!"

A warm hand touched Carin's forehead.

"Myra," she heard herself mutter. She reached up, expecting to find the pudgy fingers of the housekeeper who had tended her through past injuries. But instead she felt the lean, powerful hand of the woman's master.

Carin jerked her fingers away as if from a live coal.

"Wish for Myra if you will," said Verek's clipped voice. "I, however, am content to be spared the lashing by that woman's strong tongue, which she would deal me at the sight of a fresh bruise on you. It's enough to have the boy crying murder."

The wizard's hand left Carin's brow and slid under her neck. "Raise up," he ordered, "and take this draught. It will clear the fog."

Struggling, Carin lifted a head that ached dully. She put her chapped lips to the rim of a cup. The potion it held was warm, aromatic, and awful tasting. She drank it all.

The hand that supported her made a pretense of easing her down, but it did not so much lower her head as let her fall. No matter. Carin flopped back onto a thick cushion that smelled of calendula; these, no doubt, were the wizard's blankets that were folded under her.

"*Hyweldda,*" Carin muttered, grimacing. Her attempted scowl met resistance at her eyebrows. Again venturing her fingers to investigate, she identified the impediment: strips of linen bandages, tight across her forehead.

"So you remember the brew from the last time you needed it," Verek said. "A single draught should suffice on this occasion. You did not take such a blow to your head today as you got from the cellar floor."

Carin's eyes slowly focused on a smooth surface overhead where firelight and shadow chased each other like dancers on a stage. The blaze that lit the scene was somewhere in the vicinity of her feet. She rolled her head, seeking the fire, but found the wizard.

He sat cross-legged near Carin's left hand, coatless, with his back to the flames. The top of Verek's head nearly brushed the surface that caught the prancing firelight. Behind him was darkness, but with bright things flitting across it so swiftly that Carin couldn't make them out, only see the lightness of them in the fire's gleam.

"Where am I?" she mumbled, thick-tongued.

Verek took a water bottle from the gear that was piled beside him. He held it to Carin's lips, and with his other hand he again helped her to rise. Only when she'd taken a long sip and her head was back on its cushion did he answer.

"You are sheltered—comfortably enough, I trust—under a canvas that Lanse and I were put to some trouble to stretch over your head after the storm felled you. Barely were you down before the ice changed to a driving snow. But the worst of the gale now passes us by, here in this cleft in the rocks."

Carin's gaze shifted from the wizard's face to peer again at the bright stuff flashing in the darkness. She knew it now: Snow fell thickly in the night, large flakes that caught the light from a fire which blazed just beyond the opening of their tent. The dappled surface over her head and Verek's was the canvas that kept the blizzard off them.

She returned her gaze to his. "I fell off Emrys?" she asked, trying to remember.

Verek shrugged. "The mare did her part to ground you. She balked at more ice in her face and took cover in a stand of balsams. Evidently you were less than attentive, and so you left the saddle when she pushed in among the trees. Their branches gentled your fall. You have bruises and a few cuts, but you will mend soon enough."

Carin made a move to touch the ensorcelled band on her ankle, but she ended up only pointing at it when her muscles refused to fully make good on her thought.

"The ring closed," she muttered. "I tried … couldn't reach you … too cold …"

Verek nodded. If he spoke again, Carin didn't hear. Her eyes closed.

She drifted between sleep and wakefulness. There was movement in the tent beside her, but she didn't rouse to discover who or what. It did not touch her. After a time, all was calm. At the edge of Carin's consciousness, nothing remained but warmth, softness, the reassuring scent of healers' herbs, and the hiss of snowflakes expiring on the fire. She slept.

Some unknown hours later, Carin woke to a darkened tent. The fire had dwindled. Snow swept softly against the tent's sides. Distantly the wind roared, a noise like ocean surf pounding a far-off, rocky coast.

Much nearer, a gentle snore rose practically at Carin's ear. She rolled her head and discovered the wizard asleep not half an arm's length from her. Across his face lay a coat-sleeve, covering all but his mouth. It was a sleeve of Carin's coat. The rest of the garment was spread over Verek's shoulders and chest. Her cloak covered his legs.

We traded? I got the better of the deal, Carin thought, and slipped her hand between the blankets — Verek's — that pillowed her head.

Testing her strength and finding it much restored, she raised on her elbow to peer past the wizard. To his left lay Lanse. The boy slept so deeply that he seemed not to breathe. He wasn't making the wheezing noises that disturbed his companions most nights. Lanse slept as though drugged … or bespelled?

Stealthily Carin pushed her blankets off, raised onto her hands and knees, and crept toward the tent opening. She was at Verek's knees when one of them flexed. It nearly hit her in the face. A hand grabbed the calf of her leg and clamped down hard. She jerked her head around to see a knife coming at her, its eight-inch blade reflecting the dull fire-glow.

"*Stop!*" she hissed. "It's me."

The hand on her leg relaxed its grip but stayed where it was. The blade ceased its forward jab. For a moment, it seemed to hang in midair, only the steel catching the light, darkness enveloping the hilt and the fist that held it. Then the weapon withdrew.

Taking its place in the dim light from the tent opening was Verek's face. The coat-sleeve slid away as the wizard propped on his elbow. A few strands of black hair escaped the silver band on his brow and fell in his eyes. An impatient sweep with the back of his knife hand drew them off his face. The waning fire glinted in Verek's eyes as coldly as from steel. Chillier was his silent scrutiny of Carin.

"I'm sorry I woke you," she whispered. She cast a look at Lanse. The last thing she needed was to rouse the boy too. But Lanse slept on, oblivious.

"I have to go out," Carin said, looking back at the wizard.

Verek's sigh was part groan. He let go of her leg and sat up, sending Carin's coat falling into his lap. He buried the fingers of one hand in the heavy garment and thrust it at her.

"Then you'll need this," he growled. "Stay close and make haste. Give me no cause to chase after you in the dark and the cold."

Muttering something unintelligible, Verek lay back and rolled over on his side. His hand quested in Carin's general direction for any cover it could reach. It closed on the hood of the cloak—her cloak—that he was using for a blanket. He drew the garment up to his chin, leaving his feet and lower legs exposed.

"While you're about it, throw some wood on the fire," he mumbled as Carin turned away.

She crawled over his feet to dive through the tent's low opening. In loose snow up to her boot-tops Carin stood, and hastily pulled on the coat that Verek had relinquished to her. Soft flakes fell, swirling in weak imitation of the blizzard that scoured the canyon not half a league away, to judge by the moan of the wind that swept past this sheltered chink in the rocks.

Beside the tent was a modest woodpile, mostly buried. Carin drew out two thick branches, knocked off the snow, and fed them to the fire. The replenished flames licked upward. Their light brushed the walls of the ravine that gave Verek's party refuge.

At the base of one of those walls, where the opaque night swallowed the fire's flash, lay a jumble of broken rocks that would suit Carin's purposes.

With her needs attended to, she hitched up her trousers and started back toward the tent. But then Carin veered through deepening snow to investigate a dark shape that proved to be a horse. Emrys and the other three were well out of the weather under a rock overhang. The mare greeted her sleepily, seeming none the worse for their struggle through the ice storm.

"Did you think you were rid of me, horse?" Carin asked with mock severity. "No such luck. If you wanted to kill me, then you shouldn't have picked such a cushy spot to knock me out of the saddle." She stroked Emrys' neck. "Or were you just trying to tell me that you've had enough of following along behind a lunatic? If you don't like it, then you'll have to take it up with the warlock who's got us into this mess. I'm as stuck with him as you are."

Emrys only blinked. Her lids closed over large, liquid eyes.

Carin left the mare to rest. Jamming her cold hands into her pockets, she trudged back in the direction of the tent.

But partway there, she paused again. This fissure in the rocks that kept the storm off was too narrow and stony to sustain many trees. A few slender pines had, however, taken root. They grew skyward as straight as churn-shafts. The woodsprite might more easily find Carin in a maze than ferret out this hidden camp ... but in the wind that wailed through the treetops, was that the creature's voice she heard?

"Sprite!" Carin called in a hoarse whisper.

Nothing answered but the wind, sounding far away.

Nearer at hand the fire crackled, reminding her that the night was raw and she didn't have to be out in it. Carin brushed snow off her coat and boots, dropped to her knees, and crawled back inside the tent more carefully than she'd left it.

This time, she could avoid Verek's feet. The wizard, still on his side, had his knees drawn up as though trying to get all his lean length under the warmth of Carin's cloak. She crept past him into the mounded blankets. They seemed unfairly apportioned in her favor, now that she had her wits back and her bruised head no longer ached. By feel, she pulled out one blanket and eased it over the sleeping sorcerer. Verek straightened, muttered darkly, and rolled onto his back, but he did not wake.

Carin snuggled into her remaining covers and lay sleepless, her mind on the missing woodsprite. Six days without a peep. Six days since she'd left the creature, frail and all but helpless, in the trees this side of the plain.

Had the sprite rallied? Had it been catching up with them when the storm forced it into cover? Or did the creature remain where Carin had left it, languishing in the fir beside the stream? The woodsprite would have no company there—only the owls … or maybe those monsters from another world that had arrived by dark magic in this one.

* * *

A hand grabbed Carin's boot and shook it roughly.

"Wake up," Verek barked. "Get out of the tent, or we'll fold you up in it."

Carin kicked the hand away and sat up. What passed for a roof over her head began to jiggle. In the corner behind her, the tent left its moorings entirely.

She lunged out from under the collapsing canvas with a suddenness that made Lanse drop his corner of the tent and jump back. He stared at her as if she wore the shadow of death.

Carin tossed her hair out of her eyes and watched the boy. Lanse appeared wholly unnerved. Why? Had he been so sure she'd breathed her last, victim of her injuries, that her liveliness this morning had given him a shock?

Even if I'd hit my head hard enough to end up as a ghost, I wouldn't waste the afterlife haunting the likes of you, Carin silently promised the boy.

With a shrug she turned away, to breakfast on leftover meat and bread and then pack up the cooking gear. While Verek and Lanse went on with the business of striking camp, neither said a word—to her or to each other. But the boy cast many sidelong glances at Carin, as if making sure she'd keep her distance.

The crevasse that had sheltered them was wide enough here to accommodate horses and riders without crowding. To leave the ravine, however, required threading their way through a crack that would barely admit a riderless horse. Verek, leading Brogar, began slogging through the snow toward the fissure. But he stopped at an outcry from Lanse.

"Wait, my lord! By your leave—I would be first." The boy's voice trailed off to a mutter. He didn't look at Carin, but he jerked his head at her.

She stared at him, baffled. Verek, however, seemed to know what troubled his groom. He nodded and drew his horse aside, allowing Lanse to precede him into the crack. The boy's gelding and the packhorse strung out behind. The wizard followed with Brogar. Carin, leading Emrys, brought up the rear.

In the tunnel-like fissure, great mounds of snow were heaped at intervals, resembling cones of sifted flour. Most of it was kicked aside or beaten down by all the hooves and the booted feet going ahead of Carin. But enough remained to say what a struggle Lanse must be having at the head of this train, floundering through the stuff.

147

Why had he asked to be trailbreaker? Out of cockiness? A desire to lead, and not always follow in his master's steps?

In Lanse's face, though, Carin had seen more dread than pride. What, suddenly, was her nemesis afraid of?

The crack widened, then opened to the high-walled canyon they had traveled for days. Snow made deep drifts among the trees, but the wind had scoured clean the nearly dry streambed down the middle of the canyon. Remounted, they followed the frozen channel through a hushed world. Loud in the silence were the sounds of their passage, reverberating off the canyon walls.

Carin, lagging behind as usual but closer than yesterday, glanced nervously on all sides, instinctively hunting the phantom riders who seemed to travel with them but who existed only in the echoes. In front of her, Verek was also on his guard, but not for echoes. He scanned the canyon rim above them as though wary of attack from that quarter.

If anyone was up there, they stayed quiet. So did the weather. For four more days, Verek's party followed the streambed, through afternoons sharp but sunny and nights stingingly cold but dry. Midmorning of the following day, the wizard—now in the lead again—brought his little company out of the canyon.

The gorge had opened to a wide valley where flocks of sheep and goats grazed winter grasses. The blades showed green under a powdering of snow. At the valley's northern reach, a band of antlered beasts, stocky and short-legged, cropped the lower flanks of the mountains that rose above them as steep as temple pinnacles.

Trosdan deer. Carin recognized them from a drawing in a book she had pored over in Verek's library. She almost squealed with surprise to see Trosdan deer with her own eyes. They actually existed. Most people who lived in the south of

Ladrehdin, far from these mountains, scoffed at any mention of the animals. Purple-antlered Trosdans were supposed to be only fairy-tale beasts.

Verek turned aside from the beaten path that split the valley down its center. He headed for the northern reach where the deer grazed. But rather than approach directly, the wizard and his followers hugged the base of a wooded slope. They kept covered within a fringe of trees that straggled out from the foothills.

Through the trees, a walled town appeared, well down the valley. The track that Verek had abandoned led to the town's eastern gate. Round towers, chimney stacks, and temple spires rose above the high, defensive wall.

Carin's gaze roved from the Trosdans on the slopes ahead, back to the town that Verek was so resolutely leading them away from. She looked long at the town, and pictured hot baths, soft beds, and good food.

Drisha's teeth! she swore silently. *Couldn't we stop at an inn first, warlock?* She aimed the thought ahead, hoping to sway Verek with it. *Can't we hunt the deer tomorrow?* Folklore held that rubbing the velvety antler of a wild Trosdan brought good luck. Carin needed the luck. But she also needed a bath.

The deer saw them coming long before Verek's party reached the valley's northern tip. They didn't take fright, however. The Trosdans merely stared at the riders, their stubby tails twitching and their interest short-lived. They soon returned to cropping the grass at their feet.

As the riders neared the deer herd, streaks of color on the animals' necks and shoulders became recognizably halters and light harnesses. The beasts didn't spook because they weren't wild, Carin realized. She felt a little disappointed to know that some herdsman claimed the fairy-tale creatures. The deer looked to be tamer than the goats and sheep down in the valley.

The riders rounded a slope that jutted its foot out far enough to break the valley's contours. Beyond it was a hidden glen, slicing into the mountains that rose above. Pines and balsams shaded the glen and overlooked a scattering of oak, ash, and birch.

A largish cabin of unpeeled logs and roughhewn stones nestled among the trees. The cabin had four rubbly chimneys, one at each corner. The smoke that rose from all went straight up, scarcely wavering in the cold, still noontime. Behind the cabin stood a three-sided, slope-roofed shed, long enough to house all the Trosdan deer that grazed the flanks of the mountains—

"With room for you too, girl," Carin whispered, leaning over Emrys' neck to breathe the observation in private.

The mare's ear flicked back, then forward again. Emrys clearly shared her rider's interest in the structures. Since Deroucey, they had been nearly a month on the trail with no sign of a house or hostelry, and no cover for the horses but the blankets and saddles the weary beasts wore.

As Emrys bobbed her head and gave a soft, hopeful snort, Carin patted the mare's neck and leaned forward to whisper again.

"I bet this is why your master led us away from the town in the valley—he knew about this place. I hope we get to stay here tonight. It's a pretty little glen."

She straightened and looked at the peaks which rose, pitiless, above them. And she let herself hope for even more: maybe this was journey's end. Maybe they'd stop here at the foot of these mountains. They might spend the winter here, and Verek might abandon any thought of pushing higher up the slopes.

Carin felt increasingly optimistic as a figure came barreling out through the cabin doorway. He looked every inch the sort who would put travelers up for the winter. A smile wider than any that Carin had seen on a face since Myra's lit up the countenance of the round little man who rolled down his front steps toward them.

Verek dismounted and all but ran to meet the fellow. The two hugged each other like bears. Carin gaped at the unabashed show of affection. The wizard she knew was too aloof for such a display.

With great interest, she studied the fellow who greeted Lord Verek of Ruain like a long-lost cousin—or, possibly, as uncle and nephew. The man appeared to be considerably older than Verek. His salt-and-pepper hair, which was caught at the nape of his neck in a ponytail, fell down his back. His face was a curious mixture of doughy jowls, windburned cheeks, and rheumy eyes. Carin pictured him indoors, eating too much and straining his eyesight in dim candle-glow. She could also imagine him up on the slopes with his deer, reckless of the cold, daring bitter winds to do their worst. But his smile—the grin that welcomed Verek and gave Carin hope—was his most conspicuous feature.

Second most, Carin amended. Her gaze left the man's face to study the brown habit that swathed his rounded shapelessness. The robes were a monk's. Was it possible? Could this fat, happy elder be a man of Drisha the Divine? And could a Drishannic monk be a friend to the sorcerer Verek?

The wizard seemed to wonder as much. He stepped back from the little man who had greeted him so warmly. With his head atilt, Verek looked the monk up and down.

"What's this, Master Welwyn? When did *you* take the cloth? Last I knew, you were as much a reprobate as any—wickeder than some."

The one called Welwyn scratched his head and grinned.

"Times have changed, son. And don't *you* know it? The day is past when a funny old *wysard* can live in his cabin in the woods, reading his books and working his magic. People talk. And don't they say the craziest things? Stories were flying 'bout the evil sorcerer in the glen." He chuckled. "So I hied me down to the monastery at Cardan, took vows, and studied with 'em a couple of years."

Verek snorted. "They must have been hard up for candidates, to let *you* into the order."

Welwyn laughed. "They let me in but they didn't cloister me, not when I confessed a hankering for the contemplative life—knowing of this tumbledown cabin in the mountains that'd make a fine hermitage." He waved a hand toward the structure behind him. "When I begged leave to come home, they let me go—with their blessings, don't you know. Seems I asked too many questions 'bout Drisha's teachings." Welwyn chuckled again.

"Unwilling, were you, to take every word on faith?" Verek asked drily.

"Just keen on the details," Welwyn replied, grinning. "But while I was away," the monk added in his rich, resonant voice, "folks forgot about that wicked sorcerer. Now they call me the Merry Monk of the Dale and leave me to my books. And don't I have a fine set? Got home with twenty temple scrolls and a fair copy of Drisha's Twelve. Between those and all my old books of magic, I'll not be wanting for reading.

"But am I tying myself to the stake, spilling the beans to these two youngsters?" Welwyn interrupted himself. He looked from Lanse to Carin. At the monk's mention of "Drisha's Twelve," Carin's fingers—intact and aiming to stay that way— had gripped the reins so tightly that Emrys backed a step, drawing Welwyn's attention to the riders who still sat their horses.

"Your secret is safe, you old dissembler," Verek said. He motioned for Lanse to dismount and join them.

Carin, too, dropped from the saddle. She held back, though, several steps from where the wizard was presenting his groom.

"This, Master Welwyn, is Lanse," Verek said. "He came to my service as a boy of a scant eight years, his parents dead by wildfire. He has become, in the decade since, a most knowledgeable horseman, an archer of rare skill ... and as valued of me as my own right hand."

That's high praise, Carin thought, and pursed her lips. *But warlock, I doubt that you really value your horseboy as much as you treasure the hand that invokes your wizardry.*

"You're welcome here, my boy," Welwyn rang out. "The champion who undertakes a perilous journey must have a strong second at his side—and someone to do the cooking, don't you know!" The monk laughed heartily and clapped the pair on their shoulders.

Then without waiting for Verek to call his "footboy" forward, Welwyn turned to Carin.

"And who is this stripling, wearing his own weight in wool as green as his big eyes?"

Verek cleared his throat—nervously? Carin shot him a look. Certainly there was reluctance, if not actual apprehension, written all over her captor.

She looked back at Welwyn and walked to meet him.

"This is ... " Verek began the introduction, then hesitated.

Drisha's knuckles! Carin mentally cursed the wizard. *Can't you bring yourself to say my name? Or don't you remember it!* Quite possibly, he did not. Never in their ten weeks together had the warlock called Carin by name.

Welwyn's gaze was on her. His beefy hand with its thick, strong fingers reached for the hood of Carin's cloak and threw it back. He brushed her hair off her face. Then he gently pinched her chin, and peered at her with his watery brown eyes. Their look was kind but piercingly direct.

He picked up where Verek had left off:

"*This is* … no more a boy than I am a saint. From what I know of women—and don't you suppose there's some would say I know far too much of the gentle sex?—I will wager the farm and all the stock that this small mite of womanhood is a lass neither girl nor grown, who'll thank me to show her to suitable quarters and a bath. And that I'll do, don't you know, quick as a knotless thread slips away, when I've made her ladyship's acquaintance."

"I'm Carin," she said in a voice that was clear and firm enough to reach the deer on the slopes above. "I'm happy to meet you, Master Welwyn. Your offer is the best I've had in I-don't-know-when. I'd love to wash up and change my clothes— if Lord Verek will allow me the time." Carin cut the warlock a glance through narrowed eyes.

Verek nodded, curtly. "Get your baggage off your horse and stable the beast," he ordered. "When you have seen to the mare, then you may partake of the hospitality that Master Welwyn offers."

Carin looked back at the monk and gave him one of her rare smiles. But before she could excuse herself to return to Emrys, Welwyn had spat on his finger and was rubbing moistly at an encrusted cut on Carin's forehead.

"How did you get this wound, Lady Carin?" the monk asked in a voice that was too low to reach any ears but hers. Welwyn inspected the dried blood that came off on his fingertip. He wiped it on his robe, then licked his finger and again dabbed at Carin's brow.

She tried not to flinch from his slobbery ministrations. "I fell off my horse," she said in a voice louder than Welwyn's; better that Verek knew what they were talking about. "Or Emrys threw me. I don't really remember. An ice storm caught us, I was freezing, and I guess I passed out. Anyway, I got cut up. Lord Verek moved me in out of the cold and gave me *hyweldda* for my head."

The monk nodded, a look of satisfied relief on his face.

"Good," he said. "Don't you know, it looks just like the kind of cut a riding whip could make."

"A horsewhip?" Carin spoke out for the wizard to hear. "No, Master Welwyn, it's nothing like that. Lord Verek doesn't carry a riding crop. He would never whip … a horse."

"And don't you know I'm pleased to hear it, Theil Verek," Welwyn rumbled. He turned to the wizard. "Now I'll make bold to invite you into my humble home, and your groom and this winsome young apprentice may join us—"

The monk got no chance to finish. Verek and Carin began their protests together:

"She is—"

"I am—"

And ended together: "—no apprentice!"

Welwyn looked from one to the other, his brown eyes wide. Then he laughed … and he laughed, till his round belly shook and he needed both hands to hold it, as though it might jiggle off his frame and go rolling down the valley.

When at last his mirth had spent itself, the monk wiped the tears from his eyes. Then he put one hand on Carin's shoulder and the other on Verek's.

"And don't you know I'm delighted to hear how firmly in agreement are the two of you upon that point!" he said, and grinned like an imp. "I beg leave to amend the invitation. See to your horses, get your gear, and come into the house, all of you—be you lord or lady, lad or lass, master or novice. Fair weather find us! Our boots could freeze to the ground as we

155

stand here sorting the 'who' from the 'what' and the 'is' from the 'isn't'!"

Welwyn ushered his noble guest into the cabin. Lanse led the wizard's Brogar, his gelding, and their packhorse to the shed; Carin followed with Emrys. His master's words of praise had evidently heartened the boy: Lanse wasn't playing the weak sister around Carin, as he had been for the past five days. Even so, he stabled the three horses in his charge so that Carin could slip the mare in nowhere but at the end of the line. While Lanse unsaddled Brogar, groomed and fed the animal, she was three stalls away tending Emrys.

"What's wrong with that idiot?" Carin whispered to the mare. She slipped the bridle off. "Ever since the blizzard, he's been keen to have me nowhere near him. Not that I *mind*, but he's got me wondering ... What happened that night when I was knocked out?"

The mare could shed no light. She didn't lift her head from the oats she munched.

Carin mulled it over while she groomed Emrys with a wisp of straw. She left a more thorough rubdown to Lanse. He always repeated her attentions to the mare anyway, as though to annul them. Shouldering her bags, Carin headed for the cabin.

As she rounded its front corner, a snatch of conversation drifted out to her. She paused, listening, her eyes on a window that was open a crack to the cold but sunny day. Through the crack came Welwyn's voice, his every word distinct.

"So it's a water spell that my lady's using, eh? Don't you know it would be! And that slip of a girl came here riding the crest of it. Charms and chancels! There's tough mettle beneath her tender years. But is there naught to be done, Theil, short of proceeding down this path that you've chosen? Could you not

do the deed from the depths of Ruain and save yourself the …
ahem … unpleasantness of an encounter?"

"I tried that," Verek snapped. His voice was as curt as the
monk's was mild. "Fixing the girl to the task is like herding
hielts. She's off in all directions at once—most of them wrong.
Or else, she stands rooted to the spot, daring me to move her.
One bridge only did she deign to dismantle while I held her
head above water at both ends of it. And before that night was
over, her willfulness nearly got us both drowned. There was no
prevailing upon the girl to make the second attempt. But what
little was accomplished before we left Ruain persuaded me of
this: what *must* be done shall not be done from afar. Nor can it
be carried through at leisure. Each day that dawns brings with it
a fresh chance of disaster."

"Are you so sure of the peril?" Welwyn asked, gently.
"Mayhap, you have already done all that is needful in this
matter."

"No." Verek's reply was a firm, flat assertion. "Had the girl
done the whole of my bidding in Ruain—and not merely
acquiesced in such small measure as it pleased her to do—the
danger would not, even then, be entirely removed. The few
keys which have fallen into my hands—and the girl's—close off
only the side paths, not the center span."

Welwyn's chuckle sounded out of place amid the
doomsaying.

"'The girl' this and 'the girl' that!" he exclaimed. "Since she's
much in your thoughts, perhaps I may have leave to say what
strikes me most rousingly about this business, with 'the girl'
rising from a *millpond*. It seems to me that you've netted a
water-sylph. And don't you know what the legends say about
them? It's the wisest catch you might have made—or the most
foolhardy. She'll be a mistress true and loving, so long as you
never forget who she is. But give her less than her due and she'll

be gone, back to where she came from—and taking a big chunk of your soul with her. They say the sylphids always leave their land-bound lovers in the end. So take care, son. She's a prize, don't you know, but a hard one to hold."

Verek snorted. Carin nearly dropped her bags on the monk's front porch. She arrested their fall barely in time, and eased them down to the broad steps. Then she seated herself as quietly, with her head just below the window that was yielding such grand absurdities.

"A prize, Master Welwyn?" Verek retorted. "Be nigh on three months in her company and give me then your opinion. The girl outdoes a jennet for stubbornness; for pride, a princess. And there is no bone in her body that does not harbor suspicion. She believes the worst of me that her imagination can conjure up. And, mistrustful to the core, she'll tell me anything but the truth. A rare breed she is, I grant you, but too fiery to be a water-sylph." He sniffed. "I think, old worthy, that you've read too many hero tales. You have become in your graying years, not only *wysard* and monk, but a giddy romantic. As abundant as the stars are the objections to such a union as you propose."

"So numerous as that, eh?" the monk replied, chuckling again. "Then I'll trouble you to name me one or two. An empty sack won't stand, don't you know."

Verek's sigh was long and irritated.

"You would hear my objections, you old cadger? Very well. First is her age. Even you—famous wencher that you are—must concede that a man of my years is too old for the *fileen*."

Welwyn's laughter rumbled out through the window with a noise like turnips toppling into a root cellar.

"Too old!" he exclaimed. "Don't flatter yourself, Theil. You're a pup," Welwyn harrumphed. "This is what comes of seeing too much death, too young. Legary's early end forced you into the role of family patriarch while you were still wet behind the ears. You've never trained under a really *old* adept. I have. And I can tell you, son, that to any living *wysard* of this world, you're just a boy." Welwyn snorted. "'Too old for the *fileen*.' What nonsense! You and that young lady are nearly of an age. You can't plead antiquity to an ancient like myself. Give me better goods than that, or leave me with a sack still empty."

Carin, leaning bemused against the cabin wall, bit the back of her hand to stifle the outburst that bubbled up from within. It felt rather like a giggle. But exactly what might erupt if she let it, she didn't want to discover.

Through the window came the clink of earthenware vessels. There was a pause. Then Verek's voice cleaved the silence:

"What do you say then, old lurcher, to this impediment, which exceeds in weight all others? The girl despises me. She holds me to blame for these events and this duty that she wants no part of. I tell you distinctly, Welwyn: the minx will be my death, but never my—"

The rest of it escaped Carin as she spotted movement from the corner of her eye. She snapped her head around.

Lanse was standing in the trees at the edge of the glen, his bow raised, an arrow on the string. It would be a long shot, but the boy was—as Verek had remarked—an archer of rare skill.

Even as Carin sprang sideways off the porch like a panicked grasshopper, she commended her last breath to Drisha. How fortunate, to die on the front steps of a merry monk who could see her murdered remains laid properly to rest.

Chapter 9

A Talisman

Like a stone cast from the heavens, a large branch plummeted out of the tree above Lanse. It knocked him to the ground. He lay motionless, pinned under the bough, a crumpled form. His spoiled shot tore harmlessly between the cabin and the shed.

Flitting away through the trees, up the mountainside, was a spark like steel on flint.

"Sprite!" Carin whispered. She scrambled to her feet. Her eyes, as she flew off the porch, had not left her would-be assassin. Now her gaze followed the spark up the wooded slope, but she lost it in the brightness of the afternoon sun that slanted into the glen.

Carin took the porch steps in one leap, threw open the cabin door, and stuck her head in.

"Excuse me, gentlemen. I must tell you: Lanse tried to put an arrow in me." The two at the table under the window stared at her. "But a tree limb fell on him before he managed it. He's flat on the ground out here. Hurt, I think. You'd better come."

Both men sprang up and rushed to the door. Neither paused to don coat or cloak as they hurried past Carin. She stepped out of their way, staying on the porch while they ran to the boy.

They each grabbed an end of the big limb and heaved it off him. The wizard crouched beside the sprite's victim, his fingers probing for broken bones in Lanse's neck and along his spine. The monk stood over them, wringing his hands.

Verek rose. "Get his feet, Welwyn," he said, gesturing at the patient's boots. "I believe he'll live, but we'd best get him inside."

Between them they hauled the boy to the cabin, up the steps, and through the large front room into a bedchamber that opened off the back. Carin lingered on the outer threshold to see Lanse's unconscious body borne within and the bedroom door closed behind the boy and his caretakers. Then she was off the porch like a gust of wind, racing for the shed and for the oak grove that grew behind it, hidden from the cabin.

"Sprite!" she called through cupped hands, sending her voice up the slope, not so loudly that those in the cabin would hear. "Where are you?"

A spark came flashing through the pines, tumbling down the mountainside. "I—am—here—my—friend!" piped the fractured voice of the sprite as it leaped from tree to tree. With breathtaking speed it darted into the grove and lit in the oak nearest Carin.

"You astonishing creature!" she greeted it, hugging the tree. "I don't know what makes me happier—seeing you strong and sparky, or watching you whack that horseboy over his empty head. Thank you, sprite. You saved me again."

"My dear girl," the creature said. The woodsprite's reedy voice sounded uncharacteristically subdued. "It is my pleasure to repay in small part the debt that I owe you for my own life. But do forgive me if I confess myself troubled by what I've done. Not for all the world's timber would I see you harmed— that, you must believe. I find, however, that murder proposed is a simple matter; murder done, a bitter task."

The creature flickered in the tree bark. "For months I had thought myself ready to break open the skulls of your enemies, whenever you bade me do it or I had cause and chance to act. But now that I've struck the blow, the sap chills within me. Have I killed the boy?"

Carin patted the oak. "No, I don't think Lanse is hurt that bad. Verek said he'd likely live. More's the pity!" She stepped back and moved a little around the tree to stay well out of sight of the cabin. "You probably just gave him a sore head. He deserves worse. Lanse really did intend to kill me—I'm sure of it."

"Yes," the sprite said, flickering hotly. "I read it in his eyes."

Carin drummed her fingers on the tree trunk. "You and I are not very good at murder, are we? I couldn't finish off Verek when I had the chance. And now you're having second thoughts about breaking tree limbs over people's heads." She sighed. "We may have to get tougher. I overheard Verek talking about 'bridges' that need to be 'dismantled.'" Carin looked up at the mountains towering overhead. "Whatever he's got in mind, he wants me to help him. If I get into serious trouble, sprite, I can't afford for either of us to be too squeamish."

"I shall rise to the occasion," the sprite declared. "You may count on me. This weakness of mine is a passing fault. I regret it already. Should that knave of a horseboy threaten you again, I'll lay him low." The creature flashed in the bark under Carin's fingers.

She pressed against the tree. "I'm glad you're back, sprite. I think better when you're around. You help me work things out."

Her stomach rumbled then, so loudly that she almost jumped.

"My dear girl," the sprite trilled. "Go indoors, get warm, and eat. Your hand on this oak is like a patch of ice, and I can hear your hunger pangs. We'll talk again. I'll stay close. Meet me tomorrow in this grove and we'll continue to buck up our courage."

The woodsprite retreated up the mountainside. Carin sauntered back to the cabin. If anyone watched, they might be less suspicious of a stroll than of another mad dash.

But the front room, when Carin cracked the door to peer inside, was empty. She retrieved her bags from the porch, went in, and stood for a moment studying the monk's book-filled home.

Welwyn's cabin boasted far fewer volumes than Verek's library in Ruain, but his collection was impressive nonetheless. Shelves covered most of three walls, crammed with books to the rafters. The room had a fireplace in each corner, each hearth angled to throw its heat toward the center of the space. A couch with lumpy cushions and an overstuffed chair faced the fire in the front corner. Draped over the back of the couch were Verek's black coat and his cloak. Its red and silver clasp sparkled in the mingled firelight and sunshine that brightened the room. On a table between the couch and the chair was a squat oil lamp, poised to throw its more modest light on any book that a reader might curl up with.

The remaining wall held no books, but a great many cooking pots and bunches of dried herbs. Ranged along it was a table that could comfortably seat twelve. Abandoned mugs and a bowl showed that Welwyn had settled his guest at this end, directly under the window through which their outrageous conversation had drifted.

Carin dropped her bags beside the couch and ventured into the kitchen portion of the space. The two hearths on this side of the cabin, like those in the opposite corners, were cheerfully ablaze. A pot of stew simmered on the front fire.

She glanced at the door to the back room—one of the back rooms, actually. Lanse's sickroom opened off the library side of the common space. The cabin had another side chamber, accessed from this kitchen area. The doors to both rooms were closed. No murmuring voices reached her above the crackling of the four fires that seemed gleefully intent on making Carin's sweat run.

She shed cloak, coat, and even the quilted doublet that seldom came off. Comfortably warm in her shirtsleeves in Welwyn's toasty cottage, Carin helped herself to a bowlful of stew and a mug of the monk's stout-smelling ale. She sat down to eat, well along the table from the wizard's unfinished meal.

But her fourth spoonful of stew never reached her mouth. It was arrested in transit by the opening of the door to Lanse's sickroom. Welwyn stepped out, followed by the wizard. The little brown monk was speaking:

" — and that's the only time, eh?" Welwyn asked, holding the door for his guest. "The talent's not manifested itself — so openly, that is — on any other occasion?"

"Not so potently … no," Verek answered. The moment the wizard entered the common room, his dark eyes found Carin at the table.

Welwyn shut the door behind him. Then he turned to grin at her.

Slowly, Carin lowered her spoon. She looked from the smiling monk to the frowning warlock and tensed, anticipating at least a tongue-lashing from the latter — for her purloined meal, for Lanse's upset, or for whatever else she'd done to rouse his temper.

But it wasn't Verek who spoke next.

"Then perhaps what we need," Welwyn said, his grin almost splitting his face, "is the element of surprise."

Where there had been nothing a moment before, a knife appeared in the monk's hand. He raised the weapon and flung it straight at Carin's eyes.

"Unhh!" She toppled off her chair and rolled under the table. Above the sudden pounding of her pulse in her ears, she did not hear any knife hit the wall behind her. Coming up on hands and knees, Carin crawled between her chair and the seat beside it, searching for the weapon. But she found no sign of a knife, either lying on the floor or stuck in the kitchen wall.

Illusion, she realized. *This wizardly monk is playing tricks.*

With a heart divided betwixt fright, bewilderment, and anger, Carin raised up to peer over the tabletop. Verek looked back at her, impassive, one hand stroking his untrimmed beard, the other cupped to support his bent elbow.

Beside him, Welwyn's face wore none of the warlock's habitual guardedness. The monk beamed. With one stout hand, he motioned for her to stand.

"Excellent reflexes, Lady Carin. But not quite what we were looking for." He chuckled.

"Master Welwyn." Carin grated out his name through clenched teeth. "I'm sorry if I'm not playing the game right. I don't know the rules. And it's really not fun, anyway, to see a knife coming at me."

"Begging your pardon, my dear," Welwyn said, looking anything but contrite. "But don't you know we both should find our little game more diverting than did poor Lanse, when you were throwing the real steel at him."

"*What?*" Carin exclaimed, staring at the monk. "Sir, I don't know what Lanse—or Lord Verek—may have been telling you, but I haven't done any such thing. I swear on my conscience, the worst I've done to Lanse is throw a rock at him in self-defense. It didn't even hit him. If that cretin says I took a *knife* to him, then he's lying."

"Hold your tongue," Verek snapped. He planted his hands on his hips and glared at Carin. "You speak from ignorance and a stubborn wish to see matters as you would have them, not as they are. What Master Welwyn tells you is true. The evening of the ice storm that saw you witless with the cold and bruised in the head also found you flinging knives and flaming brands at Lanse's face—though you lay insensible of it, your mind dark to

165

the magic that you worked. What the boy has long suspected, and dreaded, has been proved: you have the power.

"Isn't this a fine mess in which I find myself?" Verek added, grumbling as much to Welwyn or the walls as to Carin. "I ride to battle with a frightened cub for a shield-bearer, and at my back an untrained adept so determined to disavow her duty that she'd deny even her own nature."

Welwyn's fat fist gave the warlock a jab in the shoulder that would have earned any other person who dared such a familiarity an immediate decapitation. Verek only turned his frown upon the monk and rubbed his bruised arm.

"And don't you know it takes tinder to start a fire? Hot air won't do it," Welwyn admonished the warlock, grinning at him. "Black clouds above, Theil Verek! This young lady will catch on quick enough, if the thing's a bit of fun and not all gloom and doom."

The wizard's frown deepened. But it could no more quell Welwyn's good humor than the black waters of a tarn could steal the blue from the skies above them.

"Allow me to demonstrate," the monk went on. He turned back to Carin. "Indulge me, won't you, my dear, and pick up that table-knife in front of you." He pointed to the place at the table where, five minutes ago, Carin had been spooning up his tasty goat stew.

Hesitantly, she did as he asked.

"Now," Welwyn said, "be so good as to throw it at me. Make it an earnest cast, as if you fain would send me to my maker."

Verek abandoned his friend then. Briskly he stepped to the front fireplace on their side — the library side — of the room, where he would be well out of the way of any but the wildest throw.

Carin shot him a pleading look. Wouldn't the warlock put an end to this madness? But Verek only fingered his chin and tipped his head, sanctioning her to do as Welwyn requested.

She looked back at the monk.

"Sir, I want to be sure I understand." Carin's voice was calmer than her thoughts. "You're asking me to try my best to kill you?"

"Yes, yes!" Welwyn cried, clapping his hands and grinning. "That's the spirit, don't you know. Hurl away! You'll see what a merry time we'll have."

Carin drew a deep breath and held it. She pinched the blade between her thumb and first finger, raised the knife above her shoulder, and threw it, strongly, at Welwyn's chest. It flew straight.

But an instant before the blade reached its target, it became a ball of light. It did not glow steadily, the way Verek's witchlight orbs shone. It shed sparks that twinkled like a thousand bright stars. Welwyn caught the ball two-handed, sending a shower of sparks down the front of his brown habit.

"Well done, Lady Carin!" he cried. "Look into these winking, inconstant lights"—he held the ball up and twirled it in his fingers—"and it's the marrow of me that you'll see in them. Now I'll toss the talisman to you, and we'll behold what you shall make of it."

Carin shook her head.

"You're not deceiving me, Master Welwyn. I've learned enough from Lord Verek to know magic when I see it." She glanced at the warlock, then back at the monk. "You've created an illusion. The knife I threw at you was real. If you toss it back to me, it'll be a knife again—and I'd rather not get cut." She held up her hand, hoping to discourage Welwyn. "Please, sir. You don't want me bleeding all over your kitchen table."

"Now, now, my dear," the monk scolded her playfully. "You're much too young, don't you know, to be tiring so quickly of our little game of catch. I swear by the light of learning that it will be no knife that reaches your hands. Come! Humor a fat old man who has no one else to sport with. Catch it!"

Before Carin could refuse him again, Welwyn had lobbed his twinkling orb. It floated above the couch, sprinkling Verek's doffed cloak with flecks of light. Then it glided over the table, raining sparks into Carin's now-cold stew.

Don't touch it! screamed a little voice far back in her mind.

Carin's hands ignored the warning. They rose, and closed around the orb. At the moment they did so, a sense of elation shot through her … a subtle thrill, akin to the pleasure of watching waves crest in whitecaps on a turquoise ocean.

The orb no longer sparkled. It—*prickled*. Carin opened her hands. There, resting in her cupped palms, was a spiny sea urchin.

"Drisha!" she cried, and dropped the thing onto the table. It rolled past her bowl of stew. With a little *clink*, it came to rest against her mug. Now it was the knife that she'd thrown at Welwyn. The change seemed to happen outside time, its reversion was so instantaneous.

The monk laughed—another great belly-shaker that threatened to pull him to pieces. He barreled over to Verek at the fireplace and thumped his friend on the back with such force that the normally undauntable wizard winced.

"A water devilkin!" Welwyn cried, almost strangling on his guffaws. "And don't you know it *would* be a sharp-spined water devilkin. Your sylph doesn't deny her true nature, Theil Verek. She shows it to you in all its prickliness!"

Neither Carin nor the warlock joined in Welwyn's laughter. Over the little man's head, their eyes locked. The expression on

Verek's face combined annoyance with some quality of emotion that was far rarer with him, and far harder to make out.

And what's he reading in my eyes? Carin wondered. Her feelings were in such a muddle, she couldn't sort one from another or begin to guess what was plastered across her face. The only clear sentiment inside her was a burning desire not to have to talk with Verek just now.

To hide her confusion, she dropped her gaze and busily began to clear away the remains of her interrupted meal.

That brought Welwyn out of his jolly fit.

"No, no, Lady Carin!" He waved her off, still chortling. "You'll not deny me the pleasure of treating you like a guest in my house. I'll be at cleaning up this mess after I've seen to the deer. It's time they were off the mountain. Now sit yourselves down, the both of you, and have some more goat. Poor fare it is. But what's in the pot is steaming yet and tastier—if my own travels tell me anything—than what you've been eating these past weeks."

Verek didn't leave his place by the corner fire, nor Carin her spot near the kitchen wall. The eyes of both were on the monk as he wrapped himself in his hooded cloak and rolled to the door.

"Master Welwyn!" Carin called.

With his hand on the latch, the little man paused and turned back to her. No part of his face was visible under his hood but a huge smile.

"Your servant, my lady!"

"Sir, can I help you bring in the deer?" Carin tried to keep the pleading out of her voice. "Before today, I'd never seen a Trosdan. And I've never touched one, of course. They're supposed to be good luck. May I go with you and help you herd them?"

Welwyn shook his head, still smiling.

"Nay, Lady Carin. Begging your pardon, but it's no job for a slim limb of a lowlander. Don't you know you can't believe everything you hear? It's only in the stories that they're such brave little heroes, rescuing princesses from the *savitar* or pulling men-of-arms from bogs. In truth, herding those fractious creatures takes one born to the mountains. They do as they please." He tipped his head back. "Drisha willing, they'll be keen to see what new beasts have taken up residence in their shed, and they'll skip down the mountain like curious kids. But if it's their usual impish selves they be, you'll not see me again for hours.

"So eat, you two, and talk a little together," Welwyn added as he headed outside. "Confession's good for the soul."

And a really bad idea around the warlock, Carin silently corrected her host.

With the monk's departure, Welwyn's cabin seemed to dim. All the cheerfulness went with him, leaving behind Verek's somber dissatisfaction with his "footboy" and Carin's dark suspicions of her captor.

Carin didn't look at the wizard. She forced herself to the end of the table that held the meal Verek had abandoned. She refilled his mug with Welwyn's potent home-brewed ale. Then she picked up Verek's nearly untouched dish of stew. He'd obviously eaten little before rushing to tend Lanse's injuries.

"This food's cold." Though Carin addressed the wizard, her gaze was on his bowl. "I'll bring you some that's warmer, if you want it."

Verek made no reply.

When the silence had stretched on for as long as Carin could stand it, she flicked him a look and found him still studying her. Then he nodded.

"Yes, I'll eat. That old meddler is right about one thing: he knows how to fix goat."

Verek pushed away from the mantelpiece and seated himself at the head of the table. Carin took his cold stew to the sideboard and ladled up a fresh serving. Her own leftovers were not only cold, but also sprinkled with Welwyn's magic sparkles. She replaced them with a steaming bowlful for herself, and opted for a cup of plain water instead of the monk's home-brew. Then she took a seat three places down from the wizard.

For a time, they ate in silence. Carin tried not to fidget.

As she knew he would, Verek at last asked her a question. It was not, however, the one she expected.

"Did you drop the tree limb on the boy?"

"Me?" She gaped at him. "Of course not. That branch just suddenly fell on Lanse. It dropped like a piece of the sky falling."

"Which is a thing that tree limbs seldom do," Verek retorted. He drummed his fingers against his bowl. "A dead branch may snap under its own weight, it's true. But the limb that fell on Lanse was green-needled and healthy—further from death than I am, I'll be bound. Neither did it simply fall. It was hurled upon him. My question is: by whom? Yourself, or the woodsprite?"

"The sprite?" Carin feigned surprise. "How could the woodsprite have had anything to do with it?" She avoided Verek's gaze. "The creature—if it's even still alive—is in Ruain, a long way from here."

The wizard snorted. "Which certainly would explain the marked scent of pine oil that rose from your coat when I took it off you, days ago, as you lay unawares, under the canvas in the snowstorm."

Carin gulped. Verek sipped his ale, studying her reaction over the rim of his mug. Then he continued:

"My faith was small, that Myra could do as I bade her and keep the creature shackled through the winter. That simple woman could as little outwit the fay as a star shall outshine the moon. But I had hoped that she might hold the goblin until we were beyond its reach." Verek sighed. "Jerold, I do not doubt, would have made a stricter warden. But to give the prisoner to him might have meant the sprite's death. Jerold does despise the creature."

The wizard pushed away from the table and stood. He went to the cooking fire, rested his hand on the mantel, and stared for a moment into the flames. Then he turned back to Carin, his eyes seeking hers.

"You see, perhaps, the problem I faced," Verek said, his voice quiet but edgy. "Leave the sprite with Myra and risk its swift escape, or consign the creature to Jerold's care and have it dead before we were a day gone from Ruain. I could hardly choose the latter, could I? Didn't I make you a promise to free the sprite unharmed, when you had done the work I set you?"

Carin reached for her water and drank half of it. Verek kept his gaze on her, obviously expecting an answer.

"Yes, that's what you promised," she replied finally, and put down her cup. "But I never thought you meant to keep your word. At least, not after that first night, when I did what you asked but you still kept the woodsprite locked away. Until it showed up in Deroucey, I suspected that you had killed the sprite before we ever left to come on this journey."

The wizard took one step toward the table and kicked a leg of it with enough force to rattle every dish on its top. Carin jumped up from her chair. She stood behind it, though it offered little protection.

"You 'suspected'!" Verek snapped. "Would to glory that you might contrive ever to hear my words and *believe* them!"

He reached for the pitcher of ale; Carin retreated a step. But Verek only poured himself another tankard full, took it back to the fireplace, and stood with the blaze behind him. As he sipped the home-brew, he seemed to gather himself, as clouds gather before a storm.

Minutes passed in silence. When the wizard finally lowered his drink to speak again, his eyes flashed.

"I make you now a promise that you may trust me to keep, as Drisha is my witness." Verek's gaze pinned Carin to the floor. "Mark me well. It will not be the sprite who endures the punishment, should the creature dare again to move against Lanse or myself. Tell your weirdling friend that I vow to hurt you in ways that it cannot imagine, if it so much as flutters a leaf at us."

Carin's scalp crawled. Possibilities that the sprite might find truly unimaginable rose, vivid, in her mind. She gave the wizard a weak nod, unable to answer him otherwise.

Verek took another sip. Over the rim of his mug, his eyes watched her until Carin could meet his gaze no longer but was forced to stare past him, out the window.

Abruptly then, the wizard reached for the nearest chair. He dragged it to the fireplace and sat astraddle it, with his back to Carin. Speaking over one shoulder, he dismissed her.

"Go. Tell the creature what I have said. I counsel you to make certain—for your sake—that the sprite fully understands the danger to you. I do not utter idle threats."

Carin fled. Collecting only her cloak, she didn't pause to throw it on but rushed out the door in her shirtsleeves. She ran to the shed and around to the oak grove behind it. Only when she was out of sight of the cabin did she take a moment to wrap up against the cold.

The sprite was not in the oaks. Nor was there any sign on the slopes above of Welwyn or his deer. Evidently the beasts hadn't been as curious about the horses as their owner had hoped. Instead of coming docilely down the mountain, they seemed to have led the monk off on a chase.

As the sun sank behind the peaks, Carin stood in the grove, calling to the sprite but getting no answer. The cold made it impossible to stand still, so she began walking, without a purpose except to put distance between herself and Verek.

She didn't get far. Twenty paces deeper into the glen, beyond the cluster of oaks, the ensorcelled band tightened on Carin's ankle.

"May your life be a misery forever!" she cursed the warlock, and burst into tears. "May you never, ever know a minute's happiness."

Carin flopped to the ground. She slapped open the buckles of her boot and yanked it off. In a growing frenzy she stripped off her stocking, baring her foot to the cold. But she felt nothing except the iron's grip. With chipped and broken fingernails, she clawed at her anklet until her skin bled. Screaming with fury, she picked up a rock and struck it blows that could have splintered bone. The iron was undamaged, though again and again she hammered at it. Her sobs alternated with shrieks of rage.

"Lady Carin!" Welwyn sounded shocked. "Stop! My dear girl—stop that, I say!"

The monk trundled down to her from the upper reaches of the glen. His hand closed over Carin's; he pried the blood-sprinkled rock from her grip.

Through her tears, Carin met the monk's gentle, worried gaze as Welwyn squatted on his haunches beside her.

"My dear girl," he said again. He took both of her hands in his beefy paws. "Things are seldom as bad as they seem, don't you know. What in this world has put you in such a temper?" Welwyn kept a firm grip on the hand that had done the pounding, but he released Carin's other one so he could wipe his stubby fingers across her wet cheeks.

With her freed hand, Carin grabbed for her fettered ankle.

"Master Welwyn," she sobbed, "I can't stand this thing a minute longer. Either that blackheart of a warlock takes it off me, or I'll beat it off. By Drisha, I swear I will!"

"Now, now, Lady Carin … do not take the name of the Divine in vain," the monk scolded her absently. Welwyn's attention was less on Carin's blasphemy than on her ankle. He studied the injuries she had given herself. He licked his fingertip and rubbed the ensorcelled anklet, cleaning Carin's smeared blood from one small section of the iron.

"Perishing oaths!" Welwyn swore then, ringingly, as though he hadn't chided Carin a moment before for the same offense. "And how long has your ladyship worn this curious bit of jewelry?"

"Day and night for six weeks," she said, still sniffling. She started to wipe her nose on the hem of her cloak. But thinking better of it, Carin bared her shirtsleeve and used that instead. Her shirt would wash.

Welwyn experimentally scraped at the iron with his yellowed thumbnail.

"Hmmm. A collar for a gallows bird is this," he muttered, more to himself than to Carin. Then he reached for her chucked stocking and boot and handed them to her. "Best put these on, my lady. The onfall of winter is no time to be going barefoot."

He hoisted himself up to stand over Carin like a large brown roly-poly while she covered her foot. Then he offered her his hand and helped her to stand. Gallantly he tucked her arm under his, and together they strolled toward the shed.

"I'll speak to his tetchy lordship, my dear," the monk said. He patted Carin's hand. "That's no fit ornament for such a well-turned ankle as yours." He winked up at her; the little man came barely to Carin's nose. "But you've the power yourself, don't you know, to rid yourself of the fetter—and not by hammering at it, either! Let's have no more of that, if you please. That's not the thing at all. What you want to do, Lady Carin, is to *think it* away—just as Theil Verek *thought it* onto you."

She shook her head. "I don't know how to do that, Master Welwyn. I'm *not* a witch."

"Said with such conviction!" The monk chuckled. "His lordship has told me how keen you are to deny your essential nature. But my dear, he's also told me how you have walked unscathed through ensorcellments potent enough to destroy any mortal being of Ladrehdin. He's told me how you opened the door to his vault of magic, there in Ruain. You lifted that latch, calm as you pleased, and you came away with nary a scorch mark on your pretty hand." Welwyn patted it again.

"Dumb luck, is all," Carin mumbled. "I didn't know what I was doing."

"Clearly!" Welwyn exclaimed. "If *I'd* been in charge of you, I wouldn't have permitted you to demonstrate your powers in *quite* so dramatic a fashion. By all that is worthy and fair! Opening that door is tempting fate, even for a well-trained adept—which you are not. Well-trained, I mean to say."

Welwyn looked toward his cabin; Carin followed his gaze. Smoke rose from all four of the cabin's chimneys. Welwyn's other guests were undoubtedly warmer, indoors, than she and the monk were, standing out here as evening closed in. But Carin held back, unwilling to go in just yet. Welwyn grinned at her.

"My dear," he said, "you confounded his lordship when you didn't lose a hand to the spells that guard the secret cave. But you almost stopped the man's heart when you spoke the name of Power and roused a wind from the *wysards'* well." Welwyn laughed. "You're living dangerously, don't you know."

"I *do* know!" Carin protested. "I'm not doing it on purpose, Master Welwyn. And I'm not 'denying my nature.' All of this is just some bizarre accident. Verek says I shouldn't even be here. But he makes me stay — I can't get away from him." She pointed at her ankle iron, and Welwyn nodded.

In the fading light, Carin looked searchingly at the monk. "Verek says I have some 'duty,' some job that I have to finish. But he's just using me. I'm a pawn — I don't have any powers of my own."

"You're rough about the edges, certainly," Welwyn said. "That's obvious, my dear. If you were *my* apprentice, I'd be honing your talents through more — *ahem* — traditional wizardly methods. But you're far from powerless. Look within. Look to your true self. You've always had the gift. It only needed the proper ... *atmosphere*, let's call it ... to flourish." The monk waved a hand in the direction of his cabin. "I saw the potency in you when you snared that prickly sea devilkin."

Carin drew back a little.

"In *me?* That can't be right, Master Welwyn. I didn't do anything except catch the creature that you conjured up. I saw what you did — raising that ball of lights, and then turning it into a sea urchin."

Welwyn slipped his arm from Carin's. He faced her and caught her hands. His stubby fingers were damp and warm.

"I'll claim no credit for magic not of my making," he said. "The sparkly lights *were* mine — a bit of my soul made manifest, if you'll excuse the romanticizing of an unbeauteous old fellow. But the water devilkin, my dear, was yours ... all yours." Welwyn's chuckle threatened to become a chortle. "Those of mundane bent have no power over the mysteries. The talisman that I threw to you answers only to the artful, each according to his — or her — own source. And your source, Lady Carin, unless I miss my guess, is the sea — that faraway sea of your own forgotten world."

Carin snapped her head around. She'd heard a familiar sound, or thought she'd heard it, off in the distance. It could have been a wind on the mountain above them. But she listened harder and caught it again—the sound of the surf breaking on a rocky seashore. Were her ears playing tricks? This mountain range rose far inland, nowhere near Ladrehdin's oceans.

Not long ago, however, Carin had crossed an ocean. She'd stood in a child's bedroom at the edge of a sea. And from that bedroom, she'd taken a piece of crystal that was shaped like a dolphin—something Verek had wanted badly enough to risk both their lives to obtain.

"What do you hear, Lady Carin?" Welwyn asked. The monk was still holding her hands. He squeezed them gently.

Carin didn't look at him. She closed her eyes, and for one fleeting moment that might have been a memory, she found herself back in her childhood home on a seacoast far beyond the void.

"I hear ocean waves," she murmured. "They're pounding the shore. They're really strong … powerful."

Welwyn chuckled. *"From water rises the wysard's art,"* he intoned as if dredging up lines he knew by heart but hadn't thought of in ages. *"Still water runs deep. But the restless sea casts forth the greatest gift."*

Chapter 10

Mysteries

The knock on her bedroom door was a gentle, considerate tapping—not an impatient, bare-knuckled rap. She knew immediately that it wasn't Verek summoning her.

"Rise and shine, Lady Carin!" The door's thick planks couldn't disguise the glee in Welwyn's voice. "You've a busy day ahead. Just peek out a window and see all that's befallen us."

"What is it, Master Welwyn?" Carin called sleepily. She sat up in bed and fumbled in the dark for her breeches. So completely did the room's shutters block light, the hour could as easily be midnight as morning. She slipped her clothes on, stumbled barefooted to the window, pulled open one wooden leaf—

"Oh!" Both hands flew to shield her eyes.

A thousand torches couldn't cast such brilliance. Carin, peering through her fingers, beheld a world gone radiantly white. Off the featureless expanse that was visible from her bedroom window, the morning sun glistened. What looked like an immense field of milky diamonds reflected the light into her eyes, nearly blinding her.

Welwyn's chuckle came through the door.

"It snowed all night, straight down—not a breath of wind to stir a flake of it. Come get your breakfast now, my dear, and then we'll be about the morning's lessons."

Lessons?

Carin pushed the shutter nearly closed. The narrow beam that shafted through the crack lit the bedroom like a column of fire. She splashed her face at the washbasin near the room's hearth and finished dressing. When she opened the door, she stepped directly into the kitchen half of the cabin's front room. Welwyn had given her his bedroom for the night. The monk had shared the other back room with the convalescing Lanse. Verek, by his own insistence, had got the couch under the books.

"Spare me another night in the company of either of those matchless fools," the wizard had growled to Welwyn, not softly enough to keep the remark from Carin's ears. "I tire of playing peacekeeper to that pair of quarrelsome bratlings. But you may tell the boy for me, if he rouses in the night sufficiently to comprehend the warning, that he has overreached himself for the last time. Should he dare again to disobey me and raise a hand to that girl save by my explicit order, I will throw him off the mountain and let the buzzards pick the flesh from his bones."

Not even the good-natured Welwyn had been able to laugh away the warlock's foul mood. The monk had exited the room almost as speedily as Carin had, leaving Verek alone with his temper.

This morning, at the long table in the front room, only one place was set. Dirty dishes on the sideboard suggested that Welwyn's other guests had already eaten and gone about their day's business, whatever that might be.

The monk said nothing of them. He greeted Carin warmly, waved her to a seat, and served her such a plowman's breakfast that three people her size couldn't have finished it.

"Master Welwyn," she began, speaking between bites of fried mutton. She had many questions to ask him. But the monk, as he dropped into a chair opposite her, held up his hand in warning.

"A master of my old profession, I truly was. But nowadays I'm only a humble man of the cloth." Welwyn chuckled. "So call me Brother if you please, my lady. If we then are overheard by any visitor to this glen, it shan't mean burning for the both of us, don't you know."

Carin stared at him. "I'll, um, try to remember that, Mas— uh, Brother Welwyn." She toyed with her food. "It's got to be a lonely way to live, staying hidden. In Deroucey when we stopped at an inn, Verek warned me not to reveal to anyone his true identity. And here you are, 'Brother,' hiding your deep, dark secret by pretending to be a monk."

"It's no pretense, my dear." Welwyn shook back the sleeves of his habit and grinned. "I took a monk's vows, and as Drisha is my witness I live by them as best I'm able." He tapped his chest. "But under these robes beats a *wysard*'s heart, it's true. I cannot change who I am. Nor would I want to." As Welwyn refilled Carin's teacup, a bit of caginess crept into his smile. "Living as I do affords me the best of both professions."

Welwyn set the teapot down, and his smile faded a little. "I will admit, Lady Carin, that any *wysard* who lives as long as I have is bound to see the *art magik* used in ways that twist and corrupt the power. If my years in the monastery taught me anything, however, it's that evil may be done by the practitioners of either profession: the monastic, or the magian."

"I'm sure you're right," Carin said. "But monks don't often get roasted over a fire. If sorcery isn't wicked, then why do sorcerers hide away? Why are ordinary people afraid of magic?"

"They're ignorant, my dear." Welwyn shook his head. "Only those who are unaware of the power's true nature presume to call it wicked."

His smile brightened. He reached for Carin's hand. "You have much to learn, and I am more than pleased to help you learn it. Let's begin with this idea of aptitude—one's natural gifts. Each of us comes into the world strong in some ways,

181

weak in others. We have no more choice in these matters than we may choose from the womb to be short or tall, well-favored or unlovely.

"Pray tell me, Lady Carin," Welwyn said, still holding her hand. "Which would you think more contented with his lot: the young man who is born with music in his soul who barely ekes out a living as a wandering minstrel? Or his brother, endowed from birth with a poet's sensibilities, who studies the law and grows wealthy in that profession but never puts to paper a single line of verse?"

Carin eased her hand from the monk's moist grasp. She cut a chunk of goat cheese to nibble while she thought it over. Then she replied, "I think the minstrel will be happier than the lawyer."

Welwyn beamed. "And why is that, Lady Carin? Surely the musician's precarious life isn't so enviable as his brother's easy living?"

She shrugged. "His brother might have money. But the musician has his freedom. He's following his heart, but his brother is just making a living. If a poet doesn't let himself write poems, if he won't let the words out, then he's put himself in a cage. He's like a falcon that's afraid to fly."

Welwyn clapped his hands.

"Exactly right, Lady Carin. And it's the miserable soul indeed, who is born with the power to partake of the mysteries but fears to embrace the gift. Down that path lies, at the end, only madness. Happy, though, are those who accept what Fate has given them, who respect the power of the *wysards* for the force of nature that it is, and apply themselves earnestly to mastering their craft."

Happy? Hardly that, Carin reflected. But she sipped her tea and kept the thought to herself. She now knew three wizards, and only this one—Welwyn—seemed satisfied with his lot.

Verek, moody on his best days, was a cauldron of seething anger at his worst. Unsociable old Jerold had sadness hanging over him like a cloud. Only this monk who lived a double life could by any stretch be called "happy."

Carin pushed back her chair and stood. Hoping to change the subject, she thanked Welwyn for her breakfast, then began to clear the table.

The monk, grinning broadly, also lent himself to the task and left hanging, for now, the question of Carin's "embracing the gift." Welwyn scrubbed dishes; she wiped them dry. He made small talk; she answered politely while she studied the white landscape outside the kitchen window.

The trampled snow on the cabin's front porch was too thin and scuffed up to show clearly how many people had stepped across it this morning. But there were dishes for four in the pile that Carin dried. Evidently Lanse had recovered from the woodsprite's attack well enough to be out with his master. Did that mean the merry monk had custody of her today?

Carin looked over at Welwyn and smiled. The monk didn't worry her the way Verek did. A sorcerer, the little brown man might be. Villainous, he was not.

Welwyn grinned back. "If I might be so bold as to advise your ladyship," he said, "you should wear a smile more often upon those rosy lips. It suits you."

He dried his hands on a cup towel. Then he crossed to the room's front door, his rolling gait taking him there surprisingly swiftly. "Bundle up, my dear," he bade her. "The most agreeable task has been given me today, to be your instructor. And if it's an apt pupil you prove yourself to be, then we'll be showing those two ornery escorts of yours a thing or two by dusk."

Sudden apprehension darkened Carin's almost-sunny mood. "Instruct me in what, Mas—uh, Brother Welwyn?" Though wary, she reached for her coat and cloak. "If you plan to teach me magic, then I can tell you already—I won't be a good student."

Welwyn sighed and smiled. "Far be it from me to criticize your ladyship. But in one regard at least, my dear, Theil Verek has your measure: you *are* rather a stubborn little jenny on that point." He chuckled. "No matter. You'll come to it when you're ready. You'll figure out for yourself who you are and where you belong. In the meantime, if this morning's lesson finds you a clumsy pupil, you'll not be the only lowlander to take a tumble your first time out."

The monk opened the door and ushered her onto the porch, into a world of crackling cold and pristine white. Squinting against the brightness of sun on snow, Carin nearly stumbled over a pair of objects that leaned against the cabin's wall. They were ungainly structures of wood and rawhide that resembled winnowing baskets, or perhaps rackets for a game of *kirree*. But they were neither. They were snowshoes.

Alongside the first pair leaned another set of similar design, somewhat wider and longer. Welwyn handed the smaller set to Carin. He claimed the larger pair for himself and walked to the porch's edge. The snow on the ground came up level with the top boards, burying the steps.

"Now the lesson begins," the monk said. He gave Carin a waggish grin. "Do as I do—and don't be discouraged if you find that it's harder than it looks, don't you know."

Welwyn positioned a snowshoe flat on the porch and put his foot in the middle of it. He crisscrossed two rawhide straps over and around his boot to bind his foot snugly to the device's woven center. In the same way, he strapped on the other one. Then he supervised as Carin secured her own bindings. It was like tying drying racks to her boots. She had to stand with her feet far apart to keep from stepping on one with the other.

The monk chuckled but said nothing as he shuffled off the porch onto the snow. He scuffed over its surface, lifting one snowshoe just enough at each step to pass its inner edge over the resting shoe. His strides looked uncomfortably long for such short legs, as he swung his foot far enough forward with each step to avoid bringing that shoe down on the other.

Almost as quickly, however, as Welwyn might have walked the distance on solid earth, he moved over the snow to a nearby stand of trees. From their midst, he took a pole—obviously planted there before the morning's lesson began—and used it for balance, like a hiking stick, on his return journey.

"And that, my lady, is how one walks on *Briga* bearpaws," Welwyn said as he neared the porch. He didn't rejoin Carin on it, but stopped about four steps away and stood there grinning. "Now you try it."

"All right." Carin squinted from the monk to her strapped-in feet. "It looks easy enough. Just slide one foot onto the snow, step out with the other a good long way … and—"

She lost her balance and slammed the moving "bearpaw" down on the fixed one. Finding it impossible then to move either foot, Carin pitched sideways into the snow with all the elegance of a falling log. The powder, like a cloud of feathers, swallowed her up. She floundered about and got snow in her eyes and mouth. The racks on her feet kept her boots up and her head down.

Welwyn laughed so hard, he would have toppled over into the snow with her if he hadn't had the pole to lean on. Carin, quite comfortable in the white cloud after the first shock wore off, wiped the flakes from her face. Then she lay still; flailing her arms only dug her in deeper. From her powdery nest, she watched the monk's round, brown body shake with his laughter. When a giggle also escaped her, Carin almost started. It had been a long time since she'd heard herself laugh.

Finally the little man wiped his watering eyes and composed himself enough to shuffle over and help her up.

"That's the spirit, my lady," he said when Carin was on her feet, awkwardly, standing with her snowshoes spread wide and feeling the strain in her thigh muscles. "There's but one way to learn to walk on bearpaws. You must stumble around until you've got the feel of them—

"Here," he added, and handed her his walking stick. "Lean on this if you start to tip over and whenever you need to untangle your paws. You'll soon learn how *not* to stand on one with the other."

And after several hysterical minutes of muddling up her feet and barely managing to keep upright, Carin had the hang of it. She shuffled along on the snow behind Welwyn like one old drunk on the trail of another. On snowshoes, the monk's rolling gait became a sort of waddling slide that, from behind, was a funny thing to see. Carin laughed at him so mercilessly that he stood aside and let *her* lead.

This first taste of breaking trail in powdery snow soon silenced Carin's giggles. Not twenty steps later, she was gasping for breath. When Welwyn shuffled past her, she gratefully—and quietly—fell in behind and stepped easily in the track that he packed for her.

They made their way to the shed behind the cabin, to find the powder as compacted there as if a legion had snowshoed across it. Soft snow was no obstacle, evidently, to a herd of Trosdan deer that were intent on getting to their grazing. Verek's four horses, though untethered, did not venture beyond the shelter. They stood under the shed's sloping roof and eyed their visitors indifferently. The fresh hay in stalls and feed troughs showed that Carin and her instructor weren't the first people to come that way this morning.

"Mas—uh, Brother Welwyn," she said when they paused on the packed snow outside the shed's open south side. "Did Lanse haul his worthless self out of bed this morning and feed the horses? That's his job. I wouldn't be surprised, though, if he moaned about his head hurting and tried to slack off." She sniffed. "He really did try to kill me, you know. I'm not sorry about the tree limb smacking him."

"Young Lanse is quite recovered in his head today, my dear," Welwyn replied. He glanced toward the oak grove, as if watching for inexplicably falling branches. "You two younglings must count yourselves fortunate to be traveling with such a master healer as Verek. He's kept in practice, patching up the one or the other of you."

"Fortunate!" Carin snapped. "That's not the word I'd use. The day I accidentally trespassed on that warlock's land has to be the unluckiest day of my life." *Well, second unluckiest,* she amended silently, remembering the whirlpool that had spun her between worlds. "Before Verek took me prisoner, I didn't think wizards and magic still existed."

This conversation was drifting dangerously close to Welwyn's earlier talk of "partaking of the mysteries." But it also brought up something that had puzzled Carin now for nearly three months. She decided to pursue the matter.

"Brother Welwyn, if you don't mind me mentioning your first profession, I have a question I'd like to ask."

"Ask away, my dear," the monk said. "I am here today to instruct you, whether the subject be of the mundane or the magical." He tapped one Briga bearpaw against the other, knocking off loose snow.

"What I'm wondering," Carin ventured, "is why there's no magic in the south of Ladrehdin. Oh, a few old women brew potions and make charms for luck. But according to the priests and all the stories that people tell their children, real magic is a thing of the past, there and everywhere. I believed the stories—until I came north and met up with that warlock friend of yours."

Welwyn chuckled, half to himself as though enjoying a private joke. "The reason, my lady, for a dearth of *wysards* southward is simple. The good folk of the plains chased us all off, long years ago. A few of our number were determined to stand their ground, and many mortals died at their hands. Those *wysards* who stayed too long and grew too weak to defend themselves did burn. But most made the decision to leave. The ones who came north hide up here still." He gestured at the peaks above their heads. "In these mountains and forests it's hard, don't you know, to find a magician who doesn't wish to be found." He chuckled again—rather morbidly, Carin thought.

"But you should know also, my dear, that the adept weren't always outcast," Welwyn went on, still smiling, but grimly. "There was a time, even in the south, when we took our places alongside the physicians and the judges and the men-of-arms. And for generations after they drove us from the plains, *wysards* lived openly in these northern woods and mountain towns."

He sighed. "Then came the first rumblings here—the first stirrings of the ignorant against their neighbors who were different, and therefore to be abhorred. Well did the gifted ones remember the horrors of the south. They didn't tarry to seek the understanding of the masses, but fled. Or changed their habits … some later than others." Welwyn brushed the snow off his brown robes and winked at Carin, with a grin this time of genuine amusement.

"Maybe I'll be pardoned now, my dear," he added, "for daring to say again that you are nowise ill-fated, but a most fortunate young adept, to have fallen into the custody of Theil Verek. His lands in Ruain are the last *wysards'* stronghold in

Ladrehdin. The people there know that the House of Verek is a house of the gifted. They know … and yet, they do not know. It's as if a spell of—how shall I call it? omission?—hangs over the whole province. Those who come and go from Ruain carry no tales away with them. And you'll not find the name of the place on any map."

That was true. In the thick volume *The Lands and Realms of Ladrehdin* that Carin had studied in Verek's library, a map had depicted the southern grasslands in great detail. But where the plains shaded into Verek's wooded highland estate to the north and east, the maps said only "The Wildes" or "The Interior," with no mention of any place called Ruain.

Boldly the wizard had identified himself in Deroucey as the lord of the province Ruain—confident, he must have been, that no one would know the name or raise a cry against its uncanny master. Whatever magic hid the place from those inimical to wizardry must be magic as old as House Verek itself, to have kept the family and its lands out of Ladrehdin's enduring folklore.

Carin shifted on her snowshoes to rest her weight on one leg and idly dig an edge of her other bearpaw into the packed surface under them. "Brother Welwyn," she said, "you seem to know a lot about Verek and that whole family. Did you know his grandfather? The old lord, Legary?" She watched for Welwyn's reaction as she named names. "Or Hugh? Ever meet Verek's father? I'm curious about him—how he died so young, when Verek was just an infant."

Welwyn's smile slipped noticeably. "Nay, my lady. You won't beguile me into telling you all I know of his lordship's affairs of clan. If it's his family you're aflame to understand, then it's him—the last man of it, don't you know—that you need to be asking. I'll tell you only this: the *wysards'* circle isn't so large on Ladrehdin these days that we can't all be acquainted with one another."

The monk looked at the mountain above them. "Of course I knew Lord Legary and Master Hugh." He sighed. "Not only that, I danced at Theil Verek's wedding—and I pray to Drisha that I won't mourn at his funeral."

With a little shake that jiggled down from his head and spread through the rest of him, Welwyn returned his attention to Carin. He grinned at her again.

"Betweentimes, we of the power have our little ways of delivering tidings, one to another. You'd learn our secrets soon enough, if you would but end your doubts and acknowledge the rare gift that's been given you." He tilted his head at Carin. "It's a good sign at any rate, young lady, that you made your way up from the south to find sanctuary with Theil Verek. Were the urge not strong within you to claim your blood-gift, you never would have made the journey alive—you nor that wandering woodsprite, either."

Carin gaped at the monk. All she could do was splutter "Woodsprite?" and hope Welwyn would keep talking.

He did. But first he gave a hearty laugh and shook his finger at her. "Yes, my lady. That temperish sorcerer who is a torment to you has told me about the sprite and the bargain you struck weeks ago in Ruain—the creature's life, for your obedience." Welwyn could hardly speak for chuckling. "It seems to me that you've gotten the better of our dread Lord Verek, for now the creature's free and you're as unruly as ever.

"I little doubt that the wight is lurking around us now"— Carin as well as the monk squinted at the nearest trees— "wishing that I would go away so it could speak in private with its benefactress. And so I will leave, soon, to discover what's become of said Verek and his second. Those two have been on the mountain with the deer since daybreak. Before I go, however, I must teach you to turn around, or you'll never get back to the cabin!"

With more easy bantering, Welwyn showed Carin how to lift and turn her bearpaws one after the other, with her feet apart so the edge of one wouldn't pin down the tail of the other. Slowly she stepped around until the toes of her snowshoes pointed back the way she'd come.

More exhilarating was the fast about-face that Welwyn taught her next—leaning on her pole for balance, kicking up, and spinning in place.

"Good," he praised Carin's efforts. "All you need now is practice, my lady. Do a few more turns here on this packed snow, then try it in the powder. If you're of a mind to test your legs, then tramp off into the trees as far as you dare. Just remember, my dear, that the winter sun sets early behind these mountains. I beg you not be late getting back, or don't you know it's his fiery lordship who's apt to be out looking for you." Welwyn's smile was not entirely innocent.

The monk shuffled off. Carin watched him until the pines at the glen's western edge swallowed him up. Then she kick-turned to face the cluster of bare-limbed oaks behind the shed.

"Sprite!" she called, not quite shouting. But neither did she whisper. The creature's presence was no longer a secret needing to be kept.

A spark shinnied to the top of the tallest oak, leaped across to another, then flitted down toward the ground—the sprite's unmistakable signal that it would meet her in the grove.

With a balanced, rhythmic stride that hardly resembled her first bumbling steps of the morning, Carin left the packed snow at the front of the shed. Behind it, she swished through the loose powder that blanketed the glen. It was tiring work. By the time she reached the grove, she was panting. She threw open her cloak and unbuttoned her coat to the fresh, cold air.

"My friend!" the sprite greeted her. "No happier sight than you have I ever seen. In this great expanse of white, the green of your eyes and the pink of your cheeks are all the more fetching."

"Good grief, sprite!" Carin exclaimed. She laughed as easily as she had with the monk. "You're quite sparkly today yourself." She meant the compliment literally. Even against the radiance of sky and snow, the creature flickered luminously. "What's with you?"

"I have been treated to a most amusing—and highly edifying—exhibition," the sprite piped, its voice gleeful. "Midst the trees above, I have seen that the mage's craven horseboy is none the worse for the bump on the head which I gave him. The knave is aslope in the mountains with his master. The pair of them are floundering through the snow, yelling at five deer in harness." The sprite trilled, the closest it could come to human-sounding laughter. "Would that you had witnessed the spectacle with me! I watched, hidden in the trees, for a long time too bemused to drag myself away. When at last they seemed to have their team in hand, I began to guess the purpose of such strange business."

"What is it?" Carin leaned on her pole and listened intently. "What are they doing?"

"The deer," the sprite said, "move over the snow on their four splayed hooves more easily than you two-footed creatures do, even with those baskets you're walking on." The spark, with a quick slide down the tree, indicated Carin's snowshoes. Then it flitted back up, level with her eyes. "I think the mage means to leave your horses here and continue the journey with the deer hauling your food and packs. The heavy beasts that you've ridden for leagues cannot travel in snow so easily as the little deer do.

"And that, my friend, accounts for my lightness of spirit today," the sprite said. "If the mage means to take you into these mountains, driving deer before him while you tramp over the snow wearing baskets on your feet, then I shall be at leisure to idle away half of every day. Hard-pressed though I was to keep up with the horses, in trees such as cover these slopes I'm more than a match for those who go afoot."

The sprite's news flattened Carin's mood like a jeweler's hammer beat gold into leaf. The oak in which the creature was lodged nearly got a hard whack from her pole. She resisted the urge, but only just.

"Sweet mother of Drisha, sprite!" she swore at it. "Slogging through the snow up these mountains is the last thing in Ladrehdin that I want to do. Unh!" Carin glanced up at the peaks and groaned. "I wouldn't mind spending the winter down here in Brother Welwyn's cabin. It'd be cramped, but at least I'd stay warm." She frowned at the sprite. "But you'd rather see me stuck in the snowdrifts. While I'm dragging myself up a mountain, you'll be flitting along, taking it easy. Every day will be worse for me, but better for you."

Carin would have kicked the tree trunk then, except the snowshoes on her feet stopped her. "You go ahead and enjoy yourself while you can. Maybe you'll feel differently when I've frozen to death in a blizzard up there." She jabbed her finger at the slopes. "Verek may last longer than I do, him being a sorcerer and all. You'll have the blackheart and that dimwit Lanse for company—until they're both dead and buried under an avalanche. After that, I guess you'll have to mope your way back down here, at your 'leisure,' and take up with Brother Welwyn."

The sprite sputtered and squeaked. But the mouth that worked in the bark of the oak could form no intelligible words beyond: "My dear girl … never … you mistake … Oh, my!"

Carin gave the creature no chance to recover itself.

"And I'll tell you something else," she snapped. "Verek knows you're here. He knows you followed us, and he's furious about you dropping that branch on Lanse's head. If he had the power to punish you, he would—severely. But he can't lay his hands on you. So he's threatening *me* with unspeakable things if you don't leave Lanse and him alone."

When the woodsprite did not immediately reply, Carin leaned toward the creature's tree, as close as her snowshoes would let her. "Do you get what I'm saying, sprite? If you make him angry, he'll take it out on me. And we both know what he's capable of. If you don't want him ripping my tongue out, or worse, then keep away from him. Stay clear of Lanse, too."

She put her hand on the tree trunk. "I don't mean to sound ungrateful," she muttered, calming down a little. "If you hadn't clubbed Lanse, he would have shot me dead. He might try again—we'll have to watch out. But in the meantime, please don't go annoying him or Verek. That warlock said he would hurt me if you even 'flutter a leaf' their way."

For a time, the glen was silent. Carin, having said quite enough, quit talking. She waited for the sprite to answer her, but the creature only flickered like a wind-whipped candle flame. No sound came down from the mountain above—no shouting at fractious deer, no belly-laughs from Welwyn.

Finally the sprite stammered out, "That—that—*coward*. How *dare* he threaten you to get at me!"

Carin eyed the spark. "Like he's never done it before? Like he didn't threaten *your* life to make me do what he wanted? Now he's switched us around. You're the one he wants to control, and I'm the hostage he'll use to get power over you."

"I won't have it!" the sprite shrilled with uncharacteristic ferocity. "I haven't followed all this way to see my presence bring harm to you. That fiend may deal with me as he thinks himself able. But while there's a spark of life within me, he won't visit my punishments upon your fair head."

Carin—surprised into speechlessness—stared after it as the creature flitted away through the trees, heading up the mountain … to do what? Confront Verek? Attack him or the boy?

The woodsprite of old—the sprite that had whimpered like a terrified child when the sorcerer captured it in his library—would have quailed at Verek's warning. The creature rushing up the mountainside—for all the world like an outraged gentleman who had gone to fight a duel—was some new being whom Carin did not know.

With the sprite's departure, the silence in Welwyn's glen took on a texture almost ominous. Not a breath of wind sighed through the treetops. No sounds came up from the valley or from the walled city that commanded all approaches to it. Sheep and goats didn't bleat; snow didn't crunch under feet or hooves. For a moment, Carin found herself mentally back in Verek's ensorcelled woodland, smothering in the profound silence which haunted that edge of his property.

But then, off the sloped roof of the shed behind her, a slab of snow slid to the ground with a *whoosh*. It broke the trance.

Carin, startled, tried to whirl but found herself anchored. She'd stood in one spot for such a long time, talking with the sprite, the cold had iced her bearpaws to the snow.

Leaning on her pole for support, she popped her snowshoes free. Then she scanned Welwyn's glen for some likely-looking destination. The monk bade her practice … and if the sprite guessed correctly that Verek intended going into these mountains on foot, then she would need all the stamina that hard exercise could build.

She chose a stand of balsams at the glen's western edge, a little north of where the monk had gone into the trees. Resolutely she made for it, keeping the upturned tips of her bearpaws high, out of the powdery snow. Every few steps, she paused to rest. Though five months of walking from the southern plains up to Verek's highlands had left Carin wiry and fit, her more recent weeks on horseback were hardly the way to prepare for a wintertime mountain hike. When she finally reached the edge of the glen, she was leaning on her pole for support and breathing heavily.

In the trees, the glitter of sun on snow lost its blinding intensity. Carin could stop squinting. As her eyes adjusted to the dimmer light under the boughs, she made out a dark and lumpy shape that was half hidden behind a tree. The snow all around was trampled and cut up, its pristine whiteness marred by spots and smears of ... blood?

Warily she peered through the trees, studying what little could be seen of the slope above. Nothing disturbed the quietness but her own quick breaths.

Stepping cautiously, Carin approached the dark lump. She was closer than she wanted to get before she finally realized what the misshapen mass was: a heap of bones, hooves, hair, and violet antlers—the frozen remains of a Trosdan deer. Whatever had killed and eaten the animal had wasted little of the carcass.

A shiver jostled her. Carin buttoned her coat to her throat and wrapped up tight in her cloak. Slowly she edged around the site of the kill, searching in the snow for tracks.

What she found made her doubt the seeing. But when she crouched beside the pawprint and held her outstretched hand over it, she knew her eyes did not play tricks. The track in the snow was of a cat's forepaw, its round footpads clearly visible; the claws that had brought down the deer had been retracted when the creature padded away from its kill. A mountain lion of the normal sort, however, this cat could not be. This cat was huge. Carin's outspread hand fit inside the track without danger of brushing a fingertip to any edge of it.

Chapter 11

Desires

The sun was dipping behind the mountains when a ruckus rose from the direction of the shed. Carin stepped from the cabin onto the porch to listen.

Mingled in the general commotion was the huffing and snorting of deer, with a buck's occasional sharp bark. Above the noises made by his deer, Welwyn's rich laughter rumbled, punctuated by a string of oaths from Verek—fair warning that the men were off the mountain.

Carin donned coat and cloak, lashed on her bearpaws, grabbed her hiking stick and a lighted lantern, and shuffled out to meet them. Following the track that Welwyn had laid down for her earlier, she covered the distance speedily.

"Good evening to you, my dear!" the monk greeted her cheerfully. "One might think you had the best teacher in the land, to see how well you're progressing. But where there was a smile on your face when I left you to your practice at midday, I now see a frown. What's fretting your ladyship?"

Carin stopped at a prudent distance from the monk and his deer herd. The beasts weren't all penned; she had no wish to spook the stragglers back up the mountain.

But the deer ignored her. Their bright eyes were fixed—not on Verek, Lanse, or the small team that the two were now unharnessing—but on a winking glow in the trees beyond.

Carin stared. The sprite's secret was well out. Even the deer knew of the creature's presence—and they were fascinated.

Welwyn coaxed the last of the herd under shelter. Then he scuffed over to stand beside Carin.

"A marvelous bellwether is your woodsprite." He chuckled. "If ever you tire of the creature, lend it to me. The last time the deer came off the slopes so docilely, it was with a corpse-candle in the lead. The beasts do fancy a light in the dusk. Brainless as moths, one might think them."

The monk was right. Now the deer turned their curious gazes on the lantern in Carin's hand.

She set the lantern on the packed snow. Standing within the circle it lit, she used the tip of her hiking stick to draw a ring in the snow the size of the pawprint under the balsams.

"Mas—er, Brother Welwyn, are you missing a deer? I found what was left of one, there." Carin pointed to the trees in the distance. "I also found a cat track, and I swear it's this big." She tapped the circle she'd drawn. "If I hadn't seen it with my own eyes, I wouldn't believe it. Sweet mercy! Just how big do your lions *get* up here?"

The look on Welwyn's face was probably the closest the man could come to a frown. He shook his head.

"The biggest cat that's native to these peaks has a paw not half so large as you've traced there, Lady Carin. But I've heard rumors, don't you know. Pray lead the way, and all shall follow. Can you show us, though evening closes in, where lies the carcass you found?"

She nodded and picked up the lantern. The deer watched her movements as if entranced.

As she stepped past their shed, Carin got her first good look at the fairy-beasts of Ladrehdinian legend. In the flesh, they were not extraordinary. About the size of roe deer but stockier in build, the Trosdans had long, thick hair. Most were tawny in color; others, grayish with white underneath. All had short, forked antlers of a shiny purple hue. Their muscular legs ended in oval hooves like miniature versions of man-made snowshoes. Born to the mountains they truly were, with warm hair coats to protect them from the snow and splayed feet to carry them over it.

Carin's own path through the snow, where she'd earlier worked her way to the balsams, was clear even in the half-light of dusk. Welwyn didn't immediately join her on it, but stopped to collect Verek and Lanse.

"I send my best pupil off to find her snow legs," the monk told them, "and what does she stumble upon? The very evidence I had hoped to show you—and to see for myself, to prove that I'm no doddering old fool who'll repeat anything I hear. Come along, you unbelievers, and let's see what her ladyship has discovered."

Welwyn followed Carin then, down the track, over snow that was hard-packed by her earlier walk to and from the edge of the glen. Behind him came Verek, trailed by a plainly unenthusiastic Lanse.

Setting its own course through the trees was the sprite. It sparked away into the night, as bold as a beacon. Carin watched its confident leaps, and wondered. Had the creature won a victory over the warlock? Or had it merely angered Verek—sufficiently to bring the sorcerer's wrath down upon her?

She waited only for Welwyn to catch up, then led him to the stand of balsams as quickly as her new skills allowed. Carin showed him the dead deer and the pawprint, handed him the lantern, and shuffled aside onto soft, unmarked snow to let him examine the evidence for himself.

Verek and Lanse were not long in joining him. Both, ignoring Carin, fastened on the cat's kill and the tell-tale track it had left behind.

"My apologies, Welwyn," the wizard muttered. "I should not have doubted you. But a mountain cat so monstrous as you described seemed beyond belief. When did you say the beast was first seen up here?"

"I don't know that anyone's actually laid eyes on the monster," Welwyn corrected him. "The first report I had of something odd skulking around the flocks was a fortnight ago. A shepherd from the valley did me the kindness of tramping up here with a warning: something was killing his stock, not only lambs and kids, but mature rams and billies. Rumor had it that a pawprint had been found in the mud of a creekbank—the track of a cat, but bigger than the hoof of a dray horse. You needn't apologize to me, Theil Verek. I thought the tale far-fetched, myself—until now."

The monk looked across to Carin. "Well done, my lady. It's a felicitous find, this. Puts us all on our toes."

"Was the deer one of yours, Brother Welwyn?" she asked.

"Aye. I missed the beast only this morning. To see its carcass now, not a bowshot from the shed, makes me anxious for the others. Not only huge is this cat, but audacious too. Methinks I'll sleep with the deer tonight."

Lanse rose from his study of the print in the snow. He turned to his host. "By your leave, Master Welwyn, I should like to take the watch. A monster this size could slaughter a horse. I pledge my word that nothing will trouble either your animals or my master's, if I am permitted to stay with them tonight."

Welwyn grinned. "You needn't ask twice, my boy. I'll take a warm bed over a shakedown in the straw any time it's offered. The job's yours. Let's hie to the cabin and get a hot supper down you, and scare up all the extra blankets we can find. You'll need them, don't you know."

Chuckling loudly, the monk headed back on the now well-broken trail, Lanse behind him. The lantern went with them.

The two who lingered did not miss it. Reflected off the snowy landscape, the half-light of dusk was as bright as a first-quarter moon. It showed Verek's unquiet eyes fixed on his "footboy." This was the first time today that their paths had crossed. If the sprite's behavior had provoked the wizard's ire, Carin might now learn, to her grief, what retribution would be exacted.

She swallowed the lump that rose in her throat and addressed her captor civilly — if awkwardly, given that they had been standing together without speaking for more than a minute. "Good evening, my lord."

Verek returned the courtesy, giving her a nod that was not as curt as he was capable of. Then all was silence. Neither moved to take the path to the cabin.

Oh, just ask him! Carin snapped at herself. Hours of waiting and wondering would be unbearable. She had to know: Had the sprite's defiance earned her a dose of hell's own strap oil?

"I, uh, delivered your message to the woodsprite, sir," Carin began, carefully. "The creature didn't listen to me. It had flashed up the mountainside before I could stop it. I've never seen it that angry. If it had been a human, I think it would have thrown down the gauntlet and challenged you to a fight."

Verek nodded. "Indeed," he grumbled. "Such was the creature's temper when it faced me on the slopes. You, I'll wager, will learn all from the sprite itself. From me, you need hear only this: the wood-goblin and I have reached an agreement. It will not ambush Lanse or myself, so long as you are not mistreated." Verek put a gloved hand on the tree trunk beside him while he widened his stance. Then he stood with his arms folded. "You, therefore, have nothing to fear from either of us. I will refrain from the diabolical brutality of which I'm often guilty."

What moved across Verek's face at this was an expression Carin found unreadable in the light of stars on snow.

"Lanse," he added with emphasis, "has pledged to make no further attempts on your life. Much impressed was that youth when the sprite came charging into our midst, flinging tree limbs about, on the prod like an enraged bull. What Welwyn and I could not convince him of, Lanse now believes: it was the sprite, not you, who brought that branch down on his head. The boy still knows you for a sneak—a listener at keyholes and windows. But the sprite has forced him to at least consider the possibility that you're not altogether a malevolent witch."

Carin struck the snow with her hiking stick. The sound of it was too muffled to vent her anger. She took a second whack at a nearby tree, knocked down a cloud of powder, and felt better.

"How many times do I have to say it?" she grated. "I'm not any kind of a witch. If I have a slight tendency in that direction, I don't consider it to be a 'gift' the way you and Welwyn do. I pray to Drisha to lose whatever it is that let me hear the voice of your wizards' well in Ruain. I don't want to hear it ever again. I don't want to bring forth sea urchins—or summon dragons." Many weeks had passed since Carin had last said the incantation that called the Jabberwock dragon. She still knew the words of the rhyme, though, and she always would.

Verek shifted slightly; his snowshoes creaked. Sounds cut distinctly through the cold, starlit evening. Carin heard the restraint in his voice as he softly replied, "We can't always have what we want."

She waited for him to break up this meeting. But the warlock made no move toward the cabin. He seemed calmer and more approachable than usual—like someone she could actually talk to.

"What's Lanse's problem with me?" Carin blurted. She jabbed her thumb toward the cabin where the boy had gone with Welwyn. "So what if I did manage to pull off a few tricks while I was out cold that night of the ice storm? I don't get why he's scared of a little magic." She sniffed. "It's ridiculous. He's the servant of a sorcerer. He's seen all sorts of things, and he isn't bothered when *you* work magic."

She cited some instances of Verek's spellcraft that Lanse had witnessed. "He didn't faint away when you used wizardry to destroy that pack of wasteland dogs. He didn't mind you casting the spell of stone over those men on the plain of Imlen. And obviously he's not afraid of Master Welwyn, though your monk friend is a wizard too."

Carin tilted her head. "So why am I so threatening to him? Why did Lanse get spooked by my accidentally working a little magic in my sleep? I'm sure it couldn't have amounted to much." She sniffed again, and desperately hoped that whatever sorcerous ability she had displayed that night had been small and clumsy.

Verek unfolded his arms and put his hands on his hips. "The talent you possess is *not* slight." He clipped his words. "Nor is your wielding of it inept when you give it full rein, as you did, unconsciously, that night." He dropped his right hand to his side and spread his fingers for an instant, as if he felt the magic flowing.

"Your questions, however," he continued in a tight voice, "deal not with your own dread of the power, but with Lanse's fear of you. And to answer you on that point, I must tell you something of the boy's history. When his parents died, I took him in—for mercy's sake, in part. But also, I knew that there was, far back in his family's past, a trace of the gift." The wizard hesitated. His eyes glittered in the shadows of the balsams. "Do you take my meaning? Or shall I speak more plainly?"

Carin shifted her weight onto one shoe and scuffed at the snow with the other. At the risk of rekindling Verek's anger against his housekeeper, she confessed what she knew.

"I heard about Lanse trying to study magic with you. Myra told me he couldn't learn it. He was hopeless at it.

"Myra also said that your grandfather had Mister Jerold as his apprentice," Carin added, touching on a subject—Lord

Legary—that Verek had warned her to avoid. But she couldn't stop herself. "Myra said Jerold turned out to be an average sort of wizard, not a brilliant one like your grandfather was wanting." And not a satisfactory replacement, surely, for Legary's dead son. How could a run-of-the-mill apprentice ever take the place of a child of the blood?

"Feh!" Verek sounded insulted but not riled. "I tell you distinctly: Myra is talking rubbish. There was a time, long years ago, when Jerold would have been celebrated as a masterful *wysard*. Eager apprentices would have flocked to him for the getting of wisdom."

The warlock paused again, and a melancholy sigh escaped him. Then he went on: "But apprentices are few now in Ladrehdin. Lanse was the last to apply to the House of Verek for training in the *wysard*'s art. In that circumstance you may, perhaps, begin to see into the heart of the boy's aversion to you … and to your displays of power."

A wind gusted through the treetops. Carin, startled, jerked her head back to look up at the branches bending above. The disturbance in the air lasted only a moment. She dropped her gaze and found Verek studying her face as though he could see it clearly in the twilight.

He chafed his arms through the sleeves of his coat. The single gust had deepened the cold, but still he lingered with her under the balsams.

"Resentment, envy … " he muttered, more inwardly than to Carin. "Treading close behind such rancor is fear. Fear is a powerful goad, but it clouds the mind. The boy sees you first as a rival, then as a more serious threat. He believes that I do not know you for the danger that you are, and he begins to think me enthralled. Wouldn't I be as wary as he is, save that I have fallen under your spell?"

Carin said nothing. The wizard seemed truly enthralled, to be going on at such length. She wouldn't risk spoiling the moment.

Verek pressed his palms to his eyes. "Something of the sort was in Lanse's mind," he said almost absently, "when he raised his weapon to you. The boy thought me so thoroughly in your power that he was compelled to act in defiance of my commands, to save his master as well as himself. His ... misreading ... of the situation has been corrected. I do not say that you need look for tenderness from him, but neither must you watch your back."

The wizard gestured at the trail that was visible as a gray ribbon through the snow. "Come. Let's not stand talking all night. It's too cold and I am too hungry. Handling sled-deer builds an appetite like a woodcutter's."

When Verek motioned for her to precede him, Carin stepped into the track. She moved along briskly with a snowshoer's shuffling stride, glad to stretch muscles that cold and underuse had made tight. However, as she passed the oak grove behind the shed, a thought brought her up short. She halted so suddenly that Verek nearly ran over her.

"Sorry," she mumbled as both caught their balance. "But it just occurred to me to ask: When you made your deal with the woodsprite—that it won't hurt you, and you won't hurt me— did you agree to take my ankle iron off? That should have been part of the bargain, because I hate the thing."

A corner of Verek's mouth quirked. He shook his head. "No mention was made of the *chalse*. And I think you will find that neither the sprite nor myself is willing to reopen the negotiations to make an amendment in your favor. The creature, I'll wager, would be no happier to have you go missing than I would. In the goblin is all the zeal, so noticeably lacking in yourself, for seeing this venture through to its end."

205

The wizard put his hand on Carin's shoulder, and she felt again the little tingle that was not fear, not revulsion, but something that nevertheless made her heart beat faster.

"So bold has the creature become, I expect we won't often be free of its presence in the days ahead," Verek muttered. "Therefore, I take this moment to speak in confidence. My gravest mistake of the past two months was to not kill the sprite when I had the chance. It was a fool's blunder, to honor my pledge to you to spare the creature's life."

He squeezed her shoulder tightly; Carin did not draw away. "And you, *fileen* ... you may yet discover that, in trusting the fetch-life, you have made an error of your own."

* * *

Their second full day as guests of the monk Welwyn began much as the first had, with snowshoeing practice for Carin and sled-deer maneuvering for Verek and Lanse. Echoing down from the slopes came their cries of *"Dey!"* and *"Doy!"* — for "left" and "right," she learned from Welwyn, who didn't leave her side all morning.

"I'll not see my best pupil become a meal for a horse-sized mountain cat," the monk teased her. "Besides, I've only these few hours to teach you to walk uphill and down — and Drisha knows you'll be doing plenty of both in days to come."

So it was true. Vanished was Carin's small hope that the woodsprite's conjecture had been wrong. The warlock meant to go on with this madness. He meant to climb into the mountains. She might have cried, if Welwyn hadn't kept her too busy to dwell on what lay ahead.

"Attend, my dear," he admonished, directing Carin's attention to a steep ascent, at the base of which they stood. "To climb such as this, turn your toes out. You'll look a bit like a duck waddling, but you'll get up it." The monk demonstrated by pointing the toes of his bearpaws outward and using the inside edges of the frames to bite into the snow. Carin did likewise, but well to the side of Welwyn's path up the slope, in case the fat fellow lost his footing and slid back to the beginning. Both of them made it up, however, to a ledge that was barely wide enough to turn around on.

"Now I'll show you the preferred way of getting down," Welwyn said, and grinned impishly. "You could always fall off the mountain—that's quickest, don't you know. But I don't recommend it. Learn the proper descent and live to climb another day."

He handed Carin cords to tie to the upturned tips of her bearpaws. Holding on to the loose ends, she started down, leaning back and pulling up on each cord in turn to keep the tips of her snowshoes from digging in and throwing her. It was rather like grappling with two clumsy pups on leashes, but Carin managed the technique without once toppling over.

Till midday she climbed and descended, practiced her turns and 'shoed round the glen, until at last Welwyn called a halt. While Carin shuffled wearily to the cabin to put a pot of leftover stew on the fire, the monk went higher up the slopes to fetch down the two deer drivers.

When they were all gathered at the table in Welwyn's kitchen, the energetic little man served them, then swallowed his own lunch before Carin had her bread well buttered. Excusing himself then, he trundled across to the back room that was his alone now, with Lanse spending nights in the shed.

From the room, Welwyn hauled out armful after armful of winter gear until the couch, armchair, and unused half of the long table were buried. There were wool blankets, fur sleeping bags and woven rabbit-skin robes, deerskin mittens lined in wool, hoods with ruffs, and knee-boots of tanned deerhide with braided tops to seal out snow. Also piled up were an ax with a leather-sheathed blade, tent poles, pots and pans, two snow shovels, an ice chisel, two candle lanterns, and a bag of tapers.

Carin's apprehensiveness eased a little with every new item the monk brought out. Foolhardy though this winter expedition was, they would continue it as well-prepared as this seasoned mountain man could make them.

Welwyn stood over his treasures, beaming like a boy with a roomful of toys. "Finish your stew, my worthies, and then we'll be about strapping all this to the sled. It'll take a bit of doing, but you'll not be wanting to leave any of it behind."

Loading the sled took most of the daylight hours that were left to them. Though Welwyn's deer sleigh wasn't much more than a long, narrow board on runners, it held an astonishing lot when expertly packed. Onto it, tied up in a tent-tarp, went all the gear except the clothing that Welwyn had laid out in the cabin. The sled also had room for the quantities of food that he brought up from his cellar: not only jerked beef and sacks of meal, but also frozen bricks of stewed meat, slabs of a heavy raisin cake, salt in a bag, sun-dried apples, pears and plums, and a cask of tea. They would eat better in the mountains than they had on the journey to Welwyn's glen.

Carin, leaving the men to ready the camp gear, retired to her borrowed bedroom to get her own things in order. Her instructions were strict: Take only one extra shirt and trousers, Welwyn said, but every pair of wool stockings that she had. For the next—how many weeks?—she must travel light but with enough clothes to keep warm and dry in ever-deepening snow.

Her packing was quickly done, her few items fitting into one sack that would be carried by a stout Trosdan deer and not on Carin's own shoulders. She set the pack beside her closed bedroom door. Then Carin stood fingering the folded papers that she'd stolen from Verek's library in Ruain.

Not since Deroucey had she had a chance to work at deciphering Lord Legary's ensorcelled narrative. And not again, after tonight, was she likely to have even an hour's privacy to devote to the task. In the mountains, Carin and her "escorts" — as Welwyn chose to call them—would probably be sleeping three to a tent.

She drew the papers from her pocket and sat on the bed. Again she used a pillowcase to cover the jumble of Legary's bespelled writing. Each time Carin snatched the linen away, a very few words appeared legibly, but only for an instant before sinking back into the prevailing chaos. She unearthed the phrases *to the tomb, his gift,* and *this House.*

The words still hidden, however, far outnumbered the handful that Carin had wrested from the narrative. At this rate, she would be years reading Legary's narrative. And she strongly suspected that, were the dead magician's words not deciphered before this journey ended, she needn't bother reading them at all.

Think, she ordered herself. *Verek and Welwyn insist that you can do magic. Can't you work a little of it on this piece of paper? Why don't you mutter a spell or recite a charm and make the words come clear?*

The problem was, she didn't know what to say. In none of the books that Carin had read in Verek's library were wizards' spells written down. Few of the volumes she'd perused had done more than mention sorcery, except for that weird text of Archamon. And it was so shrouded in spellcraft that no page of it, other than Legary's deathbed "confession," had lain open to Carin's scrutiny.

Despite her months in the company of wizards, she realized, she had only one charm to her credit. She had learned it, not from a sorcerer, but from the wisewoman who wove charms and kept chickens near the village where Carin had lived with the wheelwright's family. That same woman's whispered advice had sent her north to claim, as Welwyn put it, her "blood-gift."

"How did it go?" Carin mumbled, struggling to remember. "Something about seeing …"

With her brow furrowed in concentration, she pictured the woman named Megella swathed in layers of shawls, her calloused hands braiding into a ringlet "three hairs from the heads of three witches." Just where those hairs had come from, Carin couldn't guess. At the time, she'd thought that Meg spoke figuratively—or flippantly. Now she wasn't sure.

In any event, when the braided circlet was finished, Megella said the charm. And by looking through the ring of hair, the woman could see that which had been hidden—or so she claimed.

The words of the chant came to Carin in a rush. She spoke them without thinking:

"Peering-eyed woman, seeing all;
Keen-eyed man, seeing all;
Virile sons, nubile daughters,
Dark-eyed fey ones, seeing all."

On the paper in Carin's hand, the jumbled characters leaped into motion like a disorganized troupe of dancers fighting for position. Some letters raced to the top of the page, some wriggled to the bottom; others circled the middle. Though Legary's narrative remained as unreadable as ever, the charm of "seeing" had definitely disturbed the old wizard's spellwork.

Too intrigued by what she'd done to fear it, Carin watched the figures' pirouettes. "What you need, don't you know," she mumbled, mimicking Welwyn's catchphrase, "are three hairs from the heads of three witches." With a braided circlet to peer through, she just might make the wisewoman's charm do the trick.

But where would the necessary hairs be found? Carin ran her fingers through her own mane. From the gillie's bob of weeks ago, her hair had grown out nearly to her shoulders. *Lanse calls you a witch—and so you will be, for the sake of a little spellwork.* Three of the needed strands would come from her own auburn locks, three from Welwyn's salt-and-pepper ponytail, and the final three from Verek's head of long, crow-black hair.

The monk's plans for the twilight hours fit perfectly with Carin's. "Baths for all!" Welwyn declared when the evening meal was done and the animals were tended. "You'll not be having a long soak in a hot tub for a stretch after this, don't you know, so you might as well enjoy it while you can. You first, Lady Carin. As sure as dirt makes mud, you'll not be wanting to follow these mucky fellows."

She leaped at his offer. Armed with a bundle of clean clothes and a bar of elderflower soap, she trailed the monk into the bedchamber that had been Lanse's sickroom. It was more austere in most respects than Carin's borrowed bedroom. It had narrow pallet-beds instead of the curtained expanse of goose-down that Welwyn had ceded to her. This room, however, boasted one outstanding fixture: a brass tub, ornately worked with a rolled and filigreed lip, showy enough for a noblewoman's bower.

Carin stared at it, then at the monk. He grinned sheepishly.

"I'll never tell a soul," she whispered to him.

Welwyn only chuckled. He helped her fill the tub to the brim with steaming water. Then he left her to luxuriate in privacy.

Carin lingered as long as she thought acceptable, given that two others would want a soak as well. When she'd toweled off and got dressed, she searched for hairs from Welwyn's head.

On a table between the pallet-beds lay a comb. Tangled in its teeth were two long, white hairs. On a bed pillow, one iron-gray hair waited to be collected. Carefully she folded the salt-and-pepper strands inside the papers in her pocket, remade the bed, and gathered up her dirty clothes. Smiling, Carin opened the door and stepped into the front room.

No one was there but Verek. The wizard sat on the couch, reading by the light of an oil lamp. He didn't look up when Carin entered the room. But he spoke to her, inattentively, as though too absorbed in his book to be bothered.

"Master Welwyn begs the use of his old room for an hour or so. For two days he's neglected his prayers and those offices that a man of Drisha should perform nightly. He hopes you will not be put out while he secludes himself in there" — Verek tipped his head, indicating her borrowed bedroom — "to discharge his pious duty."

"Of course. I'll stay out here," Carin replied.

None but the walls heard.

She set down her bundle of dirty clothes and put water to heat for washing them. While she waited for the pot to boil, she followed Verek's example and scanned the bookshelves, searching for a slim volume that she could read tonight. It wouldn't do to start a story that she might never have the chance to finish.

Carin spotted a familiar title: *Ladra*. Verek's own library held a copy of the same short text. She hadn't read it there, preferring practical works like archery manuals and travelers' guides to collections of poetry. But if Welwyn and Verek both thought enough of the work to own it, she ought to take a look. Maybe it was required reading for wizards.

With the little book Carin settled at the table, near the cooking hearth to catch the firelight on her reading. As she took her seat, across the way Verek left his. He scooped up his saddlebags and retired to the back room for his bath. The door closed behind him just as Carin opened to the first poem.

Before she'd finished a stanza of it, she was trapped in the book like a fish in a weir. *It's bewitched!* cried the only corner of her mind that managed to disentangle itself.

Knowing she was under the book's spell was not the same as breaking it. Carin tried repeating the charm of "seeing" that had made a dent in Legary's spellwork. She struggled to build her proven countermeasure against Verek's spell of stone—her quickly imagined vision of dried clay flaking off soft flesh. Against Ladra's enchantments, however, none of it worked. Carin fought to close her eyes, but she couldn't. She could only keep reading.

And what strange reading it was. Every lovers' kiss recounted in verse, Carin tasted. Every blushing rose given to fair maiden wafted its perfume at her. She heard the lilting songs of the serenaders and felt the caresses of lovemaking … gentle, the touch of silk on naked skin, and passionate, two bodies twined, glistening with sweat.

Her face was hot, her breathing rapid and shallow. The book melted to her fingers. She couldn't put it down, and she couldn't stop turning the pages. Her blood, her marrow—every part of her being—devoured the erotic poetry with an exquisite hunger.

Carin did not hear the door to the bathing room open. She did not notice a scrubbed, neatly groomed Verek approach the table. But she became acutely aware of his presence when his long fingers closed over the volume and drew it out of her grasp. As Verek took it away, Carin clutched for it, desperate not to lose it.

The wizard snapped the book shut. He glanced at the title on the spine. Leveling his gaze at her, he smiled.

Carin studied his face as though she'd never seen it before. A smiling Verek was a rarity on the order of an exploding star.

"So our good Welwyn appreciates Ladra's passions, does he? No marvel—the old reprobate," Verek said. One eyebrow arched quizzically. "And you've stumbled upon them, have you? All innocent and unsuspecting, not guessing what this writer will demand of you. By the look on your face, I perceive that you are well under this *wysard*'s spell. The enchantment is a potent one." He toyed with the closed book.

Then Verek laughed—a mixture of amusement and sympathy. "Would that Welwyn had been the first to walk into this room! Ladra's dictates might have taken years off him. But the enchantress moves unwary readers to take the first upon whom their eyes shall light. You must act, therefore, as the poetess compels—distasteful though you may find it. Her magic holds her captives helpless until they've done her bidding."

Carin stared at the wizard, not sure whether to be relieved at his understanding of her predicament, or embarrassed by his unhesitating acceptance of it. Didn't he find it disconcerting that words on paper—even enchanted words—should stir in her such an overpowering compulsion?

"You'll let me?" she asked, breathless.

"*Let* you!" the warlock exclaimed. "What possible objection could I raise? Lanse is the only one among us who is both blind and stonyhearted. From neither of those failings do I suffer. When a pretty girl finds herself obliged to kiss me, I won't hinder it."

Verek walked around the table to the hearth. He watched her with an expression that was half beguiled and half unreadable, as he raised his arms shoulder high and rested his elbows on the mantelpiece at his back. He leaned against the stonework, casual in his shirtsleeves, his white linen tunic open at the throat.

214

Carin hesitated, in an agony of conflicting desires.

"Come," the wizard said. The smile played on his lips. "Do as you must—as Ladra commands—and be done with it. I won't bite you."

Carin pushed back her chair and got up from the table. Uncertainly, she stepped to the fireplace to stand facing the dark-haired, well-built warlock. Within her was a curious mix of emotions—dismay at what she was about to do, resentment of the sorceress Ladra for usurping her free will … and something that Carin wasn't prepared to put a name to, for it would require a conscious admission that what she felt for Theil Verek was not altogether a sense of loathing.

Make it light and quick! cried the only corner of her mind that could still think for itself. *Stay in control, get free of this enchantment, and don't lose what's left of your dignity.*

But when Carin had slipped her hands along Verek's freshly trimmed beard and pulled his face down to hers, what she planted on his parted lips wasn't a peck. She kissed him with all the passion that lived in Ladra's poems.

For a moment that was not measured in time, both of the wizard's hands stayed where they were. He seemed to be gripping the mantelshelf. Then his right hand let go. He cupped it around the back of Carin's head and pulled her to him, forcing her lips more firmly against his as he responded to her.

Then with a suddenness that left her gasping, he broke it off. His hands moved to her shoulders. He pushed her away and held her at arm's length.

"No," he whispered. His dark eyes filled Carin's universe. "There is much of folly in this course, and little of wisdom. I'll thank you to retire from the field before I forget that you are still more girl than woman, and this is Ladra's hunger on your lips and none of your own."

The heat that spread through Carin rose high, wave upon wave of it, a blaze that burned her everywhere—she was blushing like a panicked *callet*-fish. She slipped from Verek's grasp and retreated toward the door to her borrowed bedroom. In her confusion, she forgot that Welwyn still occupied the room.

The monk, in fact, was just leaving it. The door stood ajar, and the little man leaned against the jamb, grinning wickedly.

"My life for you, Theil Verek!" Welwyn swore. His bright gaze slid off Carin and fastened on the wizard behind her. "Don't I wish I had a pretty partridge to despise me the way this one so clearly despises you! Now it's clear, don't you know, why you claim that the girl is not your—ahem—*apprentice*."

Chapter 12

White Death

They were a week in the high mountains before Carin's legs stopped hurting. Snowshoeing uphill and down—mostly up— was a painful slog, even with five surefooted Trosdan deer, a sled, and two fellow hikers going in front to pack the trail.

Welwyn's deer were what made this march up the mountains possible, Carin had realized before they were a day gone from the monk's glen. Not only did the stout little beasts haul a storehouse-worth of supplies while breaking trail over snow that horses would have floundered in up to their girths, the deer had an uncanny knack for knowing where the trail *was*.

"The path is faint, at best," Welwyn had warned them. "In winter it vanishes under the snow. Trust the deer to find the way, or be lost in two days' time."

And so the hardy beasts led them, as they might lead adventurers in a droll-teller's tale, on long traverses up steep slopes. Gaining the crests, they kept to the ridgetops as much as possible, where the wind compacted the snow and made walking easier.

The two deer directly in front of the sled—the heaviest, most muscular of the team—bore the brunt of the pulling, while the three lighter animals in the traces ahead of them took turns at the lead. Their harness was ingeniously designed so that, with a quick interchange of iron rings and catches, the lead animal could be put in the middle of the string to rest, while those which had followed second and third moved up to take their turns at trail-breaking.

Lanse proved as sure a hand with deer as with horses. He walked behind the sled, holding a snubbing line for downhill braking. A long rein in his other hand gave him a modicum of control over the lead animal. By twitching it this way and that, and yelling "Dey!" or "Doy!" he could alter the team's course just enough—most of the time—to keep the sled from hanging up in trees or on rocks that protruded from the snow.

For all their willing work and their sure skills as pathfinders, the beasts seemed endlessly surprised by the sled that they pulled. Each time it lodged against some obstacle they'd pranced over or skirted too near, the five would strain in their harnesses, struggling to walk on, their confusion showing in their eyes when they could not progress. Then it became Carin's job to trudge to the head of the train, take the lead deer by its noseband, and force it and thus all of the bewildered creatures to back up, to slacken the ropes between the team and the sled.

By the time Lanse and Verek had the sleigh free of whatever held it, the deer would be frantic to get going again. When the wizard signaled her to release them and Carin stood aside, the team would take off at a trot, the three snowshoers hard-pressed to keep up. No amount of Lanse's shouting or hauling back on the lines would slow them until they'd made up for the delay.

The beasts had a well-developed—tyrannical, in fact—sense of time and distance and how far they ought to travel in a single day. When the miles that the deer prescribed for themselves had passed under their hooves, they stopped, no matter how early or late or how unsuitable that place for making camp.

It was then that the woodsprite proved itself to be a useful addition to Verek's party. Sparking enticingly, the creature went ahead to coax the deer into a grotto or a stand of trees, under a rock overhang, or simply around a slope to its lee side, if that was all the shelter to be found within a reasonable distance of the team's stopping.

The first few times that a clearly dubious Verek allowed the sprite to tempt the deer off the track and into cover, he carefully marked the end of that day's travel to be sure they could take up the trail again at dawn. Such precautions, however, proved unnecessary. Unerringly when they broke camp, the deer trotted back to the spot they'd reached the day before, no matter how far the sprite had led them off to an acceptable campsite. From there, the team resumed the journey, the Trosdans stepping confidently over the snow as if they harbored no doubts about the wisdom of this winter trek.

Their owner, however, had not been able to hide his misgivings. On the morning of their departure from Brother Welwyn's glen, the monk's sad looks had mirrored Carin's gloomy mood. It was the only time in their brief friendship that the little man hadn't smiled at her. He'd squeezed her breathless with his hug and whispered in her ear:

"Take care, my dear. You've won my heart. Though you must trust in Theil Verek to see you safely through this venture, if it were any man but him taking you into these mountains — not to mention stealing you from me — I'd kill him, don't you know."

From Welwyn's embrace, Carin had extricated herself before she fainted from lack of air. She'd looked into the monk's face, expecting to see his usual impish grin. But his lips were tight, and his brown eyes were as hard as granite. What she'd taken for a bad joke, the monk had meant in deadly earnest.

And so it had been a subdued party that climbed away and left Welwyn standing alone in his sheltered glen. Carin had knots in her stomach. Verek and Lanse seemed lost in thought. Both were silent except for the necessary commands to the deer and brief exchanges between themselves where the terrain demanded it. Neither of them spoke to Carin. They left her to

219

trail along, as much their unwilling follower as she had been since Ruain.

The ensorcelled fetter on her ankle kept her near. The greater range that Verek had allowed, while Carin learned snowshoeing in the glen and he mastered deer handling on the slopes, was again restricted. Now she could barely step out of his sight behind a tree or around a bend before her anklet tightened threateningly.

The only one among them who looked the least bit pleased was the woodsprite. It flitted through the trees behind Carin and hid from no one now — except the deer. One glimpse of that spark out of the corner of an eye, and the Trosdans' heads would turn. Their bright gazes would search the trees for the creature they fancied. If they hadn't made their allotment of miles for the day, the deer would keep moving down the trail while they looked for their darling, but with such inattention that the sled's chances of snagging were greatly multiplied.

Only twice did the sprite distract the team before Verek's fury cowed the creature into finding its place at the very end of the caravan. The sprite's newfound confidence, Carin observed, was not so great that the fay would risk fully unleashing the wizard's anger — not simply to prove that it *could* risk it.

Undeniably, the woodsprite now had — so to speak — the upper hand. As Verek had predicted, the creature was quick to tell Carin of their "gentlemen's agreement," as the sprite called the treaty between itself and the warlock.

"Had I thought before I leaped," the sprite confessed, its reedy voice shrill with its high spirits, "my courage might have failed me. But I was so angry at the mage's threats against you, my fair friend, that I jumped into the middle of that serpent and his detestable boy. The sap rose in me. Quickly I made my point: the mage is powerless against me unless he contrives again to catch me in a twig, as when you sneaked me indoors in

Ruain. And it's a witless seedling I'd be, to fall again into such a trap.

"'Think on this,' I advised that pair of miscreants. 'As you go afoot through these mountains, seldom will the sky be the only thing above your heads. Trees are aplenty on these slopes, stretching their limbs over you both by day and by night. You cannot keep me from the treetops. You won't see the flash of my passage if I am high above you in the branches. You won't know that I am there, readying a great bough to fall upon you. Only an instant's warning will you have as the limb cracks and plummets downward.

"'You have seen that I can do it,' I reminded those two. 'I could have killed that treacherous horseboy. Hear, therefore, my solemn promise: Harm one hair on the head of my dear friend Carin, and you'll not leave these mountains alive. I won't rest until I've crushed both your worthless skulls.'"

The sprite twinkled with excitement as it relived its confrontation with Verek. Even through her mitten, Carin felt the thrumming in the bole of the creature's tree.

"The mage took only a moment to ponder my words," the sprite went on. "Looking daggers at me, he replied in a voice that was harder than ash wood: 'Then let there be this understanding between us—you goblin. The girl will not be mistreated, but to the end of this journey she must accompany me. You will not cause harm to befall the boy or myself. Dare an attack upon either of us, and you had best be certain that we both die under the same fatal blow. Else, the one yet alive—though he survive the other by scarcely a moment—will slay the girl, no mercy shown. Do you mark me well?'

"'I do,' I told him. But perhaps you will understand, my friend—as certainly the mage did!—when I declined to approach so near as to shake his hand on our agreement. I took myself off instead to a pine. Deep in its heart, I shivered for an hour or so, marveling at my own temerity. And yet, haven't we all profited by my boldness? You needn't fear the mage or his horrid boy; they needn't fear me, and I am free to travel in your company, not skulk through the trees like a criminal."

'In your company,' as the sprite construed it, seemed to mean traveling at Carin's heels, as close as her own shadow. Yet its constant nearness did not make for easy conversation between them — not with Verek glowering at it over his shoulder if it dared to shrill out a syllable to her, and Carin too winded by perpetual climbing to reply. Only when the wizard allowed them to rest could they speak together at length, out of his earshot.

During a moment of necessary privacy, Carin brought up a matter that had puzzled her since Deroucey. As she retied the drawstring of her trousers, she asked, "Do you remember the evening we met, sprite, when I escaped from Lord Verek's cursed woods and you led me to the old oak in the wilderness north of his property? You broke a limb out of that tree, and it fell on those dogs that were going to tear me apart. Remember?"

"Assuredly I remember," the sprite replied softly. "That was the night my life began on this world. Before we met, I'd moved aimlessly through the days, friendless and afraid. You saved me from a cruel loneliness and from an existence that had no meaning. My dear girl, how could I possibly forget that night?"

Barehanded, Carin patted the sprite's tree. "Don't go all weepy on me, all right?" she muttered, a little embarrassed by the sprite's earnestness. "I'm glad to have you for a friend, too." She pulled on the deerskin mittens that Welwyn had given her and went on with her question.

"That night when you broke the branch, you told me you felt pain. It was bad enough to drive you out of that old oak, at least for a minute or two." Carin spoke quickly while their rest break lasted. "But then in Deroucey, you made the tree limbs scratch at my bedroom window. When I locked myself out, you broke me off a sliver of wood to lift the latch. Then at the monk's cabin, you dropped the branch on Lanse's head. And when the wizard threatened me over it, you went flinging branches at him, he told me."

"Indeed I did," the sprite trilled, sparking proudly.

"But doesn't it hurt you to snap off limbs like that?" Carin asked. "The first time you did it, you seemed to be in terrible pain. But now you act like it doesn't bother you at all."

The creature flickered restlessly in front of her.

"Ah, dear friend," it piped. "You've unearthed a mystery there, I confess. Precisely when the change came upon me, I cannot say. But between the evening when we met, there at the edge of the magicked woods, and the week when I slipped the mage's noose and joined you in Deroucey, I found myself more the master than the guest of the trees in which I dwell. Now I feel no pain when I cause limbs to break. I may even make them move a bit, as I made the twigs scrape at your shutters."

To demonstrate, the sprite dipped the end of a pine bough and thrust it at Carin's face. She ducked, barely avoiding a poke in the eye.

"Apologies," the creature mumbled. "I haven't such fine control of my movements as I would wish. But each day I practice a little and seem to know some improvement.

"But I digress. As to the reason for — or the source of — my new talents, I suppose it might be only that I've lived long in the trees of this world, and slowly I have reconciled myself to such a life. But I was in Ladrehdin many years before you befriended me, and only since that happy day have these new powers come to me. Therefore I think that you, Carin, must be the source of them, or at least their inspiration."

She frowned and started to object. But she broke off in the middle of a word as Verek's impatient shout drove her from the trees. The sprite, as skittish as if it were still a fugitive, flitted off in the opposite direction.

By the time the creature rejoined her, Carin didn't have the breath to argue with it. They were climbing again, up a slope so steep that even the Trosdans struggled. With the hiking staff that Welwyn had given her, Carin pulled herself along. She fixed her stare ahead, on the hem of Verek's cloak, and trudged after it. The single point of focus caught her up and kept her moving when her legs begged for rest.

Her thoughts, free to drift, went back to the sprite and its new talents. Carin couldn't help wondering about its growing mastery of its living hosts.

What was happening to the creature? Had it drawn some uncanny strength from that half-ruined stoneheap of sorcery that Verek called home? The sprite had often come to the door of the manor's decrepit hall to watch Carin practice with her first crude, homemade bow. And for the better part of a week, the creature had been locked in Verek's private sitting room, behind doors that were bespelled to invisibility. Who knew what weird forces had writhed up from the underground vault of enchantment to envelop the sprite during its imprisonment— the same way they had affected Carin in that house?

Verek's alarming speech—never far from her thoughts— sounded in Carin's head: "Exposure to the wizardry within these walls has built in you a susceptibility to the magic. You sense, at first, only simple patterns. Then you begin to see more. The time shall come when all wizardry will be present to your senses with perfect clarity."

Had something of the sort also happened to the sprite, during its captivity in that labyrinth of ensorcelled cellars and bewitched corridors? Was the creature now a budding wizard— as, indeed, Carin stood accused?

Hot from her exertions, she threw back her cloak and opened her coat. Cold air bathed Carin's neck, but that wasn't what made the hairs prickle at the nape of it. Twining with her thoughts was Verek's warning: "In trusting the fetch-life, you have made an error."

* * *

Ten days after setting out to gather "three hairs from the heads of three witches," Carin was no nearer her goal than she had been on the morning of leaving Welwyn's glen. The monk's salt-and-pepper strands lay safely folded in the papers within her pocket. With them was a single long black hair, which she'd gleaned from the couch under the bookshelves where Verek had slept during their stay with his friend. How to collect two more was a puzzle rather like the dilemma the mice had faced when they wished to bell the cat.

Though dreading the close quarters of a tent, Carin had expected nights with her "escorts" to fill out the charm's last threesome. It wouldn't need a sharp eye to spot two shed hairs from Verek's dark head against the silvery gray of the rabbit-fur sleeping robes that Welwyn had supplied them with.

The tent, however, stayed on the deer sleigh. There was no crowding under the canvas at night. As they had done since this journey began, they slept under the stars.

And a bed in the snow, Carin discovered, was a great improvement over a blanket on hard ground. Following Verek's example, she gathered enough pine boughs to spread on the snow a span deep. Over the soft needles went an oilcloth; over that, a thick wool blanket. Her fur sleeping bag topped the stack. After sliding within it, she drew a rabbit-fur robe over the whole heap and snuggled down. Carin stayed warm every night, though she might wake to a liberal dusting of new powder on her furs.

The snows, however, got heavier the higher they climbed; the winds, harsher; the drifts, deeper.

Late in their second week of snowshoeing, they made camp protected by a monstrous drift that constant winds had packed into a firm mass. No one gave, or needed, instructions as they went about the late-afternoon routine of setting up camp. Lanse tended the animals, tethering them where they could graze lichens off trees and rock outcroppings. On nothing more than that and a daily watering, the beasts thrived. While Verek got a fire going, Carin scooped up snow to melt for water for themselves and the deer.

Only wizardry could account for the speed with which Verek—working sometimes in a near white-out—kindled their evening blaze. A mortal would be long at the task that the wizard accomplished in minutes, in any kind of weather. He deigned to simplify the nightly work of making camp with only that one bit of magic: a fire that crackled brightly before Lanse had the deer unharnessed or Carin had scooped up her pots of snow.

This evening, at the base of the tall drift, Verek conjured a blaze with his usual ease. Then he got a shovel off the sled.

Wielding it with vigor, he dug into the mound of hard-packed snow, burrowing like an animal. Scoopfuls came out of the drift until Verek lay stretched in a tunnel so long that only his boots showed. In and out he crawled, bringing out more snow each time. Finally he disappeared inside and was gone for several minutes. When he reemerged, he stepped carefully up the side of the packed drift and bored the shovel handle into it, above where he had been working.

"Go in," the wizard said. He looked down at Carin and spoke between pauses to catch his breath. "Tell me where the rod pierces the ceiling. What is clearly seen from within is only guesswork from without."

She bit her lip. A snowy tomb wouldn't please her any better than the stony black pit in which he'd once buried her. But if Verek meant to put her in harm's way, he didn't need to work at it this hard. In the course of tunneling, he had shed his layers of outer garments. He now stood knocking snow off his trousers and underjacket.

And though he didn't repeat his instructions, he frowned at Carin's hesitation. In the face that looked down at her, muscles tightened, most noticeably along his jaw.

She pulled a skillet of half-cooked oatcake off the fire so the bread wouldn't burn, untended. Then Carin made for the tunnel's entrance, where she paused again, but only briefly. The smooth, white passageway into the drift was nothing like the stairway of stone that plunged to the warlock's cellar-dungeon in Ruain. This shaft did not lead downward into deathly blackness. It angled slightly upward. And at the top of the tunnel, a light showed.

Carin wriggled through and hauled herself into a small, dome-shaped room that was cleanly cut from the packed snow. The curved roof was smooth. A carved niche in one wall held a glowing witchlight orb. It bathed the snow cave with a light like the winter sun's. The wind that relentlessly whipped across the mountainside was absent here. The cave had a welcome stillness, and the promise of warmth. It would hold the heat from an occupant's body.

The den was so snug, in fact, that Carin saw right away the reason for the shovel handle that poked through the ceiling. Without an airhole or two, a person could smother in here.

She tapped the handle to get the attention of the wizard who held it. "It's coming through at the back of the cave," she yelled.

"If you want to make another hole, go toward the fire about half the length of a snowshoe before you poke it in again."

The wood withdrew. It left a puncture too small to admit wind or snow. After a moment, the tip of the shovel handle reappeared, punching through as Carin had directed.

Verek met her outside the mouth of the tunnel. "Good," he said, and handed her the shovel. "You see how it's done. If you would sleep tonight out of the wind, then start digging."

Gamely Carin commenced, while the wizard got the second shovel from the sled and attacked the drift beside her. She'd tunneled into the snow barely her own length—sweating, shedding garments layer by layer—when Verek called her to guide him in punching airholes in the second cave. He didn't offer then to finish her shelter for her, but joined Lanse at the fire.

The horseboy's getting off easy tonight! Carin grumbled silently. *Why does he get his dug for him?*

Leaning on her shovel, she watched Verek and Lanse eat heartily of Welwyn's stew. The boy had finished baking the bread Carin had started. On a bed of coals, slices of raisin cake were thawing, to be served with the dried apples that simmered to tenderness in a little water. Unvarying though the diet was, what the monk had sent them off with was far better than Lanse's cooking had been.

And it required no preparation beyond heating. The cooking chores that Carin had once gladly avoided had become easy work for Lanse. But she got the finger-numbing job of scraping the pots clean afterward, and—this evening—digging her own snow cave.

Verek saw her watching them.

"Make haste," he snapped. He waved her back to her task. "It will soon be too dark to see what you're doing. Without some brightness in the sky above to help you judge the thickness of the roof, you'll likely dig too shallow or too deep."

Carin groaned, but crawled back inside the tunnel. At the end of it she hollowed out a space smaller than the domed rooms Verek had shaped. After a time, she worked entirely by feel. With the dusk came blackness inside the snowbank—and a cold drench of dread along Carin's spine. How she loathed enclosed spaces in the dark!

A light appeared at the mouth of the tunnel behind her. "Take this," Verek called. "Make a place for it in the wall."

A witchlight orb bounded toward her. Its crinkly shell hissed a little as it struck the snow.

She was glad he couldn't see how eagerly, how gratefully she clutched at the light. She scooped out a nook to hold the orb. When a shovel handle came through the ceiling, Carin directed the making of airholes. Then she crawled out of her small but serviceable burrow, beat the snow off her clothes, and pulled on her coat.

Verek crunched down off the drift and laid his shovel aside. He motioned to the fire, where Carin's supper waited.

While she wolfed it down, Verek swigged a little *dhera* and instructed her on the finer points of carving a snow cave. "Do not neglect these things that I tell you. Before you blanket the floor and arrange your sleeping furs, make the roof smooth. Carve from it any sharp edges. Else, as your presence warms the den tonight, drops of ice water may drip on you from those nubs and ribs. Know also that you made the tunnel too straight. From its mouth, it should rise gently to the chamber of sleeping. A slanting passageway keeps out the cold.

"To remedy your error," Verek added, "block the opening once you're inside—or shiver through a night that should find you as warm as you were in Master Welwyn's lodge."

Carin almost strangled on her tea. She shot the wizard a look. This was the closest either of them had come to mentioning the *Ladra* incident. But whether Verek alluded, in fact, to her bewitchment of that night was known to him alone. His face gave no hint.

She cleared away the remains of supper, then retired to her den to follow Verek's advice. Smoothing the roof took several minutes; her jabs with the shovel had left myriad nubs and ribs. When all were removed, she wriggled back through the tunnel to collect her bedding.

Her cave proved too small to accommodate it all. Her sleeping bag would lay flat on the floor only if the foot of it extended into the tunnel.

But that wouldn't trouble her. Tonight she'd curl up. With snow gouged from the tunnel's walls, Carin plugged the passageway against a wind that, by the sound of it, was building to a gale. Up inside her den, its roar was hardly audible.

Carin slipped her boots off and nestled into her furs. For a time she lay awake, too pleased with these new—if temporary—quarters to abandon herself to sleep. She hadn't enjoyed this much privacy since Welwyn's cabin.

She felt for the papers that were hidden in her trousers pocket. If she wanted to, she could work on deciphering Lord Legary's ensorcelled writing, and the sleepers in the neighboring caves would know nothing of her secret labors.

Carin's patience, however, had worn thin with the slow cover-and-reveal method by which she'd sifted a little meaning from the jumble. Far more promising was the spell of seeing. With it, she might strip away the shroud and expose everything Legary had hidden.

Had he put pen to paper, thirty-something years ago, to confess his slaughter of his son, Hugh? Had he revealed the fate of his daughter-in-law, the young widow who mysteriously disappeared from the household? Was it written, on that paper in Carin's pocket, why the lady had left the care and rearing of her son—a ten-year-old Theil Verek—to a sorcerer who might be guilty of the most heinous crime?

Among all the questions that bounced around in Carin's thoughts, however, one especially preoccupied her. What "taint" sullied the present Lord of Ruain? Why had the old lord, Legary, hidden the *Book of Archamon* from him? Had he sensed something so malignant in his grandson that he hadn't wanted Theil Verek to have the *Book*, or the power it might give him? Perhaps Legary had prophesied the family's ruin, when his "tainted" heir came of age and fathered a son—a child without the gift and therefore doomed, perhaps, to die as Hugh had died.

If you want to know what Legary wrote, Carin's thoughts whispered, *you've got to break his spell. So get what you need and work a little magic.*

* * *

She awoke with a plan to do precisely that. And they hadn't been two hours on the trail in the brittle morning when Carin made her move.

The deer, skipping over a tumble of rocks in wind-scoured snow, managed to hook the sled as solidly as it could be hooked. Carin trudged to the front of the train, removing her mittens as she went. She got the leader by its nose strap and pushed firmly until the entire team fell back a step. When slack formed in the traces, Verek and Lanse manhandled the sled out of the rocks and onto better going. At the wizard's signal, Carin edged aside.

Away the deer trotted, huffing noisily, anxious to make up for lost time. Behind them ran Lanse, his bearpaws swishing over the snow in a fast shuffle.

At nearly as quick a pace, Verek followed. Carin timed things perfectly. She stepped around as though to point the toes of her snowshoes back toward the west, but pinned the tail of one under an edge of the other. She flailed her arms, lost her balance, and fell, straight into the wizard. With one bare hand, she grabbed for his head. Her fingers tangled in his hair.

Verek half turned, trying to break Carin's fall—trying to keep them both from toppling off the ridge.

He failed. Together they went over the edge. The wizard clasped her as tightly as she held on to him. Verek landed on his back, down the snowy slope below the ridge crest. Carin sprawled across him.

The snow slumped under them with a loud *whoompf.* Cracks shot out in all directions. A fracture broke the whiteness across the top of the slope. Snow rushed down, engulfing them in a cold, colorless maelstrom.

The force of it tore Carin from the wizard's grasp. She started down in a headfirst slide, but immediately the churning snow flipped her over onto her back. Her head popped to the surface; she gasped for air but got a mouthful of frost. Icy pain shot along the roots of her teeth.

Then her face was buried. She was rolling, tumbling down the slope. She couldn't breathe. The avalanche dragged her under.

Frantically Carin beat at the white death, thrusting upward toward the open sky—toward air—to life. She kicked with both feet, swimming as if the cascade were a great flume of water and she was a drowning diver desperate to gain the surface.

And then the snowslide crunched to a halt, as suddenly as it had begun.

Carin gulped air down a throat so frost-burned that each breath was torture. She blinked snow from her eyes and found herself gazing up at the clouds, lumpy as milk-curds, beading the sky above a pine forest. She'd come to rest with her head in the clear, and one arm free.

She jerked her other arm out of the snow and struggled to sit up. It took several tries, but finally she managed to bend her left knee, and her foot gained a purchase on firmly settled avalanche debris. But her right leg wouldn't move. It was buried deep, caught in the snowpack's vise-like grip.

Carin rested awkwardly on one buttock, propping herself with the hand that had grabbed for the wizard's head. Not a single strand of his hair twined through her bare, cold-reddened fingers. Her prize was lost in the snow, along with her mittens and at least one of her snowshoes. Its rawhide straps remained lashed to her boot, but the bearpaw's wooden frame had been ripped away.

Up the slope from Carin, there was nothing to see but the rubble of the snowslide. Verek was gone.

Chapter 13

A Watcher

"Sprite!" she shouted. "Help me!"

With fingers that ached from the cold, Carin scraped snow from around her trapped leg. She leaned back on both hands and struggled to wrench the limb free. It would not move. Snow that had been a roiling cloud of powder only moments before had set up hard and solid.

"I—am—here—my—friend!" piped the woodsprite. It jumped through the trees and lit in a snag directly overhead. "What a frightful scene! Snow spilling down the slope and sweeping you with it as if you were no more than a seedpod. Dear girl, are you harmed?"

"My leg's caught," she cried. "Give me a stick to dig with. Hurry! I think the wizard is buried."

From above came a sharp snap. A bare limb, split down its length, landed on the snow beside Carin. The wood was hard, and its splintered edge bit into the snowpack like a spade. Six good jabs, and her leg was free. No trace of a snowshoe emerged from the hole, however, when she pulled her foot out. She'd lost both her Brigas.

"Over here!" the sprite shrilled. "I see a glove."

Carin scrambled toward the creature's voice. It led her to a deerskin mitten that was lying on the snow upslope from where the slide had deposited her. She dropped to her knees, grabbed the mitten, and felt fingers within.

With a long edge of the split wood Carin scraped at the snow, removing a handbreadth at each bite. The third pass hit something. She dropped the wood and dug into the snow with fingers that felt pierced by white-hot needles. She cried out with

234

the pain but she kept digging until she had uncovered Verek's face.

It was ashen. The wizard lay unconscious. Carin leaned down, touched her lips to his ice-coated mustache, and felt no breath.

She tore at her clothes, loosening the layers—coat and doublet, and under them an old wool vest that Welwyn had insisted she wear—to get at her water flask. With cut and bleeding fingers Carin fumbled it out, unstoppered it, and splashed a cupful of the flask's body-warmed contents into the wizard's face.

Verek's eyes flew open. There came a blinding red flash, and a clap that might have been thunder except it wasn't a noise but a sensation like a hard blow, delivered in all directions at once. Carin took it like a fist in the pit of her stomach. The trees behind her groaned as if a heavy blast had struck them. The snow under her knees crumbled. A great glittering cloud of rime flew in her face and swirled around her like a blizzard.

The powder slowly settled, revealing a cavity in the packed snow, a cavity left by the wizard's sudden—and altogether unnatural—escape.

He sat at the hole's edge, coughing and gasping. The look on Verek's face mixed alarm, astonishment, and confusion. He stared at Carin. Then he twisted around to gaze at the slope down which they had tumbled.

Carin raised her flask in a hand that shook. She took a swig of warm water and wished for something stronger. Traveling for weeks with a sorcerer who made scant use of his powers, she sometimes let herself forget that he could turn nature on its head with only a muttered word or a dark thought. The avalanched mass had set up around her leg like rock. But Verek had burst from the snowpack as if from feathers.

He hacked again, in a throat that must burn like Carin's did from gulping cold air and ice crystals. Unsteadily, she offered him her flask.

The wizard accepted it and choked down a mouthful. It quieted his cough. With his eyes closed he took another sip, tilted his head back, and let it trickle down. Presently he handed the water back to Carin, drew off his mitten, and went hunting through his clothes for the flask that he carried next to his skin. His did not contain water.

Carin was too out of breath from the invisible blow to her stomach to speak, but Verek shouted hoarsely at the spark that flickered in the trees over their heads. "Sprite! Heed me."

"Wha—?" The creature sounded as winded as Carin felt. It had been close enough to be knocked around by Verek's magic. It couldn't have avoided that force that slammed into the trees.

Verek hawked and spat. "Hasten ahead," he rasped. "Distract the deer. Constrain them. Have Lanse leave tea, a loaf, and Brigas—two pair—by the trailside." The wizard's voice was gravelly, the rawness of his throat audible in every word. "The deer must race onward … tell Lanse we will follow. Go!" Verek grated. "Carry my message."

"Carin?" The sprite flickered just above her head. "Dare I leave you alone with him?"

"Blights upon you!" Verek growled. "Do as I say."

Carin studied the warlock, then looked up at the woodsprite and nodded. "Go on." She sounded as hoarse as Verek, but her breath was coming easier now. "Hot tea for my throat … it'd be wonderful."

"Then I do your bidding, magician—but at Carin's behest, not yours." In a flash the sprite sparked away, racing through the trees up the slope, apparently recovered from the buffeting by Verek's sorcery. Or perhaps, Carin thought, the creature could hardly wait to escape the affected trees and any traces of the magic that might remain in the pines.

She had another thought. "Mittens, sprite!" she cried after it. "Tell Lanse to leave me mittens!"

But she was too late. The creature had already disappeared over the ridge.

Verek took a long drink from the flask he'd pulled out of his clothes. Then he offered the *dhera* to Carin. As she accepted it, he studied her bare hands and the bloodied fingers that were missing patches of skin from scraping at the snow.

He dug back through his garments. This time the wizard pulled out a soft leather pouch that contained small, waxed-paper packets. He bit the corner off one, then held out his mittened hand, palm up.

"To lose your gloves up here," he growled, "is to risk your fingers to frostbite. Be so careless again and you may find there's no remedy for it."

Impatiently Verek crooked his waiting hand, and Carin rested her fingers in his palm. They were too numb now to feel pain, but she felt how tightly he gripped her hand.

The wizard rubbed a salve from the waxed packet into Carin's torn fingertips and over each abraded knuckle. It stung. But then it felt warm, as though she'd dipped her frozen fingers into heated oil and camphor.

Verek treated both her hands, put the medicine away, and started to pull on his other mitten. Then he stopped, frowning. With an irritated sigh, he removed the one that he wore and thrust both of them at Carin.

"Here," he snapped in a *dhera*-strengthened voice. "Keep these close. If they are not returned to me, know that you will make other restitution."

He stood up. As he knocked the snow off his hair and clothes, Carin saw that the wizard had lost more than his snowshoes in the avalanche. His silver headband was gone.

Verek looked up toward the ridgetop, studying the slope. It was neither very tall nor seriously steep. If it had been either, the slide would not have slowed as it encountered the trees. It wouldn't have deposited them where they now stood. On a steep slope, the avalanche would have roared down into the forest, ripping out trees and carrying away timber, rocks—and their crushed bodies.

Despite its relative gentleness, however, the slope did not offer an easy means of climbing out. Straight up toward the ridge crest, they might climb over snow so hard-packed by the slide that it should be stable underfoot. But hanging precariously at the top was a huge cornice that hadn't come down. Even if the overhanging snow stayed in place until they reached it—and there was no reason to suppose it would—they would never get over the suspended mass without breaking it loose.

The alternative was to climb the edge of the avalanche's path. But without snowshoes, they would plunge in up to their thighs.

Verek set off, up the packed snow. He didn't look back to see that Carin followed. The wizard worked his way at an angle toward the loose stuff beyond. When he reached the powder, he sank a boot out of sight, then punched in with his other foot.

Carin stayed on the packed surface, watching Verek wallow laboriously up the slope. Every few steps, he paused to rest. The strain of his effort showed in his heaving shoulders. It was no longer morning, but midday when Verek finally gained the ridgetop and disappeared over it.

His hard-won passage had left a path that Carin could follow. She worked her way up it, staying carefully in the track Verek had made to avoid triggering another snow-break.

When she got to the top, she found the wizard flat on his back, breathing hard. He lay with his eyes closed, and the folds of his cloak covered his bare hands.

Carin crunched past him without speaking. She walked over to pick up her hiking staff; it waited in the track of the sled where she'd dropped it. She squatted on her heels, slipped her hand out of her borrowed mitten—the glove was big for her, but warm—and studied her cuts and scrapes. Already the wizard's ointment was mending Carin's torn flesh.

She looked up to see the woodsprite returning. The creature sparked through the trees beside the trail, approaching from the west, as bright as a speck of the sun. It called to her, breathless with the speed of its travel.

"How pleased I am to see you out of the valley," it said as it came to rest. "Those provisions which the mage requested await you, not so very far down the trail. The deer were keen to push on, but I kept them in check until the boy could unload a few parcels."

"Good work," Carin murmured. "I'd love a little tea and something to eat." She kept her voice down as she eyed the prostrate figure nearby.

Verek's fur-trimmed hood was up, but a few strands of his hair straggled out of it. Carin stood and took a step toward the wizard, her fingers tingling to lay claim to the "witch hair" she still needed.

But at that moment Verek opened his eyes. He flashed her a look that could freeze stone, and Carin stopped where she was.

"Go softly, mistress," he growled. "In future, if you contrive again to throw us off a mountain, it will be you slogging back up through eighty spades of snow, with myself following at my leisure."

Carin shrugged. She backed off and dropped her gaze.

As the wizard heaved himself to his feet and started down the trail, Carin fell in behind. Even without snowshoes, the walking was good in the tracks the sled had laid down. The sun was not two hours past its zenith when they reached the supplies Lanse had left for them. The boy had even thought to drop off a pan and mugs.

The wizard scooped the pan full of snow. He set it on a flat rock out of the wind and snapped his fingers at it: they had water, boiling hot. He tossed in a generous measure of tea as Carin unwrapped a loaf of Welwyn's dense, filling cake. Made with raisins and nuts in a batter rich with eggs and milk, the cake was a meal in itself. Verek used his dagger to slice the frozen loaf. He laid the slices on the rock beside the pot of tea. Another snap of his fingers and the slices were hot, as if fresh from Welwyn's oven.

Carin poured the tea. They hunkered beside the rock to eat.

The hush that hung over the meal was the uneasy silence of two people who weren't saying what they were thinking. The sprite, lodged in a tree overhead, seemed bent on lightening the mood.

"I once saw two bear cubs slide down a snowy slope," the creature began conversationally. "They seemed to rather enjoy themselves. But then, they didn't bring the whole mountainside down upon them. What is good sport for young bears is not, perhaps, the best thing for you two-legged creatures who go over the snow with baskets on your feet."

By way of reply, Verek reached for the smaller of the two sets of Briga bearpaws that Lanse had left for them. He tested the rawhide lacings and shook his head.

"The girl won't get far over the snow on these," he said. "Oblige us, sprite, with more of your swift message-running and go tell the boy to drop off a bundle of hide thongs from among those he packed for repairs. These" — Verek fingered the strips that crisscrossed the snowshoe's frame—"are weak and must be replaced."

"Shall I also tell him," the sprite inquired as if warming to its messenger's job—"that you are safely back on the trail and will make haste to rejoin him?"

Verek nodded. "Yes. Give him what tidings you will. But now, pray begone. The miles between us lengthen with each moment you delay."

The creature sparked away. Three flashes and it had vanished into the snow-frosted treetops.

"Good riddance," the wizard muttered. He put down the snowshoe, reached for his tea and sipped it … and studied Carin over the mug's rim.

She tensed. The uneasy silence between them was ending. She was about to hear what Verek had on his mind.

He arched an eyebrow at her. "If I thought you would speak the truth, I'd ask my questions bluntly: Did you inflict upon us the events of this morning through sheer clumsiness? Or did you have a reason for tumbling us down the slope and nearly killing us both?" He shook his head. "That I can get no trustworthy answer from you leaves me to wonder at those two possibilities, the one more improbable than the other."

Verek gestured at the snowshoes. "For a fortnight I have watched you glide easily on those, handling yourself like one mountain-bred. Am I now to suppose that you lost your footing on a flat ridgetop, at *precisely* the moment which would take me over the edge with you?" He scowled at Carin. "That your foolishness was deliberately done, I can little doubt. For what purpose, however, I cannot guess. If you meant to send me to my death, why dash water in my face to rouse me to life? You only had to leave me as I lay, and the elements would have done the killing for you, cleanly and quietly."

Carin said nothing. When the mood to talk came upon Verek, silence was generally her best response.

"I wonder," he went on in a thoughtful voice. "Did you find your plan upset, when it was not myself alone who slid down with the snow? Had you meant to keep yourself back? But failing in that, you feared to let me die. Perhaps you doubted that you could manage a reascent without my help." He sipped his tea. "That would seem the likeliest case … if you hadn't grabbed me to you and held on fast, over the ridge and down, as unshakeable as a snapping turtle until the rush of the snow tore you away."

Verek pushed his hood back and rubbed his head where Carin had yanked out a hank of his hair. "I fancy that some mountain bird will weave a bit of Ruain into its nest, when spring reveals the part of me that's now buried, by your hand, down there." He gestured at the slopes that stretched below them.

Carin still held her tongue, provoking a sigh from the wizard.

He reached for the pot of tea and refilled Carin's mug and his own. Then he raised his cup to her in a mock toast. "Again you've bested me. I confess myself utterly confounded."

Carin popped her last bite of raisin cake into her mouth and chewed slowly. She washed the cake down with a little tea. Then she held up a face that she hoped looked innocent.

"I tripped, that's all." She shrugged. "Sorry. You know I'm not usually that clumsy." Carin looked at the wizard as directly as she could. Without the headband to tamp down the fires of sorcery, they smoldered visibly in Verek's eyes now. "It is lucky we weren't both killed," she admitted. "If the sprite hadn't been there to help, I probably wouldn't have got to you in time. You were buried much deeper than I was."

Verek gave her a long, searching look. Carin gazed back at him, although the urge to avert her eyes was as strong as a drowning swimmer's desire to breathe.

"Humph," the wizard grunted.

He rose to his feet. "Come." The movements of his bare hands were sharp and quick as he lashed on his snowshoes and crammed their empty tea mugs into his pockets.

Carin hastily bagged the uneaten cake. Then she strapped on bearpaws that did not need mending.

"Here," Verek ordered brusquely. He thrust the empty pan at Carin. "As you go gloved and I bare-knuckled, you'll carry this."

She took the pan in one mitt, her hiking stick in the other, and fell in behind as Verek shoved off down the trail. But before they'd gone far, Carin was crowding up behind the wizard, as near as she could get and not step on his heels.

"Lord Verek." She didn't quite shout at him, but she spoke up to be heard over the crunch of their rapid strides. "Will you tell me something?"

Verek stopped so suddenly that she couldn't avoid him: again they collided. The wizard's efforts to prop them up proved more successful this time, however. Both kept their feet.

"Excuse me," Carin mumbled as she disengaged and backed away with all the speed that was manageable on snowshoes. She looked up at Verek, drew a breath, and pressed on. "Why don't you just use your magic to take us to Lanse and the deer? For that matter, why don't you spirit us over these mountains to wherever we're going? You've got the power to do it. But you're using your magic just to make fire or boil water or heat a little bread."

Carin gestured back toward the avalanche slope. "The way you dug yourself out back there, that's the strongest wizardry I've seen from you since we left Ruain. I understand why you'd avoid being obvious when people are around. But we're alone up here." She tilted her head. "Why not cast a spell or two to make this trip go easier?"

For a moment, Verek didn't answer. He only stood looking at Carin with an expression that was quite somber—and maybe a little miserable.

Then he raised his bare hand from the folds of his cloak, and with the back of one finger stroked her cheek. Carin stood stock-still, powerless to move … or to stop the color from rising in blood-warm waves over her face.

"I make fire," he whispered in a voice like a labored breath, "because we must have it, and because my kindling of a blaze is not as conspicuous as are nature's own terrible illuminations. My escape from my snow-tomb, however, was the heedless act of a mind dazed with cold and fear. Had my wits stayed with me, I would not have made that magic; it was a mistake. It may be seen and known … by one who watches … as a manifestation of the power.

"I tell you distinctly, *fileen*: also mistaken is this notion of yours that we are alone in these mountains. There is a presence in these peaks from whom I would hide us. But I fear that I have failed to do so."

Verek dropped his hand from Carin's face, and he turned his gaze to the west.

* * *

They caught up with Lanse where he'd pitched camp at the end of the deers' day's run. The blizzard caught them all before Carin had finished hollowing out her snow cave.

Verek took the shovel from her. Tersely he ordered Lanse to see to the deer and Carin to secure their food and supplies.

As the wizard commanded, she doled out bread, jerked meat, cake, water, and a measure of *dhera* for each of them. She slid Verek's rations up the tunnel to his snow shelter, left Lanse an untidy heap he could stow for himself, and got her own provisions to her just-finished burrow in time to serve the wizard in her usual way, as airhole spotter. Reemerging to a gale that stung her face, Carin secured the camp gear under the tarp on the sled. With Verek's help, she lashed down the canvas and checked that the sleigh was reliably anchored.

The wizard saw her back to her cave, conjured a witchlight orb for her, and tossed another one to Lanse. Then he dived into his own shelter as the storm turned the close of day into a white fury of wind and snow.

In Carin's den, all was calm and quiet. She slept. The witchlight, when she woke, cast its same pleasing illumination. The wind, as she crawled partway down her cave's entrance tunnel to listen for it, had not abated. So she ate, drank a little *dhera*, and went back to sleep. Cut off from natural light, she lost track of time. The glowing orb never flickered, never faded.

This cave was roomier than the one she'd dug without help. It was long enough to stretch out in. By slouching a little, she could sit up without the top of her head brushing the ceiling. When she couldn't sleep any more, Carin propped herself up, pulled the three sheets of paper out of her pocket, and passed the time extracting more words from Legary's ensorcelled narrative.

What revealed itself, however, was hardly useful. Each quick uncovering of the bewitched paper brought up only a *was*, or a *shall*, or an *in* or an *on*. The tantalizing phrases that had once risen to view seemed more deeply buried than ever.

Carin sighed, and cursed her luck. "My fingers were in his hair," she muttered. "If I'd held on, I'd have what I need."

Carefully she unwrapped her collection: three hairs from Welwyn's head, one from Verek's. She jerked a single strand from her own mane and laid the auburn shaft beside the black one and the salt-and-pepper threesome.

Could she work the spell with fewer than the prescribed number of hairs from each "witch's" head? No, she shouldn't try it. Chanting the wisewoman's rhyme when she had no circlet of braided hair to look through had seemed to do more harm than good. Legary's writing was less decipherable now than before. Carin wouldn't risk compounding her error by weaving too small a ring of magic.

Patience, she counseled herself. *Watch for a second chance — and don't bungle it.*

Carin put Legary's narrative away, with her precious cache folded securely within. Then she snuggled back into her rabbit-fur robes and lay gazing into the witchlight, letting her thoughts wander where they would.

And as surely as the tide returns to the beach, her mind took her back to Verek's manor house. Although she'd lived under his roof for only a month—and much of that time she'd been frightened half to death—there was *something* in that ancient, crumbling mansion which still called to her.

Was it Verek's library, with more thousands of books than she could read in two lifetimes? What she'd learned from her studies there had whetted her appetite for more. In his books she might discover secrets of the apothecary's art, and in time become a healer like the wizard. She might learn to conjure fire and light. Maybe the spell of "seeing" that she meant to use on Legary's ensorcelled writing could lift the veil from all the *Book of Archamon* and allow Carin to read the mysterious pennings of generations of wizards.

But was it, in fact, her love of Verek's books that seemed to call her back to his house? Could she still be hearing, not her own yearning for knowledge, but the voice of the wizards' well?

That voice, as lustrous as sea-spray in moonlight, was overpowering. It had summoned her only once, but with such authority that Carin even now could feel the force of it as she had felt it that night … irresistible, impossible to oppose.

She couldn't think about the well of magic without also remembering the dragon that she'd conjured to those waters: the Jabberwock that had risen, howling, when Carin read aloud the incantation from the *Looking-Glass* book. She hadn't meant to bring a bloodthirsty monster into this world. But Verek had demonstrated, with a sackful of chickens, what the Jabberwock's teeth and claws could do to living flesh.

The wizard had also established that the dragon would not answer to him. The incantation that summoned it must be recited in its native language by a native speaker.

And that was her. That had to be Carin's purpose on this journey. What else could it be?

"The time may come," Verek had told her, "when I will ask you to embark with me on an enterprise that will endanger both our lives."

That time was now. This struggle through the mountains had to be their venture into danger that Verek had foreseen months ago.

Carin rubbed her forehead. What else had the wizard said? He'd called the dragon "an instrument for good." And he'd talked about killing someone … killing one person so that millions might live … so that life itself might continue, on Ladrehdin and on other worlds.

In horror Carin had recoiled from him, convinced that *she* was Verek's intended victim. But he'd denied it. "I have in mind

247

another—someone who is a more urgent threat to this world than you are," he'd said.

Carin's skepticism countered: *That warlock sees threats everywhere. He even thinks the woodsprite is dangerous*—just because the creature belonged to another world, she supposed. Why else would Verek have warned her not to trust the sprite?

She raised her head and stared into the witchlight. In the orb, Carin seemed to see the flash of the sprite. She sat up and reached for the sphere.

Its crinkly shell filled her hand with a slight tingle but no heat. The clear white light burned cool—not like the sprite, which had a sort of warmth to its nature. At least when the creature got excited and sparked feverishly, Carin could feel the bark of its dwelling-tree grow warm under her hand.

"Don't listen to that warlock," she cautioned herself in a soft whisper. "He's trying to mislead you about the sprite. He knows that the two of you together are strong enough to stand up to him. If he can drive you apart, he can weaken you."

She returned the orb to its niche. The witchlight glowed steadily, with none of a candle flame's shadow-dancing. Its stillness, however, was more hypnotic than a candle's flickering. Gradually, as Carin gazed into its unwavering light, she began to fancy that it stared back. Was the orb *watching* her?

Starting up, Carin grabbed the sphere and dug her other hand into the nook that had held it, scraping out snow to widen the space. She jammed the orb into one end of the enlarged cavity and packed loose snow in front of it to hide the thing from view, leaving one side uncovered. Only its light remained, shining into the open end of the cavity and reflecting out into her cave.

If anything peered from the orb, the watcher could see nothing now except the snow that surrounded it.

The watcher? Carin's thoughts swung round to Verek's claim that they were not alone in these mountains—that someone hidden amid these peaks might know of their intrusion and must object to it.

Who could be here in this wilderness of rock and snow? What reason could anyone have for dwelling in such awful solitude?

"Wizards have their reasons," Carin muttered under her breath. "Welwyn told you: every magician of Ladrehdin who survived the Wizards War sought these peaks, because ... " She trailed off, but the monk's voice finished the sentence in her head: *"In these mountains and forests it's hard, don't you know, to find a magician who does not wish to be found."*

At the edge of Carin's vision, something moved, briefly and gently. She sat still, alert to any repetition, however slight.

And there: it came again. Falling from the ceiling was a fine mist. No, not a mist—more like a sprinkling of hoarfrost. The delicate, feathery crystals caught the reflected witchlight like tiny cut gems.

Now the frosty shower fell faster. It cascaded from a crack that was forming in the roof of Carin's snow cave.

She grabbed for something to cover her head; she got her cloak. Diving under it, Carin half crawled and half rolled toward the tunnel that led outside. Where cave and tunnel met, she paused and looked back at the cracking ceiling.

The fissure in the roof widened, deepened—and broke. Punching through was a furry paw with its hooked claws fully extended. It was a cat's paw—but one large enough to break Carin's neck with a single swipe.

She screamed an oath. *"Drrrisha!"*

The paw withdrew, and chunks of snow filled Carin's ruined den as the roof completed its collapse. Snow buried her possessions and obscured the witchlight.

Carin wriggled into what remained of the tunnel. She hid there, her hands knotted in the folds of her cloak. Sweet *mother* of Drisha, how dark and close it was in the tunnel. Carin's breathing sounded harsh, loud in the narrow space.

But not so loud that other sounds could not reach her, from outside. There was the wind, still strong but beginning to let up. Through the treetops it moaned like a chorus of demons. Over the snow it swished, a thousand phantoms draggling ghostly trains.

Then, above the wailing of the wind, a scream rose. Human? Animal? Carin couldn't tell. It came again, as heart-stopping a shriek as she'd ever heard.

And footsteps pounded by, so close to the mouth of Carin's tunnel that she felt the jarring and got a faceful of snow grains.

Fear said to stay where she was. Reason argued otherwise. If the footsteps were those of Verek or Lanse gone to fight the cat, the battle might carry them to Carin's hiding place and bring swordsman or predator—or both—crashing down on top of her. She needed to be where she could see and evade the danger.

Carin squirmed into a night that was gusty, bitterly cold, and pitch black. She wrapped up in her cloak and stood listening for the boots that had stomped past.

From a short way off came the crunch of steps on a crust of snow. Then something screamed. Throatier than the first outcries, this was a scream not of terror, but of rage.

A man shouted. Not Verek—the voice was not as deep as the wizard's. It was Lanse out there in the darkness.

He shouted again, but his voice sounded muffled. Then came another cry—unmistakably human this time, and sharp with pain and fear.

A flash lit the darkness like a flaring torch, so bright for an instant that Carin blinked. Then the light was gone, quick as a spark. But in its wake came the snap and crack of wood breaking and the crash of a heavy bough that smashed through lesser limbs on its downward plunge. It landed with a thud— burying itself in the snow? Or was that the sound of timber striking flesh?

Clearly, the woodsprite had entered the fray—but on which side? Was the creature aiming for Lanse's skull, or the cat's?

"Sprite!" Carin yelled. She took one hesitant step in the direction of the flash and the noise.

Then a hand seized her by the collar and shoved her blindly toward the scene of battle. She shrieked and stumbled.

An arm wrapped itself around her. It hauled her upright and propelled her forward in one violent motion. Who it was that manhandled her, Carin had no doubt. She caught the scent of calendula.

"Forbear, sprite!" Verek shouted. He jerked Carin to a halt after a half-dozen steps that bruised and staggered her. His voice at her ear was as harsh as the night around them. "Accursed creature! Did I not warn you what price would be paid for treachery?"

A light blazed behind Carin, throwing her shadow and Verek's onto the snow. Was it the sprite? Or had the warlock conjured witchlight?

She tried to turn toward the beacon but she couldn't twist away from Verek. He grabbed her hair and jerked her head back, hard. Carin gasped. Pressing against her throat was an edge of cold steel.

"Do you doubt my resolve, sprite?" Verek yelled. "Then see who I have here. I do not depart from my word, you wicked changeling. If you have harmed the boy, then you'll watch my knife lay open the wench's throat."

Chapter 14

Unnatural Things

Down through the pine boughs a spark dropped. It fell groundward like a lost star.

"Stop!" shrieked the sprite. "Stay your hand, fiend! I've made no move against that detestable boy. My object was the giant of its kind that's ripped the throats from two of your animals. It's hauled one carcass away through the trees and left the boy bleeding in the snow. Shine your light on the sorry scene below me and see the truth of my words. If you would help your servant, then release the girl and hurry to him!"

The light at Carin's back flew over her head and lodged in the sprite's tree. It illuminated the carcass of a deer that lay on the snow in a mangled, bloody heap. Near it was Lanse, on his side, unmoving. The sleeve of his coat from shoulder to wrist was dark with blood, yet he still grasped his long-bladed dirk.

Behind Carin, Verek made a strangled sound deep in his throat. The knife at her neck and the hand that was knotted in her hair fell away. He darted past her to fall on his knees in the snow beside the boy. With a flick of his bare fingers Verek summoned another five witchlight orbs. They brightened the scene as if the sun had suddenly appeared in the middle of this dismal night.

Carin stumbled to the nearest tree, to lean against it and press her hand to her throat. Her hand came away spotted with blood. Crouching, she cleaned her palm on new-fallen snow and scooped up a handful to press to her neck. The cold deadened the sting of the knife cut.

For a moment Carin stayed like that, while the wind picked up the fresh powder at her feet and dusted it over her. The blizzard had died, leaving behind a surfeit of new snow with which errant gusts toyed. By the light of Verek's sorcery, Carin watched, as if from afar, as a swirl came sweeping toward them through the trees. Briefly it obscured the wizard and Lanse. Then its white needles struck her full in the face, making her gasp.

She jumped up, no longer distanced from the scene. Now was not the time for shock, disbelief, anger—all the emotions she might have vented on her assailant, if the night were not so cold and danger not still lurking, perhaps very near.

Kicking through the snow, Carin stepped to the wizard's side. Verek had finished a quick probing for broken bones; now he peeled back the boy's blood-soaked sleeve. The cat's claws had left long, deep gashes down Lanse's arm.

"Do you want me to lay a fire?" Carin demanded more than asked, biting off her words. "I suppose you'll need water—lots of it, and hot."

The wizard twisted his face up to hers and gave Carin a startled look, as though he was surprised to discover her standing there. Then he nodded. With two blood-smeared fingers of his right hand, Verek pointed at the timber that the sprite had attempted to drop on the big cat. It looked like the sprite had torn the entire top out of the tree and flung it down with great force. The broken-off limbs responded to Verek's magic by unburying themselves from the snow and splitting into firewood-sized lengths.

"Stack those for me," he muttered, his voice no longer full of menace, but subdued. "I'll kindle the blaze presently. First I must control this bleeding."

Neither of them spoke again for many minutes. Even the sprite held its tongue. It watched mutely from its tree as the wizard bent over Lanse.

Carin hauled the firewood to a spot clear of the grove. She made a platform on the snow from wrist-thick pieces of the green timber and crisscrossed those with heavier logs.

She was stacking the last of the wood when the wizard got to his feet with Lanse in his arms. Verek floundered through the powder, struggling with the boy to the mouth of Lanse's snow shelter. He paused there, to lay the boy on the snow and snap his fingers at Carin's stacked wood. It burst into flame. Then he wriggled feetfirst into the tunnel and dragged the boy in after him.

By the time Verek reemerged, Carin had one pot of water steaming, another of snow melting, and a third of tea steeping. The wizard crouched at the fire and dipped up a little hot water to wash the blood off his hands. He accepted a mug of tea from Carin and sipped it in preoccupied silence. Finally, with his tea half drunk, the wizard seemed to order his thoughts and find his voice.

"The boy has lost a deal of blood," he muttered. "When—or if—he will be able to resume this journey, I do not know. I must rely on you to take a share of the duties that were his. Will you tend the animals, give them water and tie them where they may find food of the sort they favor?"

Carin gave him a curt nod but no other answer. She rose, scooped up more snow, and stirred it into the pan where the first was melting. The deer would need several firkins of water. Then she started for the grove where the three surviving Trosdans were tethered … and where one carcass lay in the snow, bathed by the light of Verek's uncanny orbs and rapidly freezing solid.

"Wait," the wizard called, and Carin stopped.

Verek brushed past her on his way to the sled. He unlashed and threw back the canvas and shifted packs until he uncovered an item of gear that Carin had not seen since they loaded the sled in Welwyn's glen. It was the leather case that held "her" indigo bow.

The wizard drew the weapon out, braced it expertly, and put the bow into Carin's hand. She accepted it without a word, blinking from the wizard to the weapon and back again.

"The cat is most likely too gorged on the meat that it made off with, to return soon for its other kill," Verek said. "But we've hours yet until sunrise, and I would not have you straying far from the fire, unarmed. If the sprite can be trusted to look out for you—and evidently you are a better judge of its character than I am—then set the creature to watch for danger while you tend the animals."

Verek cleared his throat, then added, "Walk with me to the boy's burrow. You shall have his arrows."

The wizard started to reach for Carin. For a moment his hand hovered above her shoulder. But then he withdrew it, not touching her, and still making no turn toward Lanse's den.

"If the beast appears, cry out," he muttered. "Send the sprite to fetch me. Do not face the cat alone—unless it attacks so swiftly that you have no choice. If it comes for you, shield yourself with the deer. Better to forfeit another of the team than to lose your life."

The wizard paused. Though he stood barely an arm's length from her, Verek moved still closer until a fold of his cloak brushed Carin's fingers where they curled around her bow.

She wanted to back away, but she couldn't. Verek's eyes held her. The flash of the fire—or a glimmer of magic—reflected in their black depths.

"If you are in mortal peril," he whispered, "do not rely solely on the weapons of mortal men. You are only a novice with the bow. Your greater strength is in the *wysard*'s art. Call on the power firmly but with respect, and it will serve you."

Verek's gaze bound Carin to him another moment. Abruptly then, he stepped past her and returned to the fire.

Using his cloak to protect his hands, Verek picked up the pot of steaming-hot water and carried it to Lanse's snow cave. Carefully he slid it into the entrance tunnel, pushing it ahead of him as he crawled inside.

Shortly after Verek had disappeared within, a quiver of arrows slid down to the mouth of the tunnel. Carin stepped over and picked them up. For the first time in more than three months, she was armed.

She shouldered quiver and bow and went to water the deer. While they drank, Carin took a pine-knot torch from the fire and began the search for fresh grazing. The animals had consumed everything edible near camp. At last Carin located a lichen-covered jumble of boulders that rose out of the snow worrisomely far from the fire.

"That's a good place for a big cat to hide, don't you think, sprite?" she muttered to the spark that dogged her steps.

"Indeed," the sprite replied, its voice thin and anxious. "Do wait here and permit me to check for tracks. Such a huge creature could hardly approach through fresh snow and not leave us a sign of its passage."

Watchful, Carin stayed where she was while the sprite flitted from tree to tree, near the ground. It made a circuit of the heaped boulders. When it reported nothing amiss, Carin jammed her torch into a chink in the rocks and hurried back to the grove where the deer were tethered.

One by one, she teased the three survivors to the new feeding ground, charming each with a witchlight orb that she plucked from the trees around the cat's kill. The deer stepped along willingly, with their bright, interested gazes darting from the light Carin held to the woodsprite that sparked ahead to guide them. Their wild-eyed distress at their mates' slaughter had faded. Each deer took in its new surroundings with a brief glance, then fell to grazing as Carin tossed each orb into the rocks before retracing her steps to collect another Trosdan.

Two of the survivors were the more lightly built lead deer. The third—the team's one remaining heavy puller—was so eager to join its fellows that it threatened to drag Carin. Her third witchlight hit the snow as she made a two-handed grab for the beast's halter. When she had the animal securely tethered, Carin retrieved the dropped orb and set it amid the boulders with the other lights. They bathed the rocks in a comforting glow.

Would their brightness repel the cat?

Or attract it?

At the thought, Carin unshouldered her bow, nocked an arrow—and hit what she aimed at, but barely. The head buried up in the target pine, as far from the middle of the tree's bole as it could be and not have missed completely.

"That's not a bad try," she said aloud, determined to be optimistic, "from someone who hasn't touched a bow in months."

"A credit to her teacher," commented a clipped voice at her back.

Carin whirled. Verek stood there with his back against a tree, appraising her.

Breezy though the night was, Carin's own footsteps crunching the crusts of snow were perfectly audible over the moan of the wind. Yet she hadn't heard the wizard approach.

She heard him now, and watched him closely, as he made his way to the jumble of boulders that the deer were stripping of lichens. He pulled the pine-knot torch out of the cleft where Carin had stuck it.

Verek held the palm of his right hand so close to the blaze that it should have burned him. He never flinched. The fire slanted away from his fingers as though blown by a steady wind. Subtly, its color changed. Joining the reds and yellows were flickering tongues of blue and white.

The wizard dropped his hand. The flame licked upward again, seemingly free of his influence. But it was no longer a natural blaze. The wood and resin of the torch did not crackle. The fire didn't consume them. When Verek handed the torch to Carin, she took it knowing it for magian fire.

Verek jerked his head in the direction of their cave-pocked snowbank. "Mingle this with the flames of our campfire and they will burn high through the night. If the cat returns for the remaining carcass—and it would be bold to do so, after the uproar that met its first foray—then a blazing fire should blunt its curiosity about dens in the snow and the sleepers within." Verek folded his arms. "To judge by the state of your den, you were nearly clawed out and eaten like a snow-hare. Am I right?"

Carin nodded. She gave him a terse account of the cave-in and her escape.

"I'm freezing out here," she added. She raised the torch in one of her bare hands and her bow in the other. "My gloves and everything else got buried when my roof fell in."

A sudden gust whipped up the powder around them. In the blowing snow, Verek became a specter of the winter night. He was a white-veiled figure indistinct around the edges, faceless under his fur-trimmed hood. Carin shivered.

The apparition spoke. "I will stay out here and guard these animals. Go back to camp." Verek gestured at the magicked torch he'd given Carin. "Stoke the fire as I have told you, but do not lie out by it. Once you have touched these flames to those, the campfire will not need tending, and I want you out of this wind. Take my bed."

"Your bed?" Carin needed a moment to digest this. "Oh. Your snow cave. You don't mind me going in there?"

Verek tilted his head slightly. "While I am on watch, you may as well have shelter. I'm hardly being generous." He shrugged. "Mine is a gesture that costs the giver nothing. But it behooves one who has wronged another to make amends as best he can."

Carin stared. Oblique though it was, Verek's remark was as much an apology as she had ever heard him make.

Adding to the wonder of it, his contrition didn't seem to end there. "Sprite!" he called. He pushed back his hood. "Do you hear what we say here?"

"Every word," the creature piped from the same tree that, until a few moments ago, the wizard had stood under. "It's poor compensation you offer, you know, for holding a knife to the throat of an innocent who'd already bled on the snow for you, saving you from a cold grave. You would do better to beg her forgiveness for having so abused her."

If Carin had had a hand free, she might have put it to her throat at this reminder, to feel again the tender spot where Verek's dagger had nicked her skin. But she only stood quietly and listened.

"What must I do, mage," the woodsprite went on, as sharp-voiced as a clewbird, "to assure that you do not act again in so mistaken a manner? Shall I keep still, watching from afar and doing nothing, should danger again threaten the boy or you? If there is the least chance, that by my actions I may bring harm to my friend Carin, then I promise you, warlock, I will be as small and quiet as a bud. Let the monsters devour you! Better that, than I rush to strike your enemy and have for my reward the death of my friend."

As the sprite finished, Verek drew in a long breath through his nose. Then he let it out slowly. His right hand made a fist.

259

Carin ignored the sprite's angry sparking. She watched Verek's hand. Maybe the wizard could not hurt the sprite with his magic. But that hand would signal his intentions, if he meant to try it.

Slowly, however, Verek's fingers relaxed. The wizard took another deep breath.

"If you are quite done," he growled, "then give me leave to speak as I began. That both you and the girl have a grievance against me, in consequence of my misjudgment tonight, I acknowledge. I do not doubt that both of you will have satisfaction from me, before we three part company. Be that as it may: pray choose a better time than this to seek a reckoning. Other matters press tonight."

Verek lifted his chin. "I ask a service of you, woodsprite, on the girl's behalf. Return with her to the snow-slope where we camp and mind the sleepers and the cat's abandoned kill. If the monster comes again, alert me. I cannot watch both there and here. It's the deer, I think, that are in the gravest danger, and so it's here that I must stay. To lose another of the beasts could be our doom. We will not find the crossing of these mountains easy now, with only three Trosdans to take us over."

He pulled his hood up and tucked the fur around his face. "In this rock pile, then, is my night's burden. Yours, sprite, is with your mistress. Can she rely on you? Will you watch and neither stray nor slumber?"

The woodsprite sparked a little closer to the wizard, as though it wished to be clearly heard. "I will watch, steadfast as the trees themselves, and from a branch with a view of all that moves. I won't be caught unawares again—by man or by monster."

Verek turned away without replying to the sprite. He didn't speak to Carin either, but dismissed her with a sharp jerk of his head.

With the sprite flitting alongside, Carin walked back to camp. There she touched the magian flame to their wood fire. Instantly the fire took on a magical aura of blue and white. She huddled beside it, shivering but too keyed up for sleep.

"Sprite," she called softly.

"I'm here," the fay murmured from just over her head.

"Tell me what you saw tonight—everything that happened. Until you lit things up and Verek made his witchlights, I couldn't see what was going on. I only know what I heard."

The sprite sparked down the trunk of its tree to be level with Carin's gaze. "Alas, my friend, I do not know all that occurred. I was fast asleep until a horrible scream woke me. Terrified, I was, that you were in deadly danger. When the cry came again I leapt toward it, and I saw the giant cat rip the throat from one of your animals. Another carcass lay on the snow at its feet—the first to scream, it must have been, and the first to die.

"And then the boy was there, like a shadow in the darkness." The sprite flickered brightly, warming to its tale. "With an angry roar, the cat swiped a paw at him. He yelled out and tried to stab the monster. But the cat was too strong and too fast. It slapped at him again and sent him sprawling.

"Hardly knowing what I did," the woodsprite added, "I dropped a limb on the beast. But the cat had already taken the first of its kills in its jaws and was sprinting away through the trees. The bough I felled barely brushed the monster's flank, doing it no damage.

"And then, dear girl, you hailed me, and a moment later I heard you cry out." Distress tightened the sprite's reedy voice. "Until that instant I'd had eyes for nothing except the battle below me. I looked for you, and saw—to my horror—the mage pressing a knife to your throat.

"'What madness is this?' I thought, for a moment too stunned to do more than stare. Then the fiend spoke, and I understood. He knew nothing of the cat's attack, but believed I had dishonored our agreement and was designing for the boy's life."

Carin nodded. The sprite's account filled in the scene much as she'd imagined it. Absently she drew one bare hand out of her cloak and started to stir the fire. But then she stopped short, touching nothing. Verek's magian flames were best left alone.

Go in, she counseled herself. *It's freezing out here, even around a magical campfire.*

But Carin still had a question to ask the woodsprite, although the creature probably could not answer it any more confidently than she could.

"Sprite," she whispered, "would he have gone through with it? Would that warlock really have killed me, do you think?" Carin touched her throat, where the blood that had oozed from the knife-nick had dried into a line of hard little beads. "I remember you telling me that I didn't have to be afraid of Verek anymore. But I *am* afraid of him, sprite. I've been scared of him since Ruain, when I thought he was going to feed me to the puzzle-book dragon. And that might still be his plan." She shook her head. "I don't trust him."

The sprite flickered in its tree. It came to rest a little higher, as if trying to glimpse the blackheart who minded the deer out at the rock pile.

"I think, my friend, that you are right to doubt the wizard," it said, "and that I must be more careful of him. I was so happy to join your company, I persuaded myself that now the mage and I understood each other, and all would be well." The sprite scoffed. "I won't be a saphead anymore. You may rely on me, Carin, to watch over you as the mighty *rhonabwy* pines guard these peaks.

"But you're trembling," the creature interrupted itself. "The night is too cold. Retire and sleep soundly. I will not slumber, nor let danger approach."

Carin thanked the sprite, then took her leave of it and crawled into Verek's snow cave. The first thing she did inside was to pull the witchlight orb out of its open niche. Just as she had done in her own den, Carin carved out a shielded space for the orb so that only its light reflected into the cave.

Having taken this precaution against being "watched," she turned to examining the wizard's lair. It was roomier than hers had been, and an oilcloth and furs covered its floor completely. Verek's sleeping robes were thrown back, as one would expect to find in a bed that had been hurriedly abandoned. Carin studied the spot where the wizard's head had rested, and she smiled. There, caught in the gray fur, were two long black hairs.

Her fingers were so cold, Carin could barely bend them. But she managed to comb the hairs out and lay them side by side on the shelf of snow that held Verek's saddlebags. That was all she could do for the moment. Braiding nine hairs into a neat circle would have to wait until her fingers thawed.

The wizard's furs wrapped Carin in soft warmth. But she couldn't sleep. Her eyes wouldn't close. She stared at her prize, the dark hairs that looked like inky threads against the snow. The cat that had mauled Lanse and rousted Carin out into the night had done her a strange service. If the giant feline hadn't caved in the roof of her den, she certainly would not be here now … breathing in the herbal scents that clung to the wizard's furs and eyeing two shed hairs from his raven head.

Nothing about them should cause Carin anxiety. But she did begin to feel a sense of disquiet. And gradually, her uneasiness deepened into real apprehension.

What was here? What was worrying her?

On the snow-shelf directly behind the hairs, Verek's saddlebags rested. As Carin focused on them, she recoiled with a sensation that went far beyond worry: this was revulsion. And the longer she lay looking at the wizard's bags, the more repugnant they became.

"Sorcery," she whispered to the walls. "That warlock is using magic to guard his secrets."

What did Verek carry in his bags that he would want to protect with this powerful spell of abhorrence?

The woodsprite's pretty wand, for one thing, Carin guessed. The honey-colored stick was as alien to the world of Ladrehdin as was the sprite—or herself. And if the warlock intended to free this world of all the unnatural things in it, then he could hardly have left the wand behind, hidden in his library in Ruain, could he have?

"There," she muttered aloud. "You've put it into words. And you'll never get the thought out of your head now, will you? Admit it: you *know* what he's planning to do. You know how he means for this journey to end."

Carin shot out her hand and picked the two precious hairs off the snow near the bags. Her fingers prickled, partly with the warmth of returning circulation, but partly because the move was like reaching blindly around a rock where a snake or a scorpion might lie in wait. She couldn't yank her hand away fast enough.

She rolled over to face the opposite wall. The feeling of aversion didn't entirely leave her then, but it dwindled from an almost nauseating disgust to a mere dislike of the packs at her back.

As she lay on her side under Verek's sleeping robes, Carin fished in her pocket for the three sheets of paper and what was folded within them. Carefully she added the black strands to her collection, and refolded and pocketed the sheets.

With her prize secured, she lay quite still, closed her eyes, and took deep, slow breaths. Gradually her mind quieted. Her body relaxed. Though approaching the threshold of sleep, Carin lingered this side of it, vaguely aware that nothing remained in the cave to trouble her now. There was nothing detestable about the packs behind her. What could there be, in fine leather fitted with brass, to fill her with disgust?

Slowly, Carin rolled over. With her eyes still shut, she sat up. As gently as if they sought the face of a lover in the dark, her fingers reached for the saddlebags. They brushed the leather. Their tips slid under the flap, feeling for the pouch's lip and whatever the warlock might have stowed in his bags.

"By all that's unholy!" Carin breathed as her fingers met something that was *not* kidskin leather. This had a sliminess to it —

— And worse, *it moved.*

She gasped, jerked her hand away, and opened her eyes.

From the snow-shelf where Verek's packs had been, two grinning skulls looked out at Carin. The strips of rotting flesh that hung from them writhed with maggots. A stench of decay filled the cave. Her fingers that had touched the illusion bore a brown, mucky stain.

"Phew!" Carin clenched her eyes tight shut and willed the skulls away. "Get out of here," she told them. "You're not real — not the way you look, or the way you feel, or the way you *stink!*"

She fanned the air vigorously and waited until the odor had dissipated before she opened her eyes again. The illusion was gone. Only Verek's saddlebags rested on the shelf. The stain on her fingertips was neither putrefaction nor worm-slime, only a sooty smudge from the campfire.

"You win, warlock," Carin muttered to the packs' absent owner. "Keep your secrets. I have my own." She touched her pocket.

She turned her back to the bewitched saddlebags, curled up under Verek's furs, and tried to summon the sleep that had nearly come before. Carin's slow, deep breaths caught no whiff of corruption, only the scents of the wizard's healing herbs. Quieting her thoughts took a little longer this time. But before the night was over, she slept.

* * *

Verek evicted her midmorning.

"The boy will live," he replied, gruffly, to the question that Carin asked him over tea and a late breakfast at the magian campfire. "He is too weak to travel. We must remain here another night at least. And I must sleep. The day is yours, therefore, to do with as you will."

The wizard stood and stretched. He looked tired.

"I trust you'll be safe enough in the sunlight," he said, "for the cat is a night-hunter. But be vigilant. Game is scarce in these mountains this winter. If the beast is hungry, it may come prowling back to our small herd before darkness falls. I caution you again as I did last night: if the monster appears, summon me. Do not try to face it alone."

With that, the wizard disappeared into his snow cave. Carin finished her breakfast, then checked on the deer. The three surviving Trosdans seemed content with their new "pasture." The boulder field wasn't yet denuded of lichens. Today she could take her time and search out fresh grazing while the sun shone.

Following the trail that she and the deer had made last night, Carin walked to the grove where the cat had attacked Lanse.

The woodsprite met her there, calling down a greeting from a high branch.

"Doesn't the light of day paint a fairer face on all," the creature piped, "whether roving traveler or rooted tree?"

"Things always do look better in the morning," Carin agreed. "But this picture is missing something." She gestured at the grove. "Where's the dead deer? Where's the blood? The snow was covered with it. Now I don't see a drop."

The sprite sparked down close to the ground. "The mage busied himself early today," it said, "with removing all evidence of last night's trouble. He took the ax to the carcass and chopped off the good meat. That, he put on the sled. What was left, he burned.

"And an odd fire it was," the sprite added. "Although it consumed the deer's remains and even the blood that was spilled last night, it did not melt the snow. The mage snapped his fingers and queer blue flames sprang up everywhere. The whole grove seemed ablaze. I leaped to the far side of the snowbank to be clear of the inferno. I felt sure the pines would ignite." The sprite flickered in a good imitation of a flashing blaze.

"I'd hardly gained my new post, however," the creature went on, "before the fire died. As the mage walked away, I returned and discovered the spot as you see it now—the trees unharmed, the snow pristine, as though no violence had ever touched this place."

Carin nodded. "That warlock is good with fire. He can make it hot enough to singe the sun, or cool enough to hold in your hand." She patted the pine where the creature sparked. "I'd worry about him killing you in one of his fires, except I know you can outrun him. You must be tired, though, from all your jumping through the trees. Verek is sleeping now. Why don't you get some rest, too?"

267

"I am fatigued, I confess," the sprite replied. "But I do not wish to leave you alone, not with a giant cat aprowl on this mountain."

"I'll be all right," Carin said. "I've got my bow. And anyway, the cat will probably den up until dark. You can watch for it then. I'd sleep better tonight, knowing that you and Verek both got some shut-eye so you won't be staggering around, dead on your feet after sundown."

"You're right, my friend," the sprite said. "Without rest, I'll be a saggy stem tonight. But you must rouse me if you see or hear the cat. I'll drop a tree on it and break its back. Promise me you'll call out if you need me."

Carin promised, and the sprite withdrew deep into the grove, where the sun wouldn't keep it awake.

After the creature left her, Carin stood quietly under the trees. She studied the unmarked snow at her feet. Here, Verek's magic had left no trace of last night's events. But beyond the edge of the grove, the cat's tracks were not obliterated. They showed plain.

She unshouldered her bow, fixed an arrow to the string, and stood a moment longer, studying the cat's huge pawprints. Then she whirled and walked back to the heaped boulders where the surviving deer grazed.

For the next hour or so, Carin worked her way through the forest that surrounded their camp, searching for another good patch of grazing for the Trosdans, looking out for spoor, and practicing with her bow. What Verek had taught her in one grueling afternoon session, months ago, came back as vividly as if the lesson had been yesterday. Soon Carin was hitting her targets, not by the barest margin, but dead center.

It helped her shooting, that the day was utterly calm. Last night's wind had died. The forest was still, except for an occasional sharp report from a tree expanding in the cold.

Carin's streaking arrows hissed audibly in the silence that pervaded the sunlit, motionless landscape.

By the time she finished the circuit around their now perpetually burning campfire, the sun had passed the apex of its low arc through the winter sky. Back with the deer at the field of boulders, Carin sat down on a flat-topped rock. She laid her bow and quiver nearby, on a stone out of the snow.

Through her layered clothing she worked her hand, and drew from her trousers pocket the neatly folded papers and the strands they held. She plucked the final two from her own mane. With quick fingers, she knotted the strands together and braided the "three hairs from the heads of three witches" — auburn, raven, salt-and-pepper — into a circle that was as big around as her wrist.

When her handiwork was finished, Carin spread Legary's ensorcelled writing on her knee. As she held the braided circlet like a magnifying glass over the paper's top left corner, for a long moment she couldn't bring herself to recite the incantation. Could she bear the disappointment if this magic failed?

"Say the words," she ordered herself. "Let's see if I really have the gift."

Carin took a deep, shaky breath, then closed her eyes and muttered the charm in one exhalation:

"Peering-eyed woman, seeing all;
Keen-eyed man, seeing all;
Virile sons, nubile daughters,
Dark-eyed fey ones, seeing all."

The magic did not fail. Carin pried her eyes open and let out a little yelp. Perfectly legible through the circlet of witches' hair was the first stanza of a long narrative poem:

The evil in our midst has fled,
But not in time to save
The son I sacrificed
To arrogance.

Chapter 15

The *Wysard*'s Art

"'The son I sacrificed.'"

Glee gave way to gooseflesh that rippled along her arms as Carin read the line aloud and felt its significance sink in. Her suspicions were valid. Whether Lord Legary had delivered the deathblow himself or had ordered the execution, by his own pen he confessed himself guilty in the death of his son, Hugh.

She moved the circlet to peer through it at the second stanza, and felt her mouth go dry.

Only the issue survives —
The issue of a union corrupt,
And he with demon's taint
Upon his gift.

"Sweet mercy," Carin breathed. *He with demon's taint upon his gift* had to be "the tainted seed" that Legary had written about in his later narrative. In that second poem, the tainted one was unmistakably identified as the present Lord Verek—the warlock Carin had been living and traveling with, all these months.

"His own grandfather called him a demon," she muttered, feeling sick. "And that's coming from a murderer. Drisha's teeth, what a family!"

In two verses, Legary's ensorcelled narrative had not only confirmed Carin's worst fears, but also raised a disturbing new question. What had the elder wizard meant by "a union corrupt"? Had the marriage of teenaged Hugh and his unnamed bride been a bad match? If so, on which side?

With a mind that was divided between dread of what she might learn and determination to know the darkest of House Verek's secrets, Carin read on. Legary's words put rot in her belly.

How was I blinded?
How could I not see
The nature of the pestilence
I loosed upon this House?

"A tragic loss!" the mourners cried.
"But comfort shall you take
In the babe so gently held
In the grieving widow's arms."

Beseemly garbed in widow's weeds,
She led the progress to the tomb
And wailed and keened, and played her role
In the grotesquerie she wove.

The heir she suckled at her breast
Was two parts innocence, one part fiend.
Damn my ambitions! Damn —

A bare hand materialized as if from the ether. It snatched the paper away and almost took Carin's bespelled circlet of braided hair.

She dropped the circlet into her lap, acting more by instinct than wit. It disappeared in the folds of her green woolen cloak.

"By a cur's pocked hide!" Verek swore. "What in the name of Drisha or all that is unholy are you about here?" He stood over her, wrath personified, his glittering black eyes flashing from her upturned face to the paper in his hand.

Carin would have run, if the wizard hadn't been standing squarely in her way. Hemmed in on three sides by the piled boulders and blocked in front by a violently angry sorcerer, she could only stiffen at his feet.

For a moment, Verek was silent. His eyes skimmed the leaf Carin had torn from his treasured *Book of Archamon*. Then he cursed again, scaldingly, and crumpled the paper into a tight ball. He twisted away from her, and with a mighty heave like a spear-thrower's release, he hurled the wad at the sky. While it was yet airborne, he snapped his fingers. The paper burst into flame.

"No!" Carin shouted.

She sprang up and crashed into Verek, staggering him back a step. She beat at him with one hand as she stretched her other skyward toward the blazing wad. "Stop! It must not burn!"

The fire went out before the crumpled paper fell from the air. What landed in the snow was charred and blackened, but it was not wholly destroyed.

Carin lunged in its direction and collided again with the wizard. He caught her by the arms. His fingers clamped down with enough force to bruise her through her five layers of heavy clothing.

She cried out. Then she was hurled away from the rocks, to fly through the air as the wadded paper had flown.

Carin hit the snow near the paper, her landing so cushioned by the powder that the impact didn't knock the wind from her. She flailed at the fluffy stuff, struggling to right herself. Then her eyes fixed on Verek and she froze, as suddenly still as a portrait.

The wizard stood with his ungloved right hand outstretched, his fingers as stiff as tent stakes and all pointed straight at her. His look had something unearthly in it—something that scorched.

Carin tried to invoke divine help and found that prayer was beyond her capacity in that moment. She locked her gaze onto the wizard's outthrust fingers. Her skin burned in anticipation of the magian fire that would sear her, that would consume and destroy her, just as the wizard had sought to destroy stolen secrets.

How long they stayed like that—she sprawled in the snow, staring at the hand that could obliterate her; he leveling his fingers at her face, the look in his eyes unspeakably wild—Carin had no idea. Time ceased. She didn't even blink—

—Until, abruptly, the sorcerer lowered his hand and flung himself down on her. He pressed her into the snow so deeply that heaps of loose powder tumbled over Carin's face. Choking and spluttering, she tried to fend him off with one hand while she cleared her mouth with the other.

Verek caught the arm that pushed against him. Roughly, he hauled her up to a sitting position. He swiped at the snow on her face.

"Stop!" Carin spat. She slapped his hands away with stinging force. Then she crossed her wrists in front of her face, the same way a superstitious peasant might ward off a night-horror. She blinked to clear her vision and rubbed her face on her coatsleeves, wiping away the snow that stuck to her eyelashes. When she could see again, Carin glared at the warlock through the "V" of her intersecting wrists.

Verek, sitting before her in the snow, wore a liberal dusting of white in his hair and clothes. He was coatless, evidently having quit his cave too hastily to don his outer garments. His legs disappeared into the powder that their skirmish had churned up. Carin, with deepened alarm, tried to straighten one of her legs and discovered that his had hers pinned.

The wizard's arms were folded now. His long fingers rested above his elbows, and Carin couldn't help counting them: three fingers on his left hand, four on his right. A moment later, she cursed herself for letting her gaze linger so obviously. This warlock who seemed to know her thoughts must read volumes in a wide-eyed stare. Carin had hardly shifted her gaze from his left hand to his right before both were reaching for her again …

But slowly this time, easing their way past the mock defense raised by Carin's out-turned palms — proving that, as a counter-charm against a sorcerer, the old superstition of the crossed wrists was no more potent than the supposed power of rowan-wood had been against the sprite.

Where is the sprite, by the way? wondered that self-possessed extremity of Carin's wit that was the last to flee under duress and the first to return when her mental state improved. *What's become of its promise to watch over me?*

But maybe it was just as well that the sleeping sprite hadn't seen Verek lay hands on Carin. The creature would only shriek loudly and accomplish little to help her. Over the rock pile, there were no trees. And here in the snow, any timber dropped on the wizard couldn't fail to hit Carin as well.

The unhurried approach of Verek's fingers had closed the gap at last; he touched Carin's cheeks. She flinched and tried to turn away. But he pinned her face between his palms, forcing her gaze to meet his.

"Why do you persist in this?" he hissed, and drew her nearer to him. "How does it serve you to set your prying eyes upon my secret torments?" His warm hands slid over Carin's temples as he pushed the hair away from her face. He continued in a voice that was softly intense: "What do you care for deeds done long years ago? Aren't our present perils — and the dread of those yet to come — occupation enough for that fretful brain of yours?"

Carin found rational thought impossible with the wizard's hands on her. She caught his wrists and tugged his fingers out of her hair.

Verek let her. With her still holding his wrists, he lowered his hands to rest them on the skirt of Carin's cloak where it straggled over the broken snow between them.

She swallowed dryly, unable for a moment to speak. But then her words came in a rush.

"I persist because I want to know what kind of a man you are!" she cried. "Myra said you were a loving husband who grieved so bitterly for those he lost that he fell into madness. *Are* you that man? Or are you the devil your grandfather wrote about? 'He with demon's taint upon his gift'!"

Verek winced visibly, but he didn't try to silence her as Carin went on spilling out the words.

"I also want to know what kind of man your grandfather was. You must remember the day I found the *Book of Archamon*. What you can't possibly know is how sad I felt when I read what Legary had written on the book's final page—that poem from twenty years ago, as he lay near death. It was like I could feel the sorrow of the heart that cried those words. 'Dead was the first by guileful craft,'" Carin recited from memory. "'Dead was the third by blackest art.'

"'How the old wizard must have suffered,' I thought at the time, 'to see death come to half his house.' But then I started having doubts about him. I began to wonder about the old lord's dying confession. 'My crimes are great.' Why did he write that? 'The lad is slain.' I know he's talking about your father. But how did Hugh die? Who killed him?"

Only vaguely aware of her actions, Carin released one of Verek's wrists and pointed at the charred paper that lay in the snow not far from them. "For months I've tried to read what your grandfather hid in the book of magic. Today finally, I broke the spell and came a little closer to the truth. There on the page that you set afire, Legary wrote of a son 'sacrificed.' He called you — his grandson and heir — a 'fiend.' It's right there."

As Carin gestured again, Verek caught her hand and held it. Still he said nothing. He only eyed her with awful severity, and she felt the boldness running out of her like wine flowing from an open spigot. She pressed on before the cask emptied completely.

"What is the truth?" she whispered. "That sadness I felt when I first read your grandfather's words … Was that the sorrow of a man who was grieving for the dead children of his blood? Or was he confessing his guilt — his shame at having done something so terrible that he couldn't admit it, except in riddles?"

Carin looked without cringing into Verek's glittering eyes. "I want you to answer the question I asked you that night on the plain of Imlen: Did your grandfather kill your father? I also want to know if you're the fiend who drew a mother and her child to their deaths. *Did you drown your wife and son?* And afterward was it guilt — not grief — that drove you to madness?"

The wizard did not break his silence. Neither did he avert his gaze. He released Carin's hand and pointed without looking at the crumpled paper that lay near them. It flew to his fingers. Reaching them, the paper bore no trace of charring.

Carin stared, uncomprehending, as the restoration continued. The ball of paper that Verek cupped in his hand began to uncrumple. Slowly at first, then with astonishing speed, the wad opened and smoothed into an undamaged sheet. Even the fold lines were gone, where Carin had repeatedly creased the paper to fit in her pocket. The page from the *Book of Archamon* was as perfect as on the day she'd ripped it from the ancient volume.

Moreover, it no longer had a spell of concealment upon it. The paper lay draped over Verek's palm with its head toward him and its foot to Carin, so that the closing stanzas of Legary's narrative hung before her eyes. The lines were clearly readable. She scanned them quickly:

By the oath of my House,
And in these pages
Bathed in the light of the wisdom
Of Archamon, I swear:

The boy shall not fall to darkness.
As long as there be breath in this body,
I will guide him on the bright path,
And Morann shall touch him not!

Carin jumped as Verek pulled his other hand from her grasp. She'd forgotten that her fingers still circled his wrist.

The wizard took the smooth sheet in both his hands and refolded it. Then he slipped the paper inside his shirt. Although he sat in the snow wearing neither coat nor hood, he didn't seem to feel the cold. Carin's legs, however, were beginning to suffer, both from being stuck in the snow and from him sitting on them.

Her concern for her legs vanished immediately, though, as Verek grabbed her upper arms, seizing her this time with unnerving speed.

"By the powers, girl!" he barked, quitting his silence furiously. "No sooner does a thought pass through your head than you take it as proved! Haven't you already charged, tried, and condemned me, body and soul? Upon whom shall I call, then, to witness my avowal of innocence? Shall I swear it by Drisha? By Archamon? Is there any oath I could take that you would honor?"

Verek shook Carin hard enough to rattle her teeth. Then he pushed her away roughly, releasing her arms.

Carin nearly fell back into the snow. But she rocked upright again, flexing at the hips like a string puppet. The movement of her upper body sent one buried leg plunging sideways through the snow, nearly unseating the wizard. He caught her by the hands, steadying both of them. Then he pulled Carin to him, though she tried to hold back.

"I never thought to see a day," Verek breathed into her face, "when I would defend myself to a prying chit. Were it anyone else speaking these accusations, I'd rip the bleeding heart from the defamer's chest, set it afire, and stuff the burning organ down its owner's throat."

The wizard studied her. Apparently satisfied with what he read in Carin's eyes—a reflection of the nausea in her belly, surely—he went on. "But you, minx, may say these things and meet with nothing from me except my plea of innocence. I ask you again: By whom or what shall I swear? How do I make you accept my words?"

"Swear on your conscience," Carin whispered, looking him in the eye, "and I will believe you."

Verek's hands tightened on hers. Something went out of the wizard's dark gaze, like the fight fleeing the beast.

"If you only knew all that hangs heavy there," he murmured, "you might think it an unfit place to put your trust."

Carin shook her head. "I think it's a good sign, if it hurts you. It couldn't cause you pain if you lacked one."

The wizard brought Carin's hands together against the front of his shirt and pinned both of them there with one of his. His other hand—the mutilated one—took her by the chin. "Be assured that I note its presence daily," he muttered.

He continued then in a firm, clear voice. "On my conscience, I swear to you: I did not kill my beloved wife, Alesia, nor our son, young Aidan, whom we cherished. In the core of my heart, I may have suspected that they had not drowned by accident. But it was not until I read my grandfather's words in Archamon's great Book that I could bring myself to face the truth: that they were murdered … by one whose love of power surpassed even my grandsire's."

Verek held Carin's chin so firmly, she couldn't shut her mouth. "If you would condemn a broken man," he went on softly, "then know that he committed no crime worse than ambition. Lord Legary's ambition, it's true, led to the death of his son—that youth who was my father, whom I never knew. The knowledge of what he had done—of the grave mistake he had made—weighed so heavily on my grandsire's conscience as to make these accusations by a foolish little sylph smack of arrogance—such an arrogance as I would not tolerate from anyone but you."

The wizard's eyes held Carin through a long moment of silence, more forcibly than his hands. Then Verek turned her loose and got to his feet, not with his usual easy grace, but stiffly. "Drisha blind me," he swore. "I cannot say who the bigger fool is—you or me. For who but an ass would sit out here in the snow half dressed?"

Carin struggled mightily to stand. But the cold had prickled the blood in her legs, leaving them too numb to support her. She was sinking again into the powder when the wizard caught her arms. Before she could protest, he had pulled her out of the snow, slung her over his shoulder, and carried her to the pile of rocks where the Trosdans grazed. The deer eyed them indifferently. The affairs of men and women did not concern them.

Verek set Carin down on the same flat-topped rock he'd thrown her off of. He picked up her bow and quiver from the stone where they waited and put them into her hands. Then he stood looking down at her, his hands on his hips.

"There is not a *wysard* alive in the north of Ladrehdin," he said crisply, "who did not feel it when you broke Legary's spell of obscurity. Our incursion into these mountains could not be more obvious to an adept now, were we to blow horns and beat drums to announce our coming. I propose, therefore, to go after the cat. The beast that will not fall to steel may succumb to art— and we no longer have cause to go artless, have we?"

Verek gestured at the weapons Carin held. "Use them, but do not rely solely on them. If I flush the cat from cover, it may come here. Remember the wasteland dogs and save yourself as I once saved you."

Abruptly he turned away. With long strides, he made for the distant campfire.

"Wait!" Carin called to Verek's retreating back. "I don't understand!"

He ignored her. She watched him reach the snowdrift that held his den and Lanse's. He disappeared into the boy's cave, soon reemerged, and crawled into his own. When he came out again, he had his coat and cloak.

Verek drew them on as he walked to the grove where the two deer had died. He shouted at the woodsprite to wake up. A spark came to life in the treetops, then dropped down nearer the wizard. What passed between them was beyond Carin's hearing, but their conversation was brief. After a moment, Verek stalked off on the cat's trail. The sprite came flitting through the trees. It lit in the one nearest Carin's patch of boulders.

"Good day to you again, my friend," the creature called cheerfully. "I trust you've shunned that ill-tempered magician since we last spoke today? My, what a surly mood he's in! I am ordered—not asked, not invited, but *ordered*—to join you at these rocks. Indeed, I am pleased to do so. A chance to speak with my dear friend Carin is always welcome ... though I might have done with just a *bit* more sleep before I took up my watch."

The blood was flowing again in Carin's legs, filling them with broken glass. She stretched and kneaded them, but she didn't try to stand. The sprite obviously knew nothing of what had just happened near these rocks. She meant to give the creature no hint of it.

"Go back to sleep," she said. "Just because the wizard is awake doesn't mean you have to be. Stay in these trees close by, while I watch the deer, and I'll call you if I need you."

"That's most satisfactory," the sprite piped in tones that were already fading. "I do think I must doze again ... for only an hour ... if that will not ... inconvenience ..." The creature's sleepy voice trailed off mid-sentence.

Carin breathed a quick, soft sigh. Then she began examining the crevices in the rocks around her, searching for her circlet of witches' hair. It came to light at last, damp and limp, trampled into the snow. Carefully she worked it free, reshaped it with the tip of her finger, and sat looking at it as her thoughts whirled.

After everything it had revealed to her from Legary's ensorcelled writing, could she trust Verek's denials? If he was blameless in the deaths of his wife and son, then who was the murderer he accused?

One whose love of power surpassed even Legary's? There's no answer in that, only a new riddle. Carin frowned, toying with the circlet.

She closed her fist on it. Digging in her trousers pocket, Carin retrieved her copy of the verses that Legary had set down only days before his death. Verek hadn't discovered that page.

She glanced over her shoulder, then unfolded the paper. The stanzas on it were easily read and as familiar as the back of her hand. But was something else concealed within them?

Carin held the circlet over the page the way she would hold a sunglass that could set the paper ablaze. Quietly she spoke the charm of seeing. The words of the narrative responded by doubling their apparent size, but there was no other change. The paper held nothing beyond what was openly written there.

And as Carin reread Legary's deathbed "confession," the sigh that escaped her was one of—provisional—relief. She hadn't wanted to believe the old lord was capable of such evil, although he had seemed to think that his transgressions went beyond redemption. *My crimes ... my penance ... the lad slain ...*

"Slain," Carin whispered to thin air, "*because* of you and your ambitions, Legary, but *by* somebody else—somebody greedier than you were, your grandson claims. Who did it? Is there one killer at work in this story, or two? Did your son's murderer return all those years later to drown little Aidan and leave the House of Verek with no heir except for its present lord—the 'tainted seed'?"

Shaking her head, Carin slipped the page back into her pocket. She would find no new answers there. The solution to this puzzle lay in the narrative that she'd come so tantalizingly close to reading before losing the paper to Verek. She shut her eyes and struggled to recall the few stanzas she'd unveiled before the warlock tore them away.

What had Legary written about "the grieving widow," that mysterious lady who had lived under his roof for a decade after her young husband's death, and then had suddenly vanished? Something in the verse struck a discordant note:

> *Beseemly garbed in widow's weeds,*
> *She led the progress to the tomb*
> *And wailed and keened, and played her role*
> *In the grotesquerie she wove.*

What did Legary mean, she "played her role"? Was her grief for the dead Hugh only a pretense? Was that the "grotesquerie"? Legary's disapproval was palpable. Evidently Verek's mother hadn't been convincingly heartbroken over the death of Verek's father. She didn't convince Legary, at any rate.

Carin could picture the entire forbidden narrative as if it were an inscription carved into her thoughts, but with its middle sections defaced and unreadable. Her mind's eye went to the final two stanzas, which she had hastily skimmed while the paper lay across Verek's palm. In the closing line, an enigmatic name had appeared: *Morann.*

Who or what was that? What threat did this unknown entity pose? Theil Verek had been a boy of ten when his grandfather's pen declared that "Morann shall touch him not." Fourteen years later, Verek was a married man and had fathered a son, yet his dying grandsire had repeated the prohibition: *"Touch him not, Morann!"* What danger had hung over Verek as he was maturing into manhood? *Could it be the same menace that killed his father? The same, perhaps, that killed his wife and child?*

Carin had barely seized on that possibility when another thought came to her. This was no idle conjecture about events twenty and thirty years in the past, but a dangerous prospect for the present day. Could it be that the sinister "Morann" of Verek's youth was still out there, still threatening, and no longer constrained by Legary's interdictions against harming him?

"Maybe the warlock said as much," Carin muttered to herself. "After the avalanche, he talked about someone being up in these mountains … someone watching us. He's been trying to hide his magic. He doesn't want the 'watcher' to know we're coming."

She glanced around sharply. Then Carin pocketed the circlet, stood, shouldered her quiver and bow, and moved quietly to the patch of churned-up snow where Verek had sworn his innocence. Across it she paced repeatedly, distorting the signs of their struggle. The sprite had been too groggy to notice the traces before, and Carin didn't want the creature asking questions when it woke.

If these mountains hid a force so powerful that Verek feared to face it—and his grandfather before him had invoked taboos against it—then Carin wanted the sprite here near her, not chasing after the warlock to dash out his brains. A riled-up sprite might do just that, as a matter of honor, if it became aware of how Verek had chucked her around. But the creature's growing aggression would be better turned against the unknown threat in these mountains than directed at the wizard who might be their only hope of escaping that threat.

When the snow was too trampled to give firm evidence of the afternoon's skirmish, Carin stood still and drew the circlet back out of her pocket. It was an oddly pretty thing, with Verek's crow-black hair weaving between her rich auburn strands, and Welwyn's girding them up in light and shade. How could she have guessed that her use of the wisewoman's charm would so disturb the flow of magic on this world, that—according to Verek—every living wizard would feel it?

She peered through the ring again, studying the forest as she slowly turned. Carin's last recitation of the charm still held its power. The magian flames of the campfire—to the naked eye, cold blue in color—were dazzling through the ring, like flickers of lightning. Carin couldn't bear to look at them, even from this distance. She turned her seer's circlet upon an object nearer and dimmer: the tall pine where the woodsprite slept.

"Oh—!" She bit off a shriek of astonishment and not a little disgust. Seen through the circlet's magic, the sprite was no disembodied spark. It was ... what? A belly with its guts spilling out?

No, those weren't guts. They writhed outward from the central mass like the tendrils of a vine, twisted things that seemed to move deliberately, groping along the branches of the tree where the creature slept. Several of the tendrils had embedded themselves in the wood and appeared to be feeding on the tree. Others coiled tightly around the branches. The tendrils looked tough, wiry—strong enough to choke the life from a tree ... or a human being.

Carin gawked at the creature, trying without success to square the woodsprite's pleasant personality with its shape. It looked like an uprooted clump of the parasitic strangleweed that farmers in the south called "devil's-guts." Was this a true image of the creature's body?

She took a step toward the sprite's tree, intending to wake it and see whether that made a difference in its appearance. But a terrified scream from the deer stopped her.

Carin swiftly pocketed the circlet and whirled to face the field of boulders. As she turned, she unshouldered her bow. One hand drew an arrow from her quiver and had it on the string before her searching eyes found her target. When she saw it, she gasped.

The cat crouched on the highest rock above the deer. It stared at Carin with huge yellow eyes. Its fur, white with irregular black bands, blended almost invisibly with the snow and rocks. Nothing stood out clearly except for those eyes— their gaze unblinking, and colder than winter.

The giant dropped its head to study the three panicked deer below. Its hindquarters wiggled as it gathered itself for the jump. The tip of its tail—as black against the snow as Verek's hair—twitched with excitement.

Carin aimed her shot halfway between the head and the tail. The cat screamed and tumbled backward off its rocky perch.

But no sooner had she nocked a second arrow than the beast, spitting its rage, came sprinting around the base of the boulders, rushing at Carin over the snow. This arrow must fell the monster; there would be no time to loose another. And the prick of an arrow must be about as dangerous to the giant as a thorn in its paw. The weapons of mortal men would not stop this creature.

"Your greater strength is in the wysard's art." Verek's words flashed through Carin's mind. *"Remember the wasteland dogs and save yourself."*

A ghostly foursome of the dogs seemed to join the cat's attack—memory overlapping her present reality. Carin released the shot. At the same instant, she expelled her pent-up breath in an explosive shout of "Burn!" In the face of death, she felt euphoric—with the same sense of elation that had shot through her at the moment she transfigured Welwyn's twinkling orb into her own bit of magic, a spiny sea urchin.

The arrow struck. The cat burst into flames. Its agonized scream lasted no longer than a heartbeat. Then there was nothing on the snow between Carin and the boulders but a great heap of gray ash.

The roaring in her ears was like the sound of the surf pounding a distant shore. Carin collapsed into the snow, unable to tear her eyes from the cat's ashes.

In the tree behind her, the woodsprite was shrilling. "What's happened? What in the name of fortune has happened? What means all this shouting and screaming?" She could no more answer the sprite than if her tongue had been torn from her head.

Then Verek was there. He moved among the deer, resecuring their ropes and stroking their necks, calming the terrified beasts.

Of course. He must have been nearby all along, watching the cat's attack and magically kindling Carin's arrow at the final moment.

She watched the wizard approach her as though she were outside the event, looking in. He stepped around the ash-heap, pausing briefly to gaze at it. Then he reached Carin's side. He took her hand—she was still holding her bow—and pried open her fingers one by one. They were white-knuckled, aching from the force of her grip and as cold as death.

"Excellent," Verek murmured. "I am pleased that you have at last found the marrow of your powers."

Carin blinked.

"My powers?" she whispered, staring at him. "I don't understand you. I would have been killed if you hadn't bespelled my arrow to burn the cat."

Verek shook his head. "No magic of mine touched that shaft." He pressed the icy fingers of Carin's bow hand between his palms. "Yours was the voice that invoked the wizardry. And yours will be the magic that burns the last bridge."

Chapter 16

Choices

Lanse was strong enough to travel. But with his injured arm in a sling, he couldn't handle the lines of a deer team and sled. It fell to Verek to drive the Trosdans, which he did with a great deal of cursing and shouting.

In harness, the deer missed their dead teammates. By morning they stood in the traces forlornly, reluctant to get under way. When the sun dropped low, their uneven progress proved far easier to stop than the headlong runs they'd been making before the cat reduced their numbers.

No complaint was heard, however, from the snowshoers who followed the sled. The slower pace suited them. Lanse had to rest frequently. Carin now carried her few possessions, and what was left of the tea and dried fruit, in a pack on her back to take some of the load off the diminished team. Verek no longer stowed his heavy longsword on the sled; he wore it slung across his back, over his cloak. With his quiver, bow, and blade, and the dagger he wore at his side, he looked like a walking armory. Even that fit swordsman found breathing more difficult and rest stops more necessary as they climbed ever higher into the mountains.

The woodsprite, although it had no trouble matching their slackened pace, had developed a handicap of its own. More than half of each day, the creature slept. Often they would leave it behind as it dozed in some ancient evergreen. In a few hours it would catch up, full of apology and unable to account for its chronic drowsiness.

"Is it the cold, do you think?" Carin asked when the sprite huddled with her in a wind-whipped stand of spruces. She glanced up as a raven flew past, and watched the bird swoop and swerve in the grip of a particularly violent gust. "Or is it because we're so high? The air is thinner up here."

"I cannot guess," the creature replied, almost whimpering. "Truly I am at a loss. It's most provoking, this weakness of mine. Just as I was beginning to think myself master of the domain of trees, each day learning more of wood and how to wield it, I fall to this infirmity. I'm not much use to you like this, am I, dear girl? Should the mage break his promise to go easy with you, it's scant help I'll be if I'm a league behind and out of my senses in a pine."

It's scant help you've been for a week, Carin thought. But she suppressed the remark and told the creature little of the events that it had slept through on the afternoon of the cat's destruction. By unspoken agreement, she and the wizard had given the sprite and Lanse the same story: that the cat met its end with one of Verek's fiery enchanted arrows in its ribs.

Why the warlock favored a lie, Carin couldn't be sure. Her own reason was simple. The less evidence Lanse had of her growing powers of wizardry, the smaller the risk of rekindling his old hatred. The boy had made no overt move against her since Welwyn's glen. It was a state of affairs she wanted to continue.

But was she hiding her burgeoning abilities only from Lanse? In the dark of the night, when the snow-mantled slopes were far quieter than the turmoil inside Carin's head, the answer came as a clear *no*. Her misgivings about the sprite were growing from a vague uneasiness—planted by Verek, with his probably malicious suggestion that the creature couldn't be trusted—into a gnawing suspicion that the sprite's friendly ways might hide a harder nature.

I'm judging a book by its cover, cautioned the voice of reason. It was true that Carin's glimpse of the sprite through her seer's circlet had fed her uneasiness. *The creature comes from another world,* her rational mind argued. *Among its own kind, it might even be thought beautiful. If I find its shape ugly, maybe the fault doesn't lie with the creature, but with my way of looking at it.*

Even so, Carin couldn't shake the feeling that her magical circlet showed her something more disturbing than an unattractive body. The way the sprite's tendrils pierced the branches, they seemed to bleed a tree. Its sinews, wrapping around the limbs and coiling tight, looked like they could cut through any wood — which would explain the sprite's ability to drop tree branches on people's heads. All in all, the creature seemed as capable of choking the life from a tree as was the hated strangleweed that invaded coppices and farmers' fields down south. Maybe Carin's circlet had revealed, not just the sprite's outer appearance, but clues to its fundamental nature.

I'm imagining things, she tried to tell herself.

But maybe she wasn't.

A week after Carin used the circlet to break Legary's spell of concealment and to spy out the woodsprite, the mountains remained deserted. No mustering of wizards had descended upon them. No unwelcome visitor named Morann had appeared at their nightly camps.

So Carin dared to recite the charm again, this time turning the seeing on her "escorts." The morning was clear and cracklingly cold. She stretched herself behind a pillow of wind-drifted snow that offered an unobstructed view of Verek having his breakfast while a convalescing Lanse tended the deer. Thin, willowy Lanse …

She raised the circlet to her eye, and the boy became a brawny executioner in a black jerkin and a masked hood. Carin buried her face in the fur ruff of her hood to stifle her astonished swearing. Then she jerked her head up and peered through the ring again, only to see Lanse the executioner carrying his single-bitted ax over one shoulder as he walked to the campfire.

Carin dropped her circlet and stared. And in the pure light of early morning, the boy was himself again. He looked pinched with cold. The arm the cat had clawed was bound up in a sling under his cloak.

She marveled. Had the magic of the braided circlet revealed something of Lanse that did not lie on the surface? If so, what did his executioner's guise signify? Carin considered the three ruffians on the plain of Imlen—two of them dead by Lanse's hand, Verek had said. *That's it. The charm sees what he did in the past*, whispered some part of her that was more hopeful than convinced.

Tightly pinching the circlet's edge, Carin raised the ring to her eye once more. She must know what the magic would reveal to her of Verek—though the prospect of seeing into the wizard's depths put knots in her belly.

She looked long, her breath suspended. Slowly, Carin lowered the circlet. Her lungs resumed their work. She looked again, and her stomach settled.

The wizard was unchanged. From the glossy blackness of his hair to his long, deft fingers to the self-assured way he moved, he was the same man who had held a sword to Carin's throat in an autumn woodland and made her his.

No—not the same. The image through the circlet was not exactly right. The longer Carin studied him, the clearer the aberration became. Around the warlock hung a shadow, so faint and clinging so closely to his tangible self that it was nearly invisible. But as she watched, the shadow grew more distinct until it appeared as a somber duplicate imposed on Verek's form.

What was it? His double?

To meet one's double was unlucky in the extreme, for when a man and his wraith met face-to-face it was a sign of imminent death. Many times Carin had heard that favorite story of Mydrismas, the legend of the fisherman who saw his own wraith standing on a sandbar. His only safe path had been to address it boldly. "What's thou doing here?" he'd demanded. "Thou's after no good, I'll go bail. Begone wi' thee! Hie thee home." Whereupon the wraith had slunk off abashed, and the man met no early death, but lived to a ripe age.

The shadow that enfolded Verek, however, was not a double such as the fisherman had seen. It didn't face him. It clung to him like a second skin. And the wizard seemed as unaware of its presence as Carin had been before she trained her seer's circlet upon him.

She put the charm away. After that morning, Carin had nothing but time to mull over what the magic had revealed. Shuffling over the snow, toiling up steep slopes, burying her face in her arms to avoid the gusts that drove swirling snow plumes across the face of the mountain: Carin endured it by feeling little and thinking much. If Verek with his shadow and Lanse in his executioner's garb were images from their deeper selves, was it unreasonable to suppose that the sap-sucking tendrils and strangling sinews of the woodsprite proclaimed the creature for what it was?

* * *

A fortnight after the cat took two of their number, the surviving deer sadly showed the effects of overwork. Their long, thick hair barely hid their protruding ribs.

Carin watched them with mixed sympathy and anxiety. If the Trosdans died, the three snowshoers would break their own trail through the ever-deepening snow and pull their own sled, hauling the essentials of food, furs, tent tarp and ropes, the ax, and the bowcase that held Carin's indigo-blue weapon—discreetly returned to Verek's custody to avoid alarming Lanse. The boy would surely think his master mad for letting Carin go armed. He looked askance when the wizard handed her a shovel to carry, giving the other to Lanse.

But when Verek, in his efforts to spare the deer, abandoned his great sword to shoulder the ax in its place, Lanse could not hold his tongue.

"No, my lord!" he protested. "Do not cast it off, I pray you. Such a fine weapon—wielded by your grandsire and his before him—must not be surrendered to these soulless heights. I will carry it. My wounds are trifling. Allow me the honor of bearing the sword of Ruain, I beg you!"

Verek hesitated, holding the weapon across his mittened palms. The gold and garnets on its hilt shimmered in the cold sunshine. The warlock swept his gaze along the sheathed blade. Then he laid the weapon almost reverently on the rocks.

Carin said nothing, but she drew from her pack her only extra pair of felt-lined wool breeches. She held them out to Verek.

The wizard eyed her thoughtfully. Then he accepted the garment with a short nod of thanks and wrapped the sword in the sturdy cloth. The bundle fit invisibly into a crack where two standing stones angled together.

Your chances of returning along this trail to reclaim that heirloom are slimmer than quillwort leaves, Carin told him silently. She wasn't sure where the thought came from, but she trusted the truth of it.

Verek turned to Lanse and shook his head. "Your wounds are serious, and I would not see you waste your strength. Where we are going, we'll have more need of this"—he hefted the ax—"for hacking timber, not flesh." With a frown, the wizard quelled Lanse's further protests. He slung the ax across his back and shouted the tired Trosdans into motion.

Not another week passed before the wizard's prophecy was proved. The deer topped a rise that was thick with tall *yaran* cedars. They halted abruptly. Verek edged up to the head of the team, to stop just as suddenly. Lanse joined him.

When seconds passed with neither of them saying a word, Carin's curiosity brought her shuffling up along the other side of the deer team to stand with them. The sight that met her eyes rendered her as speechless as her companions were.

Below gaped a canyon, steep-walled and packed with a sloping mass of snow. To the left, suspended like a mountain monarch's crown above an immense ermine train, was a frozen waterfall, its facets diamonds in the sun. Down-canyon, the snow-filled chute sliced away through the rocks. Beyond, on the opposite rim, trees grew thickly. But if ever a bridge had crossed this gorge, no trace of it now remained.

Verek was the first to recover his voice. "Unhitch the deer, Lanse," he growled, "and find them something to eat. I'll be a time at this task."

Ax in hand, the wizard gazed up at the cedars that flanked this side of the canyon. He selected one which towered above the rest and struck it a mighty blow. The ax blade bit deeply.

Carin listened for the woodsprite's shrill cry, but it didn't come. Wherever the creature was—it had been absent from their company since early morning—it wasn't lodged in the cedar that Verek was felling for a bridge.

She built a fire, starting it mundanely with tinder and flint, set pots of snow to melt, and rigged a spit to roast their last hunk of Trosdan venison. The oily flesh ended up making both their supper and their breakfast. Verek had to work until nightfall to fell one cedar across the canyon's width; then he labored through the next morning to topple a second tree.

The two crashed down near each other, but with a gap between the trunks that would easily let a deer or a human slip to their deaths. Verek balanced his way along one trunk, out over the canyon to the far side. As he made the crossing, he didn't glance down. On the opposite rim, safely beyond the chasm, he took his ax to the treetops to chop through both trunks below their first spreading branches. Then he stretched his right hand above the boles. One lopped trunk rolled to meet the other, closing the gap, doubling the width of the "deck." His bridge was finished.

Wizardry for the fine touches, but sweaty work for the rest, Carin mused, watching him. Why hadn't he called on his magic to fell the trees and save himself the better part of two days' hard labor? Her breaking of Legary's spell should have released him from his self-imposed restraint, if hiding from the "watcher" was his only reason for abstaining from sorcery.

It followed, then, that there must be another reason: Verek expended his physical strength to avoid overtaxing his powers of wizardry. What had he told Carin, that evening in Ruain when he healed her fractured cheekbone with a flash of uncanny light? "The apothecary," he'd admitted, "may mix a multitude of remedies for each solitary cure that is worked through magic … and yet retain the strength, at day's end, to do other than seek his bed."

It seemed a plausible explanation, that Verek still used his powers sparingly to conserve them. But why did he find it necessary to store them up? Carin wondered. Her own excursions into the realm of magic hadn't left her exhausted. Quite the contrary. It had been as exhilarating as it was weird to craft the sea urchin from Welwyn's twinkling orb, and to burn the cat with magian fire.

Verek left his ax and most of his weapons on the far side, and returned to organize the crossing of their party.

"The deer first, one by one," he instructed Lanse. "It seems that accursed wood-goblin has deserted us, so I will coax the animals across with *Ercil's* fire. Then you and I together will convey the sled over."

He took the shovels that Carin and Lanse had carried and bore them with him to the far rim. Then, standing at the bridge's end, he conjured a witchlight orb and signaled for Lanse to send the first deer across.

The beast went willingly, single-minded for the glowing orb and never looking into the chasm that would be its death if it fell. The splayfooted Trosdan's hooves struck the timber with an almost metallic ring that sounded utterly unnatural after their many weeks of muted snow-travel.

Before the animal had taken six steps, Carin understood why Verek had bothered to chop down two cedars when one thick trunk would have sufficed—if terrifyingly—for the passage of people. The Trosdan was as clumsy on a firm surface as it was sure-footed on snow. It skittered down one bole, then the other, weaving its way drunkenly along the bridge. Carin held her breath. And when the deer stumbled into Verek and the orb, her sigh was as loud as Lanse's.

The others made the crossing just as precariously and were tethered with the first to scrape a meal from lichen-covered rocks. Verek, returning empty-handed, strapped himself into the sled's harness.

"Follow closely, Lanse, and be ready to kick the runners over should they approach too near an edge," he instructed. "I will do the pulling, but you may be called on to lift the contrivance past the rough spots."

Lanse gave him a shallow nod, looking anything but confident. The wizard faced west, leaned into the traces, and hauled the sled from the snow onto the bridge.

He barely avoided instant catastrophe. The runners—made for snow, not unpeeled timber—could not track straight over the trees' grooved bark. The sled lurched up from the depression where the two boles met, to straddle the curvature of one trunk and careen dangerously close to its edge.

With his sound arm, Lanse grabbed the sled's tail and wrested it back into the center trough. Slowly, the two men worked their way out over the gorge, Verek straining to pull the balky sled, Lanse close behind, frequently kicking or yanking it back in line.

Left to follow as she would, Carin called urgently to the woodsprite. The creature did not answer.

She eyed the canyon's width. Could the sprite leap it? Was this where she'd leave the clump of "devil's-guts" behind permanently?

Carin's conscience quashed the thought. *The creature saves me from the wasteland dogs, drops Lanse before he can put an arrow in me, and forces that dimwit and his master to leave me alone, on pain of their deaths—and I'd even* think about *abandoning it here in the wilderness?*

Working quickly, Carin gathered every bough and branch that Verek's woodcutting or her own fire-making had scattered on the snow. If the sprite turned up again before the boughs withered, they might serve it as easy stepping-stones down the bridge's length, if the lopped boles weren't themselves good highways for the creature's crossing.

Carin followed behind Lanse and wedged a bough every few steps into the crack where the two cedars pressed together. She caught the boy easily as he and his master struggled to haul the sled across. She could see neither face, but Lanse's breathing was loud and labored, while ahead of him Verek's shoulders heaved.

The sled tipped up, one runner riding perilously higher than the other. Carin crouched to study the problem. At Lanse's feet the two boles arched away from each other. One made a hump while the other dipped. The trunks—which had looked as straight as arrow shafts reaching skyward from the canyon rim—now betrayed, on their fallen corpses, their imperfections.

"Watch out!" she shouted, but too late. The sled had skidded down off the humped crest so suddenly that its tail dropped over the side before Lanse could catch it.

"Unhh!" Verek cried out as the harness bit into his shoulders. The front of the sled tried to follow its back end into space. The wizard fought it. His strength alone kept the sled from plunging off the bridge and dragging him with it.

Lanse made a grab for the rope that lashed down the sled's load. But it was too great a stretch to attempt one-armed. Unable to fling out his bound arm as a counterweight, he lost his balance and sprawled across the sled, adding his weight to the strain on Verek's shoulders. From the wizard came a sharp "Hunnh!" as though he'd been hit in the chest with a cudgel.

Carin dropped her armload of stepping-stone boughs. She grabbed Lanse's cloak and reared back, pulling with all her might.

The garment came with her—and kept coming. Lanse rolled backward off the sled, temporarily pinning one skirt of his cloak between himself and the cedar bole under him. But the unsecured edge slid unimpeded over his arm and shoulder: Carin peeled it off him as she pitched backward off the bridge.

For a moment she dangled in air, her fingers twisted in the cloth. Then she was falling, clutching Lanse's cloak as if it were a snapped rope. The part of her that could still think had only a moment in which to wonder: did Lanse shed the garment deliberately?

Carin hit the snowpack with a *whoompf.* It shuddered like a thing alive. Then whiteness engulfed her. She was rolling, tumbling inside a flood of snow. The avalanche hurtled down the chute of the canyon, gaining speed, almost noiseless. There was only a whooshing in her ears.

Breathing was impossible. Carin flailed at the churning mass, fighting to rise to the daylit world above the maelstrom. But the torrent pressed her down. She was as helpless within it as a rag doll.

Like fast-freezing slush, the flow subsided. It set up around her with crushing heaviness. Carin tried with all her strength to thrust her body upward. She couldn't move. Openmouthed, she gasped for air that did not come. The avalanche crunched to a stop and sealed her in.

Within her tomb, there was no sensation except the tight grip of the ensorcelled iron on Carin's ankle. Then that, too, was gone, spiraling down into oblivion.

* * *

The heartbeat in her ear couldn't be hers. She was dead.

Yet the sound persisted … a strong, steady *whump, whump.*

Carin forced her eyes open. She saw whiteness tinged with blue.

Ice, reasoned her muddled brain. *Dead eyes, frozen in Drisha knows how many spades of snow, might very well see ice.*

Her gaze drifted over the blue-white stuff to linger on a ribbonlike shape that was too supple to be an icicle. Carin's eyes — *they're not too frozen to move,* noted an increasingly lucid corner of her mind — traveled up the ribbon until her gaze found a throat, the hollow of it faintly pulsing in time with the *whump* in her ear.

Between them, her vision and her brain sorted it out. The ribbon was the tie of a man's linen shirt. The throat was her rescuer's.

Carin drew a slow, deep breath. Deliberately she focused her eyes beyond the shirt that her cheek pressed against, seeking clues to her whereabouts.

The blue-white light that gave an icy cast to the linen picked out rough, dark walls. As Carin's gaze climbed up them, she slowly eased her head off the chest and shoulder that cushioned her. She traced the curve of the walls; they met to form an irregular ceiling. Overhead, a few rounded nobs with a stony luster threw back the light that the darker rock absorbed.

This was a cave. Not a snow cave, but a cavern of rock thrice the size of the shelters she'd dug in the drifts. Carin rolled her head to take in the rest of it: curving walls all around; no visible opening. But a heap of woolen garments near her feet seemed to have been piled there for a reason, most likely to close a gap. Peeking from the mound was a bit of dark-green frieze cloth. Her own cloak was in the stack.

The source of the cave's blue-white illumination was a flame that burned with no wood to fuel it. It hung suspended in the air a handsbreadth above the dirt floor. It was not witchlight— that cool flame Verek called Ercil's fire, which gave off a clear light but no warmth. This was the wizard's other magian fire— blue-tinged, undying, and hot. The flame had been ablaze in the confined space long enough to subdue the stony chill.

By fits and starts, Carin sat up. For a moment, her head swam. When the dizziness passed and she reopened her eyes, she found Verek propped on his elbow, watching her. Furrowing his brow was something that might have been concern.

"Do you know who you are?" he asked. His voice, though low, filled their cave.

Carin eyed him narrowly. "You're asking me?" she rasped from a raw throat. "I've got no clue. Only what I saw in your wizards' well." She paused to swallow painfully, provoked to speech but hard-pressed to force out the words: "That other world … that ocean I crossed … my room by the sea." She shook her head. "Silly question," she grated. "I have no idea who I am."

The wizard lay back. His three-fingered hand settled on his face, hiding his eyes. Quietly at first, he began to chuckle. Then the chuckle grew to a full-bodied laugh.

Carin stared. A laugh from Verek was so uncommon, she could almost forgive him for enjoying it at her expense.

He lifted his hand from his eyes and pushed himself upright. He sat looking at Carin, leaning slightly on one arm, resting the other across his bent knees. Still he chuckled, but with his lips pressed together as though he tried hard to stop. Presently he shook himself and ran his hand over his face. The expression that emerged from behind those long, slender fingers was entirely composed, showing no trace of the amusement that had threatened to run away with him.

Verek fished in the pack that had pillowed his head. He drew out a flask, unstoppered it, and handed it over.

Carin knew its bouquet: *dhera*. A few sips of the agreeably warm liquor eased her frost-burned throat.

"The akiltered workings of your mind jolt me, at times," the wizard said. He gazed at Carin with oddly bright eyes as she drank his liquor. "The snow-slide swept you through a scattering of rocks. Though I found no injury on your scalp to suggest it, I thought perhaps you had struck against them and cold burial had hidden the wound. And so I sought to discover the soundness of your wit and the state of your memory: whether you knew your name, and mine, and were sensible of your situation. Nothing more profound than that did I ask you, *fileen.*"

"Oh." Carin's face warmed. She put her hand on her head, feeling for a knot or for soreness. There was nothing but her much-grown-out mane of wavy hair — the hair Verek's fingers had combed through while she lay unconscious of his touch.

She took a breath and tried to sound matter-of-fact. "All right then. My name is Carin. You are Theil Verek of Ruain. This place" — she indicated the cave that sheltered them — "is a mystery to me. But I'm guessing we're still in the mountains, and you're still planning to go on until we die up here."

The wizard pursed his lips. "It would seem there's nothing wrong with your memory. Be pleased to tell me how it is that you know my given—" He broke off. "Of course. You heard Welwyn call me by my first name."

Carin nodded. "And before that, I heard it from Jerold. He called you 'son' and used your name."

Verek crossed both arms over his bent knees. His eyes never left Carin's. "And so you have learned that matters of rank and title and birthright mean little in the society of *wysards*. To Masters Jerold and Welwyn and a handful of others, I am only a colt. They were deep in the magic art before I was seeded in my mother's womb."

Carin could not suppress her sharp intake of breath. Verek had never before mentioned his lost mother. Her thoughts seized on his words, struggling to shape a sea of speculations about the missing woman into a question that the wizard would permit her to ask.

But he gave her no chance. Looking aside into his magian fire, Verek almost squirmed — aghast at his own words? Quickly he returned to the subject of old wizards.

"You may think me aged," he began, but he paused when Carin firmly shook her head.

"No, I don't. Myra told me that your grandfather was at the height of his powers when he was in his eighties. She said wizards live a long time—it's the *'art magik'* in you." Carin shrugged. "I can see how time would count differently, when it's counted in wizard years."

"'Wizard years'?" Verek echoed. He looked a little startled. As he gave Carin a moment's silent study, the expression on his face shaded toward the peculiar—a look she couldn't read at all. "I have never heard it put like that," he muttered.

Then he tipped his head and continued. "It's a sad truth, nonetheless, that of Ladrehdin's small band of living adepts, I am the youngest. Hence the fatherly ways of those worthies, Welwyn and Jerold. Not so long ago, both of them—and every other *wysard* in this world—would have contended hotly with me for the right to train such a promising young apprentice as you."

Verek paused. But getting no reply from Carin, he slowly went on. "Now it appears the masters have given up hope of disciplining the young in the ways of magic. And indeed, why should we not resign ourselves to the inevitable? Magic is dying—is all but dead—in this world. On Ladrehdin, none now are born with the gift."

A chill ran up Carin's back. Out of habit, she reached to pull her cloak around her, forgetting that she wasn't wearing it. Both she and the wizard were in shirtsleeves. Her face warmed again as she imagined the warlock stripping her of her cloak and coat—and going through her pockets? Or had the avalanche emptied them for her?

"You seem troubled by my words," Verek said, his eyes missing nothing. "Oblige me, pray, with a glimpse into your thoughts."

Carin fidgeted, suddenly unsure of what to do with her hands, finding no fullness of fabric to hide them under. After a moment she simply sat on them, and shook out of the tumult inside her head an answer to give Verek.

"I'm thinking about children ... a few of them born with this thing you call a gift, but most lacking it ... and what happens to them, if an accident of birth lands an ungifted child in a family of wizards. I'm also wondering if the shortage of sorcerer's apprentices on Ladrehdin had anything to do with our leaving Ruain and coming to these mountains."

The wizard did not so much as raise an eyebrow at Carin's first comment, about children gifted and wanting. If her oblique reference to the dead sons of House Verek meant anything to him, he gave no sign of it. To her second remark, however, he offered an uncharacteristically direct response.

"Yes. I think we will find, at the end of this journey, that Ladrehdin's lack is precisely the reason you and I both are here—and the woodsprite also, for that matter."

Carin blinked at him. "You 'think'? Come on! Of *course* you know why we're here. I'm pretty sure Lanse knows what this trip is all about, too. I'm the only one who gets to lie awake nights—wondering, imagining—and dreading the day when we get to where we're going."

Verek shook his head. "You know hardly less of this affair than I do. If our presence here remains a mystery to you, it's because you will have it so."

"That's not true!" Carin protested. "I don't know where we're going, or why."

Verek sighed. He slid his hands down his shins and began to massage his ankles. "You can deceive neither me nor yourself. Look into your understanding and tell me this: What do you *suspect* our destination to be?"

She pondered only briefly before answering in a low voice, "I suspect we're going to the master wizard who made the whirlpools that brought the woodsprite and me to Ladrehdin."

Verek nodded. "Good. A plain and honest answer from you is a rarity that I treasure. Continue. For what purpose do we seek this *wysard?*"

Carin hesitated, long enough that the warlock scowled. As she looked at him, she chewed her lip. Then she muttered, "The woodsprite wants to ask the master wizard to send it back to the world it came from."

Nothing of Verek's reaction showed in his face, but his tone sharpened. "The sprite does not interest me. Pray favor me with less of that weirdling's thinking and more of your own. Tell me: Why do we undertake such a difficult journey in the dead season to find the adept who stole you from your home?"

Still Carin wavered. Her hands renewed their fidgets. One tugged at her sleeve. She shook her head. "I don't know. I really can't say. Only ... I'm afraid the sprite will be disappointed," she muttered, unable to keep the creature out of the conversation. "Somehow I don't think the woodsprite will find the master wizard willing to send it back through the void."

"Nor do I," Verek snapped. "Speak to me no more of that goblin. You hide behind it like a child clutching its mother's skirts."

He reached over and pinned Carin's restless fingers, stilling them in his warm, strong grasp. "You know our purpose here," he whispered, leaning in, bringing his face so close to Carin's that she felt his breath. "Indeed, your course has been clear since that morning in my library when we spoke of the dragon which you conjure from the words of the looking-glass book. I told you then that the creature could be used for good, not evil. By wielding it as a weapon, you may save lives without number. If you deny your duty now, it's because you find it abhorrent—as do I. But you will not persuade me that you are yet in ignorance of this thing that you *must* do."

Carin shook her head. Though the wizard squeezed her fingers painfully, she didn't jerk them away.

"I made you a promise that morning. Remember?" she said quietly. "I swore I'd never summon the dragon again. I said I wouldn't help you lay a trap and then walk right into it."

"A trap? Set for you?"

Verek's jaw muscles tightened perceptibly. His nostrils flared as he drew in a long breath. For a moment he held it. Then he let it out slowly.

Just as slowly, he released Carin's hand and raised his fingers to her face. She sat perfectly still, barely breathing, as the wizard's fingertips stroked her cheekbone, then traced the line of her jaw.

His fingers made a sudden move alongside her throat. Carin grabbed, but caught only his wrist as the wizard cupped his hand tightly around the back of her neck. As unyielding as a shepherd's crook, it pulled her to him.

"No." Verek breathed the word into Carin's face. "You cannot believe that. Even in the midst of the doubts that you harbor in droves, you cannot ignore all that you have seen and understood. You have witnessed the whirlpools that carry living beings between the worlds, and you have seen the vermin of an unearthly domain infest this realm where you now reside. You have befriended one lost creature, and watched it wax and wane on this world that can be no home to it. You've faced a monstrous cat that never was begot on Ladrehdin."

"The cat!" Carin exclaimed. She pulled away from Verek—in surprise, not fear.

He let her go. They settled just beyond one another's reach. Carin's hands came to rest in her lap. Verek's clasped his upraised knees.

Wonderingly, she asked her questions. "The cat came through the void? The same way those *mantikhora* scorpion-vermin did? The same way the woodsprite got here … and me?"

Getting only the wizard's nod for an answer, Carin pressed on.

"But—when? The woodsprite came to Ladrehdin quite a while back. You told me you felt the magical storm that brought its wand, like driftwood, to your wizards' well. And about five years ago, you saw the whirlpool that carried me, so I guess I was the second to arrive." Carin tilted her head, adding it up. "Then, barely a week before you led us out of Ruain, I was in your cave of magic watching the *mantikhora* wash into this world. So we know when all of these invaders got here."

A poor choice of words! warned the corner of Carin's mind that had the job of policing her tongue. *That makes me an 'invader' too.*

Before the thought had intruded too far, she shook it off. "But what about the big cat? If it came here in another storm of magic, wouldn't your wizards' well have shown you the whirlpool that fetched it to Ladrehdin?"

Verek shrugged. "That the waters of the *wysards* were in much turmoil at the cat's passage, I little doubt. We both would have witnessed the creature's crossing of the void—had we not, by that hour, already left Ruain."

"Already left," Carin repeated, mulling it over. If the cat had been brought across after they were embarked on this journey, how had Verek—separated from the wizards' well that showed him the magic as it happened—known about the beast's arrival?

"I sensed the upheaval as the creature neared this world," the wizard continued, as if answering Carin's unspoken question. "Though I do not know where the cat came to ground, I am certain of our location at the time. We were at the edge of the pine forests west of Deroucey, soon to begin our crossing of Imlen."

Carin slowly nodded. "I remember. You seemed wrapped up in your thoughts. When I asked if I could have a little privacy before we left the trees, you barely heard me. And when you turned around and looked at me, it was like you were looking past me."

Verek canted his head. "I wonder that you, too, did not sense the cat's passage through the void. Though clearly your susceptibility to the flow of magic was not as keen then as it has become since, still you might have felt something of the powerful tremor that I detected."

Carin shook her head. "I didn't feel anything except my saddle sores and how badly I wanted to get down off my horse. In fact, just about the time you would have been concentrating on the cat's arrival, I was trying to make you hear—in your head—how tired and achy I was from riding."

The wizard leaned slightly toward her. Carin recoiled just as negligibly before quelling her jitters. *I don't need to go into spasms of terror every time he twitches a muscle*, she scolded herself. *The fact that he's talking to me like this is proof enough that he's not ready to be shut of me … yet.*

"I do not understand you," Verek said, eyeing her sharply. "What do you mean, you strove to make me aware—inside my mind—of your complaints?"

Tersely, Carin told him how she had suspected, from her first days under his roof, that he could read her thoughts; and how she'd put the idea to the test at the edge of the plain of Imlen, in trying to convey to him by thought alone how sore and weary she'd felt.

A corner of Verek's mouth turned up, but the expression on his face was not a smile. He leaned back, and straightened one bent leg. His stockinged foot slid past Carin's. He seemed far less conscious of its movements than she was.

"Therein, I'll wager, lies the reason you knew nothing of the cat's passage," he muttered. "Your wits were too fixed on this curious attempt to speak in silence." Verek shook his head. "I cannot read your mind. If I seem at times to have done so, it is because your thoughts were written on your face. You can be as obvious one moment as you are incomprehensible the next."

The briefly straightened leg drew back and bent under him, taking his weight as he leaned again toward Carin. "If you should wish, therefore, to make me aware of a thing, then you must express the matter by means more direct than merely *thinking* it at me. I live in hope that you will tell me, in language open and simple—and before many more nights have overtaken us—that you have reconsidered your decision in the business of the looking-glass dragon. For if you hold to your resolve and refuse to summon it when the crucial moment is upon us, then I will die. Whether you will also be destroyed, I cannot say. The *wysard* who will slay me may elect to spare you—for what purposes, I leave to your fruitful imagination.

"Though I would choose life for us both, were it my choice to make," Verek went on, his eyes ruthlessly upon Carin, "I tell you plainly that it's neither my fate nor yours that most concerns me. My fears are for the blameless people of this world—and for beings equally innocent, though they follow strange ways on unknown other spheres—whose lives may turn on your decision. Exercise your office when the time comes, and you will remove the danger to Ladrehdin and to any realm from which a bridge has been built. Fail in your duty, however, and horrors not to be conceived of by the mortal mind may come stalking over those bridges to devastate worlds upon worlds."

Chapter 17

A Realm Beyond

Carin woke to an empty cave. Verek was gone.

Her heart raced. She sat bolt upright, feeling as lost as the child who had been snatched from a distant realm and set adrift in this world.

Carin's gaze darted to her knee-boots, coat, and cloak, which were piled to one side of the blue-flamed magian fire. With them was her pack, which had somehow made the ride down the snow-chute without tearing from her back.

Across from her gear was her breakfast, prepared and keeping hot by the fire: a mug of tea and slices of dried apple from the provisions in her pack, and a stale oatcake that must have entered the cave in Verek's gear. Carin had no bread in hers.

She pressed her fist to her heart, willing it to slow. "Take it easy!" she muttered. "He hasn't abandoned you ... yet."

Relief became apprehension. The tea and fruit testified mutely that Verek had been in her pack. Had he also gone through her pockets?

Carin checked, and could breathe again. Legary's deathbed narrative was still folded in her trousers pocket, and with it the magical circlet of braided hair. The loss of the paper she could endure; each line of that poem was imprinted on her brain. But she would not willingly part with the circlet before she had turned its power of seeing upon matters that were still hidden.

She swallowed every crumb and drop, then pulled on her boots and coat. Her mittens were missing, lost in the avalanche. Those on her hands when she went into the snow had been her last pair.

Carin slipped her empty tea mug into her pack, rolled her cloak into a bundle, and squeezed herself and her gear through the cave's narrow mouth. The day outside was gray, the lowering sky as wintry as the landscape. She stood on a snow-covered ledge, overlooking a field of avalanche debris. The snow, violently broken and churned, no longer mimicked an ermine mantle but resembled a battlefield. Out away from the ledge was a deep pit such as a boulder shot from a catapult might dig.

"Good. You're here," Verek snapped from behind her, dispensing, as was his habit, with the basic civilities.

Carin turned to face him. "Good morning," she said, too happy to be alive to bristle at his gruffness. "Thank you for my breakfast. Is that" — with her thumb, she indicated the battle-scar behind her — "the hole I was buried in?"

"Yes." Verek reached for Carin's bundled cloak and impatiently demanded her pack too. When she'd handed them to him, he turned without another word and tied her gear to the end of a rope that dangled down the canyon wall. His own cloak and pack were already thus secured.

Carin's gaze followed the line upward and found Lanse at the top. The boy stood on the canyon's rim, holding the rope in one gloved hand. His other arm remained in a sling, under his coat. He wore no cloak; the snowslide had claimed it.

"Up!" Verek yelled.

The gear began its climb as Lanse, backing away from the edge, disappeared from view.

Verek glanced at the mouth of the cave that had sheltered the sorcerer and his apprentice last night. He snapped his fingers. From the uncanny fire inside, the faintly blue reflection died away. His movements were quick and tense. He seemed to be in a powerful hurry to strike camp and leave this place.

"My lord," Carin addressed him politely.

The wizard half turned to her, but his eyes were on the rope. That he chafed at even this much delay was clear from his fixed study of the gear's ascent.

She persisted. "How deep was I buried?"

The question got Verek's attention. His gaze dropped upon her like a raven from the heights.

"Deep as catacombs," he said. "So deep that no air could penetrate. Had I reached you a moment later, you would not now be alive."

Carin nodded, wordlessly acknowledging what she owed him. "But how *did* you find me so fast, under that much snow? It felt like every drift from here to Welwyn's cabin was piled on me."

The wizard gestured toward Carin's boots. "You still wear the *chalse* upon your ankle. It tells me always where you are." His fingers closed, making a fist. It was not a threatening motion, but suggested possessiveness. "Had you thrown it off as you often speak of doing, you would have suffocated in an icy crypt."

"And satisfied Lanse," she said. "One of his schemes against me would have finally succeeded."

Verek shook his head. "The boy denies evil intent. He did not wish you to fall. He was struggling to save himself. You were gone before he could do anything to help you."

Carin sniffed. *Believe what you want to, warlock,* she thought. *I've seen the executioner's face.*

The rope came down in a coil, hitting the snow behind Verek with a slithering sound and terminating their conversation. He worked out the free end and wound it tightly around Carin's hips, tying the rope off into a sort of seat. Then he climbed the anchored line hand-over-hand, gained the rim where Lanse stood, and hauled Carin up more easily than the one-armed boy had hoisted their gear.

313

As she reached his level, Lanse wouldn't look at her. He busied himself loosening the hitch that had made the rope fast to a sturdy balsam fir.

It was a walk of some two hundred yards along the canyon's rim to join the waiting Trosdans at the western end of the bridge. With the deer was the sled that had caused so much trouble.

Carin eyed it, and wondered. Not only had Verek dug her from the avalanched snow—*No, not 'dug,'* she speculated, recalling the wizard's spectacular eruption from his own snowy tomb—he had also managed to right the sled and bring it across. How much had been done by mortal labor, and how much by sorcery? Either way, the demands on him had been heavy.

They lost no time in harnessing the deer, strapping on their snowshoes, and resuming their travel. Carin's hiking stick, a gift from Welwyn, was nowhere to be seen. Ruefully she recalled leaving it eastward, across the canyon. It had been her plan, after setting the woodsprite's stepping-stones, to return for it.

It doesn't matter, she consoled herself. *I couldn't hold it now, gloveless, in this cold.* She pulled up her hood, tightened her cloak around her, and stuffed her hands deep into her pockets.

The evergreen boughs she'd stuck in the cedar bridge spanned a little less than half the distance. Would they serve for the sprite's crossing? Carin watched for a spark in the trees but saw no sign of the creature.

The urge to call to it died in her throat. Over the mountain and its thick covers of forest and snow, a brooding silence reigned. It seemed to have infected her companions. Verek said nothing to the deer, never cursing them even when the beasts hung the sled on a fallen tree limb that poked up out of the snow. The Trosdans, too, were uncommonly quiet. Their guttural huffing sounded hushed.

Not much sky was visible through the dense canopy of the trees, but what showed was slaty and ominous. A storm brewing? Was that the reason for Verek's haste and the tension that showed in his every movement?

Their midday meal was a rushed affair of cold leftover venison and day-old bread. Then they were on the move again. The wizard allowed them no more than a few minutes' rest at long intervals throughout the afternoon. The going here was flatter and less taxing for the deer and the snowshoers. Beyond the gorge that had nearly swallowed Carin, the terrain was less rocky, less steep, and more densely forested.

If the gentler slopes offered an illusion of ease, the threatening sky dispelled it. Clouds hung down in a solid, gray mass. Out of the corner of her eye, Carin glimpsed lightning, but no sound of thunder broke the stillness.

As evening drew on, they pitched camp in a balsam grove protected by heavy forest, in deep, soft, unpacked snow. The loose powder made digging snow caves impossible. Verek had them stamp out a tent platform with their bearpaws. He strung a rope between two trees to support the ridge of their tent. Then he lopped enough green boughs off small balsam and spruce trees to make a pile nearly as tall as Carin. She spread the greenery inside the tent, over the platform of packed snow, in a thick layer that would keep the cold from their sleeping furs.

She emerged from her task to find Verek alone at the fire. Lanse was tethering the deer to graze what food the grove afforded them.

Quickly she scooped pots full of snow to melt on the blaze. Then she jammed her freezing hands back into her pockets. Her fingers met the circlet of braided hair and toyed with it as they had all day.

The wizard gave her no notice. He gazed steadily at the fire, as though far gone into thought.

315

Now is not the time, whispered caution's small voice.

Carin ignored it. The circlet under her fingers had been murmuring to her since this morning of questions unanswered and puzzles unsolved. If she did not raise the subject now, with Lanse absent, she might never get another chance.

"My lord?" she addressed the wizard softly.

Verek did not look up, but a throaty "Hmm?" said he heard.

"Will you let me read the rest of what your grandfather wrote about you?"

The wizard's gaze flicked away from the fire like a hot spark. When he fastened it on Carin, she flinched as if singed.

"What?" He packed the word full of such menace that Carin's stomach twisted.

But she stumbled onward. "In the *Book of Archamon* … what your grandfather wrote when you were a boy. I couldn't read that page at first, not until I made the—"

She broke off, almost swallowing her tongue. *The wisewoman's charm*, she'd started to say. Rocked back on her heels by the whopping mistake that she'd barely avoided, she cleared her throat and tried again: "—the right kind of effort. Now that I've seen part of it, I'd like to read it all. May I?"

Verek's gaze burned a hole through her. His mittened hands tightened their grip on the bow that rested across his knees.

Carin braced, hoping for nothing worse than a tongue-lashing, dreading his ready violence. But he did not lash out. He gave her a blunt answer, in a voice that was almost calm:

"No. You are not at liberty to pry into my affairs of family."

Let it go! cried her inner sentinel. But resolve's proved to be the stronger voice.

"Then why didn't you just let the paper go up in flames? If you're determined to not let me read it, why didn't you burn it, the way you started to?"

Verek's bow hand came off the weapon. Carin drew back a little. But he only raised his hand to his chin, to stroke a scraggly growth of beard.

By Drisha, he needs a bath and a barber, interjected that corner of Carin's wit which kept its own serene counsel.

Like you don't? she shot back, and ran a hand through her dirty, tangled hair.

The wizard's relentlessly direct gaze chased these and all stray thoughts from Carin's head. He stared her down, saying nothing, as still as a stone except for the gloved hand that rubbed his chin.

After a long moment of this, Carin swallowed hard and turned back to the fire. She busied herself mixing oatmeal from their dwindling food supplies with the last raisins from the almost-empty packets of dried fruit that it had become her duty to carry. Oatcake-baking had also fallen to her. It was a two-handed job that Lanse couldn't manage, even after he'd recovered sufficiently to resume much of the care of the deer.

Verek's silence stretched on. Carin didn't look at him. The bread browned under her fixed gaze, its progress watched more closely than a beetle's by a hungry bird.

He spoke. She jumped.

"I *did not* burn the leaf you tore from the Great Book," the wizard muttered, "because I *could not*. You forbade it."

Carin stared at him now, openmouthed but speechless. He could hardly fail, however, to read her question from her expression.

"Do you not remember?" he asked. "Your words were: *'It must not burn.'*"

Verek pulled off a mitten, reached inside his coat, and drew out the folded paper, pinched between two fingers. He flipped it into the fire.

Carin gasped. She grabbed the forked stick she'd been using as fire-tongs and made a stab at the paper.

The wizard parried with a bigger stick, thwarting her rescue attempt. "Leave it!" he barked. "*Look* at it."

She looked. The paper was untouched. Flames licked around it, but no edge curled or caught.

Verek finally raked it out of the coals. "'It must not burn,' you decreed. Never, therefore, will it burn." He shook off the wood-ash and slipped the undamaged paper back inside his coat.

Footsteps approached. They paused at the sled. Then Lanse came to the fire, clasping two bricks of Welwyn's frozen stew against his dirty coat with an equally grimy glove. There was nothing magical in the campfire conversation then, only worried talk of weak, starving sled-deer.

Lanse's weariness showed in his face. The boy retired to the tent as soon as he'd eaten, leaving the cleaning up, as always, to Carin. His recovery from the cat's attack had been slow and uneven—hardly a testament to Verek's powers as a healer. But if the cat was no natural creature of Ladrehdin, as appeared to be the case from what the wizard had said last night, that could explain the injury's sluggish response to his medications.

Verek did not stay up long either. He conjured a witchlight orb to help Carin with her chores. From the sled, he got his bundle of blankets and sleeping furs, and hers also. She watched him spread them over the green boughs, his in the middle of the tent platform, hers at his right hand. Lanse's place was to his left.

That was the arrangement whenever they must use the tent, although Carin suspected that all three of them preferred the privacy of separate shelters in the snow. She frowned as the sound of Lanse's labored wheezing drifted out of the tent. It was loud in the forest's stillness.

Such a deep silence hung over the trees that it brought the word "despairing" to Carin's mind. She remembered a poem she'd read in Verek's library. The poet who had used such language might have been describing these very trees, except it seemed impossible that any mortal could have ever before disturbed the snow-muted solitude of this place.

Carin, alone now with the night, glanced around uneasily, then prodded herself into motion. With a packed snowball for a dish scrubber, she made quick work of their dirtied bowls and pots, and rinsed them in steaming water from the snow-melt on the fire. With that same hot water, she washed her face, and dried on a linen chemise that she kept in her pack for the purpose. It didn't do to leave skin damp for even a few seconds in this cold. She hung the linen from a tree to dry—to freeze, rather. She'd knock the ice crystals out in the morning. Stepping a few paces into the balsam grove that enclosed their camp, she relieved herself, trained by long practice to do it quickly and hitch up her trousers forthwith.

She lingered in the grove, wanting to call to the missing woodsprite but constrained by the oppressive silence. Was the creature cut off from them? Had the canyon defeated it, despite her efforts to help it across?

Maybe the sprite is only sleeping, Carin told herself. *Which is what I should do. Tomorrow will be as long as today was.*

In the tent, she slid under the furs, into her sleeping bag, without disturbing her companions. At least, Lanse was asleep. His breathing was shallow, regular, and noisy. She couldn't tell about Verek. He wasn't gently snoring, which was the only sure way to judge the wizard's state. But he lay motionless, giving Carin no reason to think him in his waking senses.

Sleep eluded her, though. Restless thoughts lurched through her brain, in time to the annoying rhythm of Lanse's wheezing. When she closed her eyes, she saw the folded page that held

Legary's once-obscure writing … Verek flinging it into the fire … the paper emerging unscathed.

"I did not burn the leaf from the book because I could not." The warlock's words were the melody to Lanse's maddening cadence. *"It must not burn, you decreed."*

Pulsing just under that memory was another, only slightly older: Verek standing with Carin near the mouth of the rock cave, having lately played again the role of rescuer, gesturing at the ensorcelled iron on her ankle. "Had you thrown it off as you have wished to do," he'd said, "you would have suffocated in the snow."

Had 'I' thrown it off? Carin wondered. *He talks like I can get rid of that thing just like untying a bootlace. If it were that simple, I would have got it off me long ago.*

Long ago … It was many weeks now since she'd stood with another wizard and heard from him, also, a suggestion that she could choose of her own will to be free of Verek's shackle. "You've the power yourself, don't you know," Welwyn had said, "to rid yourself of the fetter … to *think* it away, as Theil Verek *thought it* onto you."

Whatever the truth of the monk's claim, Carin's fretful brain threatened to think the night away. The harder she tried to clear her mind, the louder her cogitations clamored — and the noisier Lanse's wheezing grew. Finally, with a scarcely breathed curse of "Drisha take it!" she eased from her furs and crawled out into the winter night.

The world outside the tent was a twilit fantasy so vastly altered from her earlier view of it that Carin stood dazed, unsure of her senses. The air seemed hardly to be air at all, but a phantasm of frozen mist, floating snow, and cloud draggling on the ground. It was fog, she realized as she swept a bare hand through the stuff — but no ordinary fog. It stuck to her skin like cold, wet spider-silk.

More bizarre than the air's texture was its radiance. Though the night was moonless, the fog seemed to glow. Its light was less than firelight; their dwindling campfire, some distance away, gleamed through it. The fog was dimmer by far than Verek's witchlight orb, which still illuminated the snow that Carin's washing-up had stained. Yet the stuff had its own cold, cheerless luminosity. It suffused the night with the sort of sepulchral sheen that might attend a gathering of ghosts.

Carin pushed through it to the failing blaze—this campfire was no magian conjuration that could burn unattended all night. She stirred up the embers and sat by the fire with her hands in her pockets, peering into the spectral vapor until her eyes hurt. There was nothing to see.

Presently, she looked back toward the tent. When all remained quiet there, Carin drew out the braided circlet of witches' hair.

She pulled off her right boot, then her stocking, and propped her bare foot on her clad one to keep it out of the snow. She fingered the ensorcelled anklet that had led Verek straight to her burial place under several feet of suffocating snowpack.

If you hadn't been wearing it, you would have died, Carin reminded herself.

"I don't care for 'would haves' and 'might haves'," she countered in a whisper. "I *will* have the damned thing off me!"

Eyeing the fetter through her circlet, Carin muttered the charm of seeing. And when the words were said, she gagged, nauseated. This shackle was no dead, metallic thing. It was hideously alive: a coal-black, smooth-skinned snake that clenched its tail in its teeth to hold its pulsating body tight to her ankle.

"Uggh!" Carin straightened her leg so fast that her knee popped, her nerves atingle with the need to kick the serpent off her. But immediately upon leaving the narrow field viewable through the seer's circlet, the snake became again a ring of iron.

The warlock was wise to hide its true form! Carin seethed, recalling that morning in Deroucey when Verek had concealed the ring under his hand. *I would have cut my foot off to get rid of this thing.*

Now, perhaps, such a drastic remedy would not be necessary. From the fire, Carin drew out a small branch, its tip glowing red. Gingerly she returned her girded ankle to its propped position. She gulped a breath and held it to steady both hands: the firebrand in one, the circle of magic pinched in her other and raised to her eye.

Verek's sorcery, which had been impervious, in its inert form, to furious blows with a rock, yielded instantly to this craftier attack. The snake writhed as Carin touched the firebrand to its head. Its mouth gaped open; its freed tail lashed like a whip: the ring was broken. The serpent fell into the snow, its body convulsing.

Carin scrambled away in violent haste, kicking up enough snow to bury the creature. She searched frantically for it then, peering through the circlet. A spasm in the snow attracted her hotly glowing stick. The firebrand made a snaky hiss as she punched it into the powder and under the ripple. A quick flip scooped the serpent up and sent it flying into the campfire. Its death throes lasted only a moment. It shriveled, turned to ash, and was gone.

She pitched the firebrand into the fire after it, then massaged the ankle that was finally free of it supernatural burden. Carin's skin felt smooth, her flesh unmarked except for the thin white scar of the injury that the fetter had given her in Deroucey.

As she sighed in relief, Carin glanced up and froze. The luminous fog was no longer barren. Winking at her from its oddly radiant depths were flashes and glimmers of colorful lights … vague on detail when viewed directly, but at the edge of her vision strongly suggesting eyes.

"Woodsprite?" Carin called, and jumped when her voice echoed softly off the fogbank. "Sprite," she repeated in a more cautious whisper. "Are you there?"

The only answer was a low, barely audible hum, as if a multitude of beings whispered behind her back.

Carin grabbed a large flaming branch from the fire and stuck it into the snow on her dark side, to ward off possible attack from that quarter. With urgent haste she pulled on her stocking and boot, sprang to her feet, grabbed the torch, and plowed through the fog back to the tent.

Verek was waiting in front of it. The rabbit-fur robe draped around his shoulders was frost-tipped, hinting that he had stood there for some time. His hood was back. The glow of the fog and Carin's torch lit features that were alert but not openly alarmed. The wizard's hands held no weapons. He only clasped his furs around him.

The sight of him standing calmly, unprepared for battle, reassured Carin. She stuck the flaming branch into the snow beside the tent, within reach but not guttering in their eyes.

She approached him a little warily, not at all sure of her welcome. Could the wizard fail to know that she had cast off his sorcery?

Verek said nothing. He only stood like a safe anchor in a fogbound sea. All around them the colorful lights winked, like disembodied eyes floating in icy vapor.

"What are they?" Carin whispered, edging so close to Verek that her breath ruffled his furs. "Are they alive?"

The wizard shook his head. "I don't know. We are in a realm beyond. Here are many things of which I know nothing."

A light drifted by, closer than most, and ended its existence in a brilliant green fire-flash at the corner of Carin's vision. She gasped and made a startled grab for Verek.

He flung open his robe and took her in, wrapping her tight in rabbit hair. Carin pressed against him, shivering, unable to put into words the question in her mind: A realm beyond *what*?

Abruptly the wizard reclaimed his furs and directed Carin to the tent behind him. "Go to sleep," he said. "We need not fear these spectral flickers." His fingers rested for an instant on Carin's shoulder, then withdrew. "I cannot promise that you will like what you find in this land, but tonight it may give you some comfort to know that our long journey together is nearly ended."

* * *

The lights were gone by morning, but the uncanny fog remained. For the first time since leaving Welwyn's glen, the deer seemed not to know the way. As they stood in the traces bewildered, it wasn't balkiness that hindered them, but indecision. They took a few faltering steps, then refused to go farther. They shied from the fog as if from the edge of a precipice.

Verek didn't curse the beasts. He dropped the reins and stood in silence, his eyes closed. Lanse made a nervous sentry at his master's elbow, his gaze darting everywhere as if he thought the featureless fog must have something to show him.

Carin kept close. The vapor pressed her inward, toward the nucleus of their little group. She wouldn't risk becoming separated from food, shelter, and her two armed companions in this formless, ghostly domain.

Verek opened his eyes. He flew into action, issuing commands with the brisk authority of someone who had reached a decision that must be implemented at once.

"Take the snubbing line, Lanse. You can manage it one-handed. The land here lies gently enough to pose little threat of runaway. But if need be, you will help the girl to hold the team, should nerves get away with the wretched beasts as we push on."

The wizard summoned "the girl" with a jerk of his head.

Will his lordship never bring himself to say my name? Carin wondered. Irritated but compliant, she 'shoed over the snow to join him.

He worked the second strap—the guide rein by which the lead deer was nominally controlled—out of the traces. Verek neatly coiled the long line and handed it to Carin.

"You take this," he said, "and lead the team in my tracks. Unfamiliar though this country is, I would be no sort of *wysard* if I couldn't find a seat of power that lies not a day's journey hence." He paused, eyeing the bare hands to which he had entrusted the rein. "Take my gloves." Verek pulled them off and thrust them at her. "Today I will be the one shuffling along with my hands stuffed in my pockets."

Carin gazed at him, more than mildly astonished. The wizard seemed buoyant—not quite, but almost, *cheerful.*

What you see, don't you know, is the quickening of a warrior who's primed for battle, murmured a voice in her head that so closely resembled Welwyn's, Carin was glancing over her shoulder for the monk before she realized that the thought was her own.

True to his word, Verek paced with his hands in his pockets, his head down, his eyes—closed? Possibly. Carin could not see them.

Certainly he didn't watch where he was going. He couldn't. The fog shrouded the trees so thickly that one might stub the turned-up toe of a snowshoe against a snag before its presence was guessed at. Yet the wizard avoided every obstacle, leading Carin and the deer smoothly over deep, loose powder. Her one experience with breaking trail in unpacked snow, back in Welwyn's glen, had had her floundering breathlessly through the new-fallen flakes, exhausted in twenty steps. Yet Verek tramped on all morning, setting a steady but unhurried pace that alone felt natural in this nebulous dreamworld.

"I would be no sort of wizard if I couldn't find a seat of power that lies not a day's journey hence." Carin rolled Verek's words around in her thoughts, exploring them from every angle. "A seat of power" could be a chieftain's stronghold. Landholders of all stripes flung their nets over as much territory as they could grab, but held title and blood-right through some well-fortified property that might have been the seat of the family for generations.

Worldly power, however—the kind that one amassed by running roughshod over one's neighbors—was not the sort to which Verek made reference. Of that, Carin was certain. The power he sought was the kind he could sense in the very air … the kind he could find with his eyes shut … the sort he made himself. The power to which he was leading them derived from the forces of magic.

And are you fit to be called 'adept,' if you can't also sense this power? challenged Carin's inner skeptic. She glued her gaze to the tails of Verek's snowshoes, opened her awareness to whatever might brush against it … and was rewarded, after some minutes, with a fleeting impression of blue water and summer green. Nothing more, only the colors, rich and warm and alien to winter.

The hint of warmth should have been welcome, but Carin received it with foreboding. If Verek was right, they would reach that green oasis before nightfall: it "lies not a day's journey hence." Soon, she might find her suspicions, her speculations—and her options—all at an end.

"Midday" being a matter for guesswork in the fog, they stopped after several hours, ate, and briefly rested. The deer were tethered at a patch of decent grazing, but only two gave it their attention. The animal that traveled in the middle of the string, between lead deer and heavy puller, stood listlessly, hanging its head, eating nothing. When Verek roused his party to move on, the worn-out beast refused.

The wizard's temper didn't flare. He stood looking at the animal thoughtfully. Then he turned to his companions.

"The beasts are finished. They have done what they can for us; I won't force them. Lanse, walk with me. I would speak with you regarding the Trosdans' fate."

Verek gave Carin a hard look. "Will you wait where you are? Or must I tie you to a tree to stop you wandering off?"

She shook her head. "I'm not going anywhere in this soup. I could step off a ledge before I knew it was there." She half raised her hand to him, then dropped it. "You are coming back, aren't you?"

The wizard answered with a short nod, then led Lanse into the fog. It swallowed them completely but marked their passage with a fast-moving swirl that spiraled in their wake like a whirlpool. The vapor eddied around Carin, confusing her senses until she seemed to float in the stuff, with no notion of what was "up" or "down." Reeling, she grabbed a tree, trusting it to know its roots from its crown.

Voices seeped through the fog, muffled and indistinct. Carin understood nothing that was said, but she marveled at the length of the conversation. So well did those two seem to know each other, master and servant, that a very few words usually sufficed for one to catch the other's intent. What made this discussion stretch on?

A voice—Lanse's—rose for a moment in sharp dispute, then subsided again to a murmur. If Verek was issuing orders, then it seemed his servant dared to question or even oppose them.

The fog swirled again. Wizard and groom emerged, the boy looking discontented, verging on rebellious.

Verek made for the sled, threw back the tent-tarp, and chose from the gear a single item: Carin's indigo bow. He started toward her, but as he came up to Lanse again, he stopped and held out his hand.

The boy took it. They stood eye to eye, shaking hands like equals. Then Verek drew Lanse to him and gave him as tight a hug as two men who were held apart by snowshoes could manage. When they separated, Lanse's eyes were moist. The wizard's were not, but the faint aura of excitement with which he had begun the day had given way to a stony resolve.

Verek strode past Carin without a glance. "Come," he snapped. "Follow me. We have a task to complete."

She stood riveted, stopped by a quick movement from Lanse. The one-armed groom couldn't draw a bow. But even in his weakened condition he could throw a knife. He had his dirk in his raised hand, and his anguished stare was fixed on Carin.

"Lanse—no," she breathed. Then: "Lord Verek!" she cried over her shoulder, not taking her eyes from her obviously undecided executioner.

"Hold, boy!" came Verek's clipped voice through the fog. "I told you—I need her alive. Slay her, and you assure my death. Do as I have commanded and wait here patiently."

Lanse's gaze flicked from Carin's face into the vapor over her left shoulder, then back again. He neither nodded nor spoke in acknowledgment of his master's words, but he lowered the knife.

Carin turned and hurried after Verek, but she felt the boy's stare searing a hole in her back long after the fog must have hidden her from his view.

Slip away! cried a frightened little voice over the pounding of her heart. *Without that damned shackle of sorcery on my ankle, the warlock will never find me in this ghost cloud.*

Two thoughts checked Carin's desperation, one coming hard upon the other. First spoke reason: *Lose yourself in this stuff and it's lost you'll truly be, lying dead at the bottom of a gully with a broken neck, like as not.*

The other argument for remaining with the wizard came from a source that was slower to identify itself. Uneasily, Carin recognized a close cousin of duty and conscience. It whispered to her in Verek's voice: *"Lives turn on your decision."*

The chaos in her head and heart had no power to alter her course. Carin trudged after the wizard, keeping her eyes on the trailing frames of his bearpaws, finally banishing the din and installing in its place a mind as blank as the fog. As a consequence, she lost all track of time. Whether they walked for an hour or an afternoon, she couldn't guess. Nothing got through to her until a sensation penetrated — the feel of air both lighter and warmer.

She jerked her head up.

The fog was lifting. It was no more now than a thin mist. And the touch of that mist was not colder than death, but pleasantly cool, like sea spray.

The mist cleared completely. Carin could again see the mountaintops rising above them in snow-capped grandeur. What stretched before them, however, was not a winter snowscape, but a summer meadow. Yellow and purple flowers bobbed in a gentle breeze. Butterflies darted over the blooms.

The sun was warm. Sweat began to trickle under Carin's layers of winter wool.

Verek halted a few steps into the meadow and started peeling off clothes. Carin followed his example. Cloaks, coats, and quilted underjackets hit the grass. They unstrapped now-useless snowshoes.

Carin sank into the grass to undo the thongs of her knee-boots and roll the soft leather uppers down to her ankles. On second thought, she shed the boots entirely and also stripped off her wool stockings.

Too late, she remembered her bare right ankle. Carin shot the wizard a look and found his gaze on her fetterless skin. His eyes showed no surprise, only a little bemusement.

"Come," he said, his gaze shifting to meet hers. "Pleasant as this meadow seems, our business is urgent. We cannot linger here."

Verek strode away, heading for a grove at the meadow's far edge. The trees at that meeting of grass and grove were unremarkable, but at a distance beyond them giants towered, their yellow limbs gleaming in the sun as if made of gold.

Carin grabbed her boots and her shucked backpack and ran after Verek. She'd willingly leave her heavy clothes behind, but not her pack. Over the rustling of the breeze through the grass, another gentle murmur had reached her: it was the burble of running water.

A creek cut through the grove in a series of tree-shaded pools that were made for bathing. Carin dropped her boots and her pack on the bank and had her filthy shirt off before she even thought. Covered, but barely, in an equally grimy chemise, she stared across at Verek. The wizard had jumped the creek and stood gazing at her from its other bank, his expression impenetrable.

Carin gave no ground. "I'll be a few minutes." It wasn't a request, but a declaration. "Turn your back, please."

"Make haste," Verek ordered. "We're wasting time." He spun on the ball of his foot and stepped along the far bank, disappearing into a thicket. But a moment before he left Carin's sight, his shirt came over his head. She wasn't the only one making for a bath.

The water was warm and clear. Carin had no soap; in a determined bid to feel clean again she scoured her skin with the fine, white sand that lined the creekbed. She scrubbed her scalp with it and let the briskly flowing current flush the grit from her hair.

In minutes she was back on the bank, fishing in her pack for her last clean underclothes. Carin dressed quickly, pulling on the same dirty trousers and shirt because she had no others. Her clean feet went into a pair of almost-clean stockings from her pack. She put on her boots, too, to avoid bruised feet. The floor of the grove was strewn with a variety of bone-hard, white-shelled nuts she couldn't name.

She shouldered her pack and looked downstream for the wizard. There was no sign of him.

Carin crossed the creek where Verek had, and ambled toward the thicket into which he'd disappeared. "My lord?" she called. "Are you there?"

The silence lasted long enough for a touch of anxiety to flit up her backbone. Then Verek reappeared, emerging from the thicket, dressed as before—he had no other clothes with him, either—but with his face clean and his hair wet.

Not only wet, but unevenly hacked off. It was roughly shoulder-length on his left side, but a long hank straggled down his right sleeve. The dagger that did the damage was still in that hand. In his other, Verek carried her bow and his. The one quiver between them was slung over his shoulder.

Carin stared, then shook her head. "You've botched it," she greeted him. "If you'll sit down and hand me that knife, I'll give you something closer to a proper haircut."

Verek stopped where he was, took a seat on a convenient boulder, and saying no word, presented her the dagger's hilt.

She stepped behind him, to comb her fingers through his long, wet hair and work out the snarls. Starting with the shortened side, Carin remedied the mess he'd made, then worked around to the uncut length over his right shoulder. The dagger's keen edge sliced neatly through Verek's hair, and could have severed his jugular before he knew what was happening. So distant was that memory now — of a murderous fantasy Carin had concocted before they'd even reached Deroucey — it seemed like a daydream from someone else's brain.

When she'd finished cutting his hair, Carin faced the wizard and offered him his knife back. Verek shook his head.

"Keep it. You may need it." He separated their two bows and handed her the blue one. "Take this also. I will carry the quiver for a time yet … for appearances' sake."

Carin, weaponed with a suddenness that widened her eyes, slipped the dagger through her belt, retrieved her dropped pack, and following Verek's example, shouldered her bow. Evidently he did not expect to use his soon.

He led the way through the grove and on toward the towering trees beyond. Like high hills seen at a distance, those giants were farther away than they looked. To reach them took close to an hour of walking. The sun that gleamed brilliantly off the sleek limbs was well along in the sky when they arrived, putting the time at late afternoon.

Beneath the golden-yellow giants, they walked through the ruins of innumerable stone buildings that might once have been palaces or temples. Vestiges of ancient beauty lingered in broken archways and weathered sculptures. A few splashes of bright color led Carin's wondering gaze to the shattered remains of enameled tiles and painted columns. No marvel, that the path through the mountains which led to this place was vanishingly faint, or that no trace remained of a bridge across the canyon. No travelers could have had a reason to visit this ruined city for ages beyond reckoning.

They turned a corner and found a wide, steep flight of steps, still intact amid the crumbling buildings, seemingly cut from a single enormous block of yellow quartz. The steps climbed high over their heads. From the ground, nothing could be seen of what waited at the top.

Carin snapped a glance at the wizard. He had eyes for only those steps. His gaze followed them upward and lingered long on the unseeable summit. Tautened by his upturned face, Verek's throat convulsed as he swallowed. His right hand reached for Carin's shoulder and found it with only edgewise help from his vision. He squeezed her shoulder briefly, then started the ascent.

She followed a step behind and a little to one side, craning her neck to see what might lie above. There were only the steps, semi-translucent like topaz, and over them a cluster of great golden limbs glittering against the sky.

Higher and higher above the ruined city they climbed. Eventually the steps topped out on a wide pavilion that was paved with flagstones of the same yellowish mineral. Centered below the spreading boughs of four golden-blond trees was a large pool of water that fizzed like sparkling, straw-colored wine.

From the surface of the pool a throne rose, shaped from the effervescing water as if from hardened foam. But the throne was liquid and changeable. It flowed back into the pool slowly, without splashing, as its occupant stood and glided toward them on feet that made no more impression upon the pool's surface than a water-strider's would.

Carin gaped. Approaching them was a slim and graceful woman who bore a striking resemblance to Verek. She had his long, glossy, raven hair, his obsidian eyes, his straight, patrician nose, his air of authority.

"Welcome!" the woman exclaimed in a voice that chimed off the trees above with a cold, metallic ring. "I've been expecting you. For weeks I have followed your travels with the greatest interest."

Verek, standing on the jaundiced flagstones a little ahead of Carin, made a deep, formal bow. Taking her lead from him, Carin started to curtsy, but decided it would be a preposterous gesture from one who was dressed like a boy. So she bowed, awkwardly, with little of Verek's supple grace.

The wizard addressed the woman in measured, coolly polite tones. "I had not thought to be welcomed here. Your greeting astonishes me, madam."

"Madam!" the woman exclaimed. "Is that how a son addresses the mother he hasn't seen in thirty-odd years?"

Chapter 18

The Master Magician

Verek's mother! The 'grieving widow' who had 'played her role,' had suckled an infant heir at her breast and then disappeared from the boy's life —

Everything Carin had heard, read, or guessed about Verek's missing mother came crashing into her thoughts as she stared at the woman who faced them. The lady wore a sleeveless gown of midnight purple in which green hues shimmered, the colors ever shifting as she moved. With her smooth, bone-white skin and silky black hair, she appeared to be no more than twenty-five. But what was age to a *wysard?* Carin understood perfectly well that, to a true adept, mortal years meant nothing. Even so, it was a bit disorienting to look from Verek to his mother and not be able to tell which of them should have the role of parent.

Like the voice to Carin's dilemma, Verek spoke.

"I pray you will pardon me. It is difficult to call you 'mother' when you seem young enough to be my daughter."

The woman smiled. Rather, her pouty lips twitched in what was clearly meant for a smile. The expression did not extend to her eyes: two hard, dark crystals that were very like the warlock's but as cold as his were fiery.

"I will accept that as a compliment," she said. "Allow me to return it. Time has favored you, Theil Verek. I would take you for a man younger than you are, did I not retain such distinct memories of bringing you into this world, a squalling, red-faced babe."

The lady in purple had halted her approach well away from the pool's edge. Never did her feet touch the flagstones of her pavilion. Now, with a saucy flip of her hair, she turned and glided over the water to a point near the pool's center. As she faced them again, a pale throne more elaborate than the first one rose from the water, sculpted of the gently bubbling liquid upon which she walked. Regally she seated herself. The woman did not conjure chairs for her visitors.

"I do not think you have come all this way, however," she added when she was comfortably settled, "for flattery or to hear a woman complain of her ordeal in childbed." She leveled at Verek the same sort of unnervingly direct gaze that the warlock used often, and to great effect.

He shook his head. "No, madam, I have not. I am here to beg that you will break the bonds you have built to other worlds. I come to hear you swear by the wisdom of Archamon that you will never again commit such outrages against nature."

She stared at him, her thin black brows arched in surprise.

"Much amusement it has given me these past weeks," she said, "to imagine what your reasons might be for coming here. From the several possibilities that presented themselves for my entertainment, never dared the one you name to raise its head. Pray tell me: How do my quiet pastimes, here in my private eyrie, concern the Lord of Ruain?"

"'Quiet pastimes,' madam?" Verek's restrained civility was showing cracks. His voice cut like glass. "The evil you have wrought endangers the whole of Ladrehdin. You open the gates to unfathomable perils. You invite plagues and pestilences to overrun this world, perhaps to lay millions in their graves, if not the entire populace. Nor is it to be taken lightly, the threat your 'pastimes' pose to those distant worlds now compromised by the bridges you have built. Who is to say that some small creature or wild thing which does no harm here, in its natural home, should not prove ruinous to an exotic world that can raise no defense against it?"

"Ridiculous!" The woman waved her hand dismissively. "You speak nonsense. If some venomous insect should crawl through a gate that I have opened, they who discover it need merely crush it."

"But what is the damage, madam, if some common beetle should blunder across an unnatural bridge and find itself in a world of beings no bigger than it is? Who would crush it then?" Verek asked. "Who would stop it terrorizing that realm, like a wolf among the lambs?"

She shook her head. "Your fancy runs rampant—though I do not say that such as you describe is beyond the realm of the possible. I have seen things that could not be imagined by the most inventive wit." She shrugged. "Let the tiny beings of your fantasy world look to themselves. I hunt bigger game … and when I find what I seek, it will not escape me."

"Won't it?" Verek questioned her sharply. "Will you hold it in your power, madam, as you held the giant, white-furred mountain cat?"

The woman laughed cruelly, and Carin's hackles rose.

"So you met with my cat, did you?" the woman asked with hollow mirth. "Cats are such insolent creatures—too prideful to stay where you put them. Yes, you have the right of it there. The beast escaped me. I've known nothing of its whereabouts for weeks. Pray favor me with an account of its wanderings, as you seem to have knowledge which I lack."

Verek widened his stance. "It was necessary, madam, to destroy the beast—by craft, not force. The cat, alien to this world, could not be bested here by traps or weapons of steel. Many shepherds and goatherds lost valuable animals before the creature fell to magic."

"A pity," she commented.

"A pity, madam, that those small holders lost their livelihoods?"

"Certainly not." Again the woman's laugh made Carin's spine tingle. "What do I care for peasants and farmers? It's a pity the beast was destroyed. I would have wished to have it back."

"Would you desire the return of another creature that escaped you?"

Carin started, her eyes darting from the lady to Verek. Then she became as still as the yellow flagstones under her feet. She moved nothing but her gaze, returning it by cautious degrees to the woman on the water.

The seated figure hadn't noticed Carin's reaction. But those piercing eyes might turn to the wizard's "footboy" with a great deal of interest, were Verek to reveal Carin's otherworldly origins.

Will I still pass for a boy? wondered the eccentrically calm corner of Carin's mind. *My hair has grown out, and it must appear wildly unkempt to that elegant enchantress in the pool.* Carin saw, with a sense of satisfaction that should have no claim on her attention just now, that Verek's freshly trimmed hair had dried straight and glossy. Though his beard and mustache needed clipping, he did not stand before this violator of worlds looking like a vagabond.

"Perhaps I would want it back," the woman answered Verek's question, shrugging indifferently. "Perhaps not. I have caught some fish not worth keeping. What is this creature you speak of?"

"If the wight has a name," Verek replied, "I do not know it. It seems to be no more than a living spark, flitting through the trees like a firefly. For want of a better word, I call it a woodsprite."

Carin kept her relief to herself, not daring even a gratified sigh at remaining anonymous. She did not want to be revealed to this woman. In Carin's head, reason and caution combined their voices in one loud whisper, warning that no good would come of earning the notice of this cold-eyed woman.

The lady slowly nodded. "Yes, I remember. It was years ago—one of my earliest captures, as I recall. The creature was useless, merely a flash in the trees, no more to be bottled than sunlight. I was glad to be rid of it. Do you mean to make me a gift of the thing?" She sniffed. "Pray pardon me if I am not properly appreciative of your generosity."

Verek shook his head. "No, my lady, I do not bring you the woodsprite. The irksome creature beset me through many weeks of travel, but recently it has abandoned the journey." He paused, as if in thought, then added: "It may be, however, that I will see the nuisance again, and I would fain 'bottle it,' as you say. Do you know a way that I may bring the creature to heel and rid myself of its presence once and for all?"

Her son's seeking her advice seemed to please the woman. She jumped up with less refinement than had marked her movements before, and glided over the pool's sparkling surface.

"Come," she said, gesturing toward the end of the pool opposite the steps. "Perhaps there is something, in my trifling collection of charms, that may prove useful against the pest."

She led them to a tiered dais crowded with odd ornaments. On the top shelf was a single object, a ball midway in size between a plum and an apple, perfectly round and smooth, and so black it seemed to blot up sunlight. Carin couldn't gaze at it. After a few seconds it grew enormous in her mind's eye. She felt herself falling into the sphere. Hastily she shut her eyes, and she was careful to be looking elsewhere when she opened them again.

The second tier held four objects. One was a beautifully enameled brooch in the form of a vine, its stem weaving through an elaborate spiral pattern, green leaves growing at close intervals from the stem, edged and veined with gold and amazingly lifelike. Complementing the vine brooch was a water-lily pin of exquisite craftsmanship, the delicate white flower also rivaling nature's work.

Beside the jewelry was a dull brown, rough strip of what appeared to be ordinary tree-bark. It looked as out of place in the collection as a woodsman wearing homespun in a crowd of bedizened ladies. For, lying next to the bark, was a neck-chain of silver, bearing two crystal pendants that were shaped like sleek, stylized dolphins.

To keep herself quiet, Carin bit the insides of her cheeks. She knew those dolphins. They were perfect twins to the crystal trinket that Verek had bade her steal from a child's bedroom on an unknown world. In fact, the neck-chain that bore these two had a place for a third. One silver mounting was empty.

Carin's gaze darted from the necklace to the woman who walked on water. The lady stood now in the edge of her pool, studying the dais with a thoughtful air. The part of Carin's wit that was busily rethinking four months of conjecture and guesswork took a moment to note the obvious:

Behold the master magician. Here is the one who brought me to Ladrehdin, and the woodsprite before me. Here stands the wysard who frightens Verek so badly that he won't say her name.

The sorceress seemed unaware of Carin's scrutiny. She held out her hand, palm up, with her slender fingers forming a cup. Something flew into her palm from the third level of the dais. That tier held a jumble of twenty or more objects, some as mundane as the tree-bark, others magnificent, crusted with gemstones.

The woman held up the item that she'd summoned to her hand. It was a small, bejeweled, ruby bottle.

"This might contain the creature that plagues you." She gave Verek a hopeful look. "The difficulty, however—as I have discovered by dint of much trouble—is that the charms may act in unexpected ways. One does not always get what one seeks. There's nothing for it but to make the magic and observe the results." She twiddled the bottle coquettishly. "Shall I open the void and see what takes the bait?"

"Stay a moment, if you please, my lady," Verek replied, his tone smooth now, and engaging. With the manner of one who was feeling more at ease in strange surroundings, he slipped his bow and quiver from his shoulder and laid them casually at the foot of the dais.

"I am bedazzled by these charms of yours," he went on, his voice more than conversational. He sounded almost teasing. "Pray favor me with a lesson in their natures and their uses. What is the meaning here, for instance, in this row of blackened, misshapen lumps?" Verek gestured at the bottom tier of the dais. It held nothing recognizable, only a multitude of fist-sized chunks that looked as if they'd been in a fire.

Carin's circumspect gaze shifted to the warlock. What was he doing? For the love of Drisha, he couldn't be falling under the spell of this woman, could he? Such malevolence as Carin felt from the sorceress must beat at Verek's magian sensibilities like a dark storm.

But the witch proved as willing to show off her amulets as any mother would her children.

"The many burnt ones are my failures," she said cheerfully. "I keep them to remind me of how much remains unknown and lies beyond the craft of even the most skilled *wysard*. This next row holds the charms I have yet to test." She gestured at the tier from which she had taken the ruby bottle. "You may judge for yourself, from their number, how great is the task that awaits me."

"I think it must be—and has been—considerable," Verek murmured.

"Quite so. Look to the second row," the woman said, "and you will see those few with which I have tasted success, only to have it spoiled by bitter disappointment. You came here to condemn me, Theil Verek, though I perceive that your censure is turning swiftly to admiration. Well should your disposition soften toward me. I have been years at this task, searching in distant places for that which Ladrehdin now lacks. And little it's gained me, save the virtue of patience."

Verek nodded. "I am moved to commend you, gracious lady, for the fortitude you have shown in the face of many setbacks."

He indicated the single item topping the sorceress's collection, the weird black ball. "Perhaps I may guess the importance of this extraordinary object. It is the 'bait,' isn't it, with which you caught your greatest prize?"

"It is indeed." The woman's eyes shone with a cold sort of pleasure. "And if you displease me no more, with words of reproach, but continue to honor me as a son should honor his mother, then I will permit you a glimpse of that most valuable catch."

Verek made a courtly bow. "I am undeserving of your kind favor, my lady. If I may impose upon your patience a little longer, however, I crave to know the story of this pretty piece." He pointed to the necklace of crystal dolphins. "Why it should catch my eye above the other jewels of your excellent treasury, I cannot say. Except I have never seen its equal," he lied. "There is that about it which intrigues me."

The sorceress was looking ever more content with her wayward son.

"You've a sharp eye," she purred. "Yes — that little bauble held great promise. It found for me a world much like our own Ladrehdin. In that realm, I could sense an age-old magic. But the power had long been neglected. It slumbered in deep

342

abeyance. My excitement was great when I opened the void and drew on that ancient force. 'Here I will find an apprentice strong in the power,' I thought, 'to train up in the ways of wizardry. I may also discover a pool of new magic to mix with the ebbing waters of Ladrehdin and return this land to *wysards'* rule. Far too long have the monks and the mortals held sway.'"

"Long indeed," Verek said, nodding. "But what did you find across the void?"

"My hopes were blighted there." The woman frowned. "Nothing appeared in the vortex but an artless girl-child, small and frightened, utterly without value. Didn't I say that I have caught some fish not worth keeping?" She sniffed. "From a sea of sleeping magic, I hooked nothing but a fingerling!"

Carin almost choked. Verek appeared to be holding himself together with some effort. When he spoke again, however, his voice betrayed nothing but polite interest.

"And did you throw the fingerling back, my lady?"

She scoffed. "Certainly not. In the beginning it could be the work of years to breach the void but once—though swifter have come my successes of late. I would not waste my strength or deplete the power of this place"—she gestured at the bubbling pool under her feet—"to return to its native waters a gasping fish that was more easily thrown away on Ladrehdin. The sprat fell out of the vortex far from here. What became of her, I've no idea. It's of no consequence. What matters is the charm's failure to net me something useful from such a promising world.

"Perhaps," the woman added with the suddenness of one to whom a thought had just occurred, "perhaps, my son, you and I may join our talents for another try." She smiled at Verek in a way that made Carin's skin crawl. "Together, we would be formidable, you and I."

The wizard inclined his head in a noncommittal nod. "I believe, madam, that such an alliance would not be wise. Assuredly, it is not the reason for my coming here."

He lifted his chin and continued, "You have been generous, in telling me what I needed to know about these things." He indicated the dais with its ornaments. "The task will not prove as overwhelming as I feared it must be. You have destroyed the greater number already." Verek pointed to the bottom row, the one covered in charred rubble. "Those remaining are a most manageable lot."

Striking with the speed of an adder, the wizard grabbed the black ball off the top of the dais. He dropped it down the front of his shirt, had one hand on the dolphin necklace, and was reaching for the strip of bark before the sorceress could react.

"No!" she screamed. "Leave them!"

She raised her hand. Yellow fire like a streak of sulphurous lightning leapt from her palm and hit Verek in the chest.

He went sprawling. The necklace clattered from his grasp onto the flagstones. But he regained his feet like a practiced fighter, coming up in a crouch, ready to parry the next blow.

None came. The sorceress lowered her hand.

"Trickster!" She said it with a sneer while backing with undignified haste toward the center of the pool that supported her. "I have been beguiled by pretty manners and a handsome face I would fain love. But now I see your treacherous heart. No, Theil Verek, you will not have what you came for. Return to me my property and be gone! Your business here is done."

"Far from it, madam," Verek said, straightening. Gingerly he rubbed his chest where her thunderbolt had hit him. "I mean to end these otherworldly trespasses of yours before the agents of ruin can pour through the gates that you have opened. There must be no further delay—

"For years I did nothing," he added, speaking quickly. "I refused to understand the danger. I denied there was any need to act. In the beginning, your transgressions were easy to ignore, they happened such long years apart. But your most recent offenses have been separated by only weeks. And with those, your scheme ends. I have come in all haste, through winter winds and snows, to stop these outrages before you have done irrevocable damage. You will relinquish to me the five talismans with which you have violated the sovereignty of other realms, and you will stand aside while I destroy those as yet untested."

"Certainly not!" the sorceress cried. "Go! Leave me at once, or—" She broke off, but the black fury in her eyes delivered the threat more convincingly than any words could.

"Or what, madam?" Verek pressed her. "Or die? Do you intend to murder me—as you murdered my family?"

Carin made a little strangling sound at the back of her throat. She could no more stop it than she could stop her heart. The two combatants were too intent on each other, however, to notice her.

"Of what do you suspect me?" the sorceress murmured, her pale face flushing, but not with shame. The set of her head and the gleam in her eye spoke to Carin of excitement, not guilt.

"I do not 'suspect,' madam," Verek snapped. "I know. I know you killed my father. How you did the deed, I am not certain. A simple poisoning seems likely. Had you worked the black art against your husband, my grandfather would have known of it. And he did not know of your perfidy, madam, for ten long years."

The woman smiled, as if enjoying a private joke, but made no reply.

"What gave you away?" Verek demanded. "An unguarded word ... or a gloating look such as you now wear? I remember little of that night—only my grandsire storming through the

345

house in search of you, shouting his rage, and you nowhere to be found. Your escape—by the barest of margins, it must have been—left him in a frenzy. He was in no fit state to offer solace or explanation to a boy who was suddenly bereft of his mother."

At this, the sorceress looked slightly surprised, perhaps startled to think that her son might have missed her. Verek, however, shook his head and rushed on:

"I needed no comforting—maternal affection was never what I had from you, was it, madam? I soon put you out of my mind … except for a few dark recollections that filled me with terror. My grandfather never spoke of you again, but threw himself passionately into my training. It was only later that I realized how desperately he tried to counter your early—shall we call it 'influence'?—upon me. He bent every effort to teach me the ways of Archamon."

"Archamon!" The sorceress spat the name. "The ancient magician you hold in such high regard was afraid of the power. He taught his followers to fear it. Legary could have been the greatest adept ever to practice the craft, had he not been too timid to use the vastness of his strength."

"Not too timid, madam," Verek retorted, shaking his head again. "Too wise. It is a pity he lacked wisdom to see the danger you posed to his House and his honor."

"'House' and 'honor'!" the woman sneered. "Spoken like a true squire of Ruain. Shall I tell you of Legary's 'honor'? Shall I tell you how he slighted his son when he realized that milksop, Hugh, had barely a trace of the gift? Legary scoured the countryside then, searching for a fit apprentice to take the boy's place. He found no candidate but that peasant Jerold. Even so long ago as that, the gift had become rare in the children of Ladrehdin. He did his best with Jerold, but that ingenuous one could never hope to achieve Legary's mastery."

"No," Verek quietly agreed. "None could."

"But then the great *wysard* came to me with a proposal," the sorceress said, smirking. Carin was hanging on her every word. A quick glance at Verek showed him equally attentive, but with a fierce frown on his face.

"I remember that meeting as if it were yesterday," the woman said. "Indeed, is it not whispered of yet, whenever *wysards* gather to lament their loss? Do they not speak in awe and disbelief of the only time a sage of Archamon trafficked with a necromancer of the West?

"'By the Powers!' Legary swore to me. 'If I cannot procure by natural means an adept worthy to follow me as master of Ruain, then I shall contrive a chimera. My inept son is now of an age to marry. Be a wife to him and give me a grandchild deserving of my name and both our lineages.'

"I agreed at once," the woman said. "We of the West had also remarked with much dismay the shrinking pool of candidates for apprenticeship. Something had to be done. I was eager, therefore, to mix my blood with a man of Ruain's in hopes of reviving our dwindling power."

"And so I was born," Verek commented dryly.

"And so you were." The sorceress nodded. "You were hardly more than an infant when we knew we'd succeeded. You possessed a gift such as none had boasted since Legary's generation."

"By 'we,' I take it you mean yourself and my grandsire," Verek interposed, his voice a rapier. "For my father did not survive my infancy, did he."

"Hugh was weak," she snapped. "I had you. I did not need him."

"*Only the issue survives,*" Verek recited. "*The issue of a union corrupt — and he with demon's taint upon his gift.*"

"What?" the sorceress demanded, sounding puzzled.

Carin eyed the wizard. What had it cost him to speak aloud his grandfather's words of condemnation?

Verek shook his head. "You would not know the verse, madam. My lord Legary wrote it after you had fled his house and lands. He was horror-stricken at what he had done—his House dishonored, his son murdered, his grandson corrupted. And all for arrogance and ambition."

"Ambition is no bad thing," the sorceress said. "You would do well to show more of it. In your veins flows the blood of the two most powerful *wysards* Ladrehdin has produced in eight hundred years, and yet you do nothing with the gift but mix herbs and heal sick peasants."

Verek glared at her. "And how is it, madam, that you know how I spend my time?"

The woman laughed, prickling Carin's neck-hairs.

"I have my ways—my spies, I should say. Perhaps you believe I have taken no part in your life for thirty years and more, but I had word of you and *yours*, whenever I cared to."

The wizard bared his teeth like a cornered animal. So contorted were his features, Carin could not bear to look at him.

"Did your spies tell you," he snarled, "how Legary rejoiced with a loud voice when my son was born, that the child carried no trace in his veins of your foul blood?"

"They did," the sorceress replied coolly.

Verek took a step toward the pool. "Did they tell you how my wife and son delighted in daily strolls to the lake of the lilies?" His voice was a low rumble like an approaching firestorm.

The sorceress shrugged. "Those two were not worthy of you. The woman you took to wife had nothing of the gift in her family for generations. Your child was utterly artless. How could such a son be heir to the legacy of Legary and Theil Verek? They were in the way. It was my hope that, once they

348

were dead, you would marry a canny woman and sire a child I could proudly claim as a scion of my own blood."

She shook her head and stood for a long moment looking disdainfully at Verek, her eyes growing harder than glacier ice.

"How you disappointed me!" she cried. "For one brief moment, when you summoned horrors from the depths of your craft to ravage the woodland where I drowned them, I exulted. 'His grandfather has lost him!' I thought. 'Theil is mine again. I shall give him all the knowledge Legary has denied him, teach him to *use* the power, not fear it, and together we will wrest from other worlds potent magic and invincible weapons.'"

She scoffed. "But your show of force left you cowering in the face of your own strength. In terror that you might come to know all the evil that you are capable of, you crawled back into your apothecary's workshop. There you have remained for twenty years, as bloodless as your father and no fit ruler of Ruain."

She spat into the fizzy pool. What hit the water was hard and as yellow as citrine.

"I renounced you then, Theil Verek, and I have not concerned myself with your affairs since that time—not until I realized it was you, my weakling son, blundering through these mountains toward me."

Carin could no more look at Verek's face than she could stare into the sun. He burned with unearthly ferocity. Every line of his body was tensed to spring. Surely he must attack this murderess.

But it was the witch who pressed the assault.

"Who guards your property and your interests now, in your absence?" she demanded. "Jerold?" Her laugh was short and malicious. "Only a fool would leave undefended a place of power that is unrivaled in this world. Do you think other *wysards* do not know what a vastness of *gê* force flows in

Ruain's waters and caverns? Do you think none would take that stronghold from you, given their chance?

"The thought grows strong within me that *I* shall take it, *Lord* Verek." She spoke his title scornfully. "I shall be mistress of Ruain, and with the power of that place I will summon to my service an army of fiends like these."

The sorceress waved her hand peremptorily. A moment later, over the western rim of the pavilion clattered the venomous pair whose arrival in Ladrehdin Carin had witnessed from the safety of Verek's enchanted cave. Long, low, scaled bodies, each with eight muscular legs, the forelegs bearing massive, serrated pincers ... the powerful tails ending in stingers that arched over the backs.

Mantikhora, came the name into Carin's thoughts, the only name she could find for creatures that were part crocodile, part scorpion. The Ladrehdinian fable that supplied it to her was gory with details of the monsters' feeding habits.

Their mistress waved her hand again. The mantikhora stopped in their tracks halfway to the pool. The sorceress laughed her wicked laugh.

"It seems you are right, my tender son, to fear the beasts that creep upon other worlds. For who on Ladrehdin has shoes big enough to squash *these* vermin? With twenty more like them, I will overrun king's soldiers and Drisha's priests alike. I will lead the adept in a new Wizards War—and this time we shall prevail. We will come out of the West and out of the North, down from the mountains and down from our eyries. And those of the Power will rule this world again, as *wysards* once reigned—as *I* reigned!—before the magic faded and those fools among the adept gave heed to Archamon and his creed."

She looked at Verek with open contempt. "Prepare to join your milksop father, your feckless wife, and that artless whelp of yours. You have made a deadly error in coming here. I will yield neither these waters nor, from this day forward, those incomparable depths in Ruain to such a jellyfish as you."

The sorceress flung up her hand. The fire that shot from her palm was not sulphur yellow this time, but a smoky flame, dark as burnt ocher.

Verek's reflexes were lightning. The flame hit the flagstones just behind him, gouging out a chunk of the quartz. As he dodged aside, his right hand stretched toward the murderess, his fingers stiff and extended.

What flew from them was invisible to Carin, but not, apparently, to the sorceress. Instantly a wall of water boiled up before her, a liquid shield. Sparks from Verek's counterattack scattered harmlessly off its furiously bubbling surface.

The woman threw another ocherous bolt through the shield. This time the flame caught Verek a glancing blow to his side. He collapsed to the flagstones, howling in agony.

He is powerless against her. With sickening force, the realization hit Carin in the pit of her stomach. *The witch stands invincible in wysards' waters, drawing strength from their depths. But the power of the warlock's enchanted pool is far beyond his reach, a months-long journey to the east.* All the care Verek had taken to hoard his energy for this meeting had been pointless—and he must have known it would be.

The sorceress raised her hand to deliver the deathblow. Her eyes were cold as a snake's.

"Touch him not, Morann!" Carin screamed.

Her words rang from the mountains above them like an echo, but in a voice that was not Carin's. The echo repeated her command in the deep, stern timbres of a man: *"Touch him not, Morann!"*

"Legary!" the sorceress cried, looking wild-eyed over her head, spinning on her pool's surface like a leaf in a foaming eddy. "How … ?"

The woman called Morann abruptly ceased her search of the cliffs and leveled her gaze at Carin. The look from those eyes dropped Verek's "footboy" to her knees.

"You!" the sorceress spat, her entire body quivering with rage.

"Now, Carin!" Verek shouted, his voice etched with pain.

Came the majestic echo from the mountain: *"Now!"*

Carin's prior practice of the incantation from the *Looking-Glass* book, learning to say it in the space of four rushed heartbeats—in hopes of catching Verek unawares—saved her life. As Morann's hand came up to slay her, Carin rattled off the rhyme in a single outrush of breath:

*"'Twas brillig, and the slithy toves
Did gyre and gimble in the wabe:
All mimsy were the borogoves,
And the mome raths outgrabe."*

A hill rose steeply from the liquid under Morann's feet and tumbled the sorceress into the pool. She came up spluttering, staring in disbelief at the uncanny hillside.

Attacking the slope with their corkscrew snouts was a colony of *"toves,"* those otherworldly badger-beasts. Squawking miserably down at the "toves" from their nests atop the hill were thin parrots with messy feathers. Squeaking at the entire assembly in sharp, shrill voices were creatures like piglets.

Carin paused only to gulp a breath. Her heart was thudding against her ribs as she delivered the potent line of the incantation:

"Beware the Jabberwock — !"

The odd but harmless heralds flowed back into the bubbly water of Morann's pool. Rising in their place came a bat-winged dragon fiercer than Ladrehdin's worst firedrake of legend. The dragon's talons were swords; rows of knife-edged teeth lined its gaping jaws. The roar of the Jabberwock shook the limbs of the blond trees that grew over the pavilion.

Morann screamed. Her hand came out of the water, shedding fizzy droplets, to flutter urgently at the vermin that waited on the flagstones west of the pool.

The creatures roused. They advanced upon the pool, their claws clacking like bones rattling, their stingers probing over their backs.

But huge as they were, the mantikhora were no match for the *Looking-Glass* dragon. One swipe of a taloned forearm snapped the nearest of the pair in two. The Jabberwock dragged the broken creature into the pool, snipped off the stinger, then swallowed the body, head first. It downed the pincer claws the way a visitor to the seaside might enjoy a meal of lobster.

Carin heard labored, half-demented laughter. She tore her gaze from the Jabberwock to discover Verek struggling to sit up, grimacing with pain but watching the scene in the pool with deliriously bright eyes.

"Behold, Morann!" he shouted. "Here is the novice who is strong in the Power, the 'sprat' you stole from a sleepy sea of magic. You did not know what a gift your net had drawn up from that world. This is one fish, madam, that you should have thrown back!"

Morann's answer was another shake of a trembling hand. The second mantikhora swerved away from the pool, avoiding the fate of the first. With mindless tenacity it crawled over the flagstones, making for the injured Verek.

"No!" Carin yelled.

She scrambled to her feet, unshouldering her bow as she did so, and sprinted to the dais where Verek had laid his weapons. The fingers that plucked a jasper-tipped arrow from his quiver were as steady as a surgeon's. There was no fumbling as Carin set the arrow on the string. She drew and let fly, sending the arrow off with a mad howl of *"Burn!"*

The missile pierced the mantikhora between two of its scales. Fire spouted, engulfing the body. It made a hissing crackle like a hibernating beetle cooking in a firelog. In two seconds, nothing marred the flagstones but a heap of ash.

Carin nocked another arrow and whirled to face the pool. Her conjured dragon needed no help, however. The Jabberwock had eaten all of its mantikhora except for a few bits of scaly hide. Now it lunged for the only other being within its reach.

Morann had not recovered her footing on the waters of her wizards' well but struggled in the foam, a panicked swimmer. Her purple gown and her long black hair floated around her like seaweed. Smoke wisped from her clothing and her hair, as if they were slowly being burned off her by the liquid—was it acid?—in which she floated. She seemed on the verge of drowning in it, but she managed to hit the dragon with a dark flame snapped from her palm—

—A flame that only strengthened the creature. Where, before, the dragon had been pale as straw—the color of the magical waters from which it rose—it now took on the deep, burnt shades of a thing forged in fire. Where it had been fizzy, same as the liquid in the pool, it became sleek, or glazed-over, as if hardened by the witch's touch.

The Jabberwock struck. Morann screamed in inhuman terror as the dragon's foreclaw swept her out of the water and into its maw.

"Stop!" shrilled the woodsprite's unmistakable pipe of a voice from a golden-blond tree above the pool. An enormous branch plummeted down, bludgeoning the Jabberwock on the side of its head. The dragon roared—displaying between its fangs a shimmering strip of Morann's gown.

Carin looked for blood in the water. She saw none.

Drisha is merciful even to the wicked, ventured the imperturbable part of her wit. *The witch died quickly, not torn to bits and swallowed piecemeal.*

Now the dragon was beginning to fade, its form becoming as liquid as the unnatural stuff of which it was fashioned. The creature could not reach Verek or Carin out on the pavilion's dry flagstones. It was confined to the waters that gave it shape, and brief in its existence on a world not its own.

It waned, but it did not weaken. An instant before the Jabberwock vanished, it hooked a claw into the huge branch, now floating in the pool, that had struck it from above. With a howl the dragon flung the branch on a long, arcing flight that ended with the limb slamming like a battering ram into Verek's outstretched ankle.

When Carin reached him, the wizard was curled on his side, groaning between clenched teeth, gripping his ankle with one hand and pressing his other to his side where Morann's thunderbolt had ripped into him. His eyes were tight shut, his face twisted with pain.

As Carin brushed his sweat-soaked hair off his forehead, Verek opened his eyes and gazed up at her. The magian flame was scarcely there, heavily veiled, no more menacing than candleglow.

Weakly he shut his eyes again, rested his cheek on the flagstones, and unclenched his teeth. What rolled off his tongue was a mostly unintelligible string of oaths, followed by a muttered: "Didn't I tell you that deuced woodsprite was not to be trusted?"

Chapter 19

Ruptures in the Void

Verek twisted his head a little to look up at Carin again. "You have my thanks for my life," he whispered.

She shook her head. "Don't thank me yet. We're not exactly out of the woods. You're hurt, I don't see how you can walk, and we have a long journey back through the snow to reach Ruain. What do I do now? Should I go get Lanse?"

"No!" Verek exclaimed. His hand left his side to grab for her. "No. There's no time. It will soon be dark; you would lose your way. And I have no wish to be alone and helpless in this place when the witching hour comes. The death of its powerful mistress will not pass unnoticed."

Or unavenged?

Carin glanced at the sky. The sun was behind the mountains but its glow would light this high, pale pavilion for an hour yet. Whatever the night might bring them, she had time, before it fell, to prepare.

She shrugged out of her pack and dug around in it for the grimy chemise that she'd changed for fresh at the creek in the grove. She cut the garment into strips with her—Verek's—dagger and laced the strips into one long bandage. Not bothering to ask his leave, she pried his fingers off his ankle and wrapped the bandage tightly around it, over the soft-tanned leather of his boot, snugging it up to counter the swelling.

Verek groaned anew but did not protest. "Yes," he murmured when Carin had finished. Experimentally he straightened the leg. "That makes the agony rather more bearable."

He tried to roll onto his back, but the injury to his side fetched him up short. Carefully he pulled up his shirt to reveal a purplish bruise that covered half his abdomen and extended over his ribs into his armpit. Revealed also were a folded sheet of paper and a ball of abysmal black. Both fell to the flagstones as Verek pulled his shirttail loose.

"Damned uncomfortable place to keep things," he muttered. With his elbow he rolled the ball toward Carin. "Put that in your pack, if you please. It falls now to your charge."

"It's horrible," she said, but she picked it up and thrust it deep into her pack. She took care not to look directly into it.

"Yes, it is. It's the talisman of those vermin that fell before you and your dragon like wheat before the scythe."

"The dragon isn't 'mine'," Carin grumbled, settling down cross-legged on the flagstones beside Verek. "I may use the Jabberwock, but I didn't create it."

She picked up and twiddled the folded paper.

"I guess I don't need to read this now, to have my questions answered. Why didn't you tell me long ago what I wanted to know? Why wouldn't you admit that they were all one blackheart? The 'master *wysard*' who wielded the power of passage between worlds, the victim you meant for the dragon to take, the 'watcher' in these mountains, the murderer of your family" — *not to mention, the cold-eyed snake who was your mother* … Carin would have swallowed her tongue before she'd mention *that* aspect of Morann's multiple identities — "they're all the same." She jerked her head toward the pool where the sorceress had disappeared down the Jabberwock's gullet. "Why wouldn't you just say it? If you only knew how my brain has struggled to make sense of it!"

Verek gazed at her with pain-clouded eyes, his hand again pressed to his side.

"Had I told you all of it, *fileen*," he murmured, "wouldn't you have thought I was dragging you into a blood feud? Could I have persuaded you that my cause was nobler than common revenge?"

Carin heaved a sigh.

"If you'd told me all of it, my lord, I would have *understood*. What you've said about otherworldly 'bridges' and 'opening the gates,' inviting alien plagues and pestilences into the world—that all sounds quite menacing, and I can see why the gates have to be shut and the bridges torn down." Carin glanced at the ash heap where her flaming arrow had destroyed the vermin from another realm. "Things like those horrible *mantikhora* should never be allowed to cross from their world into another one. It's taken me a while, but now I get it. I get why you've been so determined to come here … and, um, pull up the drawbridge." Again she jerked her head at the pool.

"But if I had thought you were out to avenge the deaths of your family, if you'd said that the 'master *wysard*' was a murderess, if I'd known that's why you needed me here …"

Carin paused, suddenly shy about saying more. She went on in a lowered voice. "Before I came to you in Ruain, I felt lost. Just knowing that you wanted—you needed—my help … that would have given me a place to be and a reason for being there. Don't you see? If I had known the whole story …" She flicked the folded paper between her fingers, then shrugged one shoulder, powerless to make herself any clearer.

Verek managed for a moment to look thoughtful before grimacing again in pain.

"When I last saw Myra," he grated through his teeth, "she told me I had a poor understanding of the fair sex." His words came easier as the spasm passed. "I believe she may have been right. I have, perhaps, lacked perception." He hesitated, then tried to smile. "Why, for instance, a woman would pack along her flimsies under such circumstances as these, would have eluded me—before now. If you've any more to spare, I could wish for a bit of your linen to bind this other wound." Verek pressed both hands to his side. "It has me in misery."

He still needs you, badly. The thought whispered to her, half comforting and half terrifying. Carin ducked her head, fishing in her pack, avoiding the touch of the smooth ball that rolled among her smallclothes and woolen stockings. She came up with the chemise that served her for a face towel.

"This is all the linen I've got left, and it won't be enough."

She began tearing it anyway, making strips. "The air's warm here," she said, and eyed her patient's tattered attire. "Almost too warm." Carin shot a glance at Morann's pool, which continued to fizz and bubble and send up the occasional small jet. Verek's wizards' well was colder than ice, but Morann's looked—and felt—hot. "Maybe I could rip up your shirt. You don't need it in this heat."

Verek shook his head. "My shirt, I must put to a better use than bandages. I fear that I've come to this task wholly unprepared and made a proper mess of it. Having won no assurances from you that you would speak the incantation when required, I had assumed that we would both be dead by now and would have no need of linens, or packs … or painkillers."

He groaned, then softly added, "I must ask you, therefore, to make do as best we can. Be pleased to help me shed the garment, then listen to all that I say to you."

Carin helped him work his shirt over his head. What the effort cost him was clear from his sharply indrawn hisses of pain and the pallor of his skin when the garment was off and she eased his bare, muscular shoulders down to the flagstones.

He was silent for minutes then, breathing shallowly, his eyes closed. The bruise up Verek's side stood out like a blot of ink, spreading, streaked with scarlet, and ringed in unhealthy shades of green and yellow.

Abruptly Carin turned her back to him, pulled off her shirt, shed her chemise—her last—and drew her filthy overblouse on over her bare skin. While the linen was still warm from her body, she ripped the chemise into strips and joined them to the too-short bandage that the first had made.

It was another ordeal for Verek to sit up while she wrapped his torso. But when it was over he breathed without so much pain, and he managed to make his wishes known: Carin was to tie up in his cast-off shirt all those amulets from the third row of the dais, which Morann had said were yet to be tested for their ability to link Ladrehdin with other worlds.

"And mind that faithless sprite," Verek growled. "Take care that the creature doesn't club you with a tree limb."

The sprite. Carin had been keeping one ear and half an eye on the goblin since its failed attempt to rescue the sorceress. The woodsprite remained high in a tree over the bubbling pool, sparking a little, emitting a mournful wail every few minutes.

Carin called to the creature but got only its loud lamentation in reply. At the dais she worked quickly and looked up often. Morann's collection stood directly under a thick limb that could crush an ox. The sprite, however, stayed where it was, never shifting from its high perch.

She knotted the amulets securely within the shirt and started to tote the bundle to Verek.

"No," he called, watching her in the still-luminous twilight. "Leave it beside the pool. Bring me instead the talismans that have proved their potency."

Handling these more warily, Carin picked up from the second tier the vine brooch, the water-lily pin, and the shred of tree-bark. On her way back to the wizard she scooped the dolphin necklace off the flagstones where Morann's warning thunderbolt had made Verek drop it.

The crystal dolphins tickled Carin's palm—an altogether unnatural sensation to emanate from such sleek, smooth carvings. She tipped the crystals out of her hand and carried the two pendants by their chain to avoid the unnerving touch of their energy.

Reseated on the flags beside Verek, she spread out the charms.

"I remember, my lord, what you shouted that night when I journeyed to the child's bedroom and picked up another one like these." Carin gestured at the dolphins. "You yelled at me to throw you the crystal. You said you couldn't withstand the thing's pull upon me. Now I'm wondering: Were these two dolphins calling to the one that I was carrying and threatening to snatch it—and me—*here*, to this place? Did I nearly end up back in the power of the sorceress?"

Verek nodded. "She very nearly had you then, and I doubt she even knew it. I believe the crystals act for themselves and need no magician's voice to stir in them the power they possess."

Carin considered that in silence. Then she left off her study of the dolphins to raise her eyes questioningly to the wizard's.

"The last time I saw the one that I brought through the void, it was lying at the foot of the steps that go up from your cave of magic to your library. Where is that dolphin now?"

"Still there in the cavern of *wysards'* waters, but resting now on the bench of the fish ... that emblem you have favored since you first entered the chamber and embarked with me on this quest," Verek replied quietly, speaking more easily from the small measures of relief that Carin had dealt his injuries. He'd also fortified himself with a long drink of *dhera* from the flask in his hip pocket—that being the only bit of vital gear he hadn't left behind.

Carin's eyes did not stray from his. "Then … there's a link—a bridge—from this place to there. The crystals make the connection. Can't we use that bridge to go home now, tonight?"

The wizard smiled, a bit crookedly.

"Indeed, *fileen*, it is my fervent hope that you will cross that bridge only a few hours hence. First, however, there is the matter of returning these errant pieces"—he gestured at the charms—"to their proper places in nature's design. And if you will loosen my boot—not the one that covers the break, thank the powers for small kindnesses, but the other one—within it you will find another lost thing that needs to go home."

Carin reached for Verek's boot-top, undid the braid that secured it just below the knee, and pushed the soft leather down his stockinged shank. Peeking over the cuff of the boot was a stick the color of pale honey and gleaming like waxed wood.

"Sprite!" she yelled, snatching the stick from Verek's boot. She sprang to her feet, waving it. "I have it! I have the beautiful wand that must have come to Ladrehdin from your homeworld. And didn't I tell you I would refuse to return it until you could make the journey with me? Come down and join us, sprite. We have plans to make. There's no point mourning the death of the 'master magician.' She won't send you home. But I'll do my best to get you there."

The creature did not reply. But its wailing quieted.

Carin, too, grew silent as she considered what "getting there" might actually mean. She sat down again and twirled the wand through a moment of deep thought. Then she laid it on the flagstones beside the other talismans, reached over and laced up Verek's boot, and finally raised her eyes again to the wizard's.

"I see—only too plainly, I believe—some of what has to happen next," she murmured. "But maybe I'm guessing wrong. Will you tell me now what you're thinking?"

Verek nodded. Quickly and quietly he set forth his scheme, with no apology or expression of regret. Carin's part in his plan was largely as she'd envisioned it, although he made it sound considerably less frightening than it played out in her mind.

When he'd also described, briefly, his own intentions once Carin had gone about her task, she sat frowning at him. Then she shook her head.

"No, sir. This plan of yours won't do."

The wizard stared at her, one arched eyebrow giving him a look more intimidating than questioning. "Oh?"

How does he manage it, in just one word and it so short? Carin's skin prickled at the undertones in that brief query, but she resisted the urge to scoot backward on the flagstones to evade his reach. The warlock was hardly in a position to punish her for disobedience. *His 'footboy' is driving the horses of this coach,* advised the voice of reason, *and his lordship knows it.*

She shook off the muse and answered him. "In the first place, sir, I'm not at all sure that I can do my part alone, without your help."

"You must." Verek scowled. "You can see that I am unfit for the journey and could be no help to you, only a hindrance. In any case," he added, his expression turning unreadable, "you are the novice who brought ruin to the most powerful *wysard* on Ladrehdin, and you spoke with the voice of one who, in life, was much that woman's better. I doubt that there is anything you cannot do, if you are strongly minded to accomplish it."

Carin mulled that over. After a speechless moment, she moved on to her next objection.

"Well, the other thing is, I need to know just what you mean when you say you're 'going where the tides of magic carry you.'"

Verek sighed. "I was a great fool," he muttered, "to let wrath and the lust for vengeance drain me of the last dregs of my strength. I came here not for revenge, but to save uncountable lives. Isn't that what I have told you? Is that not what I tell myself? And yet, when the *daēva* stood over me, I squandered myself in unwinnable combat.

"The keys to many realms awaited me there." He gestured at the dais, which was empty now of all but the charred rubble at its base. "I had only to sweep to safety these few charms" — his hand waved listlessly over the select pieces that were laid out on the flagstones — "and then obliterate the rest. At one stroke I might have removed the danger to a score of worlds. I threw away the chance. Like the greenest pup I went for the throat when nothing was within my reach but the hock. And like the pup, I got badly gored."

The wizard held out his right hand, palm up. In the dusk a tiny flicker of white light appeared and then was gone, lasting no longer than a spark struck with flint and steel.

Verek clenched his hand into a fist and tapped it on the flagstones in quiet frustration. "Not even *Ercil's* fire may I conjure now. Those talismans that you have bundled and left for me at the water's edge will suffer no blow from this hand." The fist opened. The fingers returned to rest on his bandaged chest.

"Neither of us," Verek went on, fixing Carin with a gaze that glittered in the waning light, "must be here tonight to explain to dead things and crawling horrors what has become of their mistress. The only course I may follow, therefore, is as I have told you. When you are safely embarked, I will slip into the pool with that pack of charms and let magian waters have their way. With a little luck and by the mercy of the powers, I may wash up in some *wysard's* well—Master Welwyn's, if I might so dare to hope, or another among the elders of the craft who will not refuse me aid."

Carin didn't bother to ask where Welwyn's pool of enchanted waters might lie. All these Ladrehdinian wizards seemed to have one. The monk's might rise in his ornate bathtub, for all she knew or cared.

"It's ridiculous," she snapped. "You'll drown. I saw how close you came to dying in the magic waters of your own cave. And don't forget that I took that plunge, too. That water was so cold, it burned.

"But this stuff"—she pointed at the bubbling liquid of Morann's pool—"looks like it could peel off your skin, then boil what was left." Carin shook her head. "No, sir. If you 'slip into' that pool, it's your corpse that will bob up in some other wizard's well. Unless, of course, the tides of magic just carry you out on a sea of oblivion and leave you to float in darkness for eternity."

Verek opened his mouth, looking as if he meant to argue. Carin cut him off.

"And what about Lanse?" she demanded. "If you go to your death in this pool, what becomes of him? Are you just going to abandon him here? ... Lanse, who's served you faithfully since he was a boy? Drisha knows *I* don't much care what happens to him. But it seems cruel to leave him alone in these mountains with his bad arm, almost no food, and no company except for those worn-out deer—

"Or do you think that 'dead things and crawling horrors' will be good company for him," Carin asked, savage in her worry for Verek, "when they find no one up here on these flagstones to blame for the loss of their mistress? I suspect that

Lanse, waiting out there in the forest for you, may not be out of reach of the evils of this place."

As she finished speaking, the look on the wizard's face was so melancholy that Carin felt like crying. Her eyes, however, remained dry.

"Didn't I tell you, weeks ago," Verek whispered, his anguish shadowing his gaze, "that you would put little faith in my conscience if you knew everything that hangs heavy there? I have known, since this journey began, that Lanse's fate could hardly help but be as you describe it: abandoned at the last, to fend for himself as best he may."

The wizard was silent for a moment, his eyes closed, his thoughts turning inward.

Then he looked sharply at Carin, and his expression hardened.

"Confession is good for the soul. Do the monks of Drisha not say it?" Verek's voice was cold. "Let me confess, then. On the day last autumn when I learned that you had defied the spells guarding Ruain's wellspring of power, to open the eternally hidden door to the cavern and witness my torments, I determined then that you must die."

Carin caught her breath with a grunting, throaty sound like she'd been stabbed in the back. Which, in a way, she had.

Verek half reached his hand to her. But he let it drop and went on speaking in a tight voice.

"'The girl grows too powerful, too quickly,' I told myself. 'Use her strength to seal the ruptures in the void. Then destroy her. She is a great threat to Ladrehdin. Woe to us all, if ever she fathoms the depths of the potency that surges in her. When mind and magic join within, then she may rise with the virulence of the mythical Ashen Curse that overwhelmed the ancients. No—she must not be allowed to live in this world that is not her own. She must die before the wellspring of her art becomes a torrent that sweeps all before it like pebbles in the flood.'

"Your execution, I planned from that moment, to be carried out the instant you no longer served my designs."

Verek eyed her, awaiting her reaction. But Carin had recovered herself. When she gave him nothing but a look that was as steady as his, the wizard tilted his head quizzically and went on. His voice was hardly above a whisper.

"You were many days under my roof. From the looking-glass book, you read to me. Hardly an evening passed that we did not speak together — to argue, as often as not. But even in your obstinacy I found much in you to ..." He paused, choosing his word. "To value. I weakened. Even before we had departed Ruain, I knew I would not find it in myself to slay you, when the time came."

Carin leaned toward him. "But you had a stand-in."

Verek nodded. "In my cowardice, I appointed Lanse to be your executioner. For months I have felt sick with self-loathing each time I looked that boy in the eye, to know that at the end of this quest I would ask him to kill for me, and afterward abandon him to these haunted wastes."

The wizard ran his hand over his face. His skin, in the deepening dusk, was as wan as a ghost's.

"You are quite right, *fileen*," he murmured, his voice eerily emotionless. "Almost certainly I will die in the waters of the *wysards*. And to a terrible grave I will carry the memory of my shameful words to Lanse:

"'Kill the girl,' I told him as we spoke in the fog beyond your hearing. 'If she returns to you without me at her side, or if you should discover her wandering these barrens alone, then you will know that I am dead and all my plans have come to nothing. Slay her at once. Take care that she does not kill you first,' I warned him, 'for if the girl outlives me and wins her freedom from the one we have come here to challenge, then she will have proved herself a more formidable sorceress than ever you suspected.'"

Verek's hand shot out; he took Carin by the wrist. His grip betrayed no weakness. "So you see what folly it would be to attempt to fetch Lanse to my aid. The boy would kill you before you spoke a word in my behalf."

His fingers slid off Carin's wrist. He snatched the dolphin necklace from the flagstones and thrust it at her.

"This alone I can offer to redress the wrongs that I have done you and the boy. Return the other talismans to their natural homes—that is paramount. Against that task, all else pales. But when you have broken the bridges between the worlds, make these"—Verek shook the crystals—"take you to Ruain. Upon your safe arrival tell Master Jerold all that has happened here. He will know how to contact Welwyn and others of the elders. Together those old worthies may contrive a way to collect Lanse from this desolate place, particularly now that it has no awful mistress to oppose them."

Carin sat quietly, taking in the wizard's litany of revelations, the feverish gleam in his eyes, and the crystal dolphins that dangled from his fingers. Slowly, she reached for the necklace and pulled it from Verek's grasp.

As if her action had been their cue to speak, a multitude of voices rose out of the twilight, murmuring distantly, indistinctly, but with a malevolence that twisted Carin's gut.

"Go!" Verek shouted. "The horrors of this place would not wait for midnight. They are abroad. Take the talismans and be gone!"

Carin stuffed the dolphin necklace into her trousers pocket. Then she grabbed her pack and swept into it the vine brooch, the lily pin, and the shred of bark.

"Sprite!" she yelled, leaping to her feet. "Get ready! We have to go. Break off a sliver or a scrap that I can carry you in." She slung on her pack, shouldered her bow and Verek's quiver of arrows, and picked up the honey-colored wand.

"Come on," she ordered the wizard in the same unyielding tone that he'd often used with her. "Get up. Prop against me. Or if you've got to crawl, then crawl. One way or another, I'm getting you to the pool."

"No!" he shouted. "There is no time for me. Go! Now."

"Don't argue," Carin snapped. "Give me trouble and we'll both die. I won't leave you here alone to face whatever is on its way. Get on your feet—or foot."

She crouched beside him, offering him her shoulder to brace on. Verek uttered every swearword in the language of Ladrehdin and a good many in tongues Carin had never heard. But together they struggled upright and hobbled three-legged to the pool, their arms around each other, the wizard leaning on her.

When the toes of their boots overhung the pool's rim, Carin pulled the necklace out of her pocket. She slipped its chain over Verek's head and settled its paired pendants on his chest.

"Are you mad?" he breathed into her ear. "Without the crystals, you'll be lost."

"I count two between us, sir." Carin closed her fist around one dolphin and yanked, hard. The silver chain bit into Verek's neck. He flinched as the pendant came away loose in Carin's hand. "One to guide my journey home," she said, stuffing the unchained dolphin deep into her pocket, "and the other to take you there. Think of that crumbling mansion in Ruain and be still while I do the same."

Carin slipped her hand between Verek's bandaged chest and the lone crystal that now hung around his neck. With fingers that did not shake, she raised the trinket to her eyes. In a mind that was as clear as daylight she pictured the wizard's cave of magic, the bench that bore the carved shape of a fish—and the twin to this dolphin, which Verek had said rested beside that symbol.

The air above Morann's pavilion was utterly still. Through it cut the dark, muttering voices that approached from all sides. The speakers were below them yet, emerging from the rubble of the ruined city. But soon they would make the climb up the steps to this high, stone-paved altar.

Carin ignored the voices. Her mind's eye sought the absent dolphin. Her head cleared of everything except the search for that talisman. It was out there, waiting to form—with its twin that she held—a bridge to take Theil Verek home.

There —

A red-tinted rectangle rose from the ensorcelled waters of Morann's pool. It resembled the cover of a book.

No, it's got to be the doorway, Carin told herself. *It's the door from the library that leads down to the cave. That red is the glow of the cave walls shining up the stairwell.*

Nothing else appeared, neither the stone bench upon which the crystal rested nor the crystal itself. The illusion was not nearly as detailed as the image Carin had twice summoned of the child's bedroom that had originally housed the trinket.

But perhaps it would have to do—given that incandescent eyes without bodies were appearing over the pavilion's edge. Carin viewed them through the red rectangle as if through a sheet of diaphanous paper.

Verek seemed to reach the same conclusion about the adequacy of her vaguely drawn doorway. His unkempt mustache tickled her ear as he whispered into it: "Come back to me, Carin." His lips brushed her cheek.

Then he was twisting out of her grasp, grabbing the bundle of untried amulets that waited on the rim beside him, falling with it through the doorway. The dolphin necklace went with him, pulled from Carin's fingers, leaving her holding only the honeywood wand. Her conjured red rectangle closed behind Verek like a book slamming shut.

He was gone. There was no splash, not so much as a ripple in the pool. In that, at least, she had succeeded. Her injured warlock had not plunged into deadly wizards' waters.

Carin blinked. She was alone on the pavilion with the woodsprite and a swarm of stares. The eyes glowered hotly at her as they neared, watching her maliciously ... hungrily.

"Now, sprite!" she yelled. "Put yourself into my hand, or stay behind. I'm going."

From above came the sound of timber snapping. Carin braced for what might prove to be a fatal blow. But better to have her brains splattered across Morann's flagstones than to fall to the bodiless horde that approached.

What hit the paving, however, exactly where Verek had stood a moment ago, was a spindle of golden-blond wood no longer or heavier than a pipestem. Carin crouched and picked it up. In her other hand, she held the honey-colored wand steady before her gaze. She gave the wand her absolute attention, barring from her consciousness the muttering voices and the glaring eyes.

A tree. Almost instantly the image of a tree rose from the ensorcelled waters at Carin's feet. Never mind that it had limbs like the arms of a misshapen ogre, or that the sky behind it was not blue, but a coppery orange. The apparition was clearly a tree, and welcoming in its familiarity.

From her crouch on the pool's rim, Carin sprang for the tree. She kept her gaze fixed on a bent but sturdy-looking branch that resembled a crooked elbow—a promising place to land, compared to what she was fleeing.

As her boots left the flagstones, something brushed Carin's heel. The touch sent cold shudders up her spine. She smelled decay, fetid and old and sallow. If an odor could have a color, this stink would be a sickly yellow. Over Morann's pavilion spread something ancient, age-ambered, and rotting.

Carin did not take her eyes from the tree that waited to receive her. She saw nonetheless, at the edge of her vision, that all the stares which glowered at her did indeed arise from shapes. The shapes might, if one were generous, be called bodies. Her fleeting glimpse of Morann's vassals, even more than their stench, made Carin want to vomit.

Chapter 20

A Quickening of Magic

The journey to the ogreish tree took ten forevers. The tree grew no closer or larger, though Carin had the distinct sense of moving toward it. What flowed past her was not water, was nowhere near as heavy as water, yet she had the impression of streaming through some fluid medium. She seemed to hear the ocean, as if she were holding a seashell to her ear.

The sound of it, distant and rhythmic, bore no resemblance to the shrieking of the whirlpools that Carin had witnessed in Verek's cave of magic. It was a great relief to not be spinning furiously in such a vortex as those. She was making this passage between worlds with magic that, unlike Morann's contortions of power, flowed smooth and straight.

Out of the corners of Carin's eyes, all was blackness. It wasn't a night sky; there were no stars. It wasn't a thick, stifling darkness such as she had endured in Verek's cellar-dungeon. This was a blank—an absence—a void. She could not look down to see what, if anything, passed under her feet. She couldn't move her hand to her pocket for reassurance that the unchained crystal dolphin—her safe-conduct back to Ruain—still nestled within. None of her muscles answered her. Carin could verify only that the honeywood wand was still in her grasp. It appeared in her outstretched hand, between her eyes and the tree.

She could not feel the woodsprite's slim spindle. Whether it made this journey at her side, gripped in her other hand, was open to question.

Questions ... Carin mused in a mind that was dragging behind, ratcheting down to become as unresponsive as her body. *Answers have come to many. Are there others I should be asking?*

She meditated with slow deliberation but could not order her thinking. After a time, her brain slid into a state neither awake nor asleep. Cotton wool packed her skull.

But occasionally a thought penetrated like a needle sticking a pincushion. Then, for an instant, Carin had the wit to worry. What was she doing out here—wherever "out here" was—on this mad errand for a moody magician who had long plotted her murder? And why should it please her to imagine Verek at home now, back in his manor of magic, being clucked over by a beaming Myra?

Drifting gradually, cloudily into Carin's field of vision, and wisping its way strand by strand into her consciousness, too, came a patchy blanket of mist. It threatened to obscure her target tree.

Carin was straining to see through it when the mist suddenly lit up, as if aflame with the orange light of what seemed to be a rising sun. As the sunlight rapidly strengthened, the mist thinned, then broke away, drawing back under a coppery sky.

The sunrise revealed an alien landscape that was stirring to life. Carin watched rock after rock roll down to a creek to drink, like a flock of gray sheep that gathered on the brook's banks. A forest of trees stretched their limbs in the orangey morning light and yawned sleepily.

In Carin's hand, the honey-colored wand lifted delicate wings, twitched its antennae, raised itself on threadlike legs … and flew away, making straight for the twisted tree that she had intended landing in.

The wand—

Better call it a fly, advised Carin's reengaging brain, which took in the scene as though she found it all perfectly natural.

What once was wooden suddenly looks quite like a long, slender fly that ought to be swatted, doesn't it?

The fly flitted into the tree just ahead of Carin. It lit in the crook of the elbow that she'd wanted to settle in.

Another gnarled limb of the tree came swinging round to slap at the pest, but it missed. The limb caught Carin a clout that sprawled her facedown in the damp soil of the creekbank. She barely missed the flock of rocks.

"Humph!" came the tree's startled exclamation.

"Ooh!" cried the rocks in chorus, scattering like the sturdy sheep they resembled.

The rocks rolled off a ways, then stopped to stare at Carin. At least, they seemed to be looking at her. Nothing that hinted of eyes appeared in their mossy—woolly?—surfaces. But at a safe distance the flock regrouped, murmuring in a dialect that seemed to consist mainly of astonished "ohs" and "oohs." Gently they rolled into each other like incredulous spectators nudging one another with their elbows.

Carin sat up slowly, to avoid alarming the ...

"What are they, sprite?" she whispered to the spindle that had indeed made the journey through the void, gripped nerveless in her other hand. "This is your land. Tell me if I should call them rocks, sheep, or the people of this country."

The sprite flickered in the splinter of wood that it had stolen from Morann's giant trees. "My land, Carin?" the creature shrilled. "I cannot claim this place. Nothing here is familiar."

"*What?* What do you mean?" she almost shrieked, eyeing the spindle sharply. "This is the homeworld of the wand that you risked your freedom to touch. See?" Carin pointed at the long, slim fly buzzing past. "There it goes—just a stick, we thought. But in this world, it can fly. Here, the trees have got arms and the rocks jump around like spring lambs. What an upside-down place!"

She looked around, marveling not only at the wonders of this world but at how calmly she accepted them. It was as though, having committed herself to cross the void and walk on this ground, she was immune to the shocks that should attend such a journey.

The woodsprite whimpered.

"Maybe you've just forgotten," Carin murmured. "You were stranded a long time on Ladrehdin. Wouldn't it be wise to roam through these trees? Maybe they'll jog your memory."

"I don't wish to do it," the sprite said, a quaver in its voice. "I will, but only to please you. This place frightens me. Promise me, my friend, that you will not abandon me here. Let me take a quick leap to the tree that overgrows the creek, and then I will return at once to my splinter. Do not move a handsbreadth until I am safely back in your care, I beg you."

"I won't go anywhere." Carin gripped the spindle tightly, trying to reassure the creature. "Take as long as you like to explore this place. I'll wait."

The wood in her hand trembled. There was a spark so intense, Carin felt the warmth of it. Away the sprite flashed, into the tree that had tried to swat a fly but had cuffed instead its otherworldly visitor.

The woodsprite screamed. Quick as it touched the twisted tree, it sprinted away to another, and then another. It disappeared into the alien forest in a series of panicked twinklings. The sprite's screams died on a vaguely malodorous breeze.

"Come back!" Carin yelled.

Some of the lively rocks had rolled hesitantly after the sprite, but they didn't follow it far. They murmured among themselves and shifted as if craning their nonexistent necks for a better view. Nearby, every tree that the sprite had touched slapped frantically at its trunk in the manner of men knocking ants off their exposed skin.

Carin waited only a moment, holding the spindle high, scanning the forest for the flash of the creature's return. Then she was on her feet, dodging the blow that one annoyed tree aimed at her, scattering alarmed rocks in all directions as she plowed through the flock.

"Sprite!" she cried, running after the creature. "Come back!"

She swerved to avoid another agitated tree that waved its limbs menacingly. And as she swerved she collided with something soft and fleshy. It emitted a muffled "Umph!" Carin sprang back, then stopped to stare at the thing that blocked her way.

It was, to all appearances, a mushroom. *No, not to 'all' appearances,* she corrected her first impression. This mushroom stood taller than she did. And it had teeth. The thing snarled at her, showing canines that would have looked more at home in the mouth of a wild boar.

Carin whipped out her dagger and backed away. The mushroom came after her, snarling loudly. She lunged at it but barely nicked its smooth, colorless stem.

The thing screeched like a hell-wain. From the gills on the underside of its cap, spores showered down. They engulfed Carin in a cloud that stank of sulphur.

She fell sideways to the spongy ground, her limbs leaden.

The mushroom toppled over backward. It disappeared at once under a swarm of rat-sized creatures that resembled bouncy, round-bodied spiders. The scavengers tore the mushroom to bits, swallowing chunks of it and carrying off neat slices of its gilled cap.

Desperately Carin tried the counter-charm that Verek had taught her to break the spell of stone. It didn't work. Her petrified limbs ignored her frantic commands to stand and flee.

This was no magic that afflicted her, but an unearthly case of mushroom poisoning. She could do nothing but lie on her side on the evil-smelling loam and watch the spiders consume every scrap of the fungus.

In a little while the spiders finished their feast and scurried away. Carin breathed a prayer of thanks to Drisha or whatever gods ruled this place. Evidently she was not to the spiders' taste.

But her relief was short-lived. Padding toward her now was the soft, unmistakable slap of bare feet.

Carin couldn't roll over to see what came. The footsteps stopped behind her. Something squeezed her thigh. A wheezy voice chortled gleefully, emitting satisfied little sounds that, in human speech, might have been "Ah!" and "Mmhh!"

A net settled over her from head to toe. It tightened painfully, its strings cutting into her skin, as her captor dragged her away, over the humus, up a hill, into a little cranny ringed with rocks. Carin eyed the stones closely—with her face jammed against them, she could hardly help it—and again she offered up thanks. These appeared to be rocks of the usual sort, not given to rolling around or elbowing each other.

New sounds arose at Carin's back: the crackle and sputter of burning wood, the rattle of a pot against its hanger, a sluicing sound as someone or something poured water into a kettle.

Carin went cold. Evidently she *was* to this creature's taste.

She clenched her eyes shut and tested her hands, willing them to move. She could feel them both, one still gripping the dagger, the other holding the woodsprite's spindle. But neither betrayed the slightest inclination to do as she commanded them.

"Carin!"

Her eyes jerked open and she beheld a familiar spark racing up the hillside—but through the stones? She stared. What kind of topsy-turvy world was this, that could turn a sprite-of-the-wood into a rock-troll?

"My friend!" the spark wailed as it darted into a stone inches from Carin's face. A shape like a blubbery mouth worked in the rough surface. "My dear girl! What a disgusting place this is. The trees are *meat*. From one to the next I leapt in horror before I fell to the ground, sick and exhausted. There I made the astonishing discovery that saved me. These things which seem rocky"—the spark fluttered in its stone—"are in fact woody knobs, with their roots stretching deep in the dirt. My *dear* friend! I cannot think that woody stones littering the soil under fleshy trees make a fit abode for such a one as I. Won't you rise, and take me up in my splinter of Ladrehdin, and quit this place at once?"

"I would if I could," Carin mumbled with tongue and lips that were not wholly stopped by her paralysis. "The trouble is, I can't move. Sprite, peek over my shoulder and tell me what kind of a creature has me in its net."

The sprite flicked over Carin's head, then returned, sparking in a state of deepened agitation.

"It's a furry thing half your height," the fay reported in a frightened whisper. "And it is sharpening a fearsome-looking blade and humming quite happily to itself as it works. I do not like the look of this."

Carin strained to hear the activity at her back. Faintly came the hum of her captor's song and a sandy *swish-swish* like steel on slipstone. Her stomach turned over.

"Listen to me, sprite," she hissed. "You've got to distract that thing. If it comes over here waving its knife, then you must draw it away and keep it busy until I can get back on my feet."

"But how—? Oh!" the sprite interrupted itself. "It comes. Oh, my! What a dreadful grin the thing unveils through all that hair."

The sprite leaped over Carin again, taking the fight to the hummer. "Stay back!" shrieked the fay. "Leave her alone."

A startled "Yah?" burst from Carin's captor. Bare feet went slapping down the hillside. The sprite's piping voice followed, fading with distance.

"Thank you, you brave little wood-goblin," Carin whispered to the vacated hilltop. All was silence for a time except for the bubbling of a pot on a crackling fire.

Now that she was in no imminent danger of going bodily into that pot, the sounds of cooking made Carin's mouth water. Her last meal had been consumed at midday—how long ago? It seemed only yesterday, but vague memories of a journey stretching to infinity hinted that Carin might now be more than a day's travel from Ladrehdin, even by a magical path.

She tried her fingers again. Those gripping the dagger twitched. The mushroom's poison was wearing off—and quickly, now that the ebbing had begun. The first signs of returning mobility spread through her as warmly as *dhera*. A few minutes later, the sprite flicked up the hillside to find Carin sitting up, her captor's net thrown off, the spindle of Morann's wood close by her left hand, and the dagger ready in her right.

"Alders and ironbarks!" the sprite cried triumphantly. "That thing with the big knife is a bigger coward than I am. It fled to the next hill over and hides there now, peeking out from under the rocks like a great furry mouse."

Carin looked where the sprite indicated and saw a gently sloping hill much like the one they sat atop. Just visible in the rocks was a ball of brown fur, unmoving except for an occasional shudder.

"You're no coward, sprite," she corrected her friend. "You've saved my life again. I'd be boiling in the pot right now, just stewed meat, if you hadn't chased that thing away. But as long as it stays clear of us, I think I'll help myself to some of its hot water."

At the fire, Carin sat where she could keep an eye on the hairy hummer. She shrugged off her pack, bow, and quiver. A quick examination showed the weapons to be undamaged, though she had lost patches of skin from her arm, scraped off when the hummer dragged her on her side up its hill.

Carin dug her tea mug from her pack and dipped up boiling water from the hummer's pot. A cautious sip confirmed that the liquid was, in fact, water. She dumped in a little tea, and while it steeped she threw a handful of dried fruit into the pot to stew. It was a meager meal but her pack held no other food.

Theil Verek, she thought ruefully, *wasn't the only one to go off unprepared.*

The woodsprite settled into a woody knob at the hill's summit. From its watchtower it kept an alert and impatient vigil, whining at Carin to hurry.

"I am hurrying," she mumbled around a mouthful of fruit. "But while I eat, why don't you tell me where you disappeared to, that last week we were in the mountains. What became of you? And why in the name of Drisha did you try to save that witch from the dragon? Verek told me you'd be treacherous. I didn't believe him, but you worried me when you dropped that limb on the Jabberwock."

The sprite, so distracted that it hardly seemed to know what it said, babbled out a rambling story. Carin pieced together the essential points: The closer it got to Morann's citadel, the sleepier the sprite became, until it could barely rouse itself for a single hour in a day to follow its companions. Well after they had crossed the canyon, the sprite groped its way over the cedar bridge. Then the uncanny fog caught it, and its movements through the trees became leaps of faith. Each time the sprite jumped, it did so blindly, unable to see whether any tree waited to catch it. The forest west of the gorge was thick enough, fortunately, to bear the creature up through an exhausting day of such travel.

When the fog lifted, then the sprite knew where it was. Long forgotten, or long-suppressed, memories surfaced … of the grove, the ruined city, the topaz steps leading to Morann's high altar, the golden-hued trees that overhung her wizards' waters. The sprite had been there before. In fact, the creature had arrived in Ladrehdin by way of those waters, and it had dwelled for a time in the ancient grove. But Morann's inability to enslave the wood-goblin had infuriated her. The creature eluded her just as it would later frustrate Verek. So Morann drove the sprite away, with a spell that blotted out the creature's memories of her realm.

Upon its reapproach to Morann's stronghold, the sprite encountered that spellwork anew, and felt so wearied, so sapped of life, it thought it might die. Such persistent and powerful magic should have kept the creature at bay forever. But the woodsprite that returned to the sorceress was stronger than the otherworldly being she had exiled years ago. It defied her ensorcellments and came flashing through the grove, leaping into the golden trees just as the Jabberwock took her.

"I could think of nothing then," the sprite admitted, "but keeping the enchantress alive. Without her, how was I to return to my homeworld? I never meant to oppose you, Carin. I had no idea of anything but saving the witch from the dragon, then forcing her — somehow — to send me home."

Carin nodded. "I understand. It's too bad, though, that the dragon clubbed Verek with the tree limb you gave it. That was sort of an accident, but he'll never trust you now."

She got to her feet. "But it doesn't really matter if he trusts you or not, I guess. If we manage to find your homeworld, then you'll never see him again."

That sounded final, in a way that made Carin pause. She needed a moment to refocus.

When she did, she reached for her pack and dug out the vine brooch, the lily pin, and the bit of tree-bark. She laid them against the sprite's woody outpost so the creature could feel them.

"Let's keep looking, sprite, until we find where you belong. Which of these do you want to try next? One of them must be the bridge that will take you home."

Eagerly the sprite flitted over the talismans, biding for a moment within the bark. Even so, it could not say whether that object had arisen on its own world.

"But it seems like our best choice." Carin spoke cheerfully, trying to boost the woodsprite's spirits as she returned the two pieces of jewelry to her pack. "So let's see where this scrap of another world takes us."

She shouldered her pack and weapons, held the spindle up for the sprite to reenter, and headed downhill with both that wood and the tree-bark gripped in her left hand, leaving her right to wield the dagger. But it seemed word had spread among the meaty trees, hairy hummers, sulfurous mushrooms, and rolling sheep-stones of this place, warning them away from the armed stranger. The trees kept their twisted limbs to themselves, none offering to swat her. The sheepish rocks scattered before her. Of mushrooms and hummers, nothing could be seen.

On the creekbank, Carin halted and turned, holding the dagger out. A few of the braver sheep-rocks that had trailed her from the base of the hummer's hill fell back again, "oohing" their consternation.

Assured that no denizen of this place contemplated an attack, she stuck the dagger in her belt and held out the bark. "If you're ready, sprite," she whispered to the spindle, "we'll be going. I think we've worn out our welcome here."

The woodsprite answered with a quick, silent sparking. Carin hung the toes of her boots off the clay bank, over the sluggishly flowing brook as though she stood on the rim of a wizard's well. She turned her attention to the tree-bark.

And she'd hardly filled her lungs with the fusty air that came off the water before the image of yet another tree rose like a mirage. This tree's limbs, however, were well-formed, and shaggy, covered with the same sort of bark she held in her hand. Carin eyed a high branch that offered numerous hand- and foot-holds. She crouched, and sprang for it.

Again came the sensation of arrowing through a black nothingness that had to be *something*. It streamed around her, fluid and floaty. Again she heard an ocean, distant but familiar. She entered a period of torpid thought that faded to semi-awareness.

This time, one observation rode out the cotton-witted part of her journey. At the moment Carin jumped from the creekbank into the void between the worlds, an exhilarating little thrill shot through her. She knew it now—that sense of elation—as the quickening of magic. Her passage through the void was her own wizardry—not Verek's, not Morann's, but hers. Maybe she wasn't in perfect control of this magic that she made, but it was born of her own gift.

It took a frightfully long time for the shaggy tree to emerge from the backdrop of nothingness to loom below her. But finally she was landing in its branches.

Carin dropped the shred of bark to gain a free hand with which to steady her arrival—or fend off a blow, if this tree was so minded. But the tree accepted her as it might take a high-flying falcon into its limbs, with the slightest nodding of its small, green, juniper-like leaves and no exclaiming or thrashing.

The scrap of bark tumbled into a heap of others so similar that Carin couldn't, from her high perch, make it out. The snow under the shaggy tree was strewn with shredded bark.

Snow? Yes. The scene was wintry. This tree and a scattering of others rose above a rolling, snow-drifted landscape. The air was cold and fresh, and it chased from Carin's nostrils the last whiffs of decay from Morann's necropolis and from the world of carnal trees.

The woodsprite gave a little cry that was half delighted, half perplexed. It flashed from its spindle to enter the tree that held them. The sprite flickered down the bole, then jumped into a nearby shrub.

Carin watched the creature's explorations with quiet pity. She already knew the sprite must soon return to her, for this was not its world. This was the domain of …

She scanned the horizon for confirmation, and saw it. Gliding silently over a snowdrift, its white fur almost invisible, was the beast that so clearly belonged here. A huge cat with a thick ivory pelt was hunting its dinner. The magnificent brute paused under a tree, well removed from Carin's, and reared up on the trunk. With long, sharp claws it shredded the bark, like a house cat sharpening its claws on a length of firewood, or on a leg of its mistress's prized dining table.

Here was no one to scold it. The cat moved off. When it had disappeared in the snowdrifts, Carin wriggled out of her pack and fished out the next talisman. This one was the water-lily pin—not an obvious emblem for a woodsprite, but they were running out of possibilities.

Like a lamp that had only a little while left to burn, the sprite leaped with an unsteady flicker into the branch that held Carin. Without a word it crept back into its spindle, woefully signaling its readiness to resume their journey.

Carin gripped the piece of jewelry tightly, as if to force it by strength of will to take them to the world they sought. With narrowed eyes, she stared at the pin.

Nothing happened. No image rose before her gaze.

As the seconds passed, she began to feel the cold. Her heavy woolens were long gone, stripped off and abandoned in Morann's ensorcelled meadow.

"Beggar it *all*," Carin swore with a passion that would have done Verek proud. "If I'm going to freeze to death or starve in the snow, I would rather have done it on Ladrehdin."

Her voice cut cleanly through the cold stillness. "Sweet mercy," Carin muttered then, when she saw what she had done. Her swearing might have been the death-cry of an expiring deer, the way the cats reacted. Two of them appeared at once, prowling sinuously toward Carin's tree, their blue eyes upturned to study her.

"Mother of Drisha!" she cursed again, but softly now, calling on a divinity that might or might not hold sway in this domain. Could such gigantic cats climb?

While the down-to-earth side of her wit weighed that question, a more abstract corner wrestled with a possibility that could not be ignored. Had her inexpert wielding of magic thrown her into a predicament from which escape was impossible? The snow under Carin's tree showed no evidence of a stream or a pool, frozen or otherwise. For the first time, no waters were in sight, magian or otherwise. Without water to support the magic of it, maybe no talisman could work.

Hastily Carin repacked the unresponsive pin and took out the vine brooch. Below, one cat had reached her tree. Launching itself nearly halfway up the trunk with a powerful leap, it began climbing. Thus was her first question answered.

Carin raised the vine brooch to her eyes and gathered her wits to study it with mortal intensity. She had to make it work.

And like anything stared at long and hard, the brooch gradually began to reveal aspects that had earlier escaped her notice. Carin saw the network of veins in its leaves, the tiny spike at the base of each midrib, the fine hairs along the tendrils that coiled from the main stem.

But ... should it appear to move? Wasn't this certainly a delusion, this strong impression it gave, that the elaborate spiraling pattern of its stem was slowly unwinding?

No. Her eyes weren't tricked. The brooch was no longer an exquisite jewel fit to fasten a lady's cloak. It was a long stemmy vine, writhing in Carin's hand as though it had enough sense to realize it shouldn't be there.

Out of nothingness, a green lacework of leaves fell like a hood over Carin's head. Tough green strings bound her feet and legs. The vine in her hand made itself fast around her wrist, stabbing its spikes into her skin, securing its tendrils to some nearby anchor that indisputably was not the shaggy tree of the cats' world.

A multitude of shrill, reedy voices rose around Carin, piping away like the woodsprite made legion. She could pick out no intelligible words, but the voices seethed indignation.

Around her neck a wiry stem wrapped, pulling tight as a garrote. The last thing Carin heard was the woodsprite's protests shrilling above the rest:

"No! No! Stop! *Angwid,* stop this. Make room. She is a friend. She's brought me home."

Chapter 21

Broken Bridges

"Carin, dear girl. Do wake up, I beseech you."

Cool, sweet water dripped on her lips. Her tongue licked it off and sought more.

A veritable flood came then, pouring into her open mouth.

Carin sat bolt upright, spluttering. Her eyes flew open to behold a mass of leaves, tightly bunched, looming in front of her face like the wildest jungle greenery.

She recoiled, one hand flying to shield her throat.

"Be easy!" the greenery cried. It slithered backward a short way, spilling some of the water that it cupped in its leaves. From the mouth working in the stem came a voice she knew well. "It's your faithful woodsprite that you see in this spindly excuse for a vine."

"Sprite!" Carin exclaimed. She struggled to take in everything at once: the soft green creature before her; the smooth, water-washed boulder under her; the verdant expanse like a seaborne pasture that floated all around her; a cloudy, green-tinted sky and a breeze that smelled strongly of cabbage. "What—? How—?"

The breeze chilled her skin. Without conscious thought Carin reached for her shirt collar to pull it higher around her neck. But her questing fingers found no cloth. She glanced down, and stared. Where once her whipcord figure had boasted few curves, she now had, as Myra would have said, some meat on her bones. But she wasn't wearing a shirt. From the waist up, she was naked.

"Drisha's teeth!" Carin swore, her voice raspy and choking in her bruised throat. "Sprite! What's been going on here? Where's my blouse?"

"My apologies, dear girl, for the unseemly conduct of my people," the sprite piped in a thin, strained tone. "It was all I could do to keep them from strangling you. When you, um, arrived so suddenly, crowding in on them as you did, you put them quite out of temper." The vine leaned closer. It seemed to shiver.

"I *crowded* them?"

Carin crossed her arms over her chest and glanced around. The boulder she was sitting on rose out of an ocean that was choked with greenery. Everywhere—except for a band of open water immediately surrounding her vantage point—vines and water-weeds slithered and writhed, riding the gentle swells. At the edge of the open water waited a tangled, lush mass that reared above the ocean's surface—clenching, then spreading, uncountable stems and tendrils as though dreaming of getting them around her neck again.

In the distance, a few hummocks bulged up from the general mass of greenery—other boulders perhaps, but all of them completely buried under the rampant plant life. No rock or soil showed anywhere. A sloping contour on the far horizon suggested a possible surface of land rising above the level of the sea, but it too was wholly overgrown. If any beach existed at that meeting of water and land, it was invisible beneath an unbroken mat of green. Every surface inch, from sea to shore to distant hilltop, wore a solid carpet of plants.

"I don't know how they could be more crowded than they already are," Carin murmured to the solitary vine beside her. "But I suppose I *am* taking up space. And they don't appear to have any to spare."

"No, indeed," the sprite muttered. "I confess myself quite surprised by such a profusion."

"But you recognize this place? We *have* found your home?" Carin eyed the sprite, secretly satisfying herself that its current accommodation was not the same as the spiky length of vine that had been the talisman of this world. The sprite's vine was smooth-stemmed, and noticeably more spindly than the erstwhile "brooch." She glanced around for the talisman that had pricked droplets of blood from her wrist with its sharp little spines. But that particular specimen seemed to be gone, disappeared into the general glut of plants.

The sprite's vine bobbed as if nodding. "So much has come back to me, Carin, like a flood in my mind. Being here now, twined around this boulder, rooting into its crevices … I do know this place. Or I knew it, once. All these weeds …" the sprite muttered. It shook itself drearily, the way a man who felt helpless might shake his head. "Where are the groves like temples? Where are the noble trees reaching for the sky?" The vine twisted away for a moment, as if scanning the horizon, then slithered up to Carin again.

"Well," she murmured, rubbing her throat and fingering the welts the vines had raised there and on her wrist, "you were away for a long time. Things change."

"Indeed," the sprite replied, sounding far more subdued than Carin would have expected from a traveler who had longed for home and finally reached it. "But what a great change has been wrought in this world! I find much of what surrounds me at this moment to be quite unrecognizable." The sprite shivered again.

Both were briefly silent, Carin casting about for something to say. She had never let her thoughts dwell on what would happen if the woodsprite actually succeeded in returning to its homeworld. The prospect of saying good-bye, of parting permanently from the creature, had always belonged to the far future — a circumstance to confront only when she must. Even so, she had imagined a deliriously happy woodsprite, not a stringy vine with drooping, quaking leaves.

The damp breeze that played over Carin's bare skin sent another shiver through her. "I would, uh, like to get my shirt back," she murmured as she hugged her body. "Do you know what the plants did with it?"

The sprite lifted its leaves, a gesture of apology.

"It's gone, Carin. Your garment was fashioned of linen. They took it away to give it a proper burial, as they honor the remains of any dead thing that once was living wood or herb. That custom, at least, does not appear to have changed during my absence."

"They buried it?" Carin gawked at the sprite, grasping the implications. "Beggar all!"

Hastily she took inventory, beginning with her feet. She still wore her leather boots. Her woolen trousers hadn't been taken, though they bore moist green stains that suggested her landing in this world had not merely crowded, but crushed some of the throng. Her dagger with its gilt haft and steel blade remained stuck in her leather belt. Her pack, sewn of sturdy wool frieze, was with her yet. Also remaining was Verek's quiver of varnished leather. But the arrows it had held and her treasured bow were gone.

She held up the empty quiver questioningly.

"Shafts of wood, you know," the sprite mumbled. "They interred your bow also."

Carin's quick check of her trousers pockets found the crystal dolphin and her circlet of braided witches' hair undisturbed. But the linen papers that had held Legary's narratives were missing.

She dug through her pack and discovered that it, too, had been turned out. The grasping tendrils of the undertakers had not bothered with her spare pair of woolen stockings, her pewter tea mug, or, more importantly, the abysmal talisman of the *mantikhora*'s world or the water-lily charm. Apparently they hadn't recognized the latter as floral. Carin's last pinch of tea, however, and the few bits of dried fruit that had made up her rations were gone to their final rest.

Carin swore again, silently. *You haven't got a prayer of finding what they took*, she warned herself, looking around at the entwined mass that surrounded her.

A grumbling rose from it, a legion of voices less shrill than the indignant piping that had greeted her arrival, but perhaps more threatening for being muted. Out in the crowd, a spark flashed, reminiscent of the woodsprite's way of sparking when it traveled through trees. But here, the flashes were few, low, and brief. None flitted far. The plants seemed too jammed together to have much individual freedom of movement. Bodily, however, the green mass was bunching itself into a wave, the plants piled up, ready to topple, ready to sweep over Carin and bury her along with the boulder she had temporarily taken for herself.

You don't stand a chance against that lot. Leave your things and get out of here.

Carin pulled the stockings from her pack, knotted them together, and covered her bare breasts with the makeshift bandeau. Then she withdrew the final pair of amulets. The woodsprite was home, as was the talisman of this world. She could do nothing more here, and there was no sense prolonging the good-byes. The mutterings at the edge of her lagoon were sounding ever more hostile. Better to leave at once than to pit the sprite against its countrymen any longer.

"I'm going to miss you," Carin murmured to the vine that was weaving in front of her. Her tears welled up, and she found it hard to continue. "You're about the best friend I've ever had," she managed finally, speaking rapidly and trying not to choke up. "I'll always remember you, and how you saved my skin so often that I lost count. But it's time I went, sprite. When I'm gone to the next world —"

She broke off, uncomfortable with the sound of that. She held up the water-lily pin and rephrased: "I mean, when I head out on the next leg of this journey, then you can get on with celebrating your homecoming."

The vine slithered high up the boulder, its clustered leaves coming close like a child nestling up to share a treasure. For Carin's eyes only, the sprite opened its massed greenery to reveal the spindle of wood that it had taken from Morann's grove.

"I hid it," the sprite whispered. "I would not let them bury it. Now I'll wink back into it and slip into your pocket, and we will leave together."

"*You* leave?" Carin demanded in a husky whisper. "Have you lost your mind, sprite? You're home! For years you've struggled and schemed to make your way back to your native world. In the time I've known you, that's practically all you've talked about. But now you're telling me you don't want to stay?"

"I no longer have a home here, Carin," the sprite murmured. It wrapped a tendril around her wrist, the same wrist the spiky talisman had bloodied. "Had I known what this world had come to, I never would have wished to return." The sprite's vine coiled as if preparing to lash out.

"Look around you!" it demanded. "The weeds have overrun and ravaged this place. There are no trees left. If, as I suspect, the trees have all been strangled, then I will never leap to the sky of this world to see a woodland stretching before me for leagues. I will find no timber here, only soft and yielding stems that revolt me with their flabbiness." The sprite hissed its disgust. "This is a wilderness of weeds. I have known a world of robust wood. Trees live for centuries. Weeds die in a season. Generations without number have come and gone here on Angwid while I lived in the forests of Ladrehdin."

The tendril tightened, cutting into Carin's skin until it threatened to draw new blood. She winced, tried to pull away, and felt the filament dig deeper.

She stiffened as the sprite twined more tendrils around her bare arm.

"You cannot leave me here, my friend," the creature said, with a chill in its voice that Carin had never heard before. "I would die in a matter of days. Take me back. In the world of the magicians, I am strong. I am as I should be. There, I may live to the age of that ancient oak to which I led you safe from the dogs."

Carin held still, at pains to give the vine no reason to further constrict around her.

"Everything we've been through together!" she murmured. "Is it all for nothing? I have kept my promise and brought you home. Now I must go on with …"

She hesitated, chewing her lip, remembering what Verek had said. *Fail in your duty*, he'd warned, *and horrors may come stalking over those bridges to devastate worlds.*

All around Carin writhed the sprite's countless kindred, choking this world. As she looked from them to her friend, her gut twisted. *Strangleweed.* What the circlet of witches' hair had revealed to her: here she was seeing it firsthand, with no intervening magic.

This is what Theil Verek fears, Carin thought. *Just such a scourge as this. If he were here now, he would ask you: Why have you come on this journey, if not to break every bridge, if not to sever every remaining connection between the worlds? If you fail, this could be Ladrehdin's fate — every native life strangled, an entire world choked under a pall of alien weeds.*

She had hesitated too long. The woodsprite knew her: it could read her doubts.

"No!" the creature shrieked in a voice so high it hurt her ears. "You will not leave me here to die!" Innumerable tendrils shot forth from the vine, wrapping Carin in such a weight of greenery that it almost yanked her off her boulder.

As if the sprite's outcry had been the signal to strike, the emerald horde that waited at the edge of Carin's lagoon raised an answering cry. In one tangled mass the vines splashed through the water toward her. Their onslaught sent waves sloshing over her boulder.

"All right, sprite!" Carin yelled, half crushed in the creature's grip, trembling under this foretaste of what would happen if the mob fell upon her. "I'll take you! Now turn me loose."

The sprite gasped, as if only then realizing how tightly it held Carin. The wiry tendrils released her. As she pulled herself up to the top of her boulder again, her heart pounding wildly, the sprite's vine uncoiled and slithered around to encircle Carin's outpost. It raised its leaves in a wall of green.

A span from that wall, the advancing horde stopped. Carin could make out many distinct varieties in the throng: rushes, nettles, thistles, thorns, plants that resembled cattails and arrowleafs and lettuce. But predominant were the twining types: climbers, creepers, bindweed, devil's-guts. Their voices shrilled with cries that Carin took to be curses. They did not seem to be sparing their fellow, the woodsprite.

"Get ready!" Carin yelled, trying to sound in control, though gooseflesh crawled up her arms. "When I tell you to—not before—jump into your stick and we'll go."

"Quickly!" the woodsprite shouted. "The weeds are apt to strangle us both."

The sprite was sparing only a few tendrils now to grasp its spindle of Morann's wood. The rest of its sinews were twined in its defensive shield.

Carin raised the water-lily pin to her eyes and tried to think of nothing else. Surely there was enough potential in this green-clogged sea to excite the magic of a water spell.

But the charm failed. No image rose to point the way to the next stop on this mad journey.

Carin slipped the pin down inside her boot and held up the final talisman: the dark orb that repulsed her. She held it gingerly between her thumb and first two fingers. Under her gaze the ball wavered, as though it didn't fully occupy the space it was in and kept trying to slip back through the void to the world that had spawned it. Looking at it made Carin sick. Her gorge rose, and she had to shut her eyes.

She needed protection—something to put between herself and whatever this thing was. Carin fingered her braided circlet of magic. Three hands would have served her well just then: one to hold the witches'-hair amulet to her eye, one to grasp the ball at arm's length … and one to break the bridge.

She managed it with two hands, even as badly as both were shaking.

The talisman of the *mantikhora*, as Carin described it through the circlet, lost its dizzying, wavering quality but it seemed to tense up, like a balled fist ready to strike. It commanded her attention. At the edges of both her vision and her consciousness as she gave herself to the magic, only traces now remained of the woodsprite's world. Faintly Carin heard the mob's shrieks and perceived the shuddering of the woodsprite's green wall.

"Quickly, Carin!" she heard the sprite scream. "I cannot hold them off!"

"Now!" she yelled.

A noise like the surf pounding a far shore drowned her voice. As if from a distance she saw her hand—the one that gripped the orb—go for the spindle of Morann's wood, extending the ring and little fingers to snatch it. Carin ripped the spindle from the woodsprite's hold. A stringy tendril came with it, torn from the creature's body. And in that same moment she was hurtling off the boulder, into the void between the worlds.

"No!" The woodsprite's shriek followed her. "Carin! Don't leave … me …" The cry dwindled into nothingness.

Toward the realm of the *mantikhora* Carin did not rush, as before, with a feeling of direct movement. This time, she fell. So frightful was the sensation of sliding headlong down a steep slope that she would have screamed, had it been possible. But she could not scream.

Nor could she release the spindle that dangled accusingly between her fingers. She could not hide it in her pack, out of her sight. She could only stare, for what seemed an eternity, at the black ball and at the golden wood that peeked from behind it like the sun returning from an eclipse. Tears blurred her view of talisman and traitor's token, but she could not blink them away.

Mercifully Carin's wits dulled, and layered guilt, shame, and horror under a heavy blanket of woolliness. She grew detached. Her existence both inside and out was, for a long time, without meaning.

If she had not been viewing the ball through the magic of the circlet, she might well have missed the danger as it gradually unfolded in front of her. The circlet, however, revealed the orb's metamorphosis by slow degrees and in sharp detail. What Carin had taken for a clenched fist was, in fact, a curled-up body. Legs—many legs—began to fan out from an expanding central bulk. Eyes glittered at her from shiny blackness. Fangs popped from a newly formed mouth.

Now Carin found that she could scream. And she did so, loudly, as she hurled the fanged thing down to a desert floor that was gradually rising to meet her.

The orb-beast landed atop a creature that was griffin-sized but shaped like the winged fruit of a maple tree. Immediately the beast tore the two wings off its victim and fell to eating.

Carin watched the severed wings flutter over the sand and felt the shock of recognition. They were exactly like the artifact she had picked up from the rim of Verek's ensorcelled pool on the night the *mantikhora* came to Ladrehdin. That artifact was no giant dragonfly wing, as she had thought at the time.

Below her, a swarm of the maple-seed creatures filled the air, whirling rapidly on their paired, translucent wings. One of the creatures dropped too low. The orb-beast grabbed it, bit deeply, and sent two more wings drifting over the sand.

The rest of the swarm whirled away, fleeing the danger. Carin alone kept falling toward it. She put out both hands in an attempt to stop.

Only then did she see that her right hand was empty. In ridding herself of the orb-beast, she had also cast away the spindle of Morann's wood. The spindle was somewhere down below, in the sands of an alien world. And if she did not get it back, that scrap of Ladrehdin could make a new bridge to this place. Over the bridge, the vermin of these desert sands could crawl into her adopted homeland and devour it the way the orb-beast was devouring the winged creatures.

Carin pocketed the circlet of witches' hair and fished out the crystal dolphin. With her free hand, she began to describe circles in the air while she yelled *"Burn!"* with every particle of magical conviction she possessed.

She conjured a wall of flame that rose around her, keeping pace with her descent to the desert floor. The sand looked soft but Carin hit it with a bone-jarring jolt. Drawing breath painfully, she sucked in lungfuls of hot air.

Through the blazing curtain that warded them off, Carin gazed at a collection of freaks. The creatures she had named *mantikhora*—half crocodile, half scorpion, and huge—were in their element here. Several lolled in a wide, sluggish stream that gleamed silver under a glaring sun. The stream flowed, not with water, but with something resembling liquid metal. A *mantikhora* splashed through the stuff to get away from Carin's curtain of fire, and the droplets it flung to the streambanks beaded up like molten steel.

The *mantikhora* paused in its retreat when a second orb-beast scuttled across its path. The newcomer was hurrying toward the beast that had arrived in Carin's custody. What the two fanged things would have done—fought, or mated, or joined forces— Carin did not discover. The *mantikhora* grabbed the newcomer with one scorpionlike foreclaw and downed the orb-beast in a bite. Nothing but a leg escaped those crocodilian jaws.

Carin's beast—the predator she had been carrying around with her from world to world—escaped the fate of its fellow. She'd landed near it, and the fire of her magic curtain proved too hot for the beast. Reluctantly the orb-thing moved away from the stream and away from the remains of the two whirly-winged creatures it had killed.

And as the thing moved, Carin saw the woodsprite's spindle. The stick of wood was half buried in the sand under a gnawed sliver of flesh. Or maybe that was a fragment of shell. It was hard to know what to call the winged creatures' remains.

Experimentally she moved toward the carcasses, and her wall of flame moved with her. She took two more steps and the blazing curtain touched the remains. The overheated air became unbreathable then as smoke and fumes rose from the burning shells.

But she needed only another quick step, and her fire-curtain cleared the spindle. Carin fell to her knees and dug the wood from the sand.

Still kneeling, she spared one last glance for "her" orb-beast, the talisman of this world. The creature, obviously hungry after its inert stay atop Morann's treasure dais, had found its next meal. Its fangs were deep in the throat of an animal that was neither jackal nor buzzard, but combined the worst of both.

You've done your duty by the orb-thing, Carin thought. *It's back where it belongs. Now get out of here!*

She held up the crystal dolphin and locked her gaze on it. An answering image rose amid the fumes and smoke. Carin saw Verek's well of enchanted waters, the cave that contained it, the four carved benches arrayed around it like the points of a compass, one of them bearing the outline of a fish. And resting on that bench was the mate to the crystal in her hand.

The flames died. Around her streamed the coolness of something that was not air. Yet Carin could breathe it, more easily than she had breathed the scorched air of an alien desert.

The stupor came and claimed her. For ages, timeless boundless ages, she could not think. She could barely feel, engulfed in emotions that were impossible to sort through, although she had an eternity in which to try.

* * *

Carin could not say whether her arrival made any splash in the wizards' well, but the shock of those glacial waters hit her

400

like a sledge. She fought to remain conscious. If she blacked out and sank, she would drown.

"Verek!" she screamed. "Help me!"

He didn't answer. His cave of magic was empty. The glow of the walls reflected redly from the waters of the pool and from the facets of the stylized dolphin that lay on the bench. But the glow picked out no wizard waiting to pluck Carin from the pool.

By a racking effort of willpower as well as muscle, she got both hands above the ice. She flung the spindle and her crystal onto the cave floor. They clattered noisily across it, the ringing of one as resonant as a brass bell; the chiming of the other, brilliant and high.

Her gasping breaths were also loud as Carin pulled herself through the glacier, almost swimming. Her arms ached from the exertion. Her legs were beyond feeling. They trailed stonily in her wake. Stroke by laborious stroke, she covered the distance to the pool's rim. Her fingers touched the steps that led up from the depths. She got her knees under her and crawled from the well.

Carin collapsed onto the floor, there to draw deep, tortured breaths and shiver violently. She was deathly cold, but not wet. The liquid glass of the wizards' well had no power to dampen clothing or hair, although it could drown a swimmer as surely as any ocean of water.

How long she lay on the rim, trembling, Carin couldn't guess. Too many journeys through the void had hopelessly addled her sense of time. It seemed another eternity, though, before her teeth stopped chattering and sensation returned to her flesh.

When her legs would support her, she stumbled to the bench of the fish. She gazed at the crystal dolphin that Verek had placed there. The charm did not rest directly on the stone. It nested in a coil of auburn hair—Carin's hair, from the shearing that Myra had given her when this quest began.

Hardly knowing what she did, Carin dug into her pocket and pulled out the circlet of *wysards'* hair. Carefully she reshaped the ring of interwoven black, auburn, and salt-and-pepper strands. She looped it over the crystal so that it, too, touched the coil of her hair. From the floor she picked up the dolphin that had accompanied her to distant worlds before bringing her safe to Ruain. She nested that crystal in the circle alongside its translucent twin.

Carin shrugged out of her pack and empty quiver and sank to the floor. She leaned against the bench that held the mated charms. Absently she rubbed her wrist, until she realized that the thorn-pricks and welts inflicted by the vines of Angwid had healed, leaving behind only a tracery of pale scars.

After a moment Carin reached for the golden-blond spindle that had also attended her travels. The wood was the stuff of Ladrehdin but it had no place here, not in the province of Ruain. The wood came from the far west of this world, from the giant trees that guarded Morann's necropolis.

Call the woodsprite with it, whispered a little voice that Carin didn't want to hear.

"The sprite is dead," she rebuffed the thought aloud. Though she spoke softly, her voice filled the cave of magic. "If its kindred didn't rip it to pieces for protecting me, then it shriveled up and died soon anyway. Weeds die in a season."

Carin cradled the spindle in her hands. Then she stood up and stepped to the rim of the pool.

"It is the custom of those green things of Angwid to bury their dead properly," she said, speaking formally now. "How should I settle these remains? This splinter of wood is not the sprite's body, but the creature fashioned it for that purpose. And it served the sprite well, much as a body would have served it, for a time that I cannot reckon by the seasons of this world."

The voice that answered her this time did not arise in Carin's thoughts. It emanated from the waters of sorcery.

"Burn it," chimed the tinkling, silvery, seashell song of the wizards' well. *"That is seemly."*

Carin nodded. Respectfully, gently, she laid the spindle at the edge of the pool. She stood over it with her head bowed. Fixing her gaze on the wood, she whispered the command: "Burn."

The spindle blazed for the briefest instant. Then the fire died, and nothing remained on the pool's rim but a film of white ash.

A wind breathed through the cave and swept the ash into the waters of the well. Droplets like diamonds formed around each particle, then slowly sank into the pool's depths. Carin gazed after the diamonds until they vanished from sight.

Abruptly she stepped back from the rim and dropped to a crouch. She worked her fingers under her boot-top and pulled out the last magical charm: the one talisman—or entity—that she had failed to return to its proper place in the cosmos.

"Will you face the *wysard* and say that you have fallen short?" asked a voice that could have come from heart, soul, or sorcery, for all Carin was able to name it.

"No," she answered. "Take me there."

Her free hand swept a dolphin off the bench, disrupting her previous attempts at unification. Carin's gaze pierced to the core of the water-lily pin.

The magic awakened, filling her, answering her as it had not answered on the cats' world or on the woodsprite's. This time, an image rose from the waters of enchantment.

The image showed Carin no alien landscape, but a place she knew. Framed in the vision was Verek's upstairs sitting room, a fireplace of gold-veined marble in one long wall, the wall hung on either side of the chimneypiece with paintings — two portraits, two landscapes. One of those landscapes was of a lake of blue water and white lilies, in a woodland of sheltering oaks and bright flowers.

"Take me there," Carin whispered again. She stepped over the rim of the wizards' well into the image —

— And into Verek's quarters. Before she had time to blink, she was standing in front of the painting of the lake where Verek's wife Alesia and their child, Aidan, had drowned years ago.

Carin looked at the lily pin in her hand. It was unchanged. This charm was simply what it appeared to be: a lovely piece of jewelry.

In its beauty she found understanding. The charm had failed her twice on other worlds because the place it was linked to, here on Ladrehdin, no longer existed except in art and memory. Verek, mad with grief, had annihilated the lake of the lilies. Only the wizards' waters of Ruain knew the place now, and that power could do nothing more than send Carin here to view a painting of the lost lake. The jewel in her hand was as much a relic of a bitterly remembered past as was the rendering that hung on Verek's wall.

Carin placed the pin on the mantelshelf near the painting and stood contemplating it. Had the Lady Alesia once delighted in the bauble? Had Morann used the pin as a point of focus to manifest the black art that killed the lady and her son? Carin could readily imagine a vortex erupting from the lake, catching mother and child unawares, whirling them into the tangled, long-stemmed water lilies, there to drown.

"That was the first," she whispered to the empty room. "The first whirlpool the witch made never left this world."

Perhaps it was the success of that early attempt that had encouraged Morann to cast a wider net, beyond the void, to catch up other innocents. Some, like the white-furred cat and Carin herself, must have come from worlds that were not so very different from Ladrehdin. The talismans of tree bark and crystal dolphin were as unchanged as the lily pin, when they made the passage between the realms. Other amulets, however, took on an aspect in one world that was unrecognizable in the next—a honeywood wand that, in its native domain, had the power of flight; a black orb, smooth-skinned and featureless, that swelled in the heat of its desert world to become a bloated, fanged predator.

Somewhere between the extremes fell Angwid, choked by its unchecked profusion of plant life. Angwid's talisman was identifiable on both sides of the void. Yet the woodsprite had no more recognized the vine brooch as the token of its homeworld than Carin had grasped the significance of the crystal dolphin that Verek had used her to retrieve.

"Used" her? Yes, as the wizard had used her to return all the talismans—living or inanimate—and thereby break the bridges between the worlds; as he had used her to consign the woodsprite to its death.

"*I cannot send living flesh through the void.*" Verek's frank admission, spoken months ago in Deroucey, came back to Carin. "*That is a power beyond my craft.*" Had the wizard known, so long ago—or had he only hoped—that the mastery he lacked was not beyond the talents of his apprentice?

Carin spun around, suddenly unwilling to be discovered here in Verek's private apartments. She breathed easier to find the door to his suite tight shut in the other long wall of the sitting room. When no sound reached her from beyond that threshold, she rushed to the exit, the wider door in the interior wall, which opened to the upper corridor of the wizard's sprawling house. It yielded easily, not locked, nor bespelled to invisibility the way it had been when Carin last tested it. Hastily she left the wizard's quarters and hurried down the hallway to her own.

Her bedroom was just as she'd left it, with one exception. At some point in her absence, a small chest had been installed at the foot of the bed. Carin lifted the chest's lid, and smiled.

Folded within was her whole wardrobe, the clothes that Myra's skillful needle had fashioned for Carin during her month's stay under Verek's roof. There was a linen shift, which could be sashed at the waist and worn alone or slipped under a well-made kirtle of red wool. Beneath those garments lay her favorite pair of soft, gray trousers.

The chest also held one of Verek's shirts. It was made of pearl-white linen, sewn from the best fabric the nobleman's wealth could buy. The shirt had been cut down in sleeves and shoulders to fit Carin's smaller frame. After Myra had "borrowed" it for her, that afternoon when everything else Carin owned was rain-soaked, the shirt had never found its way back to the wizard's wardrobe. It had fallen under the housekeeper's needle to become Carin's own.

Carin tossed the crystal charm on her bed. She had taken the dolphin from its magical mate to ensure her safe return from the realm of the lily pin. But within the familiar walls of Verek's home, she needed no such protection.

She slipped Verek's dagger from her belt, pulled off her stained, travel-worn knee-boots, shed stockings and breeches that were so stiff with dirt and sweat they could stand on their own, and untied her makeshift bandeau. Through the folding doors into her private bathing room, Carin burst almost at a run and splashed into the pool's warmth. Thrice she soaped from the ends of her hair to the tips of her toes. Then she sat, up to her chin, on the steps that descended into the tub and let the flow of the natural hot spring rinse away the last traces of alien worlds.

Carin studied the room's walls of glowing rock—so like the enchanted cave deep under this house ... and yet, so different. "One delights while the other daunts," Verek had once remarked. Here in the bathing room off Carin's bedchamber, nature's forces expressed themselves in pleasing energies that eased taut nerves and calmed troubled thoughts. Below, however, in the cave, forces worked that were alive with age-old magic.

That cavern could be a place of peril for anyone who dared to venture there. Hadn't she seen Verek almost drown in his own wizards' waters? Hadn't Carin come to grief there, twice suffering the agonies of that unearthly cold? And yet, the cave of magic did not terrify her now, not like it once did. The voice of the power that lingered in that place had spoken to her ... and she, to it.

Carin splashed from the tub, squeezed the water from her hair, and toweled off. In a drawer of the mirrored dressing-table that stood beside her bed, she found a flask of a creamy hairdressing. A dollop smoothed the snarls from her wet mane. Combed out, Carin's hair fell halfway down her back.

She drew on her gray trousers and white shirt. They were cut generously enough to accommodate her filled-out bust and hips. The fitted kirtle, alas, would be hopelessly small on her now.

In her bare feet, Carin padded onto the second-story landing. She hurried downstairs to the foyer and along the passageway that opened off it, and stepped into Myra's kitchen.

The housekeeper was sitting at the table polishing the silver. She greeted Carin's entrance with wide, startled eyes, a gaping mouth, and a tongue that—for the space of two heartbeats—had nothing to say. Then the torrent began, washing over Carin, as welcome as rain in the desert.

"Oh my, dearie!" Myra jumped up from her work with surprising agility for one so stout. "Oh, my! Drisha be thanked! Here you are, sound of life and limb, and I never heard you come in at all. And you to your bath already — that great, damp, ruddy mane gives you away." The housekeeper rounded the table to catch Carin up in a hug that was a womanly version of Master Welwyn's lung-collapsing embrace.

Those two would get on well, Carin thought, squeezing Myra with arms that couldn't quite reach around the woman's bulk. *Do they know each other, I wonder?*

Abruptly Myra held Carin off. She looked her up and down with a delighted but puzzled smile. Then she began poking and prodding her like a hairy hummer checking its quarry for meatiness.

"Why, dearie!" the woman exclaimed. "I wouldn't have thought it likely, in this twelvemonth and six, that you could bloom from stripling girl to shapely woman. But here's the proof, standing before me and rounding into those curves that I despaired of ever seeing on your bare-boned frame."

This twelvemonth and six? A year and a half? Carin did a quick mental calculation and faltered over the answer. But she smiled as she greeted the housekeeper.

"I can't tell you how happy I am to see you." Carin took the woman's hand. "We've got so much to talk about. Do you remember, you once said you wanted to hear all about my adventures? Well, I've had lots of them, and I'll tell you everything. But first, Myra, I have to know: Where is he? Where is your master, and how is he getting along on that ankle? I'm sorry I had to send him back to you so bruised and battered. But is he mending? Can I see him?"

Myra's look of puzzlement deepened, and her smile vanished. She shook her head. Like a woman who suddenly felt old and tired, she lowered her bulk to a seat at the table.

"Oh my, dearie!" she cried. "Why do you ask me such things? How am I to know where my master is or how he fares?" She choked back tears. "I have not seen my lord since he rode away with you and the boy. And that, dearie—as you must know—was the winter before last."

Chapter 22

Through Eternity

Carin collapsed onto the bench beside Myra, staring at the housekeeper as if the woman were delusional. Then she jumped up and dashed to the side door that opened to the courtyard. She flung it open and stood on the threshold, studying a remnant of Jerold's magic garden.

Where well-ordered beds of gentians and daffodils had once bloomed between expanses of manicured lawn, she saw rank shrubbery and grass grown tall. But clearly she'd come back to Ruain in springtime. The air was warm and fresh. The wildflowers that peeked through the undergrowth were the early bloomers. And beyond the wall that enclosed the grounds, the tops of the trees in the woodland were showing green, putting on their new leaves.

Carin returned to the bench and settled again beside Myra, willing herself to a patient untangling of this mystery but hardly knowing where to begin.

"It's been a long six months, I'll grant you, Myra. But it can't be more than that. The flowers are up and the trees are budding. Didn't we ride out—your master, Lanse, and me—only last winter, two weeks before Mydrismas?"

"Dearie, I well remember your leaving," Myra answered softly, but with a look that suggested Carin was the deluded one. "How I'd hoped to celebrate the festival here, with a great feast, all the old stories, and a young *wencel* again in the house to enjoy them. But nothing would suit my master save that you ride away, west toward the mountains, when the wise must count it folly to make such a journey in the dead season. It was bitterness to my heart to watch you go, for well sure I was that

I'd nevermore see the three of you alive." She sighed. "But my master bade me stay to my duties and keep the house open for no less than a year and a month—longer, as I chose—against the return of any or all of you."

Myra brightened a bit. "And didn't it happen, just as he foresaw, that one of you should come straggling home, nearly a full year after you'd left?"

Carin shook her head, bewildered. "Who, Myra? Who came back? Not your master?"

"No, dearie, not my master. 'Twas young Lanse who rode in late one afternoon last autumn, mounted on his lord's great brute, leading his own horse and that coddled black mare that you had such a fondness for."

"Lanse!" Carin exclaimed, rising from the bench and halfway to the door before caution settled her down again.

The master of that idiot commanded him to 'Kill the girl,' whispered her native wariness. *I'd best keep clear of my assigned executioner.*

"Is Lanse here now?" Carin asked. "And is Emrys in the stable, and Brogar too? We left the horses on the mountains' lower slopes with a monkish friend of your master's called Welwyn. Do you know him?"

Myra waved her to silence. "One thing at a time, dearie. Yes, Master Welwyn was known to this house from before the day that I came to service here, though he's not darkened the doorstep in …" She paused, frowning with the effort to remember. "Why, dearie, it's decades now since he's been. He came to the marriage feast of my lord and his lady." Myra sighed as if at a bittersweet memory.

"As for Lanse and the horses," she continued then, "nay, they've been gone these six months. The boy rested here only a fortnight, eating as much as I could feed him. He was bone-thin, pale and gaunt as a wraith. He would not tell me much of what had befallen, only that the three of you had crossed a canyon into a land where decent folk had no business to be. His lord took you off into the fog, and neither of you ever came back, he said."

Carin nodded. "The path we had to follow took us far from Lanse."

Myra frowned again, looking slightly accusatory. "The boy said he waited—close on a month, by his reckoning—and killed the last of Welwyn's deer for meat to live on. When the fog lifted, he tried to find you both, but there were … things, he said … that would not let him pass beyond the edge of the forest into a meadow where he knew you'd been. He could see your coats and cloaks piled in a heap amidst the flowers—what he thought were flowers. But he saw them turn white and waxy, then they shriveled and blackened, and he knew they were not flowers, but those ghoulish herbs that grow on burial grounds. Corpse-beards, some call them, or ghost fingers. Whatever were you doing in such a place as that?"

"Lord Verek had, um, private business with somebody who dwelled past that ground," Carin murmured, wincing a little to think that the field of "flowers" she'd sat in had actually been a boneyard, bespelled to be unrecognizable. "He took me to help him. Lanse had a hurt arm and couldn't use a bow. I could— and I did, when I had to."

Myra nodded. "*Och*, the poor lad's arm was paining him still, when he struggled home all those months later. Loath he was to come back alone. But when he thought it certain that his lord and you were lost, he took what he could carry on his back and walked down the mountain. How he made it out alive, I cannot say. The boy was as tight-lipped as Jerold used to be— Drisha rest the old goat's soul."

"What?" Carin exclaimed, her chest constricting. "Jerold's dead?"

"Aye, dearie." The housekeeper gave another weary nod. "The old magician passed on in his sleep a year ago—about the time of the equinox last spring. His garden's gone to seed without him. I haven't had the heart to muck about in his flowerbeds. He never let anyone but himself touch his garden in life, and it strikes me as unseemly to be interfering with it now he's gone. So 'tis run wild."

Myra beamed with a sudden thought, the gist of it easily read in her eyes before she said it aloud. "But now you're back, child, maybe you'll trim it up and make it lovely again. Old Jerold would want you to have the charge of it. He grew fond of you in those few weeks we had you with us—though you might not have thought it, the way he growled and grumbled to catch you on the garden paths."

Cheerfulness being the housekeeper's natural state, Myra hung on to her smile as though determined to banish from her kitchen all cares and woes.

"Well now, dearie," she declared briskly, rising from the bench. "Though you've come home with more meat on your bones than when you left—not like poor Lanse—I daresay you'll be wanting your dinner. There's a good bit of rabbit stew left from yesterday. It's plain fare I've been eating, here by myself. But with my master's bonny ally in the house again, I'll be pleased as pepper to put a good meal on the table for you. So have your fill of the rabbit now, dearie, and let me be seeing what's in the larder for something better tonight."

With that, Myra went to work. She ladled up a great bowlful of stew and served it to Carin with a hunk of fresh bread, a crock of sweet butter, and a mug of small mead. Then she flew into the preparations for an evening meal that would be, by the look of the meats and vegetables she arrayed on the sideboard, a feast that a king and his entire court wouldn't have risen from unsatisfied.

Only when the stew was in front of her did Carin realize that she was ravenously hungry.

Well, you should be, commented her composed inner observer, which seemed to find nothing bizarre in the notion that she had been away from Myra's table for a year and a half. *By rights you ought to be starved, considering that your last meal was a mug of tea and a handful of fruit, eaten nigh on a year ago by Ladrehdinian time.*

As she wolfed down the leftover rabbit, Carin pondered the problem. How could a journey that had taken her to the western mountains in a single winter account for an absence from Ruain that Myra reckoned at eighteen months? Had she really been wandering around "out there," roving through the void, for more than a year? Carin had no way to judge. All those seeming eternities that it had taken her to cross from one world to the next had estranged her from the flow of time. It meant nothing to her. She'd lost all feeling for it.

But what was "time," if not change? Carin's passage through the void had changed her. She only had to look at the new fullness of her body to know it.

Maturity was a thing of experience, however, as well as of time. Which of those had played the bigger part in her transformation, she couldn't say.

Carin looked up from her bowl to find Myra studying her. The woman wasn't much given to long, thoughtful pauses. But for a moment she stood silent, absentmindedly wiping her hands on a dishcloth and neglecting the feast that she had begun to prepare.

"Dearie, you were a waif when you left this house," Myra said, her words mirroring what Carin had been thinking— "thin-whittled, wearing a boy's clothes, and with your hair bobbed as short as a gillie's. It does my heart good to see that great ruddy mane of yours spilling down the same as it did before my master bade me cut it."

Myra hesitated, then added, "I've seen many an odd thing in this house, but I don't know that I've been more wonder-struck than I am today. A slip of a girl you were when you left here, a kitling bound to my master and in his care. Now you've come back to his house making your own way, a woman whole. It's odd …" Again Myra paused.

A moment later, she shook her head. "But what am I going on about? A girl ripening to womanhood is nothing to marvel at. 'Tis only the natural way of things. If there is one among my master's young confederates who has dealt me a shock, I must say 'tis not yourself, but that headstrong Lanse."

"Why?" Carin asked. "What did he do?"

The housekeeper sighed. "'Tis a great worry to me that the foolish cub did not stay here at home where he belongs. He was wasted away and near dead with weariness, yet the boy resaddled that great brute Brogar and rode off on his own, refusing to say where he was bound. He would only bid me tell his lord—should our master return in his absence—that he had taken the other horses, his gelding and your mare, to stable them at our neighbor Cian Ronnat's. Though he would speak nothing to me of his schemes, I think Lanse went seeking his master. He will not give our Lord Verek up for dead, but intends to find him—or find death for himself, I fear, in trying. These six months, I've had no word of him."

Lanse is looking for his master, Carin silently agreed. *But maybe he's also seeking the one his lord ordered him to kill.*

She scraped her bowl clean, washed down her last bite of bread with her last swallow of mead, and rose from the table. "Thank you, Myra, for everything. For the food, for my clean clothes, and especially for still being here. I'd have sat down and cried if I'd come back and found you gone too."

The housekeeper waved away the sentiment but rounded the table and gave Carin another breathtaking hug. Before Carin excused herself then from the kitchen, she asked again: had there really been no sign of Lord Verek within these walls?

"I've got my reasons," she replied to Myra's baffled look, "for believing that your moody master should have been home long before now. In fact, after he left me he would have had time to return here and say good-bye before Jerold died. Lord Verek intended to get back last spring and send Lanse help, right away. I'm trying to work out how Lanse could have come home alone so many months overdue, and how I got here even later — and why neither of us found Lord Verek here ahead of us. This shouldn't have happened …

"Lanse can ride a horse into the ground looking for his master," Carin added, "but I've got my own ideas about where to find him."

"Oh my, dearie!" Myra exclaimed, wringing her dishcloth. "Don't be reckless, child. If you take a notion to run off again, like Lanse did, I'll be sorely vexed."

Carin mumbled something noncommittal. Offering what she hoped was a reassuring smile, she took her leave of the housekeeper and hurried from the kitchen to the foyer. Hesitating there, she looked down the hallway toward Verek's library.

But Carin chose the stairs instead and dashed up to her bedroom. From the clothes chest she fished out a clean pair of stockings, covered her bare feet, and put on the old, scuffed squaretoes that had stayed behind — her plain country boots that had been deemed unsuitable for mountain travel in wintertime.

At the dressing table, Carin ran a brush through her now dry hair. She cinched up her shirtwaist with the red sash that contrasted nicely with the gray of her trousers.

Drawing a deep, steadying breath, she stuck Verek's dagger through her sash. She pocketed the crystal dolphin. Then she headed down the corridor to explore the suite of rooms that she had never seen, in the weeks of her first stay under Verek's roof.

His upstairs sitting room held no great interest now. Carin had come to know it well enough during the woodsprite's captivity in a potted tree at the room's single, recessed window. Even so, she paused to study again the paintings that hung two by two on either side of the chimneypiece—the portraits, of the lovely Lady Alesia and a dark-haired, bright-eyed little boy of about five; and the landscapes, of lost lake and mountain pinnacle.

Carin narrowed her eyes at the latter. The painting, unless she was much mistaken, depicted the western mountains that Verek could have no great reason to love.

The man must have a taste for suffering, she thought. Why else would he display on his walls the faces of his dead wife and child, the scene of their deaths, and a view of their murderer's stronghold?

Shaking her head at the wizard's taste in art, Carin turned from the paintings and approached the doorway to the rest of his private apartment. It, like the hall door, was unlocked. She stepped through onto a small landing at the head of an ironwork spiral staircase. She glanced down the stairs but could see little of the room below.

Off the landing, however, another door opened to a large but plainly furnished bedroom. It had a fireplace, with a table and a chair where the wizard must often have taken his meals when his brooding, secretive ways kept him from joining Carin and Myra in the kitchen. His bed was large, and raised on a platform under the room's windows. Like the bed Carin had slept in at Deroucey, Verek's had a canopy of wool curtains that could be closed for warmth or privacy. The bed was dressed simply, with a heavy, dark-blue blanket over plain white sheets. Beside the bed was a cushioned bench, convenient for sitting and pulling off boots.

At the far end of the room, light spilled through an arched opening in the thick stone wall. The light had a familiar quality—steady, unflickering, like sunlight through clouded crystal.

Carin crossed to the arch and discovered another private bathing room, its walls glowing with the same soft light that lit her own. Here, however, there was no pool. Instead, water cascaded from a slot high up the wall. The cascade fell into a wide, shallow floor-basin, and from there drained out of sight. The water-sculpted caverns that underlay this house, this age-old seat of the family of Verek, did not merely provide a footing for the edifice. Here and down the hall past Carin's bedroom, the hot springs flowed into the house and had been channeled, by some ingenious past builder, into places for cleansing body—and soul?

On the bathing-room wall opposite the waterfall, a mirror hung. Under the mirror, a shelf of marble held only a hairbrush. Any other implements that might once have rested there—for grooming a cropped beard and narrow mustache, for instance— had gone with the wizard on his travels. At the inn in Deroucey and again at Welwyn's cabin, but not at Morann's enchanted brook, Verek had taken the time to use them. In between, he'd looked as scruffy as Carin.

She left the waterfall murmuring to itself, as it must have done for at least a millennium, and walked back through the bedroom to the staircase that spiraled to the ground floor. Carin descended into one large and startling room.

If the bedchamber above revealed almost nothing of its owner's personality, here the wizard's mark was everywhere. The section of the room nearest the stairs was obviously his herbalist's workshop, where he mixed the salves and draughts and healing powders that cured all manner of infirmities with uncanny speed. There were boxes and bins of dried herbs, bottles and jars of oils and ointments, balances for weighing them, mortars and pestles for mixing them, and little pots to hold the finished compounds. The air was fragrant with laurel, lavender, and many other healing herbs, but most distinctive was the musky scent of calendula oil.

Strange how a whiff of the calendula got Carin's heart racing. She stood for a moment breathing it in, feeling her face grow warm and her insides sort of soften.

A little deeper into the room, the herbal fragrances gave way to the acrid odors of metalworking. On a well-used bench were tools for shaping iron and wood, and beside them a frame made to hold a painting. The frame was only half finished, but elaborately carved and ornamented in gold and enamel inlay, decorated with a delicate tendril-and-blossom design. Carin appreciated the craftsmanship without a pang. The ornamentation did not remind her of the woodsprite so much as it summoned thoughts of Jerold, master of the garden and onetime sorcerer's apprentice.

As Carin stood in Verek's ground-floor workroom, taking in the proofs of his talents, she was also reminded of what Myra had told her on her first morning under the wizard's roof: "Apothecary and alchemist he is, and herbalist, metalsmith, and worker in stone. There's little in this world that my master cannot turn his hand to."

The one section of the workroom that Carin had yet to explore occupied the best-lit spot, under a row of windows that stretched the length of the back wall. She walked to the windows, turned—and inhaled sharply.

"Myra, my talkative friend," she whispered to the absent housekeeper, "you might also have mentioned that your master knows his way around a canvas."

On an easel rested a nearly finished work—a portrait, in a style too similar to those hanging in the sitting room to leave any doubt about whose hand had produced them. The scene was of ocean waves lapping at a sandy beach, with a small, neat cottage in the background, an inviting cluster of boulders to the fore … and seated on the highest rock a girl, auburn-haired and exactly matching Myra's long-ago lament: "She might be elves' kin—all wide eyes and lanky limbs … so thin that a good wind could blow her away."

In the girl's hand rested a sea urchin redder than her flowing mane. She held the water devilkin fearlessly despite its poisonous spines. A wry smile quirked her lips as though she enjoyed some private joke. Her gaze was direct, locking large green eyes with the painter's as he worked.

He caught me better than any mirror ever did, Carin marveled, staring at an image of herself that was so true to its time, she half expected the girl to step off the canvas, shrug one shoulder, and introduce herself as Carin's left-behind younger life— because the girl in the painting was the very image of the starveling she had been when this quest began. But Carin was older now, and changed in ways that went beyond the flesh.

For one thing, offered that little interior voice which insisted on being unhelpful, *you have killed. Not once, but twice. You have taken the life of an enemy and of a friend. And the friend may have been the truest you'll ever know in this or any world.*

Carin shook herself to silence the voice. Leaving the windows, she walked the length of the workroom and found the door that she expected to find at the end of the great space. This one, like the others to Verek's private apartments, was unlocked and unguarded by any spellcraft.

It opened on the winding stairs that descended to the cave of the wizards' waters. Carin glanced down at the reddish glow that emanated from deep underground.

"Soon," she whispered. "Not yet." She stepped onto the narrow landing, lifted the latch of the door that closed off the head of the stairs, and entered Verek's library.

The room was exactly as she had last seen it. Her neat stacks of books still covered the floor, the work of a busy month spent bringing a semblance of order to the wizard's collection. That old habits were hard to break was evident from the fire crackling on the hearth. No one had used the room for a year and a half, by Myra's reckoning. Yet the housekeeper had dutifully made a fire, just as if she'd been expecting her master or his book-loving apprentice to be at work here, as was the habit of both.

Wait—had no one been here? The longsword lying on a bench at the fire disproved Carin's first impression. It was the weapon that Verek had discarded beside the mountain trail, in favor of an ax when it became impossible to carry both. The spare trousers Carin had given for wrapping and protecting the steel were nowhere to be seen. Undoubtedly Lanse had not bothered bringing her garment home. That the boy had somehow lugged the weapon down the mountain, with no deer to help him haul any of the gear he required for his survival, earned him Carin's grudging respect. She didn't like Lanse and she'd never trust him, but his loyalty to his master was something she must honor.

From the paired benches at the fireplace, Carin stepped to the big oak desk under the windows and gazed at the *Book of Archamon*. Without hesitation she opened the ancient volume to its last two entries. Legary's narratives covered facing pages at the back. Neither, now, wore a spell of concealment. The page Carin had worked so hard to decipher lay as open to her study as the final entry—the wizard's deathbed narrative—always had.

Carin sat at the desk and pored over the left-hand page, nodding as all the intriguing words and phrases she had patiently teased from the once-bespelled writing fell into place. The account spoke of Legary's anguish on the night he realized that the necromancer he had forced his ungifted son to marry had murdered Hugh, soon after giving birth to Legary's adept but "tainted" grandson:

> *The evil in our midst has fled,*
> *But not in time to save*
> *The son I sacrificed*
> *To arrogance.*
>
> *Only the issue survives —*
> *The issue of a union corrupt,*
> *And he with demon's taint*
> *Upon his gift.*
>
> *How was I blinded?*
> *How could I not see*
> *The nature of the pestilence*
> *I loosed upon this House?*
>
> *"A tragic loss!" the mourners cried.*
> *"But comfort shall you take*
> *In the babe so gently held*
> *In the grieving widow's arms."*
>
> *Beseemly garbed in widow's weeds,*
> *She led the progress to the tomb*
> *And wailed and keened, and played her role*
> *In the grotesquerie she wove.*

The heir she suckled at her breast
Was two parts innocence, one part fiend.
Damn my ambitions! Damn my pride!
— Created in my scheming;
Left to fester in her spleen.

Ten years' corruption, ere I saw
The damage that was done.
Wickedness ill-used his reason;
Darkness flickered in those eyes.

I raged and ranted,
Threatened death
To the one who stained
This honored House.

"The choice was yours!" she sneered at me.
"Would you hear the voice of Power with one
Ungifted at your side? Or honor with
A worthy heir this ancient lineage of the adept?"

"Sorceress!" I screamed. "Prepare thyself for
Dark descent to formless void and endless night.
In farsinchia *shall we meet again —*
Two perverters of the age-old light."

Quick as arrowflight, she was gone,
Back to craggy heights beyond
The river wild and canyon deep.
But on the wind came words to burn like fire:

"'Wife of Hugh,' you named me.
For pride of House, you threw him to me.
How unworthy was that weakling pup,
Of one who wields the Power potent!

"With disdain I felled the firstling.
But with his seed was made the one
Who shall rule in his place.
And mark me well, Fool Legary:
The boy is his mother's son!"

By the oath of my House,
And in these pages
Bathed in the light of the wisdom
Of Archamon, I swear:

The boy shall not fall to darkness.
As long as there be breath in this body,
I will guide him on the bright path,
And Morann shall touch him not!

"He did not fall, Lord Legary," Carin whispered to the empty library. "You did not fail. The darkness didn't take him. But you were never sure, were you? Though you raised him as your own and trained him in the bright ways, you were never sure of him. You always wondered: *was* Theil Verek his mother's son? Was he a fiend, a blackheart, a dark wizard who could turn the 'gift' to evil? You doubted him, and he couldn't help but know it."

Carin laid her finger on the right-hand page, as though the long-dead wizard she addressed could see the gesture. "Then came that terrible day, fourteen years after Morann fled, when she sent the vortex to kill Theil's wife and the little boy who bore no trace of the taint. Theil went mad. He cursed the woodland and the lake with a kind of evil that could only come from the worst perversion of the power.

"You were sure, then, that you had failed. You were certain—weren't you, Legary?—that Theil was forever lost in the darkness and could never find the bright path again. And so you killed yourself stopping the madness, saving Ruain—saving, maybe, the better part of Ladrehdin. Who knew how far the curse could reach, how much destruction it could do? You stopped it before it spread to the plains and the seas and all around this world. You gave your life to stop it, but before you went to your grave you confessed your part in all the wickedness, you confessed your guilt. And then you hid the *Book of Archamon* for fear of the evil that your grandson might work with the vastness of the knowledge it contains."

Carin tapped her finger on the final three lines of the book, lines written more than twenty years ago by the dying Legary. She looked up, speaking to thin air.

"And yet, you still hoped. You wanted to believe that Theil would carry on as your heir, as master of the House of Verek. Maybe he'd marry again, and father another innocent child to follow him as lord or lady of Ruain. You hoped that he could make for himself and for your 'ancient lineage of the adept' a future that was worthy of his inheritance."

Carin glanced again at the right-hand page and reread the lines she knew by heart:

> *"The evil toucheth not this child!"*
> *I rejoiced in the knowledge of it.*
> *I cried it from the turrets,*
> *I declared it from the treetops.*

The blood of my son's blood is clean!
The evil that slew the first
And tainted the second
Hath no power over the third.

The raven heard my shouts of joy;
The black raven carried my news abroad.
Of my happiness, the enchantress did learn;
All my joy, the sorceress did blight.

From weak seed, and flawed,
Sprang innocent youth.
From the womb of guiltless Alesia
Came the child of shining spirit.

To the lake of the lilies walked mother and child;
From waters ensorcelled came never they home.
Dead was the first by guileful craft;
Dead was the third by blackest art.

The second — the troubled, the tainted seed —
Vented wild rage upon the living wood.
Dead and barren, as his heart within,
Left he the woodland with fury spent.

"Stop him!" shrieked the man of the green.
"Wilt thou suffer the spread of his venom
O'er all the Land of Ruain, and the blighting
Of all bright flowers within thy vast domain?"

"Stop him!" I cried to the four winds.
"Halt this furious plague.
Stem the life-force's ebbing;
Let not the curse prevail!"

The winds took heed:
An edge was made.
Within these walls and past the wood
The poison floweth not.

But I have paid the dearest price
To invoke the forces primal;
They draw me now into the tomb,
Where lie the first son and the third.

My crimes are great, my penance vast;
What punishment can harm me now?
The lad is slain, the infant drowned;
The tainted seed is future's hope.

By the oath of my House, I command thee:
Touch him not, Morann!

"She didn't touch him, Legary, not in any way that mattered. She didn't corrupt him. And now, sir, I'm going to fetch him home."

Carin shut the book and pushed back from the desk. She strode across the library, returning to the door that opened on the stairwell. Down the stairs she plunged, deeper and deeper under the house, bursting at last into the cave of magic with a bolder step than she had ever before dared.

At the rim of the wizards' well Carin skidded to a stop, pulled the crystal dolphin from her pocket, and glanced at its mate. The other dolphin rested like a tiny anchor on the bench of the fish. She raised her crystal to her eyes and conjured an image from the enchanted pool—the image of the child's bedroom, colorfully decorated with paper fish, waiting on the world that was her natural home but could never be the abode of her heart.

"Take me there," she commanded.

The journey was one easy step from the pool's rim onto the floor of the child's bedroom. And a moment's study of the pleasant room, with its window that looked out upon the sea, revealed what had upset Carin's plans for Verek's prompt return to his own ancestral home.

On the child-sized desk, under the shelves that held books and stuffed animals, lay a slip of paper. Carin picked it up.

It was only a brief note of instructions for taking a medicinal draught that Verek the apothecary-wizard had once prepared for her. "*C – Drink the liquid. Leave the dregs. – V,*" it read. Simplicity itself except for the large, flowing capital letters, written in an elegant hand, decorated with a pattern of tendrils and dots that brought to mind a grape-laden vine.

"Oh! I forgot," Carin murmured, though in fact she remembered the writing perfectly.

After the wizard's note to her had served its original purpose, she'd used it for a bookmark. And in that capacity — Carin having forgotten ever to remove it from the pages — the paper had mistakenly journeyed to this world, tucked out of sight between the red and gold covers of the *Looking-Glass* book. No wonder Carin had managed, at the edge of Morann's ensorcelled waters with horrors creeping toward them, to conjure up — not the crystal in Ruain that would have built Verek a bridge home — but this very personal specimen of the wizard's singular ... one might say spellbinding ... penmanship.

On the desk, the puzzle-book lay atop its companion volume, *Alice's Adventures in Wonderland*. Carin fingered the book. She knew the "Jabberwocky's" source, *Through the Looking-Glass*, almost by heart, she'd studied it so thoroughly with a deeply interested and attentive wizard. But she could not remember ever having read the other book, though surely she must have, if this bedroom had been hers in a forgotten childhood.

"Later," she whispered. "I can read it to him later—after I've found him."

Carin stepped through the bedroom door into a hallway, and went looking for her misplaced magician.

She found him at the living-room fireplace. He was crouched over a pot of something that smelled vaguely fishy, and he stirred it unenthusiastically.

Verek was barefoot and wearing the garb of this world— blue denims that fit him admirably, and a white knit shirt that was a little tight. His long, clean, shiny hair was pulled back and tied at the nape of his neck. His hair fell far enough down his back to partially obscure what was written on his shirt, but Carin would have had to be blind to not instantly recognize the opening stanza of Lewis Carroll's "Jabberwocky," done up in old-fashioned black-letter.

"Beggar it all, my lord," she swore serenely from the entryway. "I seem to have erred in sending you through the wrong door, by way of the wrong bridge, to the wrong planet."

With a clatter, Verek's stirring spoon hit the firedogs. In one smooth, fluid motion he whirled and stood. His movements gave no hint of cracked ribs or broken ankle. Gone also were his beard and mustache, shaved off. Without them he looked maybe twenty-five.

"Great merciful powers!" he swore, staring as if Carin were a phantom. "I've gone mad."

Carin shrugged. "How would you know the difference? You've seemed half crazy since the day we met. But I wouldn't say you were any worse demented than I've come to believe is normal for you."

A smile pulled at the corners of Verek's lips. It did not fully succeed in lifting them, but from his eyes it shone unreserved.

"By Drisha!" he thundered. "It *is* you."

Disdaining to go around the wickerwork chair that stood between them, he vaulted it, providing positive proof that his fractures had healed. Carin barely had time to take one long step to meet him. Then she was in his arms, having the breath crushed out of her for the second time that day.

Verek didn't release her as quickly as Myra had. But when he did finally hold Carin off, to look her up and down, he seemed again to doubt his own senses.

"I perceive, *fileen*," he muttered softly, his eyes drinking her in, "that Myra has at last managed to put some curves on that lathy frame of yours. As I recall, she was much given to bemoaning your lack of them."

Carin shook her head. "I've eaten only one meal with Myra since I returned from the 'errand' you sent me on. It's not your housekeeper's cooking that gets the credit. I've traveled the void, and out there everything's different. Time is meaningless. In some ways it passes quickly, and in other ways it doesn't pass at all. Out there, time just seems to go its own way."

She paused, wanting better words to describe for him her indescribable journey through eternity. But all Carin could think of was how long it had been since she'd last looked into his eyes. "I've been away from you for a time that I don't know how to measure," she murmured. "But Myra says it's two winters. Did you think I'd never come?"

Verek tilted his head. "Two winters? Not here. By this sea I have waited for you, and the days have been hot, summer days." He studied Carin's face with an intensity that was as unsettling as ever, but she felt no compulsion to pull away.

"It's done?" he asked then, but so absorbed in his inspection of her that Carin hesitated to reply for fear of distracting him. Slowly, she nodded. When that didn't break the spell, she reached up and gently brushed back a few strands of his hair that had worked loose from his ponytail.

"Yes, it's done," she murmured, still teasing the wayward strands off his lean, strong face. "Things are back where they belong. Now there's nothing in this world—or any other—to keep us from making up for lost time."

The smile won out. Verek looked at Carin without a trace of his usual cool reserve.

"Breath and blood!" he swore. "I thought it would never be, but at last you are—"

His actions finished the thought. He slipped his hand behind Carin's head, his fingers twining in her freshly washed hair. He pulled her face to his, meeting her parted lips with his. The kiss was long, deep, and passionate enough to earn a place in Ladra's bewitchments—though the magic of Ladra had nothing to do with it.

When they finally broke apart, Carin took her wizard by the hand. "Sweet mercy!" she murmured. "Come on—let's go home."

"Soon, *fileen*." Verek squeezed Carin's fingers. "Very soon."

Something unsettled had come into his look. Not a frown—at this particular moment, he seemed incapable of expressing a frown. But he also seemed torn—like a man who was fiercely inclined toward one direction, but felt the pull of an iron hand in another.

He tipped his head to indicate the room where they stood.

"Before we go, walk with me through your former home, and tell me what you can of this place. Let us see if we can discover who you are."

END of BOOK TWO of WATERSPELL

About the Author

Deborah J. Lightfoot got attached to history through her grandfather, a High Plains cowboy. From her mother, an artist and avid reader, came her love of books and all things mysterious and magical. Deborah has had a fondness for dark horsemen since Richard Boone's Paladin rode through TV landscapes wielding a six-shooter instead of a sword. Six-shooters figure in her award-winning books about the American Southwest: *Trail Fever* (William Morrow) and *The LH7 Ranch* (University of North Texas Press). Swords and sorcery provide the thrills in *WATERSPELL*, an intricate fantasy trilogy with medieval overtones and a few nods to history. A journalism graduate (summa cum laude) of Texas A&M University and an Authors Guild member, Deborah is in educational publishing as a freelancer for a national nonprofit organization. Besides writing, editing, and ingesting books, her pleasures include traveling abroad and hiking the Yorkshire moors, Canada's Pacific Rim National Park, and while living in Mexico part-time, that country's La Primavera Bosque. On the Web: djlightfoot.blogspot.com

CPSIA information can be obtained at www.ICGtesting.com
Printed in the USA
LVOW060243291111

256902LV00002B/23/P

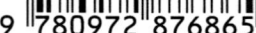